THE TATTOO THIEF

Alison Belsham initially started writing with the ambition of becoming a screenwriter and in 2000 was commended for her visual storytelling in the Orange Prize for Screenwriting. In 2001 she was shortlisted in a BBC Drama Writer competition. Life and children intervened but, switching to fiction, in 2009 her novel *Domino* was selected for the prestigious Adventures in Fiction mentoring scheme. In 2016 she pitched her first crime novel, *The Tattoo Thief*, at the Pitch Perfect event at the Bloody Scotland Crime Writing Festival and was judged the winner.

THE
TATTOO
THIEF

ALISON BELSHAM

Leabharlanna Poiblí Chathair Baile Átha Cliath
Dublin City Public Libraries

TRAPEZE

An Orion Paperback

First published in Great Britain in 2018 by Trapeze Books,
an imprint of The Orion Publishing Group Ltd
Carmelite House, 50 Victoria Embankment,
London EC4Y 0DZ

An Hachette UK company

1 3 5 7 9 10 8 6 4 2

A CIP catalogue record for this book
is available from the British Library.

ISBN (Mass Market Paperback) 978 1409 1 7513 1

Typeset by Input Data Services Ltd, Somerset

Printed and bound by CPI Group (UK) Ltd, Croydon CR0 4YY

www.orionbooks.co.uk

For my beamish boys,
Rupert and Tim

One, two, cut a tattoo,
Three, four, flay some more
Five, six, my bloody fix
Seven, eight, will not wait

i

I peel away the blood-soaked T-shirt from the unconscious man's back to reveal a spectacular tattoo. The photocopy I take from my pocket is crumpled but it's good enough for me to check against the image on his skin. Thankfully, there's just enough light from the street lamp to see that the two designs look the same. A round Polynesian tattoo in heavy black ink adorns the man's left shoulder, an intricate tribal face scowling from its centre. Spreading out from the edges is a pair of stylised wings, one extending down the man's shoulder blade, the other extending across the left side of his chest. All of it is speckled with blood.

The images match. I have the right man.

There's still a pulse in his neck, but it's faint enough to reassure me that he won't cause any problems. It's essential to do the job while his body's still warm. If the corpse cools, the skin stiffens and the flesh becomes rigid. That makes the job harder and I can't afford mistakes. Of course, flaying the skin off a living body means so much more blood. But I don't mind blood.

My backpack is lying nearby, discarded as I pulled him into the bushes. It was easy enough – the small park was deserted at this hour. It only took one blow to the back of his head and he crumpled at the knees. No noise. No commotion. No witnesses. I knew this was the route he'd take when he left the nightclub because I'd watched him take it before. People are so stupid. He suspected nothing, even as I walked towards him with a wrench in my fist. Seconds later, his blood was spreading across the ground from a wound at the temple. The first step executed most satisfactorily.

Once he was down, I hooked my hands underneath his armpits and dragged him as quickly as I could across the stone paving. I wanted the cover of the shrubs so we wouldn't be seen. He's heavy but I'm strong, and I was able to pull him through a gap between two laurel bushes.

The exertion has left me breathless. I hold out my hands, palms down. I see the ghost of a tremor. Clench fists, then open again. Both hands flutter like moths, just as my heart flutters against my ribs. I curse under my breath. A steady right hand is essential to carry out my assignment. The solution's in a side pocket of my backpack. A packet of tablets, a small bottle of water. Propranolol – the snooker player's beta-blocker of choice. I swallow two and close my eyes, waiting for them to take effect. At the next check, the tremor is gone. Now I'm ready to begin.

Taking a deep breath, I reach into the bag and feel for my knife roll. Satisfaction floods through me as my fingers touch the soft leather, the steel outlined beneath. I sharpened the blades with great care last night. Intuition, you might say, that today would be the day.

I drop the roll onto the man's back and untie the cords. The leather unfurls with a soft clink of metal, the blades cold beneath my fingertips. I select the short-handled knife that I'll use for the first cuts, marking the outline of the skin to be removed. After that, for the flaying itself, I'll use a longer, backward-curving knife. I buy them from Japan and they cost a small fortune. But it's worth it. They're fashioned using the same techniques employed for Samurai swords. Tempered steel enables me to cut with speed and precision, as if I'm carving shapes out of butter.

I put the rest of the knives on the ground next to his body and check his pulse again. Fainter than before but he's still alive. Blood seeps *from his head, more slowly now. Time for a quick, deep test cut into his left thigh. There's no flinch or intake of breath. Just a steady oozing of dark, slippery blood. Good. I can't afford for him to move while I'm cutting.*

The moment has arrived. With one hand holding the skin taut, I make the first incision. I draw the blade swiftly down from the top of his shoulder across the jutting angles of his scapula, following the outline of the design. A red ribbon appears in the wake of my blade, warm as it runs down onto my fingers. I hold my breath as the knife carves its path, savouring the shiver that rolls up my spine and the hot rush of blood to my groin.

The man will be dead by the time I finish.

He isn't the first. And he won't be the last.

I

Marni

The needles punctured the skin faster than the eye could see, depositing dark ink into the dermis and leaving a bloom of bloody roses oozing on the surface. Marni Mullins wiped away the beads every couple of seconds with a fold of paper towel so she could see the outlines on her client's arm. A slick of Vaseline, then the sharp dig of the needles into the flesh again, creating a new black line that would last forever. The alchemy of skin and ink.

Marni sought refuge in her work, mesmerised by the hum and the soft vibration of the tattoo iron in her hand. It was a temporary escape from the memories that plagued her, the things she could never forget.

Black and red. The imprint she dug into the yielding skin. Her client flinched and jerked under the pressure of the needle heads, even as Marni used her wiping hand to keep his arm still. She knew all too well the pain he was experiencing. Hadn't she endured too many hours at the sharp end of a tattoo machine? She could sympathise but it was the price that had to be paid – a moment to be endured for something that would last a lifetime. Something that no one could ever take away from you.

She used her forearm to push a lock of dark hair from her forehead and swore under her breath as it slipped back into her eyes. Angling her lips to blow the hair to one side, she dipped the seven-tipped needle into a small pot of water to change the ink from black to slate grey.

'Marni?'

'Yeah. How you doin', Steve?'

He was lying face down on her massage bench. He twisted his head towards her, blinking and grimacing. 'Can we take a break?'

Marni glanced at her watch. She'd been working on him for three hours straight and she suddenly became aware of the tension that had built up in her shoulders.

'Sure, of course.' Three hours was a long session, even for a regular like Steve. 'You're sitting like a champ,' she added, putting her iron down on the equipment stand next to her stool. It was something she always said to clients, regardless of whether they were sitting like a champ or not – and Steve, with all his fidgeting and moaning, definitely wasn't.

But she needed a break too as she was starting to feel claustrophobic. It was always that way at conventions – artificially lit halls, stale air and noisy crowds. The lack of windows meant you couldn't tell if it was light or dark outside, and Marni needed to see the sky wherever she was. In here, the air was thick and hot, the hall crammed with bodies being tattooed and a crush of voyeurs watching the needles. All this was underscored by blaring rock music and the continuous grind of the tattoo irons on bloodied skin.

She took a deep breath, rolling her head across her shoulders to release the tension in her neck. The sharp smell of ink mingled with blood and disinfectant hung in the air. She peeled back the black latex gloves and thrust them into a rubbish sack. Steve was stretching and flexing his arm, clenching and opening his fist to get the circulation back. He was paler than he had been when she'd started tattooing him.

'Go and get a snack. Come back in half an hour.'

Marni quickly wrapped the bloody design in cling film to keep it clean, and pointed Steve in the direction of the cafeteria. Once he'd gone, she pushed through a knot of people on the stairs to reach ground level and burst outside through a pair of fire escape doors. Sucking in a lungful of cold air, she realised she'd escaped not a moment too soon. She leant back against the cool concrete wall and closed her eyes, concentrating on decompressing, letting the combined weight of the people and the building lift from her chest.

She opened her eyes and blinked. The artificial glare of the hall was now replaced with bright sunlight. Gulls wheeled overhead, screeching at one another, and at the bottom of the deserted side street a slice of the sea shimmered invitingly. She tasted the salty air with relish and then arched her back until it hurt. Bones clicked and crunched as she rolled her shoulders. She had to wonder if she was getting too old for tattooing. But there was nothing else she could do – and truly, nothing else she'd damn well want to do. She'd been inking people since she was eighteen, nineteen long years, tattooing thousands of square metres of skin in that time.

Thrusting a hand into her bag to check she had a packet of cigarettes, Marni set off through the warren of narrow streets that made up Brighton's Lanes. It was a bank holiday weekend and tourists thronged the alleys, drawn like magpies to the vintage jewellery and antique shops, or looking in the chi-chi boutiques for the ideal wedding outfit or perfect pair of brogues. All her favourite cafés were packed, but she didn't mind. Today she'd rather take her caffeine fix in the open air, so she emerged from the Lanes onto North Street and cut through to the outdoor café in the Pavilion Gardens.

There was a long queue of people waiting at the serving hatch, which meant she'd probably be late getting back for Steve, but an extra few minutes out in the fresh air would make it worthwhile.

She looked up at the sky. Pale blue. Not the bright azure of a summer's day, but a soft periwinkle, diluted by wisps of dissolving cloud, fading to a hazy grey horizon that merged with the sea. Perfect for a spring bank holiday weekend.

'What'll it be, love?'

'Black Americano. Two shots, please.'

'Right you are.'

'And a muffin,' she added as an afterthought. Low blood sugar. It wasn't the best choice of food for a diabetic but she could adjust her insulin dose later to compensate.

Chattering sightseers emerged from the Pavilion, still amazed by what they'd seen inside. It was a Disney palace built in Regency times, a wedding cake concoction of onion domes, spiky towers and pale creamy stucco which always made Marni think of Scheherazade and the *One Thousand and One Nights*. She'd fallen in love with the place on her very first day in Brighton. She sighed, looking round for a place to sit. All the benches were taken and people sprawled on the lawns, eating and drinking, laughing or lying peacefully in the sun.

Then she saw him and her stomach contracted. She turned straight back to the serving hatch, hoping that he hadn't seen her. She wasn't in the mood for an encounter with her husband this morning. Her ex-husband, to be precise – unpredictable at the best of times and always challenging in terms of the mixed emotions he stirred up. Together since they married when she was eighteen, apart for the last twelve years, but there was never a day when he wasn't in her thoughts. Co-parenting complicated a relationship that the term love-hate could have been invented for.

She risked a quick glance, and watched Thierry Mullins striding across the grass with a thunderous expression clouding his features. He looked shifty, glancing from side to side and over his shoulder. What was he doing out here? He was supposed to be at the convention hall – he was a member of the organising team.

'Two pounds forty, please.'

Marni paid for her coffee, grabbed the cardboard cup and sidled around to the far side of the café to avoid being seen by Thierry. Her hands shook with adrenalin as she lit a cigarette. How did he still have that effect on her? They'd been divorced for longer than they'd been married, but he still looked the same as when she'd first met him. Tall and lean with a handsome face, his black skin darkened by the tattoos that had kick-started her life-long fascination with this living art. Just as often as she tried to avoid him, she felt drawn to him. They'd nearly got back together on a score of occasions, until her instinct for self-protection had slammed on the brakes. But moving on from the relationship? She'd given up hope. She took a deep drag of her cigarette. Caffeine, nicotine, deep breaths. She closed her eyes, waiting for the chemicals to make themselves felt.

She dropped the stub of her cigarette in the dregs of her coffee and looked around for a bin, spotting a green plastic dumpster at the back corner of the café. She raised the lid with the foot pedal and, as she dropped the cup inside, a rush of putrid air overwhelmed her. It was a stench far worse than the usual smell of a park bin on a balmy day. Bile rose in her throat as she peered into the dark interior. And immediately wished she hadn't.

Amid the crushed Coke cans, discarded newspapers and fast food wrappers she could see something. Pallid and glistening shapes that swiftly materialised into an arm, a leg, a torso. A human body, unmistakeably dead. She saw a flurry of movement – a rat, gnawing at the edge of a dark wound. Disturbed by the onslaught of daylight, it disappeared back into the rubbish with a squeal.

Marni stepped back, letting the lid come crashing down.

She fled.

2

Francis

Francis Sullivan closed his eyes as he allowed the communion wafer to glue itself to the roof of his mouth. He tried to focus on the murmurs of the celebrants and the congregation around him, but his mind was elsewhere.

Detective Inspector Francis Sullivan.

He let the words roll silently over his tongue. That would be him, tomorrow, first day on the job. The shock promotion had made him, at twenty-nine, the youngest DI on the Sussex force. He was more nervous about it than he had been on his first day at secondary school. It was a good thing, but terrifying. It showed a huge leap of faith by his superiors. Sure, he'd passed the exams he needed to with flying colours. He'd performed well for the interview board. But why promote him so soon, given his relative inexperience on the job? Because his father had been a celebrated QC? He hated the thought.

His new boss, DCI Martin Bradshaw, had looked less than thrilled when he'd told Francis of the promotion. He hadn't congratulated him, either. It made Francis wonder if Bradshaw had been totally behind the decision, or whether he'd simply been railroaded by the other members of the interview board.

His stomach lurched as his thoughts turned to Rory Mackay. Detective Sergeant Rory Mackay. Passed over for the job and now assigned to be his number two. He'd met Mackay last week. A formal introduction in the boss's office, during which the infinitely more experienced DS had made it clear that he wasn't impressed. He'd worn the expression of a man who'd found the remaining half of a maggot in the apple he'd just bitten. Francis had kept his cool with polite detachment – he was aware of the risks of trying to become too chummy with your team – but he could sense theirs was going to be a prickly relationship.

The man was willing him to fail. And Francis knew that he wasn't the only one.

'The blood of Christ.'

Francis snapped open his eyes and raised his head to receive the scant sip of wine from the chalice.

'Amen,' he murmured.

So be it.

But was it too soon? Throughout the selection process, he'd felt calm and confident. Exams had never been a problem for him. But had his success on paper created expectations that he'd find difficult to live up to on the job? The dangers of early promotion were mythical in the force. He'd heard stories in the cafeteria, apocryphal or not. Running before you could walk. Failing to get results. It wouldn't need to be a catastrophic mistake for him to end up sidelined at this point, just a couple of tough cases that went cold.

Anxiety dulled the pleasure of his achievement. *Detective Inspector Francis Sullivan.* He hadn't been sleeping since he'd heard the news. And the mental focus he'd need to rely on had evaporated. Damn it. He might be wet behind the ears but he wasn't stupid. The team he was taking charge of didn't think he could do the job. Didn't think he was ready for it. He needed to get them on side from the very first day, on the very first case. Otherwise, they'd be proved right – he'd fail. They could see to that. Bradshaw and Mackay would be watching and waiting. They'd find ways of tripping him up.

He glanced up at the carved figure of Jesus, suspended on his cross above the chancel. The Son of God was giving him a reproachful look, and Francis looked down again quickly. He muttered the bare bones of a prayer, crossed himself and rose to go back to his pew, feeling admonished for his distraction.

He sang the final hymn on autopilot, taking no meaning from the words, then knelt to pray. He refocused for a couple of minutes on his reason for being here – a thought for his mother, an intercession for his sister. A benediction for their carers. Nothing for his father.

The vibration in his trouser pocket didn't give him enough time to get to his phone before the notification sounded. A bleeping that seemed longer and louder than usual in the silent church. Heads turned and a woman hissed her disapproval. He scrambled to mute his phone, glancing up at Father William.

Francis bowed his head in regret, then surreptitiously read the text that had come in.

It was from DS Mackay.

Starting work a day early. Dead body called in. Pavilion Gardens.

As soon as it was decently possible, Francis left his pew and headed towards the open doors at the back of the church. In the porch, Father William pursed his lips before speaking.

'Francis.'

'I can't apologise enough, Father. I thought it was switched off.'

'That's not my worry. You looked troubled throughout the service. Do you want to talk about it?'

'I would like to,' said Francis. He meant it. 'But I have to go. A body's been found.'

Father William crossed himself with a silent murmur, then

put a hand on Francis's forearm. 'So much evil abounds. I worry for you doing this work, Francis. Always walking on the edge of despair.'

'But on the side of justice.'

'God is the final arbiter, remember that.'

A middle-aged woman jostled Francis with her elbow. He was taking up more than his fair share of the vicar's time.

The final arbiter. Francis chewed the phrase over. In heaven, maybe. But down here on earth it fell to people like him to chase down the evil that men do. His job was to track killers and bring them to justice. The first had just come calling and he was determined to succeed, so help him God.

And if there was no help coming from above, he'd damn well manage it on his own.

3

Francis

Francis inched his car along New Road. Even with his blue light flashing, the bank holiday crowds weren't accommodating. Shared bloody space – it meant nobody knew who owned which bit of the road and everybody assumed they had right of way. He gave a short blast of his siren to shift a slow-moving family out of his path, raising his eyebrows as they glared at him.

He pulled up by a row of benches in front of the Pavilion Gardens. A woman feeding ice cream to her children scowled at him for driving where she was walking, but most of the small crowd of people that had gathered there were too busy craning their necks at the police activity on the other side of the fence to take any notice of his arrival. He was relieved to see that the whole area had been taped off and that several uniformed officers were maintaining the cordon.

He showed his warrant card and was quickly waved in. Rory Mackay spotted him straight away and came towards him, his bulky figure swathed in a white paper SOCO suit.

'Sergeant Mackay,' said Francis, with a nod. 'Give me a run-down on what we've got.'

'You'll need to cover up first, boss,' said the DS, giving him a withering look. 'I've got a spare suit in the boot of my car.'

Francis followed Mackay to a silver Mitsubishi parked with

several other cars just inside the North Gate, on the other side of the gardens. He was silently spitting that he hadn't anticipated the need for a crime scene suit. And that he hadn't thought to come to this side where he could have parked more easily.

'Thought you'd be here a bit quicker, given it's your first case.'

Francis felt his shoulder muscles contract. 'I was in church, Mackay. I shouldn't have got the message at all. Or at least not until I got outside.'

'Right you are.'

Francis saw the smirk that drifted momentarily across the sergeant's features.

Mackay opened the boot of his car and tossed Francis a SOCO suit. Francis took an inventory of the boot's contents as he pulled it on. Three boxes of Stella, bottles, and two boxes of Heineken, tins. Barbecue coal. It was easy to tell how Mackay had been planning to spend his Sunday.

'Should be your size. Careful putting it on – they tear easily.'

'I have worn them before,' said Francis.

The suit was a size too small, the trouser legs too short. Rory propped himself against the side of his car, sucking on an e-cig as he waited.

'Let's get on,' said Francis, still adjusting the sleeves of the suit to his satisfaction.

Mackay slammed the boot and they set off back towards the café.

'Desk sergeant took a call at 11.47 a.m. reporting a dead body in a dumpster behind the Pavilion Gardens Café. No other details at that point.'

'Any idea yet who made the call?'

'Woman's voice. She hung up before the sarge could ask her name.'

'But we've got the number?'

'It was a pay-as-you-go.'

That was the first thing that would need to be followed up.

'The body?' continued Francis.

'Male, naked. Very obvious bang on the head and a significant wound to the left shoulder and torso. No ID as yet but he's got a number of tattoos which should help.'

'Find anything else?'

'We'll be able to search the dumpster once the body's been removed – we're just waiting on Rose.'

Rose Lewis, the forensic pathologist. A safe pair of hands – Francis had worked with her on a couple of cases during his stint as a DC.

'Right, I'd better take a look,' said Francis.

As they walked back down towards the café, Rory took a call. 'Yes, sir, he's here now, sir . . . I've secured the area and put SOCO to work. Liaised with pathology, yes . . .'

Rory fell silent for moment, nodding. 'Yes, I think his phone's switched on now. He was in church.'

Francis could hear by Rory's tone what he thought of that. He sped up his pace – this wasn't exactly the start he'd envisaged for his first case.

Rory led him across the grass and around the side of the café. There was a green plastic bin towards the rear of the building. Francis picked up the stench of the contents as they drew nearer, and began breathing through his mouth. He felt his gag reflex tighten and saliva flooded his tongue but he fought against it. White-suited SOCOs swarmed the area, scouring the ground, measuring distances and taking photos.

'Open it up,' said Rory.

DC Tony Hitchins was standing guard over the dumpster. As Francis and Rory approached, he used the foot pedal to raise the lid, trying to avoid looking inside as he did so. Francis pulled on a pair of latex gloves and stepped forward.

Hitchins was looking distinctly off-colour, and as Francis came level with him, he saw the constable's stomach and chest start to contract. His lips were clamped together in a thin line.

'If you're going to puke, Hitchins, get out of my crime scene.'

Francis caught the lid of the dumpster as Hitchins made a dash across the lawn. He only just managed to scrabble under the blue-and-white tape before bending double and depositing what was left of his Sunday breakfast in the grass.

'For pity's sake,' said Francis, and Rory shook his head. But their eyes didn't meet. There wasn't a policeman on the force who hadn't thrown up after seeing a body at one time or another, and probably more recently than any of them would care to admit.

Francis turned back to the dumpster and steeled himself to look inside, hoping desperately he wouldn't repeat Hitchins' faux pas. Not today.

And there it was. His body. His first victim as senior investigating officer. This initial encounter was something akin to a blind date, with an individual he would come to know extremely well over the coming weeks and months. He'd learn more about the victim than he knew about members of his own family – and he'd likely discover secrets that would shake the victim's family to its core. For now, the man was a stranger – grey, slick-skinned and decomposing, rotting like the garbage which surrounded him. But with his team, Francis would burrow under his skin to see what made him tick and who might want him dead.

Francis mentally logged the shocking image. Limbs twisted, skin like putty, and red-black flesh where his face and torso had become rat fodder. Even the man's own mother wouldn't recognise him. This image would fuel Francis's outrage and keep his focus sharp.

'Sergeant Mackay? Sergeant Mackay?'

A voice from behind made Francis turn round. Rory was already walking towards the tape perimeter where a man with a camera slung round his neck was standing. Press.

'Tom,' said Rory with a nod. 'Thought you'd pitch up sooner or later.'

'Your bad penny,' said the man, grinning. 'What you got, Mackay?'

'Nothing for you,' said Rory. 'We'll release information to the press when it's appropriate, not before. Now fuck off.'

He turned and walked back over to Francis. 'Watch out for that one. Tom Fitz of the *Argus*. All over bloody crime scenes like a rash.'

'How does he get here so fast?' said Francis.

Rory shrugged. 'Monitors the radio, buys the desk sergeants drinks.' He was clearly unimpressed.

'Well, keep him sweet,' said Francis. 'You never know when the press can be useful.'

'Rose is here,' Rory said abruptly. He obviously had no interest in pandering to reporters.

'Detective *Inspector* Sullivan,' came a friendly voice.

Francis turned to face Rose Lewis, who was directing a partially recovered Hitchins to set her various equipment bags down nearby. She was so petite that even the smallest crime scene suit swamped her and she had to stand on tiptoes to see over the edge of the dumpster.

'Ooh, nasty,' she said. She turned to Hitchins. 'Can you find me a step ladder so I can take photos?'

'Yes, ma'am.'

'Congratulations are in order, I believe?' said Rose, as Hitchins went off on his mission.

'Yes, thanks,' said Francis. 'Enjoying your bank holiday weekend?'

'I am now. Your first body in charge?'

He nodded.

'Then you'd better bloody solve it, hadn't you?'

He knew that better than anyone.

And the consequences of failure.

4

Marni

It had taken all of Marni's courage to make the call. Knowing that she was talking to a cop on the other end of the line had left her almost as shaken as discovering the body in the first place. She'd kept it short and refused to give a name. Anything to do with the police was still a trigger for her, carrying her back to a time she'd rather forget. She'd sworn that she'd never, for the rest of her life, get involved with them again.

By the time she returned to the convention, Steve had been waiting half an hour for her and it was another half hour until her hands had stopped shaking enough for her to carry on tattooing him. But he hadn't seemed put out once she'd reluctantly admitted what had happened. Not surprisingly, he'd shown a prurient interest in her discovery.

'I've never seen a dead body. Did it really smell as bad as they say? Did the police come straight away?'

It made Marni's head ache and she cancelled her final appointment of the day. When the convention closed for the night, she felt wrung out and emotional. The image of the dead body kept springing into her mind and the stench still seemed to hang in her nostrils. If only she hadn't gone to the Pavilion Gardens. Talking to the police had raised her anxiety levels still further as the memories she'd worked so hard to suppress reared back into view.

Once her kit was stashed for the next day, Marni walked alone along the seafront in an effort to clear her head. She couldn't stop thinking about what she'd seen. The way the man's wet skin had glistened as the light fell on it. And those dark patches. At first, she'd taken them to be bruises but then she realised they were tattoos. The image was like a freeze-frame glued behind her eyelids – and each time she saw it, the details became clearer. The tattoo on the right-hand side of his torso – a pair of praying hands. And on one of his calves, a study of Saint Sebastian in black and grey, the arrow wounds picked out in red.

She tried to push thoughts of the body out of her mind to concentrate on where she was going. The front was busy with people and traffic. A high-pitched whine grew louder behind her, and she turned to see twenty to thirty mopeds streaming along the road, each vehicle decked out with mirrors, raccoon tails, pendants and flags. The mods were in town for the bank holiday and the riders were just as distinctive as the bikes, in their parkas, striped blazers, Hush Puppies and The Who memorabilia. The noise of the mopeds jangled her nerves as they passed by.

It was getting dark now. The sodium glare of the street lamps tinged everything a soothing deep amber, but Marni longed for somewhere darker and quieter. Relishing the cool air that bit the back of her throat, she dropped on silent feet down a flight of stone steps to the beach.

The tide was out and she walked over the crunching shingle to the water's edge. It was cold and dark here, the cacophony of the pier obliterated by the roar and hiss of the waves. The sound was as mesmerising as the grating buzz of the tattoo irons. She inhaled deep breaths of salt-laden air, massaging the over-worked muscles of her right arm as she walked. Tomorrow would be another long day of tattooing.

She scanned the deserted beach, her gaze coming to rest on a decrepit hulk standing a couple of hundred feet from the shore.

This was all that was left of the West Pier. Silhouetted against the dark sea, it had been left to rot after being gutted by fire. No longer umbilically attached to the shore, it was now an island haunted by the ghosts of long-forgotten holiday-makers and small-time local gangsters.

Her thoughts returned to the discovery of the body. What would have happened to the man in the dumpster if she hadn't found him? Would he have ended up in a landfill site somewhere, slowly dissolving until there was no trace left of him apart from his bones and his fillings, his tattoos vanishing as his corpse was devoured? Did inked flesh taste different to the rats that nibbled on the body? Or to the squirming maggots, fat and white, burrowing into the exposed red flesh? She shuddered to think about it.

Whoever had put him in there was almost certainly responsible for his death. She hoped to God the police would be able to find out and track down who did it. It was an unsettling thought that this sort of stuff went on so close to home.

Marni shivered. She'd come out here to clear and calm her mind for sleep. Fat chance. She tugged her light cardigan around her shoulders and turned back towards the lights of the Palace Pier, as alive and buzzing as the West Pier was dead. The wind dropped and for a few short moments she could hear her own footsteps crunching on the shingle slope. The beach that swarmed with people during the day was a lonely place at this hour.

Then a woman screamed.

Goose bumps skittered across Marni's skin like wind across the surface of a pond. Her chest tightened and she whirled around, staring into the darkness.

A second later there was a shriek of laughter, the same woman's voice, joined by a man. Marni took a deep breath and tried to calm herself down but her heart was pounding. The beach was deserted as she cut an angle towards the stone steps back up to the promenade.

She glanced ahead towards the Palace Pier. Shadowy figures were moving between the sturdy metal pillars that anchored it to the shore. Male voices rang out towards her through the spume-laden air.

'You alone, love?'

Marni turned away. He could rot in hell for all she cared.

'Come on, come and join us for a bit of fun.' A different voice, closer this time.

Marni ignored it, climbing up to the promenade as fast as she could.

As she walked back home through the night-time quiet of Kemptown, her thoughts kept coming back to the same thing. The Saint Sebastian tattoo on the man's leg. She knew why. It reminded her of Thierry's work, particularly the way the arrow wounds were picked out in red. *Thierry*. Why had Thierry been out in the Pavilion Gardens when he was supposed to be at the convention?

Please God, don't let this turn into something.

Could the tattoo on the man's body really be one of Thierry's? It was unlikely, and if it was, it probably meant nothing. Of course it meant nothing. She was making connections with the past that weren't rational. But when it came to Thierry, she never was rational. He had an emotional hold on her that only seemed to grow stronger, try as she might to deny it. Of course there was no connection between Thierry and the body in the dumpster. It was just her obsession with the man that dragged him into everything that happened to her.

As she turned into Great College Street, she could see a light on in the front room of her house. Alex was home. An eighteen-year-old boy didn't need to see his mother in this kind of state. She took a deep breath to compose herself and pulled her phone from her pocket. Even though she spent most of her time avoiding him and trying to suppress her feelings for him, it always seemed to be Thierry she needed at a moment of crisis. She dialled, waiting for an answer, hoping for reassurance.

'Thierry?'

All she could hear was white noise. Then bar noise.

'Marni?' His French accent changed the sound of her name.

'Obviously.'

'Marni! I'm in the bar with the guys. Come and join us. Charlie and Noa want to say hi.'

Charlie and Noa were Thierry's colleagues at Tatouage Gris, Brighton's only all-French tattoo studio. She could hear their voices in the background, as well as women's laughter. Tattoo groupies, no doubt, in town for the convention. Thierry was mad if he thought she'd be interested in joining them.

'No. You come here – I need to talk to you.' Suddenly she was desperate to see him and in the same instant she hated herself for it. He was an addiction she just couldn't seem to kick.

'About what?'

'I've had a really bad day.'

She heard Thierry sigh.

'Thierry, I found a body.' Her voice was an octave higher than usual. 'I'm scared . . .'

'Whoa, slow down. What are you talking about? Did you call the police?'

'Of course. But I need to discuss something with you.'

'No. I'm tired, *chérie*, and I'm not interested in dead people.'

'Thierry, come on. What if it was someone we knew? What if it was Alex?'

'It wasn't. I spoke to him an hour ago. He was feeding Pepper. You're out of dog food.'

Pepper. Her bulldog.

'Come on, Thierry. Please.'

Thierry made the vocal equivalent of the Gallic shrug, a nonchalant grunt that she used to love. 'If this is a plot to seduce me . . .'

'For fuck's sake.' She hung up on him and went inside.

'Mum!' Alex came into the hall and greeted her with a hug. 'How was your day?'

Marni squared her shoulders and smiled. 'Great. Did some good work on one of my regulars and a couple of walk-ups. Yours?'

Alex shrugged. 'Revision. Boring.'

A bowl of pasta and a glass of wine later, and Marni sank down onto the sofa to catch the news. Alex wanted to watch football but she had the remote. In retrospect, she wished she'd given in to him straight away.

. . . police are appealing for the anonymous caller who alerted them to a dead body found in Brighton Pavilion Gardens to come forward to help with their inquiries. The man, found in a rubbish container, has yet to be identified . . .

'Okay, Alex, let's see if they've scored yet.' She tossed him the remote, trying to hide the sudden tremble in her hands.

'No, wait – there's been a murder, right in Brighton. Nothing ever happens here.'

But Marni didn't want to hear more. 'You'll miss a goal,' she said.

With few facts to report, the news moved quickly on to another story and Alex flipped channels. They hadn't missed a goal and it turned out to be a dull match.

Alex grew restless. 'How was the show today?'

'It was good. Your father does a great job there – Brighton's always the best of the conventions.'

'Mum, do you think you'd ever get back together with Dad?'

Marni swallowed a gulp of wine the wrong way. She shook her head as she coughed. 'Where did that come from?'

'You still get on when you're together.'

'Sure.' It all seemed so simple to someone his age.

'And I know Dad would want it.'

Would he? Or was he having too much fun as a single man in a profession that afforded ample opportunities for flirtation? Marni sighed. 'The problem with your father isn't that he doesn't like the idea of being married. He's just not very good at the practical side of it.'

'No one's perfect, Mum. Not even you.'

Marni Mullins didn't dream. She couldn't afford to – dreams were too painful. She lay awake, eyes wide open in the black void. She'd long since given up on sleep but her mind wandered, untethered and unfocused. Alex's words rang in her ears.

Nothing ever happens here.

Only now something had happened and she was being drawn into it. A man was dead. And there was something about him tugging at the dark recesses of her mind. Something familiar. But what was the link? If he was a local man, who had been tattooed locally, she might know him. But that was hardly likely. Thousands of people in Brighton had tattoos. And even if Thierry had tattooed him, what of it? Did that implicate him in some way?

Marni snapped on the bedside light, blinding herself. She squeezed her eyes shut and fought back against the sob rising in her chest. There couldn't be a connection. It was just her mind in freefall between wakefulness and sleep. She sat up and the room spun. Bile burned at the back of her throat.

She ran to the bathroom, dry heaving, and bent over the toilet bowl with gritted teeth. Saliva flooded her mouth and she took deep breaths to counter the feeling, finally bringing herself under control. She slumped down onto the floor, her eyes watering. She blinked. There was blood spattered across the white tiles. In the distance, she heard the harsh grating of metal doors clanging shut. She saw brick walls painted institutional grey. Her belly and breasts were tight and taut in the last stages of pregnancy. Footsteps in the corridor, her blood running cold, an explosion of pain. She was crouching, bleeding and cramping, crying for help. Receiving only another kick in the gut . . .

She opened her eyes and the blood was gone. The dead body and the Saint Sebastian tattoo had triggered her. She needed to know, one way or the other, whether the tattoo on the murdered man was by Thierry. Hopefully not and then she could forget the whole thing.

Back in her bedroom, she looked for her phone and Googled the number for the Brighton Crimestoppers line.

It rang. And rang. And rang.

Marni waited. She didn't know why. It was twenty to three in the morning and there would be no one there to take her call.

Finally, she gave up. She tossed her phone aside and lay back, waiting for the fears to come crowding in.

5

Rory

The rancid stench of death assaulted Rory's nostrils before he'd even made it through the morgue doors. Within seconds the smell became a taste in his mouth. He started to cough and made a beeline for where he knew Rose Lewis kept the Vicks VapoRub. At the same time, his ears were hit by a barrage of choral music playing at high volume. Rose Lewis's morgue definitely wasn't the place for a hangover – he knew that from past experience.

'Morning,' shouted Rose over the noise. She was bent over the body of a naked man, a scalpel in her hand.

Rory nodded at her as he slicked translucent gel across his top lip to counter the rotten apple smell of the embalming fluid and the sharp vinegar tang of formaldehyde.

'*Membra Jesu Nostri*,' said Francis, who'd followed Rory in and was now waiting for him to finish with the Vicks.

Rory didn't have a clue what he was going on about.

'Damn, you're good, Sullivan,' said Rose, crossing over to her sound system and turning the volume down. 'Composer?'

'Buxtehude.'

'Of course. It's particularly suitable for work. The libretto details the individual body parts of the suffering Jesus. But you know that already.'

Rory handed Francis the pot of gel without commenting. The intellectuals, showing off to each other. It seemed to be a game they liked to play, seeing who could be the smartest. But it didn't solve cases and if Sullivan thought he'd be impressed by it, he'd need to think again.

Truth be told, the morgue wasn't Rory's favourite place, so he tried to minimise his time there. It wasn't that he didn't like Rose – she was always perfectly polite to him, if maybe a little patronising – but her self-assurance in the harsh glare of the polar white surroundings made him feel belittled at times. Of course, the work she did was valuable, but DNA evidence and blood spatters weren't everything, just part of the bigger picture. There was a growing tendency to view science as the whole case, instead of what it really was – a support tool to solid police work.

He pulled on a pair of latex gloves and followed the boss over to Rose's work station.

This was the only body on view, but the steel drawers that lined one wall held plenty more. Rose and her team worked their way diligently through them, piecing together the stories of their lives, prising secrets from their blood, flesh, bones and teeth. He wondered what she'd be able to tell them about dumpster man.

The body that lay in front of her on the autopsy table was partially covered by a white rubber sheet. Flat on his back, there was a cut from his sternum to his pubis, and Rose had started to remove his organs for further investigation. Rory studied the cadaver. The facial features were indistinct. The rats had stripped away the skin and flesh unevenly – part of one lip was missing, his nose had been chewed and both cheeks were mauled. A section of his torso had been similarly savaged. On the rest of his body, the skin was grey. Rory had seen enough recovered bodies over the years not to be fazed but he stole a sidelong glance at Francis. It wouldn't quite be fair to say he was rattled – in fact, he looked interested. But there was a tightness to his jawline that hadn't been there earlier.

Rose would have already photographed and measured the body. She would also have scraped the detritus from under the man's fingernails and logged each of his wounds and his tattoos in her taped report, pausing the music to record each detail. Right now, she was examining the inside of his mouth with gloved fingers. And next – the final indignity of an unexplained death – she would investigate his anus for signs of recent sex or sexual assault.

The two policemen watched her in silence until she finally switched off her dictaphone and looked up at them.

'Conclusions, Rose?' said Francis.

She killed the music. Thank God for that. It had been getting on his nerves.

'Conclusion one: I'm going to be in trouble with Mike for working on a bank holiday Monday.'

Francis shrugged. 'If I had my way, killers would only strike nine to five, Monday to Friday.'

Rose laughed.

'Just think of the overtime,' said Rory. 'How's Laurie?'

'True enough. Brownie points to you, Rory, for asking. He's good. Just started big school and loving it.'

'And this?' Francis nodded at the body to pull them back on track.

Rose flipped back to being business-like in a second.

'Right, here's what I've got so far. My estimate of the time of death is twenty-four to forty-eight hours ago but I can't tell you for sure if he was dead or alive when he was deposited in the dumpster. I assume your team will be checking when those bins were last emptied.'

'Hollins is on it,' said Rory.

'And the CCTV on New Road?'

'Hitchins,' said Francis.

'The Tweedles,' said Rose. 'Stay on their case – they can be a bit slow.'

'Don't I know it,' muttered Rory.

Tweedle Dum and Tweedle Dee, as Hitchins and Hollins were known around the station. They bore an uncanny resemblance to each other, both with unruly brown hair and physiques that were one doughnut on the wrong side of fitness.

Rose looked at Francis and then at Rory.

'You lucked out having this one as your number two, Francis.'

Francis nodded but stayed silent.

He can't even bring himself to agree? thought Rory.

'Rory's one of our most experienced,' continued Rose. 'He knows what he's doing, so use his knowledge.'

The boss frowned. Rory suppressed a smirk – it wasn't exactly a vote of confidence in Sullivan from Rose.

'I'm sure Rory will let me know if I'm ever doing anything wrong,' said the boss. There was an edge to his voice.

Rory sniffed. He suddenly felt as uncomfortable with the turn the conversation was taking as Francis evidently did. Rose was stirring, and Rory had to ask himself why. What was her agenda?

'He wasn't killed outright by the blow to his head,' she said, thankfully turning her attention back to the body.

'Are you certain of that?' said Francis. He peered at the partially shaved cranium. Rose turned the head slightly to one side so they could both see the bloody indent in the skull.

'Absolutely. That wound wouldn't have been fatal. It did fracture his skull and it would have rendered him unconscious. Might have resulted in lasting brain damage.'

'So what did kill him?' said Rory.

'It was a combination of factors,' said Rose. Her voice rang with confidence in her findings. 'After he'd been hit, he was unconscious. My guess is that he was still alive when abandoned.

There was significant blood loss and that, coupled with prolonged exposure, is what killed him.'

'Blood loss from his head? The wound doesn't look that big,' said Francis.

'Some from the head, but mainly from this wound here.' She indicated the large bloody area of exposed flesh on the man's shoulder and torso.

'I thought that was rats, post mortem,' said Rory.

'Not entirely. This is where it gets interesting, why I called you both in so quickly.'

Rory studied the bloody pulp.

'Take a closer look,' urged Rose. She turned to the bench behind her and picked up a magnifying glass. She gave it to Francis. 'See? There are cut marks. As far as I can make out, they were made with a short, extremely sharp blade.'

Francis bent down and examined the area with a gloved hand. 'I see what you mean.'

He handed the magnifying glass to Rory and stepped back. Rory examined the wound. Rose was right. There were unmistakeable cuts to the flesh that couldn't have been made by animals.

'Jesus!'

He noticed the boss wincing at his choice of words. Trust his luck to get stuck with a God-botherer for a DI.

'Do you think these were done before or after the blow to the head?' he asked.

'I'm only guessing at this point, but probably after,' said Rose. 'There's a level of precision that suggests the victim wasn't struggling at the time. But the cuts aren't deep. They weren't intended to kill. It looks more like someone deliberately cut skin and flesh away from his body. But it's hard to be sure. There are as many bite marks as cuts.'

Rory continued to examine the exposed flesh. 'The cuts all

seem to be around the edges of the wound.'

'The perpendicular cuts, yes,' said Rose. 'But here and here in the centre there appear to be some cuts horizontal to the dermis.'

Rory blinked and looked again. He could just see, amid the torn and dirty pulp that the flesh had become, several small, straight lines cutting deeper into the substrate. His stomach muscles clenched and he had to clamp his jaw shut for a couple of moments, until the feeling of nausea passed.

'Let me see,' said Francis.

Rory handed him the magnifying glass with relief.

'What does that mean?' he said, peering through it.

'It means, Francis, that your victim was flayed. Most probably, judging from the blood lost from his body, while he was still alive.'

6

Francis

Black jeans, black T-shirts, shaved heads or dreadlocks. Bare. Tattooed. Skin. Gallons of ink embedded in living flesh flowed past Francis and eddied around him so quickly he couldn't make out what the images were. Dark black, smudgy blue or brightly coloured flashes. What the hell was he doing at a tattoo convention on a bank holiday Monday? He'd sent a grumbling Mackay back to the scene of the crime to conduct another fingertip search of the area, looking for pieces of flesh that might have been cut from the body. He, meanwhile, was here to track down the mysterious caller. They'd linked the phone that made the call to a local tattoo artist. Her website told them she was at the convention, and the chances were that she'd have more information. He wanted to find out why the woman had been so evasive.

Francis felt painfully self-conscious the moment he stepped into the main hall of the Brighton Conference Centre. He must have been the only person in the building without a tattoo – and certainly the only person wearing a suit.

Taking a deep but reluctant breath, he moved forward into the throng.

People swarmed by him, bumping and pushing, treading on his toes, craning their necks to see into the booths. Then there was the noise. Each booth emitted heavy metal loud enough to drown out that of their neighbours.

And above it all, he could hear a constant high-pitched electrical whine. He couldn't locate the source until his eyes came to rest on a man's naked back. A woman was tattooing him – the noise was the collective drone of the tattoo guns. Blood oozed from the black lines she inscribed. Francis could taste its copper taint in the air and felt repulsed.

The hall was airless and far too warm. He pushed his way to the end of the aisle, desperate to find an open space. He'd never understood the appeal of getting a tattoo, and en masse like this, he understood it even less. Surely all these people had looked better before they'd permanently marked their bodies. There was something tribal about it all. But what tribe, what meaning?

'Excuse me?'

He caught a passing man by the shoulder. The youth turned his head to look at Francis. There was a blue spider's web tattooed across the top left-hand side of his forehead, disappearing beneath his hairline.

'Yeah?'

'I need to find a tattoo artist called Marni Mullins.'

The boy pulled a folded piece of paper from the back pocket of his jeans. It was a schematic of the convention hall with the booths numbered. He turned it over and consulted the list of tattoo artists on the other side.

'Marni . . .?'

'Mullins.'

He looked down and Francis could see the rest of the spider's web and the heavy outline of a word tattooed under his short blonde hair. He squinted at it, but couldn't work out what it said.

'Stand twenty-eight.'

'Thanks,' replied Francis.

'No problem, mate.' Then he disappeared back into the

seething throng before Francis could ask to look at the diagram to work out exactly where stand twenty-eight was. No matter. Presumably they were arranged in numerical order. With a sigh, he launched himself back into the crush.

Three girls in strapless 1950s dresses, with Marilyn Monroe hair, propelled him along in a cloud of cloying perfume. Their arms, shoulders and chests were spattered with brightly coloured tattoos of flowers, bluebirds and love hearts. He hung back to escape from their gaggle of noise, only to find himself in the middle of a different gang: goths with hair as black as their inkings. He checked the stand numbers and ducked across to the next row.

Francis elbowed his way along, glancing from side to side. A girl lay virtually naked on a massage table as two heavily tattooed men worked simultaneously on a spectacular Chinese back piece. A man sat silently with his eyes shut, tears washing down his cheeks, as a girl made deft strokes on a geometric pattern on his forearm. Sharing the same booth, a man was tattooing the top of another man's skull. *God, but that had to hurt, didn't it?* The guy being tattooed wasn't even wincing.

Finally, he came to number twenty-eight. A female tattoo artist was busy working on a customer who looked far too young for a tattoo. Was this the woman whose phone they'd traced? She was small and wiry, perched on a stool and concentrating intently on a huge scarlet and pink chrysanthemum tattoo on the girl's leg. Her unruly dark hair was pulled up into a crooked ponytail but more of it had escaped than was being held in place. She wore faded denim dungarees over a white vest, and both of her muscular arms carried full sleeve tattoos in swirling blues and greens.

Francis stared at her for a moment. Would she help or did she have something to hide? There was a certain sector of the public that seemed to relish being able to associate themselves with a murder, but not this woman. She'd been determined to remain anonymous.

He coughed loudly to catch her attention. 'Are you Marni Mullins?'

The woman was tattooing high up on the inside of her client's thigh. The girl moved her other leg restlessly, and the small sighs escaping her lips sounded to Francis as if they were as much from pleasure as pain. Unperturbed, Marni Mullins continued shading flower petals in deep pink ink.

He spoke again and this time she raised the needle from the downy skin before looking up to see who was addressing her.

'That's me.'

He saw now that she was older than he'd expected – well into her thirties, with small crows' feet just visible at the corners of her eyes.

'I'm fully booked for the rest of the afternoon,' she said, dropping her gaze back to her work.

'I'm not here for a tattoo.'

Marni Mullins looked up at him again, this time giving him more of her attention. She shook her head, as if realising she'd made a mistake.

'No, obviously not. What do you want?'

'My name's DI Francis Sullivan. I'm looking into an incident that occurred yesterday in the Pavilion Gardens. I'd appreciate it if you'd put down your tattoo gun and talk to me.'

'Machine.'

'What?'

'It's a tattoo machine, or a tattoo iron. We don't call it a tattoo gun.'

'Tattoo machine, whatever. I need to talk to you.'

'Why would you want to talk to me?' Her tone was hostile.

'I have reason to believe that you found the body and made

the anonymous call to Brighton police station yesterday. Is that the case?'

The girl being tattooed was suddenly interested and looked round to see who Marni was talking to.

'You know someone who's been murdered?' she said. She had a lisp, Francis noted.

'No,' said Marni. 'It's a long story.'

'I'd rather discuss this in private,' said Francis.

Marni Mullins' forehead creased into a frown. 'Give me an hour then, if you want privacy. I can't stop in the middle of this.'

'You're obstructing a police investigation.'

'And you're costing me money and my professional reputation. I'll be done in an hour and if that's not good enough for you, you'll have to arrest me.'

This wasn't the way to keep his witness co-operative. He attempted a more placatory tone. 'Okay. We'll talk in an hour. Where?'

'Meet me in the convention office on the ground floor. Bring coffee.'

The girl grinned at him. 'You'll have time to get a tattoo.'

Francis ignored her. 'I'll see you in an hour,' he said to Marni.

'Stiff,' muttered the girl under her breath, settling herself back down on the bench.

'Policemen,' said Marni Mullins, obviously not caring that Francis was still within earshot. 'They never get it. You try to help them with something and they think they can walk all over you. Bloody bastards.'

7

Marni

Two hours later, Marni pushed open the door of the tiny convention office, wondering whether calling the police had been the right thing to do. The appearance of the gangly young police officer at the front of her booth had unnerved her and she wasn't happy about the prospect of having to go through the whole thing again, face to face. Now, as she stepped inside, the room seemed smaller than ever with Francis Sullivan's long limbs concertinaed onto the chair behind Thierry's desk.

Bulging files, piles of papers, precarious towers made from boxes of convention programmes, half-drunk cups of coffee and an overflowing bin – it was all far too familiar. Marni lifted a stack of documents off the chair opposite Francis before sitting down. She watched him warily as she did so. He looked young for a detective inspector – and completely out of place. No one wore a suit to a tattoo convention. Ever. In her world, men who wore suits were generally not good news.

However, even she couldn't miss a certain boyish charm about him. He was interesting looking – spiky red-blonde hair, with a slightly crooked mouth and hawkish nose. His mood didn't seem to have improved by being kept waiting. He glared at her from across the desk.

'Sorry to have kept you,' she said. She doubted that it sounded convincing.

He replied with the smallest of nods, then pointed to one of two takeout coffee cups.

'You found the body, didn't you?' His tone made it clear that it wasn't really a question.

Marni took a sip of coffee. It was cold.

'I called it in.'

'You didn't leave your name.'

'That hardly seems to have mattered. You know who I am, evidently. How does that work?'

DI Sullivan frowned at her.

'I could charge you with wasting police time and money. I've spent half a day tracking you down from your mobile phone number.'

This was typical. Of course, he hadn't come here to thank her for doing her civic duty. It was just the usual shit – she had done something wrong and it was his job to reprimand her for it. She was wasting her time and there were clients waiting.

'Sorry,' she said, pushing back her chair as she stood up to leave.

Sullivan stood up faster and blocked the door.

'I haven't finished with you yet,' he said. 'I need to go through exactly what happened when you found the body. We can do it here or I can take you down to the station.'

Marni sat down again. Dammit! She couldn't handle a police station. Why had she gone out to the park the previous day?

'What do you need to know?'

Sullivan sat down again too.

'Right,' he said, 'from the beginning and don't leave anything out.' He took a smartphone from his breast pocket and detached a stylus from it, ready to write.

Marni took a sip of her coffee, grimaced at the lack of sugar, and then ran through the details of how she found the body. It only took three minutes – getting the coffee, smoking the cigarette, opening the dumpster – but he wrote down every word. She didn't tell him that she had been lurking there to avoid Thierry.

'Did you notice any tattoos on the body?' he said.

'Yes ... a vague impression. But I can't remember what they were.'

The policeman put his hand, palm down, on a brown envelope that was lying on the desk.

'He had quite a number of tattoos and I need to know who did them.'

'Why?' Her heart began pounding.

Sullivan picked up the envelope. He spread a sheaf of eight-by-ten photos across a space on the desk's cluttered surface. They were all black-and-white close-ups of tattoos – a Saint Sebastian, a pair of praying hands, an eagle perched on a skull, a coil of barbed wire around an upper arm. Marni bent forward to inspect them.

'Looks like the guy was quite a collector,' she said.

'A collector?'

'A tattoo collector,' she explained. 'Look, these are all by different artists.'

'You can tell?'

It was her turn to give him a withering look. 'They're all completely different styles. Mostly good work, but it's quite a mixture.'

She looked at each one closely. The praying hands were good, really good. He must have paid a fair amount for them. She put the image down and picked up the next in the pile. It hit her like a sledgehammer between the eyes. She dropped the photo in the sharp realisation that she was almost certainly looking at a tattoo by her ex-husband. The Saint Sebastian tattoo in the picture had all the hallmarks of Thierry's work – just as she'd suspected.

'You recognise it?'

She shook her head quickly. Too violently.

'Please, Ms Mullins. It could have some bearing on the case.'

Marni felt anxiety building in her chest. She didn't want to get mixed up with the police again and that could happen only too easily if Thierry was somehow involved. She wanted no part in it. She shook her head and said nothing, willing Sullivan to leave her alone.

'If you don't tell me something that you know, that's relevant to my case, I'll have to arrest you for obstruction. So, if you know who did that tattoo, it would be in your interests to tell me.'

Marni closed her eyes and pursed her lips. Could it really be linked to the man's death?

'It looks like the work of my ex-husband.' Her voice was a whisper.

'What did you say?'

Marni paused and swallowed. Her mouth was dry.

'My ex-husband.' Loud enough this time.

'His name?'

'Thierry Mullins. But you can't really think that means he has something to do with it? The man had lots of tattoos from different designers.'

He ignored her question.

'Can you tell me where I'm likely to find Thierry? I need to have a word with him – he might be able to help identify the man.'

'We're sitting in his office.' She answered him on autopilot.

A few minutes later, there was the sound of a foot hitting the bottom of the door and Thierry Mullins appeared, clearly unhappy at having been summoned to his own office. He glared from Marni to DI Sullivan and folded his arms defensively across his chest.

'Whatever it is, I don't have time for it.'

It was the first time Marni had seen him to talk to in several months. Despite co-parenting a teenager and all the joint history that brought, she usually tried to avoid direct encounters with him as far as possible – apart from Sunday night. But now he was here, she drank him in. She could smell the scent of his sweat mingled with his cologne. He looked tired, and there was more grey in his hair than when they'd been together. Her eyes roamed over the dark tattoos on his muscular arms until she had the sense to look away.

He had been, for a short spell at least, an excellent husband. Through all the turmoil of their early years together, he had stood by her, marrying her when they discovered she was pregnant, helping her get over the trauma of what happened, caring for Alex when she couldn't ... But that was a long time ago. Their marriage had lasted a scant seven years before his eyes had begun to wander.

Of course, he was still a great father to Alex – she would never deny that. And he had a lot of good qualities besides. A bon viveur who was the life and soul of the party, humorous, kind-hearted, generous with his praise, if sometimes quick to anger. He was a brilliant tattooist of religious iconography and he made a more than decent job of putting on a great tattoo convention. But she hated him. At least, she told herself she hated him – and this was for her own protection. There was too much darkness in their shared past. Even if hearing his French accent could make her think of doing things that would have seemed indecent even when they were still married.

'Marni?' Thierry was looking down at her with concern.

Francis Sullivan stepped in and took over. He held out the picture to Thierry.

'Did you do this tattoo?'

Thierry glanced down at the picture and then back at Marni.

'What's this all about?' The question was clearly directed at her.

'Mr Mullins . . .'

'You're police, aren't you?'

'Yes.'

He turned to leave the room. 'If you're here to harass my wife, I would think about it very carefully.'

'Thierry.' Marni reached out a hand to touch his arm. 'Wait.'

'Come on, Marni, let's get out of here.'

'Mr Mullins, if you do that, I'll come after you with a warrant. Now, please, just answer the question. Did you do this tattoo?' The DI was still holding out the photograph.

Thierry stepped forward. He was several inches taller than the policeman and bulked out with muscles.

'What if I did?' His voice was practically a growl.

'We're trying to identify a body. Can you help?' Francis's voice had taken on a new tone of weariness.

Thierry looked at Marni.

'Someone, somewhere has to know what's happened to this man,' she answered, struck anew by the horror of what she had seen. She nodded at Thierry to take the picture.

He studied it carefully.

'It's possible,' he said.

Marni put out a hand towards Thierry's laptop, which was lying at one end of the desk.

'Why not check? If you did it, there'll be a picture in your archives.'

Thierry bent over the desk and fired up his computer. The three of them huddled in silence as he searched. Finally, he clicked on a folder headed 'Tattoos by subject'. It opened to show a list of files with headings such as 'Virgin M', 'Vengeful angels',

'Lucifer'. He chose a file labelled 'St S'. A succession of images of Saint Sebastian tattoos spread across the screen. He flicked past several but each one had significant differences to the one in the photo – a different placing of the arrows in his torso, his head bent to the other side.

'Wait,' said Marni. 'That's it. Go back.'

Thierry scrolled back up.

'You're right,' he said. 'They're the same.'

'Who was the client?' said Sullivan.

'I don't remember the name of every person I've ever tattooed. There have been hundreds.'

'What about the date?' said Marni. 'The photo file will have a date – then you can check your appointment book for that day.'

Thierry clicked through the file directory.

'May the fourth, twenty-ten.'

Marni and Francis waited in silence as he loaded his calendar. The only sound was the clicking of his fingers on the keyboard.

'Evan Armstrong. I remember him now. A big guy. Bastard ran out on me without paying.'

'Yes, he was about six two,' confirmed Francis.

'He already had a few pieces when I worked on him,' said Thierry.

Francis took the opportunity to thrust the rest of the pictures at him. 'These are his other tattoos. Did you do any of them?'

Marni shook her head but Thierry took his time leafing through them.

'No. He already had that barbed wire. What a crap piece.' He moved on to the praying hands. 'This is much better ...'

He carried on flipping through the photos. Marni peered at them over his shoulder.

At the last picture, she gasped. Thierry swore softly in French. They were gazing at a colour picture of a torso. The whole of the left shoulder was a bloody mess. The wound extended down the man's back and around his chest. Francis snatched the picture back.

'Sorry. You weren't meant to see that.'

'Rats?' said Thierry.

'Yes, but . . .' Francis took a deep breath. 'We think someone cut away a piece of flesh from that area as well.'

Marni's head snapped up to look at him. 'Let me see it again.'

He handed her the still and she studied it more carefully this time, the colour draining from her face. She traced the outline of the wound with a finger and then passed her hand across her face as if to try to erase the image from her eyes.

'I know what this is,' she said slowly, pointing to the wound with her finger. 'Look at the shape – it's symmetrical. Someone's taken a tattoo from his body.'

ii

I enjoy working with living flesh.

The soft rasping sound of a blade tugging against the skin. The copper smell of deep scarlet. The warmth of fresh blood cascading between my fingers.

I miss them.

The skin dies as I take it from the body. But for a while it's still warm and pliant. Sticky on one side with clotting blood. The other side might be smooth or it might be hairy. Soft if the skin is from a woman, usually slightly rougher if it's from a man. Though not always. Some men have very soft skin.

It's time to find my next victim. It's time to sharpen my blades. It's time to get back to work. The list is still long.

8

Francis

As he opened his office door, Francis wondered if he dared congratulate himself on getting off to a flying start. Getting a fast ID on the body could make all the difference to solving a murder case – most murderers have some sort of link to their victim.

'Rory,' he called out as he sat down.

Rory appeared in his office doorway.

'Any confirmation that our body is actually who Mullins says it is?'

'Aye,' said Rory, holding out a clutch of pictures. 'I got these off Facebook, Evan Armstrong's page. There's no doubt that he's our man – the tattoos on show match the ones on the body.'

Francis studied the pictures. They were various holiday shots of Evan Armstrong in shorts and T-shirts.

'You'll need to get an official identification by his next of kin, though,' added the sergeant.

'Yes, thank you, Rory. I'm well aware of that.'

That, of course, was the downside to having discovered the identity of the body. The worst part of the job. It wasn't a task Francis could delegate to a member of his team – it was his duty to break the news to the family. This was something the team couldn't afford to get wrong, because being asked to identify a body was the most harrowing thing a grieving parent or spouse would ever have to experience.

Francis had seen the distress of a woman who, when asked to identify a rape and murder victim believed to be her daughter, collapsed as she gazed down into the face of a dead stranger. She'd prepared herself to be reunited with her child, but even that scant comfort had been snatched away from her – and she was plunged right back into the maelstrom of not knowing. It was something he never wanted to see again.

That wouldn't happen this time. Evan Armstrong was dead and his family had a right to know. Driving to their home in Worthing, Francis felt as if he was arriving with a dark cloud in his wake. A mantle of pain that would envelope them for the foreseeable future. And only the scant comfort that might come if he could bring Evan's killer to justice.

'Do they know anything yet?' said Angie Burton, accompanying him in her role as family liaison officer.

'There's been no missing person report, so it's hard to say if they even realised he wasn't around. He didn't have a police record, and we've got nothing on any of the rest of the family. Chances are this is going to be a bolt out of the blue for them.'

Angie was quiet but she didn't show any signs of nerves. She had an attractive, open face and an easy manner. Her role was to be a comforting presence in the family's moment of distress, and they wouldn't realise that her real task was to mine them for information about the victim and his life.

'We're here,' said Francis, pulling up outside a 1930s semi with fake Tudor beams and imitation leading glued to the windows.

Angie shook her head sadly as she stepped up to ring the doorbell.

'Evan, isn't it?' she said.

Francis nodded, as they heard footsteps coming towards the door.

Once they were sitting down with cups of strong but milky tea, Francis couldn't put it off any longer. Both Evan's parents were at home – they were retired – and they sat looking at him in worried expectation. Evan's mother looked as if she was about to cry, even though they hadn't said anything yet. The silence in the room stretched out.

'They're from the police, you said?' Evan's father was clearly addressing his wife.

'We are,' said Francis. 'I'm Detective Inspector Francis Sullivan and this is WDC Angela Burton.'

'Angie,' she added.

Francis paused, staring out of the window at the allotments beyond the end of their garden. An elderly woman was digging feebly with a fork and it mesmerised him for a moment.

Don't make them wait any longer. No, give them a couple more seconds before torpedoing their existence . . .

He swallowed, then spoke. 'Mr and Mrs Armstrong, when did you last see or hear from Evan?'

That was all it took. Evan's mother clutched the front of her blouse and let out a gasp. Her body crumpled back in her chair, like a deflating balloon.

'He didn't phone at the weekend. I said there was something wrong.' She spoke to her husband and he immediately put his arm around her.

'Wait, Sharon. Let the man finish.' His face had turned ashen and Francis heard a tremor in his voice.

'On Sunday morning, a body was discovered in the Pavilion Gardens in Brighton. We have reason to believe that it might be Evan.' He didn't want to mention to them that the body had been found in a bin.

'That's why he didn't phone,' said Sharon Armstrong. 'He must have been dead when I tried to call him.' Her voice had taken on the high pitch of hysteria and her eyes darted around the room, not settling on anyone or anything.

Angie went and knelt by her side, putting an arm around the back of her waist and using her other hand to cover Sharon's hands.

'You're sure it's him?' said Evan's father, his voice cracking.

This was the hardest part. Francis explained, as gently as he could, that his facial features had been obscured. He didn't mention the rats. He told them that they thought it was Evan because of the tattoos on his body. And he asked them about the tattoo missing from his shoulder.

Afterwards, although he could remember the facts they'd told him, Francis couldn't recall a blind word of the conversation. A cup of tea was spilled and Angie fetched a glass of water for Sharon, who at one point seemed to be on the verge of fainting, while Dave Armstrong sank into stony-faced silence after looking at the photos of the remaining tattoos.

'I knew those tattoos were a mistake,' said Sharon, clutching the water glass with white knuckles. 'They got him killed, didn't they?'

'You don't know that,' said her husband. He turned to face Francis. 'Do you?'

'At this stage, we can't speculate about a motive, or exactly what happened to him. But you knew he had a tattoo on his left shoulder?'

Dave nodded. 'Some sort of tribal design. On his shoulder and down his chest and back. It was his most recent one. Done just a couple of months ago, I think. He sent us a picture of it.'

Francis's heart skipped a beat when he saw the photo. It was a picture of a topless Evan Armstrong, taken from behind, showing an intricate geometric design tattooed around his left shoulder and stretching down his back and the side of his ribs. They hadn't seen this tattoo in his Facebook gallery. At a glance, Francis could see that it fitted approximately to the shape of the wound on the dead body. He needed to get this picture over to Rose Lewis. Then he needed to find out what monster had done this and why. What in Evan Armstrong's life had caused him to end up murdered and dumped? There was nothing on his social media that hinted of criminal involvement, but that didn't mean it wasn't the case. In the meantime, he hoped the Armstrongs could derive some comfort from Angie, from God or from whatever reserves they might find within themselves.

When he got outside, he checked his phone. Several missed calls and a message from an unknown number. He dialled in and listened.

Hello, DI Sullivan. My name's Tom Fitz, I work for the Argus. *I was wondering if you had a word for me about the discovery of a body behind the Pavilion. I understand you're in charge of the case. We want to run a piece on it tomorrow, so I'd like to know who the victim was and what you think happened to him. You can reach me on . . .*

Francis cut off the call. Not a chance.

He drove back to the office in a sombre mood, the age-old question preying on his mind. Why would God have created a world with such evil in it? Why would someone cut a tattoo from a man's body and leave him to die? Was it a punishment or an act of revenge? Or could it be something to do with a cult? Maybe the design of the tattoo carried a secret meaning . . . He was at a loss. By the time he parked his car back at the station, he was experiencing the visual disturbances that heralded the onset of a migraine. Where the hell would he find the answers?

9

Francis

DCI Bradshaw had called the whole team together for a review of progress on the case so far. Francis was late. It was a characteristic he couldn't bear in others, so it galled him to be guilty of it himself, particularly in front of his new boss. He made his best attempt to slip into the room silently and unseen.

'Good of you to join us, DI Sullivan.' DCI Bradshaw's voice bounced off the walls of the open-plan office and reverberated through Francis's chest. 'I imagine you have a reason for being late?'

Someone let out an exaggerated sigh and he heard one of the DCs whisper to another, 'We'd never get away with it.' He was a long way from earning the team's respect.

'I was breaking the news to the victim's family, sir.' It was like being back at school.

'Well, I hope you got some useful information.' A sneer made Bradshaw's face even uglier than it was in repose.

'I think so, sir.' It was incredibly difficult to keep the sarcasm out of his voice. 'I now have some information on the victim.'

'We'll come to that in a moment, Sullivan. Carry on, Rory.'

So, arriving late meant that Francis had ceded his position to his deputy. He couldn't afford to let this happen.

'Shall I . . .' he interjected, shifting from behind DC Hitchins so the chief could see him properly.

'Do you know where Rory had got to?'

Francis shook his head.

Bradshaw raised his eyebrows and nodded towards Rory.

'Rose Lewis has performed the autopsy and should be getting test results back to us by tomorrow p.m.,' said Rory. 'A search of the site suggests that the victim was bludgeoned on the paving close to the café, then dragged out of sight into the bushes.'

'Do we have an approximate time of death?'

'Sometime between midnight and six a.m. on Sunday morning. The autopsy results should enable Rose to narrow it down further.'

'I've just spoken to Rose on the way back,' said Francis.

Bradshaw nodded at him to continue.

'She's putting the time of death between two fifteen and two forty-five, based on the core body temperature and the cessation of rigor. Heat building up inside the dumpster will have shortened rigor mortis and kept the body warmer for longer. She found early signs of putrefaction, also accelerated by the temperature.'

'Anything else?'

'The lividity pattern was set by the time we removed the body from the scene. Blood pooling occurred in the position in which he was found, meaning that he was dumped there either prior to or within about an hour of his death.'

Francis glanced round the room when he finished talking but none of the team met his eye.

'Right, let's talk about the victim now,' said Bradshaw. 'Rory?'

'The victim's name was Evan Armstrong.'

'Yes, we all know that now,' said Bradshaw. 'Why was he killed and who might have done it?'

Francis seized the moment. After all, it was his investigation.

'The shape of the wound on his shoulder suggested that a tattoo had been cut away from his body. I've just received a photo from his parents that confirms this theory.'

'Any clues as to why someone would do this?'

Francis shook his head. 'Nothing yet.'

'This woman, the tattoo artist, she couldn't tell you?'

'It's a fresh theory, sir. I'm just about to put the team on it.'

'Well, don't fucking sit on the information. Get going. We need to know everything about Armstrong. Address, job, who his friends were, what he did in his free time. Come on, Sullivan, you know the score.'

Of course he bloody did – and he'd be right on it if he didn't have to waste time in meetings like these.

'Yes, sir. Burton's with the family now. She'll get what she can from them.'

'And what about the CCTV on New Road and around the Pavilion? Turned up anything interesting yet?'

'Hollins?' prompted Francis, determined to show that he'd had the team doing something.

'Hitchins,' said Hollins.

DC Hitchins looked from Francis to Bradshaw.

'Nothing with an obvious link to the crime,' he said. 'Saturday night was busy. Lots of extra people around for the tattoo convention. Looks like the clubs were heaving. Lot of drunks in the street, plenty of chancers wearing hoodies . . .'

'Not good enough,' said Francis. 'Find out from Armstrong's friends what his movements were that evening and take another look.'

'Did anyone report him missing?' asked Bradshaw.

'Not so far, boss,' said Rory.

'Why am I not bloody surprised?' muttered Bradshaw. 'Okay, get on with it. I want suspects up on this board by tomorrow lunchtime.' He rapped on it with his knuckles. 'One last thing.

Who spoke to the press? There's a piece in the *Argus* this morning, pure bloody speculation. But you need to get a lid on it fast.'

Then he jabbed his forefinger towards Francis. 'And you, Sullivan, in my office now.'

'Yes, sir.'

Francis followed Bradshaw along the corridor and up the stairs until they came to his office on the top floor. He had a feeling he was in for a further bollocking, as if a dressing-down in the incident room wasn't enough already. The DCI ushered him inside impatiently and didn't invite him to sit, despite sinking into his own chair with an audible sigh. Francis stood to attention in front of the desk, waiting for the inevitable.

'Listen, boy, I don't want to show you up in front of your team but you're going to need to do better than that. I recommended you for promotion because I thought you could do the job. It was a huge risk.'

'I know, sir, and I'm immensely grateful . . .'

'I couldn't give a shit about your gratitude. I put my trust in you and, so far, I'm getting nothing in return. There are too many unanswered questions. What's the motive? Robbery gone wrong? I take it you didn't find a wallet on the body or you would have had the ID sooner. Have you spoken to the uniforms who were out on Sunday? Get hold of the duty inspector for the night and ask him for a list of reported incidents.'

Bradshaw was a man who relished the sound of his own voice, and Francis knew from experience the best thing to do was to let him go on until he ran out of steam.

'What else did you learn from the woman who found the body? Couldn't she tell you any more? Come on, what've you got for me?'

'No, sir, she was quite reticent about coming forward. There was no wallet found on the body. However, we did find a sizeable amount of cash in the pocket of his jeans, so I don't think robbery was the motive. Hitchins is following up with uniform branch and Angie Burton's questioning the next of kin.'

'And what's the problem with your witness? Why wouldn't she give a name at first?'

'She appears to be quite hostile to the police.'

Bradshaw rolled his eyes.

'So you need to find out why. It could have some bearing on the case. People aren't normally hostile to us for no reason.'

Francis wondered whether to bring up his theory about a tattoo having been removed from the body again. But Bradshaw was already red in the face and Francis wasn't sure his blood pressure could take it.

'The husband. Did he have anything useful to say at all?'

'Nothing really, except the victim failed to pay him for the tattoo. Though that's ancient history.'

As he said this, Bradshaw bristled and sat up straighter in his chair.

'The victim owed this man money and then turns up dead? There's your first bloody suspect for the incident board. Get him in and question him. And don't waste any more of my bloody time doing your fucking job for you or Rory will be running the show and you'll be on traffic patrol for the rest of your damn career.'

iii

It takes only seconds to make a clear assessment. It'll be better to take the head off the body so I can work undisturbed. Scalping is an incredibly delicate task. Removing the head in the open will require a saw and will result in an inordinate amount of blood. He's still unconscious, his breathing ragged, but it's a comforting sound as I think through the logistics.

Not here, in the underground car park, where I surprised my victim from behind with an ether-soaked rag. Not in my anonymous white transit van. Not back at the farm – I don't want the hassle of cleaning up the evidence and then taking the body away. But I'd like to leave another little calling card for my favourite city. First time, it was the Pavilion. Perhaps I should tuck this one away under the pier. There are dark spaces there to hide the body and the blood will have been washed away by sunrise. Perfectly anonymous – and by the time he's discovered in some dark recess, there'll be nothing to link me or the van or the farm to the crime.

A small grunt from the boy – for he's hardly more than that – tells me that the ether's wearing off. I quickly undo the lid of the brown glass bottle and douse the rag. The boy breathes it in with a sigh, as if greeting an old acquaintance, leaving me free to get on with my planning.

There's a meat saw here in the van that should make speedy work of his neck. My watch shows it's close to two a.m. Plenty of time. I could be back at my workshop before dawn and if the head's still warm, it'll still be easy enough to peel away his tattoo before the skin stiffens. After that, there'll be no hurry disposing of what remains of his head.

With a plan in place, it's time to get to work. I secure his wrists and ankles with cable ties – he's bound to come round again before I've finished with him. Then I wrap a large bath towel around his head, securing it at the back in a bulky knot. There can be no damage to the skin of his scalp – dead skin doesn't heal and any small nick will be a blemish forever on the preserved tattoo.

Forty minutes later, I'm driving along Madeira Drive, past the top of the pier and down towards Kemptown. I don't pass another car on the road. Thankfully there's no moon tonight – just velvety blackness which will swallow us up as we head down the beach. I pull into a row of deserted parking places and stop the van. I wait for a few minutes but it's deathly quiet. No one would be out walking their dog at this hour. I have to trust that I'm alone.

The boy starts moaning and writhing in the back, terrified. The stink of piss and fear gives me pleasure, and I play with the idea of letting him stay awake until the saw blade takes him back down into the darkness. But there's no point risking a struggle that could see his precious head being ground into the shingle. A minute later, when the ether has made him docile again, I open the doors at the back of the van. No one sees me dragging him across the pavement and onto the shingle. No one sees me squatting, at the water's edge, as I start to cut. Or hears the rasp of my serrated blade tearing through his flesh or the grittier sound of it grinding across his bone. The ferocity of the waves sees to that. We are totally alone as his body slumps into the shallows. There's no one here to see the ribbons of blood dissipating into the black water of the creeping Channel. None but a solitary seagull, its eyes darting in search of junk food. And me, of course.

Back in my studio, I stand face to face with the severed head. His brown eyes are open. In the absence of life they look like glass eyes.

The spider's web is quite visible on the left-hand side of his forehead, but a fine growth of stubble blurs the outline of the giant spider that sits on top of his cranium. I caress the dome of the skull, enjoying the rough nap of the shorn hair against the soft pads of my fingertips. It won't stay, though – the hair will be chemically removed during the tanning process. His head is still warm, the skin still soft and pliable. I turn it around and read the legend incorporated into the strands of web issuing from the spider's abdomen.

Belial

The name of the Devil in sinuous Gothic script wrapped around the back of his skull.

"'And what accord has Christ with Belial? Or what part has a believer with an unbeliever?'" I whisper softly, picking up my knife. A favourite verse of mine from Corinthians. I'll show that bastard who didn't believe in me. I'll show him what I can do. When your own flesh and blood rejects you, the fires of ambition burn that much more brightly, don't they? You want to prove yourself successful as an act of vengeance.

All that remains is for me to start slowly peeling the flesh away from the bone.

10

Rory

Rory Mackay was in his element, delighted to see the boss floundering in that briefing. Arriving late would have scored Sullivan's first black marks with the chief and it had gone from bad to worse with every answer. Meanwhile, Rory himself would make sure he got every ounce of credit due to him for any contribution he made and, with any luck, Sullivan wouldn't last much past his first case.

But for now, the team had a job to do and at least, for once, the victim wasn't a child or a sexually exploited young woman. This one shouldn't prove too hard to solve. If the motive wasn't a robbery, then it would be a falling-out of thieves and Rory had a handle on most of the villains that called Brighton home. He'd wager money that the killing was gang related but the new boss was wet behind the ears. When Sullivan made a total cock-up of things Rory would be able to step in and become a DI himself, no doubt about it.

Despite Bradshaw's grumbling, the incident command board wasn't looking too bad for thirty-six hours in. There were pictures of the body and of the crime scene pinned up, and now they had an ID. Once they dug around a bit in Evan Armstrong's past, Rory felt sure they'd come up with a list of suspects too.

'Mackay. A word.'

Rory looked up from his desk to see DI Sullivan standing in the doorway.

'Boss,' he said, getting to his feet.

He followed the DI into the glorified pigeonhole he'd been assigned on his promotion. The threadbare carpet still bore cigarette burns from the days when it was legal to smoke at work, but then the youngest DI on the force was hardly going to get a corner office with a view.

It should have been mine.

Francis sat on one side of the desk and Rory sat on the other. Rory said nothing, watching as the boss settled into his chair and fingered the corner of a manila folder in his in-tray. He had the look of a schoolboy who'd been torn off a strip. There were red patches on both his cheeks.

'Right, we're bringing Marni Mullins and Thierry Mullins in for formal questioning. Get the team onto it now. I want to see them both this evening, before they've had time to discuss their alibis.'

Their alibis? Was he serious?

'Sure, boss. You think they're involved? Together? I thought they were divorced.'

'They are. Apparently.' They'd definitely shared some sort of rapport in the convention centre office.

Rory gave him a questioning look.

'I think it's highly unlikely either one of them had anything to do with it,' said Francis. 'However, we need to tick all the boxes. Evan Armstrong had a tattoo cut from his body, so this case is going to generate a hell of a lot of interest from the press. We can't afford to miss something obvious.'

Rory could hear an echo of Bradshaw.

'A fishing expedition, in other words?'

The DI sighed and tilted his head to one side.

'Have we got overtime for this, boss?' said Rory. He knew full well that they hadn't.

'Get out and get on with it. I'll deal with Bradshaw if there's any problem about overtime.'

Interesting. The boy had a temper on him and it looked like he wouldn't be afraid to take on the chief.

'And keep this under your hat – I don't expect to see it reported in the *Argus*.'

It sounded like an accusation. He'd changed his tune over keeping the press sweet.

It was after ten p.m. when Rory peered through the rectangular window in the door of the interview room to take a look at the witness. This was a deliberate tactic – interviewing witnesses when they were tired made them more vulnerable. A small, dark-haired woman was sitting at the table, twisting the sleeves of her cardigan nervously, her face wearing the guilt-ridden expression of someone who could only be innocent.

He grabbed the door handle and went into the room.

'Marni Mullins, right?'

She glared at him without speaking.

'I'd like to ask you a few questions about what happened in the Pavilion Gardens on Sunday.'

'I've already spoken to your DI. I don't have anything further to add.'

'However that may be, I need to take a formal statement from you.'

He got out his notebook and licked the tip of his pencil. 'Now, Ms Mullins, please tell me exactly what happened when you went to the Pavilion Gardens on Sunday.'

'Haven't you forgotten something?'

'Have I?'

'You haven't read me my rights.'

'Because you're not under arrest. You're here to give a witness statement.'

The woman stood up, pushing her chair back. 'Then I'm free to go.'

It was a statement, not a question.

Rory stood up too. 'Ms Mullins, it will make all our lives easier if you just give the statement and answer a few questions voluntarily. We need you to answer these questions and if you don't do it now, we'll have a warrant drawn up.'

'Just tell me one thing straight, Sergeant. Am I or am I not a suspect?'

She might not be a suspect but she certainly wasn't going out of her way to help. And it wasn't as if she'd have anything useful to tell him anyway.

'You're not a suspect. But a man has been murdered, and you found the body. What you can tell us might shed some light on who did it, even if it means nothing to you. Please sit down and we'll get through this as quickly as possible.'

Marni Mullins sat down again, reluctantly. Something told Rory that she knew her way around a police interview, and she certainly seemed to have some prior knowledge of police procedure. Not so unusual perhaps, given the world she moved in.

'Now, tell me what happened on Sunday.'

'I went to the Pavilion Gardens for a coffee. I found a body in a dumpster. I phoned the police.'

Round One to Marni Mullins.

Rory settled into his chair. 'The short version. Nice. Now, tell me properly, in full technicolour detail, about what happened on Sunday morning.'

It took him six attempts to get the level of detail he needed, but finally he felt he'd extracted any and every fact that could have been of any conceivable use to the investigation. When they finished, she looked worn down.

'Thank you for your co-operation, Ms Mullins. You're free to go.'

She stood up, not looking him in the eye.

Rory walked towards the door to show her out. With his hand on the door handle, he paused and turned towards her.

'Just one last thing,' he said. 'Where were you on Sunday morning between one a.m. and five a.m.?'

Marni took a step back, using one hand to steady herself against the table. 'You can't ask me that.'

'I certainly can. Where were you on Sunday morning between one a.m. and five a.m.?'

'I'm not a suspect.'

Rory remained by the door. He could hear her breathing, shallow and fast. She was frightened.

'I was asleep in my bed. At home.'

'With your husband?'

'Ex-husband. I'd be the last person he'd want to sleep with.'

Her voice cracked as she spoke, and she reached for the paper cup of water that still stood on the table. As she raised it to her lips, her hand was shaking so violently that most of the water splashed out onto the Formica table top.

Rory felt pleased with himself. Hopefully Sullivan, watching via CCTV in the next room, would have picked up on some of his interviewing technique. As he led Marni Mullins out of the interview room and towards the reception, they passed her ex-husband in the corridor, being escorted up for his interview. It was past one a.m. now, and being kept waiting for several hours had done little to soften his mood.

'*Merde*,' said Thierry, glaring at Marni.

She looked away without saying anything.

'Nice way to greet your wife,' said Rory. 'Not surprised you ditched him.'

The look she gave him when he said that was every bit as

hostile as Thierry's look had been to her. It was definitely them against the police, rather than her against him. Rory showed her through the reception area to the main doors, wondering about their relationship.

'Am I free to go now?' she asked.

'Yes. But we might need to talk to you again.' That, of course, would depend on what Thierry Mullins told them in his interview, but he wasn't about to share that with Marni.

Rory took Sullivan's place as an observer when the DI went in to interview Thierry.

'Where were you on Sunday morning between one a.m. and five a.m.?' said Sullivan with no preamble.

Bam! Straight in with no subtlety. No building up a false sense of security with his suspect. *Idiot.*

'Sleeping mostly.'

Sullivan stared him down. Mullins was justifiably indignant about being dragged in here after helping to identify the victim earlier but the boss wasn't having any of it.

'Sleeping mostly? And what about the times when you weren't sleeping?'

'I was in bed for the duration.' Thierry Mullins evidently wanted to close down this line of questioning.

'Where?'

There was a long silence. At least the boy knew better than to prompt his suspect.

'I picked up a girl. Went back to her place. I can't remember exactly where it was.'

'Where did you meet her?'

'In the Heart and Hand.'

A grungy pub on North Road. Rory knew it well enough, though he didn't drink there. It wasn't the sort of place where being a policeman would go down too well.

'The girl's name?'

Mullins looked blank and shrugged. 'Linny? Lizzy? Something like that.'

'Mr Mullins, would you recognise her if you saw her again?'

'Of course I would. She had a mermaid tramp stamp on her arse. It's not a big deal. I was drunk, so I don't remember the details.'

'I'm afraid we're going to have to check them out more thoroughly.'

'Why? You think I had something to do with Evan Armstrong's death? I'm a suspect?' Mullins literally spat out the words.

'He did owe you money, didn't he?'

The tattooist grunted and turned sideways in his chair so he didn't have to look at Francis. In other words, Francis had blown it. He'd lost what scant co-operation there was and he wasn't going to get anything of any use out of Thierry Mullins now.

'I want my lawyer. No more questions.'

This was going nowhere fast and when Rory's phone rang, he answered it without compunction.

It was the duty inspector. He sounded out of breath.

'Mackay? We've got a body. Just called in. Down on the beach, under the Palace Pier.'

II

Francis

The chances of getting any sleep that night had gone from slight to zero, Francis reflected as they came off Old Steine at speed. Rory drove straight across the empty roundabout and, in an illegal manoeuvre, brought the car to a standstill on the wide apron of pavement at the entrance of the Palace Pier. There were already two uniform branch cars pulled up, and an ambulance stood, engine running, on the pedestrian crossing zig-zags on Madeira Drive.

'That lot might as well piss off,' said Rory, as they jogged over to the stone steps that would take them from the promenade onto the beach.

Francis agreed. There was no point in the ambulance. Processing the scene would take several hours and then the body would head straight for the morgue.

'Unless Hitchins needs hospitalisation after throwing his guts up,' Rory added.

They picked their way over the shingle towards the scene.

'Fill us in, Sergeant,' Francis said, as a giant of a man in police uniform approached them.

'Body under the pier, called in by a young couple about an hour ago.'

'Definitely dead when they found him, or her?'

'Him. His head's missing.'

Yes, definitely dead.

'Let's take a look.'

The sergeant led them into the inky darkness under the pier. There were a number of uniforms unspooling blue-and-white tape to wrap around the giant pillars that supported the iron and wood structure above.

'What were the couple doing under here?' said Francis.

Rory guffawed.

'On their way home from a nightclub,' said the sergeant with a completely straight face.

The penny dropped and Francis felt his cheeks reddening.

Rory said nothing. He didn't have to. He pulled a black plastic vape out of his pocket and sucked on it as they walked across the shingle.

The body was lying near the water's edge, face down. The stump of the neck was a bloody mess that looked black in the dull light of the sergeant's torch. The man was naked from the waist up, but still wearing blood-stained jeans and trainers. There was a wallet-shaped bulge in the back pocket of his trousers. One of his feet was just within reach of the waves.

'Tide coming in or out?' said Francis.

Rory looked along the beach for a couple of moments.

'Coming in, boss, but it looks like it's just about reached high water.'

'If it has further to rise, it'll compromise the scene. We need to work fast.' Francis glanced around the area. 'Right, no one comes within this perimeter unless they have business here. Rory, we need crime suits. Sergeant, find out how long until SOCO gets here and get some bloody lights set up.'

Rory set off up the shingle back to the car.

'And get a search underway for the head.'

By the time Rose Lewis arrived ten minutes later, Francis was suited up and in control of the situation. SOCO set up their huge LED lamps, allowing Francis and Rose to inspect the body more closely. In the powerful beam, the man's skin took on a greenish tinge and the stump of his neck changed from black to dark, glistening red. Quivering blood clots clung to the mangled tissue, like giant globules of jelly. The skin at the perimeter was torn and ragged, chewed up by whatever had inflicted the cut. His torso was heavily tattooed and there were more tattoos on either arm – dark black shapes that from the wrong angle made no sense to Francis. Rose instructed one of the SOCOs to take photographs, while she measured the body temperature, ground temperature and air temperature to help her assess the time of death.

Francis used a pair of disposable tweezers from Rose's evidence collection kit to extract the wallet from the pocket. It was a brown leather gate-fold, sodden and heavy. With gloved hands, he gave it a cursory check for ID. There was money, and a wad of receipts, but nothing that gave any clue as to who its owner was.

He dropped it into a plastic evidence bag. If the receipts weren't too wet, they might yield useful information.

Together, Rory and Francis contemplated the body.

'Tattoos,' said Rory.

'These ones are intact,' said Rose, following his train of thought.

'Yeah, but it means he'll more than likely be on our database. Some of them look gang-related.'

Tattoos meant criminal connections in Rory's book. Maybe he'd been guilty of the same thought process himself up until recently – but now he wasn't so sure. The thorough checks they'd run on Evan Armstrong had turned up nothing.

'I'll take his prints back at the morgue,' said Rose. 'This is an unstable scene and I want to get him out of here as fast as we can process him.'

'Was he killed here or just dumped?' said Francis.

'Too early to say. Decapitation means a shitload of blood, wherever it happens, unless it was done post mortem.'

'Was it?'

Rose shone a small hand-held torch right into the stump. She was silent for a moment. Francis suddenly became aware of the sound of the waves tugging at the shingle beneath his feet. He had to take a half step back to keep his footing. Everything was unstable. You could think you'd got a handle on your life, but there was always an undertow ...

'No. Our boy was decapitated while still very much alive – it's obvious he's lost a lot of blood, which wouldn't have happened if he'd been dead when his head was removed.'

12

Thierry

If he never saw another policeman for the rest of his life, it would be a lifetime too soon. Thierry Mullins muttered to himself as he strode down John Street away from the police station. *Merde!* He nearly ploughed into an old woman with a shopping trolley as he turned the corner into Edward Street, but he was far too angry to stop and apologise. He was on a mission and if there was going to be any apologising done it would be coming in the opposite direction. His bloody ex-wife. *Putain!* While you always lose the good ones, somehow you never manage to escape from your mistakes.

Sixteen hours in a cell. He glanced at his watch, newly returned to him by the desk sergeant on duty. No phone call, no access to a lawyer. *But then he wasn't under arrest so why should he need a lawyer?* That's what they'd said. But he knew his damned rights, and his had been infringed. Fucking *flics*.

The smell of hot pastry drifting out of a takeaway shop made him pause. They had virtually starved him. The curling sandwiches of stale white bread filled with stinking tuna that he'd been offered at various points throughout the night weren't remotely edible. Each time he'd pushed the paper plate away across the table. He'd been running these last twenty-four hours on their shit coffee and nothing else.

Then the duty sergeant had come into the interview room, when they knew they would have to release him or charge him anyway, and told him that they'd been able to verify his alibi. They'd found a girl called Lisa with a mermaid tattoo, who'd admitted under some duress that she had indeed brought a man back to her flat from the pub on Saturday night and that he'd been there with her until approximately nine a.m. the next morning. The sergeant seemed to find it hugely funny that she didn't remember his name either.

Thierry came out of the shop with a sausage roll. It was now almost lunchtime and he'd wasted a whole morning. He'd missed two appointments at the studio, which was money he could ill afford to lose. Hopefully, for the clients, Charlie or Noa had picked up the slack, but that still didn't help him.

Edward Street became the Eastern Road, and as he passed Brighton College, he wondered if that jumped-up little git of a DI had spent his formative years inside its redbrick buildings. He crossed the road and turned into College Place and then turned again into Great College Street. Marni's house – or to be more accurate, his house – was halfway down on the right-hand side. He banged on the door, resisting the urge to peer through the window. He should never have relinquished his front door keys, though at the time it seemed like the right thing to do. Now Marni had the house and Alex, while he lived alone in a miserable one-bedroom flat that had mildew in the bathroom.

He glared furiously at the front door that used to be his own and his anger flared as he was kept waiting. It was only when he shouted and kicked the bottom panel with his foot that the door finally opened.

Marni blinked up at him, a wave of panic passing across her features. She stepped back, slightly stunned.

'Marni?' His anger evaporated for a moment as the old instinct to protect her kicked in. It had been his default mode for so many years.

'Thierry.' She tried to close the door in his face.

'Wait, will you?' He stuck a foot into the narrowing gap.

'You scared me.'

'And you got me pulled in by the police.' He could guess what had scared her. When was she going to leave the past behind? 'Let me in.'

He pushed against the door and they tussled for a moment. Thierry prevailed and pushed past her into the hall. He stood panting for a few seconds.

'Tell me what frightened you, Marni.'

'Nothing. I'm just on edge. All this ... it's bringing up the past.'

He'd been right. She turned to face him. She looked tired. He knew that look – it meant she wasn't sleeping and she probably wasn't eating properly. She wasn't coping on her own. But did this mean she needed him around? And was he prepared to make that commitment again?

'You know Paul's still in prison. There's nothing to worry about.' His tone softened slightly.

'He may be locked up, but he always has ways of getting to me.'

This wasn't why he'd come to see her and he didn't want to dig into things best left forgotten. 'You shouldn't have got yourself mixed up in this, Marni. I can't afford more run-ins with the police.'

She sighed. 'I know. I'm sorry.'

'They kept me up all night.'

She looked shocked. 'Wine?'

It was the least she could do. 'What's open?' he asked.

'A Côtes de Blaye.'

Thierry wrinkled his nose. It wasn't one of his favourites.

'After an apology,' he said, tilting his head to one side.

'For?'

'*Merde!* I've just spent sixteen hours in a police station because of you.'

'They've only just let you out?'

'*Oui.* Thanks for your concern.'

Marni shrugged. 'How would I have known they were still holding you?'

'They seem to think that because that man who was killed once owed me money, I might have been the killer.' He sighed. 'Why did you have to tell them the tattoo on his leg was one of mine?'

'Come on, Thierry.' Marni shook her head defiantly. 'I made one anonymous call to the police. Jesus, I found a dead body. Do you think I should have ignored it?'

'Sure. Someone else would have seen it.'

He followed her to the kitchen. Their kitchen, that he had designed, and that he and Charlie had built together. Those had been the best days of their marriage. They'd left their troubles behind in France and started a new life in Brighton. Marni's wounds had begun to slowly heal as she tended to her baby son, and for a short time, Thierry had thought the future would be easy.

Marni uncorked a half-full bottle of red and split it between two glasses.

'Remember,' she said, handing him a glass, 'I have to set an example to our son. You might feel that it's okay to run away from your responsibilities but someone round here has to be the adult.'

'What responsibilities?'

Marni rolled her eyes. 'Providing for your son, for a start,' she said.

Thierry grunted. This old complaint. He'd heard it too often. He had nothing more to say.

'Drink your wine and get out, Thierry. I'm too tired for this shit.'

He sniffed the glass.

'It's off. The wine is off,' he said with a shrug. 'And stop obsessing about Paul. You need some sleep.'

Marni's look was as sharp as the Sabatier knives he'd left behind in the kitchen drawer.

'He sent me a letter.'

'When?'

'A couple of months ago.'

She hadn't said anything to him at the time. The realisation stung.

'What did it say?'

'I didn't open it.'

The look of fear had returned to her features, and suddenly he wanted to make things okay for her. 'You know it means nothing, babe. He's playing with you. He's locked away and he can't get to you.'

'The letter got to me,' she said.

He raised a hand in supplication.

'Do you have it still? Can I see it?'

'I threw it away.'

He could tell she was lying but he was too tired to fight with her.

'Okay. I go now.'

As he retreated down the hall, Alex appeared on the stairs. He was still in his pyjamas and his eyes were heavy with sleep.

Merde.

'Dad? What are you doing here?'

'Your father's just leaving,' said Marni.

She caught up with Thierry and propelled him towards the front door.

'Leave me alone, Thierry. Don't come back. You remind me of Paul too much.'

If there were words in her arsenal that could truly wound him, these were they. If she was still thinking that way, things could never be right between them. He felt a lump form in his throat and he turned away so she wouldn't see his face.

Marni opened the door and pushed him onto the front step.

'Who's Paul?' he heard Alex saying from the stairs.

The door slammed and he was on his own.

iv

It's a process. Skinning. Curing. Soaking. Liming. Fleshing. De-liming. Bating. Pickling. Degreasing. Tanning. Neutralising. Fatliquoring. Samming. Settling out. Drying. Every step is important to produce the softest, most pliable leather.

People don't think of human skin as leather, but you have to understand it results in a most pleasing product. Especially tattooed skin. It always surprises me that they don't tattoo animals before killing them for their hide. The results would be unique and beautiful.

This scalp, with its twisted spider's web, will make the most extraordinary piece. Scalping is an incredibly delicate operation. You need to work slowly, so you don't tear the skin. It's very fragile before it's been tanned. But at the same time, you need to work fast. Warm skin is flexible, giving – but cold skin becomes stiff, making the work hard. It took me two hours to gently separate the boy's scalp from his cranium, cutting and peeling back a centimetre at a time.

Now it's soaking in brine to preserve it. This is merely the first stage of its journey from skin to leather. The salt draws the moisture and kills the bacteria. The detached scalp writhes under the surface of the water like a fat koi carp.

I have a special job. It's a privilege, really. The Collector allows me to prepare these skins for him because he recognises that I have a unique talent.

Which my own DAMNED FATHER never did.

Why did I think of that all of a sudden? I can't let my father into my head while I'm working. When he's inside my mind, my hands shake. I lose my focus. And the more I try to banish him, the more he makes his presence felt – undermining, belittling, confirming the worst truths about myself.

I close my eyes and take a series of deep breaths. I refocus my thoughts on the Collector.

The Collector has made up for the failings of my real father. The man who let me down so many times, so often. Where my father saw me as a failure, the Collector sees the good in me. He's given me purpose in my work. Smoothing the skin. Softening it. Stroking it. Transforming it into something so much more beautiful than when it was alive. I get to peel it off a living creature and transform it into a work of art. Art is more important than life.

My job is very therapeutic.

13

Francis

Francis knew he was at the right place when he saw the sign along the top of the shop front. 'Celestial Tattoo' in black cursive writing across an explosion of red and pink chrysanthemums, just like the one Marni Mullins had been tattooing on the girl at the convention. So this was her home turf. He stared through the windows at the darkened shop. He could make out a small counter, with a row of mismatched chairs to one side. The walls were covered with tattoo designs, as you'd expect. Behind the counter there was a shelf holding rows of candles, a few books and a variety of other objects he couldn't quite make out in the semi-darkness.

Despite an 'Open' sign hanging on the back of the door, the place looked distinctly shut. Francis tucked his battered document case under one arm and put his hands up against the glass for a better view inside. There was a door at the back of the shop and he could just see a glimmer of light around its edges. Maybe she was here.

He rapped on the glass door and then tried the handle. It swung open, squeaking loudly on stiff hinges.

'Hello?'

He stepped inside. A snarling explosion of fur and snapping teeth burst through the door at the back and catapulted itself at his centre of gravity. He fell back against the glass, which shattered around him, smelled the hot stink of a carnivore's breath and felt grabby jaws trying to make purchase on his arm. The beast's teeth closed around his sleeve instead, tearing the fabric. Sullivan gasped, flailing to get away.

'Who's there?'

A light snapped on above him.

'Who is it?' Marni Mullins' voice was on the edge of panic.

'Francis Sullivan.'

'Who?'

'DI Sullivan.'

'Christ. Pepper! Come here, Pepper!'

The slavering bulldog ignored his owner and continued to rip at Francis's sleeve.

Still winded, Francis looked up to see Marni silhouetted in the doorway at the back of the shop.

'Do you have no fucking control over this dog?' he asked, trying to wrench his arm away.

'Pepper!'

Francis struggled into a sitting position and put the palm of his free hand across the top of Pepper's muzzle. He leaned in closer until his face was right by Pepper's ear. Pepper growled low in his throat, adjusting his grip on the material of the suit. Glancing furiously at Marni, Francis bit down hard on the thin flap of the bulldog's ear.

With a yelp of surprise, Pepper let go of Francis's arm. He tried to shake his head, but Francis still had him by the ear.

'Jesus, what are you doing?' Marni caught hold of Pepper's collar, at which point Francis released his bite. He wiped his mouth with the back of his hand, grimacing.

'You need to get that dog to training classes, Ms Mullins.'

Francis struggled to his feet, gingerly avoiding shards of broken glass, and retrieved his document case from the floor. Marni dragged the monster across the shop, pushed him through the door to the back and slammed it shut. Only then did she seem to realise the damage that had been done to the front door. She raised a hand to her mouth.

'I'm sorry,' she said, shaking her head. 'Are you hurt?'

Francis touched the back of his head where it had made contact with the glass door. He felt a bump and then looked at his fingers. There was blood on them.

'Of course,' he said, holding up his hand for her to see. 'And you're damn lucky it wasn't worse. As for this suit, it's ruined.'

'I'll replace it,' said Marni quickly. There was a tremor in her voice.

'Too right you will. You need to get a muzzle for your dog. Or better yet, get rid of it.'

Marni bent down and started to pick up the largest shards of glass from the floor.

'He's a guard dog.'

'What if a child had walked through that door?'

He saw her hackles rise. 'It's unlikely. This is a tattoo shop.'

'Could I have some water, please? I can still taste dog in my mouth.'

She headed to the back of the shop. When Francis hesitated at the connecting door, Marni Mullins looked amused.

'Oh, don't worry about Pepper. If I invite you in, he'll be fine.'

He tentatively followed Marni into her studio and looked around. Just like the front of the shop, the walls were covered with her artwork – some of it drawings and watercolours, some of it close-up photographs of tattoos. The space was cluttered – as well as her desk in the corner, there was a massage bench and a large, old-fashioned barber's chair. A glass-fronted corner cabinet housed a collection of crystal and real human skulls, some painted like Mexican Day of the Dead sugar skulls.

'Sit,' she said, pointing to the barber's chair. 'Whisky?'

Francis shook his head. 'I don't drink on duty.' He hardly drank at all but that was none of her business.

While Marni phoned someone to come and board up the broken door, Francis sipped his water and contemplated Pepper. The bulldog eyed him warily in return but remained outstretched on a grimy cushion under the desk. A couple of times he rubbed at his bitten ear with a paw. Eventually, he lumbered over and butted Francis's leg with his flat-nosed muzzle.

By the time Marni returned from measuring the door, the dog was lying on his back with his head on one of Francis's feet.

She eyed them suspiciously. 'You a dog person?'

'No.'

He unzipped the leather document case and took out a large glossy photograph.

'What can you tell me about this?' he said, holding out the picture towards her.

It was a blow-up of the tattoo that had been cut from Evan Armstrong's shoulder. Marni took the picture and scrutinised it.

'This is the guy in the dumpster, yes?'

Francis nodded.

She looked back at the picture.

'Polynesian tattoo, but that doesn't mean it was done there. He could have got it anywhere. It's good work. Do you know who did it?'

She was calmer now that her attention was focused on the tattoo.

'I was hoping you could help me with that. His parents gave us the photo, but they don't know anything about his tattoos. Or his private life, for that matter.'

Marni frowned. 'I can't just look at a tattoo and say who did it. You do know there are tens of thousands of tattoo artists in the world?'

'I realise that, but . . .'

'And it's not like we sign our work.'

'No initials even?'

'There are one or two artists who do – the ones with their heads stuck up their own arses,' she said. 'But, no, most tattooists don't feel the need to leave their name on a stranger's skin. It's enough of a privilege being able to ink people in the first place.'

'But you knew the Saint Sebastian was by Thierry?'

Marni levered herself up to sit on the massage bench. 'I know Thierry's style particularly well.'

'But you don't recognise the style of whoever did this? It's not a local artist?' He studied the picture again himself.

'No, I don't think so. I'm not really into tribal or indigenous work.'

They fell silent for a moment.

'Why does it matter?' Marni asked.

'What?'

'Who did the tattoo. Could it have some bearing on the case?'

Could it? Francis honestly had no idea. He was chasing anything to find a lead.

'I can't rule it out at this stage.'

'Is Thierry a suspect?'

'I can't discuss the details of the case.'

Damn right he couldn't, because there was nothing to discuss. And if she couldn't help him, it was time to get going.

He stood up to leave.

'Give it to me and I'll ask around for you.' She hopped off the bench and took the picture from his hand. 'Will the artist be a suspect?'

'Can you think of any reason why someone would cut a tattoo from the victim's body?' he countered. 'Is it a thing?'

He needed to understand why it had happened.

'"Is it a thing?"' Marni's eyebrows shot up. 'What do you mean by that?'

'Retribution in the tattoo world, or some weird tattooing cult ritual? I don't know what you people do.'

'*Us people?*' Marni shook her head. 'You think we're a cult? Fuck, no, cutting tattoos off people isn't any kind of "a thing".'

Pepper's ears pricked up as Marni raised her voice.

'Listen to me. You might not want a tattoo or even like tattoos. Fair enough.' She glared at him. 'But, boy, do you have a problem with your attitude. People with tattoos are not members of a cult. They're just people – who happen to have tattoos. That's all they have in common. Twenty per cent of adults in this country, in fact.'

Francis raised his hands in supplication. 'Sorry. I didn't mean anything by it. I'm feeling my way here . . .'

He'd touched a raw nerve. Something, or someone, had hurt Marni Mullins.

'Yes, you meant something or you wouldn't have said it.'

The barrier had gone up. Francis looked around the room for inspiration, but there was nothing that he could relate to and use to form a bond.

'Honestly, I'm sorry.'

Marni rested back against the massage bench again. 'So tell me, what's your problem with tattoos?'

'I don't have a problem with tattoos,' he said slowly. That wasn't strictly true but he needed her help. 'But I don't get them, either. I mean, why would you let anyone permanently mark your body like that? It doesn't make sense to me.'

'Self-expression,' she said simply.

Francis didn't really know what she meant by that.

'My mother always said . . . tattoos are the outward sign of internal damage.' It came out in a rush.

Marni looked furious. Evidently it hadn't been the right thing to say.

'You can't believe that.'

'No . . . But then why do they have them?'

'They *can* be a sign that someone's been hurt – but it's usually a positive thing . . . Empowerment, hope, a determination to be strong.' She closed her eyes momentarily, then held his gaze with heightened intensity. 'I lost a child. My back piece is a memorial to that child, my way of holding him with me forever.'

'I'm sorry,' said Francis. He felt like he'd been prying where he had no right to.

'But more often people are tattooed for simply aesthetic reasons,' she continued, 'or because all their friends have them, or as a gesture of love or respect. We're not all the same sorts of people so we don't all have them for the same reasons.'

'No, I can see that. I realised that at the convention.' He looked at her sheepishly. 'So, will you help me?'

Her look was cold. 'I'll do what I can, ask around a bit. But don't hold your breath, Frank.'

'Francis,' he said through gritted teeth.

She was obviously a woman who made assumptions too. However, she was his only pass into the world of tattoos. He needed her if anything about this murder hinged on the missing tattoo. Evan Armstrong's flayed shoulder certainly suggested it did. And now they had a second body which was heavily tattooed as well.

He needed her if he was going to solve this case before they had another victim on their hands.

V

I'm becoming famous! They wrote an article about me in the local paper. Of course, they don't know my name or who I am. But my activities are causing some excitement – and not a little fear creeping through the community, or so I hope. I wonder if the Collector has been reading all about me. I wonder if he's proud . . .

I know that some killers court publicity, writing to the press and sending messages to the police. But I don't think I'll do that. My mission is rewarding enough and it's always the letters that get those idiots caught. I'm not going to make their job any easier for them. Instead, I'll just enjoy reading about my exploits in the Argus.

It's annoying that they get so many details wrong, but then I'm the only one that really knows what's happened to each of my victims. They can only guess, and fill in the blanks with their fear and prurience.

I wonder if they'll write a book about me one day.

Of course, I'm the only one who can tell my story with any accuracy. How my brother, Marshall, stole my birthright. He should never have been born – my mother nearly miscarried him. He became the blue-eyed boy as soon as he could walk and talk. He was younger than me but he was sharp. He learned how to run rings around me and how to shift the blame for his petty misdemeanours onto me. I had taken the cake from the larder. I had spilled black ink on the cream carpet. I had cut the heads off all the alliums and the roses in my mother's garden. His cherubic features made him easy to believe and, behind my parents' backs, he taunted me and made my life a misery.

He poisoned my father against me and then took control of the family company. Kirby Leathers. Set up by my great-great-grand-father a hundred years ago. The company should have come to me. I would have nurtured our family business and it would still be in the family. But, no. It went to my brother. Daddy's favourite.

But that's just the start of my story.

14

Rory

Rory could smell whisky on the man's breath straight away. He clutched the takeaway coffee Rory offered with a wizened claw of a hand. The long nails were grey with dirt, the skin as yellow as the man's eyeballs.

'Thanks.' It came out as little more than a croak.

Rory dropped down next to him on the narrow bus shelter bench. It was past two a.m. and the night buses were few and far between. It was unlikely that anyone would join them at the bus stop.

'How've you been, Pete?'

'Comme ci, comme ça,' said the man, with a reedy laugh. 'You know 'ow it is.'

Rory nodded. The story was always the same with guys like Pete. A scramble for work, a scramble for money, a scramble for booze.

'Keeping an ear to the ground?' Rory asked.

Pete glanced around suspiciously, even though there wasn't another living soul in sight.

'Thing is . . .'

'If you've got something for me, you know I'll pay.'

Pete remained silent but his eyes lit up at the mention of money.

'Listen,' said Rory, 'you might be able to help. We got a body called in yesterday morning. A small guy, young-ish, prison tattoos. Heard anything on that?'

'Where was he?'

'Down near the front.' Rory didn't want to give him too many details. Pete was as leaky as a sieve and would think nothing of selling information in the other direction if he could.

'I heard a couple of deals were s'posed to go down over the weekend. Word's out that one of 'em went wrong. Would that fit with your timing?'

Rory shrugged.

'Who were the deals between?'

Pete rubbed a finger and thumb together, giving Rory a meaningful look.

Rory knew this would be coming and fished a small roll of notes from his trouser pocket. He peeled off a twenty. Pete gave him an incredulous look – twenty wasn't going to do.

Rory shook his head, retaining the cash. 'I need names, Pete.'

Pete sighed theatrically. 'Make it worth me while, then.'

Forty pounds changed hands and Pete reeled off a litany of local dealers. Rory knew of all of them, and knew that a couple of those mentioned were serving time.

'Come on, Pete. This is bullshit. Something better or I'll have that money back.'

Pete raised his claw-like hands defensively. 'Okay, seriously. The Collins brothers. There's been trouble brewing there for a time.'

'Between them and who?'

'There's a Romanian gang tried to move in on their turf.'

This was hardly news to Rory, but it could explain the body under the pier. On his way home, he became more convinced by the theory. Turf wars between the local drug gangs were nothing new and accounted for a large part of the violent crimes in the city. The information wasn't worth forty quid, but it was worth keeping Pete on side. Very occasionally he did come up with the goods.

When he presented the theory to Francis in the station the next morning, he could see that the boss was sceptical.

'Is this just a guess by your informant, or did he give you anything solid?'

'He doesn't exactly follow rules of evidence,' said Rory. 'But it gives us something to look into. After all, the guy's covered in prison tattoos – it's reasonable to assume he's in one or other of the gangs, and that this killing, or even both, might be gang-related.'

'We'll assume nothing.' The boss's tone was sharp. He didn't like the fact that Rory had come up with a lead.

'So let's see if your tattoo woman can throw any light on where else he might have got those tattoos.'

Rory's moment of smug satisfaction at stealing a march on the boss was to be short-lived. The door to the incident room opened and Hollins escorted Marni Mullins into the room.

'Thanks for coming,' said Francis, going over to greet her.

'Did I have a choice?' She looked nonplussed. 'I really have told you everything I know.'

'I know, and we're grateful for that,' said Francis. 'I wonder, if I show you some pictures of tattoos, if you could tell me about them.'

She shrugged. 'Sure.'

Francis led her over to an unused desk at the far end of the room and spread out an array of photographs, close-ups of tattoos on pale, bloodless skin. Rory could see from the backgrounds that they'd been taken in the morgue.

'This man was found dead early on Tuesday morning. We suspect some of these tattoos are gang-related.'

Marni bent over the pictures. After looking for a minute, she rearranged them into the semblance of a body shape. A torso, arms and legs that were a mess of badly executed, blurry black tattoos – symbols, numbers and skulls.

'Was he murdered?' said Marni.

Francis nodded. 'Decapitated.'

Marni Mullins studied the tattoos again and then pointed to one of the pictures.

'Some of these are very interesting.' She no longer sounded nervous.

'It's fairly obvious he's in a gang,' said Rory. 'We suspect it was a drugs deal gone wrong. His fingerprints should tell us a whole lot more than these scratchings.'

The boss glared at him before directing his next question to Marni.

'Ms Mullins, do any of these have special meanings we should be aware of?'

Marni pointed at the picture she'd picked out a moment before.

'This,' she said. 'It's a classic gang symbol.'

The tattoo she indicated was a five-pointed crown.

'What did I tell you?' said Rory.

Marni's head snapped round at him. 'You know it?'

'A gang's a gang – there aren't that many to choose from in Brighton.'

Marni sighed. 'This isn't a local prison tattoo. The crown signifies the Latin Kings. They're a gang operating out of Chicago. The five points show affiliation to the People Nation gang. As far as I'm aware, neither of these gangs has branches in Brighton. Another thing, this has been done using an electric tattoo iron. Prison tattoos are made with sharpened ballpoints and boot polish.'

Francis Sullivan was trying to hide a smirk. Smug bastard, thought Rory.

'Some of these are home-made tattoos,' said Marni, pointing at a couple that were cruder in execution, 'but that doesn't mean they were done in prison. The dots and the number fourteen – it's all American gang stuff. Three dots mean *mi vida loca* or "my crazy life". Five dots mean time in prison, symbolising the four corners of the cell with the prisoner inside. And the number fourteen claims membership of the Nuestra Familia gang in northern California.' She turned around to face Francis. 'I think what you have here is a very confused wannabe. He's probably no closer to being a member of a gang than I am.' She directed her gaze at Rory. 'In other words, if you think this is a gangland killing, Sergeant, you're barking up the wrong tree.'

What makes her the bloody expert? thought Rory irritably.

'And what about this?' Sullivan was pointing to a tattoo of a snarling wolf on the outside of the victim's right calf.

Marni looked at it for a couple of minutes, tracing the outline with her finger.

'Ah, that's a beautiful piece of work. He would have paid good money for that and it's nothing to do with prisons or gangs. It's also fresh. His taste in tattoos is maturing. Was maturing.'

'Tell me,' said Francis, 'how do you know if a tattoo has been done by hand or done by a machine?'

'Amateur tattoos done in prison or at home are easy to spot,' said Marni. 'The lines are thicker and the work's crude. They also tend to be blurred at the edges. See, look at the difference between these two.' She pointed to the crown on the man's torso and the word 'HATE' which was emblazoned across the knuckles of his left hand. 'Prison tattoos are always black as there's no access to coloured ink inside.'

Rory feigned disinterest, earning a filthy look from the boss.

'It's worth knowing, Sergeant,' he said. 'Tattoos are featuring in more and more cases.'

'Yes, sir,' he replied through gritted teeth.

'Thanks for coming in,' said Sullivan. 'I'm sure this information will prove to be useful.'

Rory doubted it. It had told them precisely nothing, while shooting down what was a perfectly reasonable theory.

Marni watched as Francis gathered up the pictures.

'Goodbye, Mrs Mullins,' he said, leading her across to the door.

'Marni,' she said. 'I haven't been Mrs for fifteen years.'

'Right, Marni it is from now on,' he said.

Sickening. But what a pretty shade of pink the boss's cheeks turned when he blushed, thought Rory, as he pinned the pictures to the incident board.

15

Francis

Francis watched Marni weaving her way along the crowded pavement just ahead of him. There were too many people moving to get out of the downpour for them to walk side by side. She was taking him to see another tattooist, Ishikawa Iwao, her mentor and a tattoo historian, in the hope that he could tell them something more about Evan Armstrong's shoulder tattoo. God knows if he could help, but Francis was running out of ideas. Bradshaw had spent the lunch hour breathing down his neck and he needed to find an escape from the Chief's rancid tobacco breath. As soon as he was back in his office, he'd called Marni and asked for help once again.

'This is it,' said Marni, over her shoulder.

She ducked out of the rain into a doorway, which opened directly onto a flight of stairs. Inside, the walls and ceiling were painted black and the carpet was so old and worn that Francis couldn't have hazarded a guess at its original colour. He followed Marni up the stairs, which took an abrupt turn after half a rise. A skinny girl in a black mini-dress pressed herself into the corner to give them space.

'Plod,' she hissed into Francis's ear as he passed her.

How in God's name did they know? Always. Did he emanate some sort of smell or was it the cut of his suit? Was there a certain cast in his eye that gave the game away?

'Not here for you, dear,' he murmured to her as she continued down the stairs.

Marni looked back at him questioningly, and he raised his eyebrows.

The stairs opened into a narrow corridor with doors along either side. The air was hazy and smelled heavily of incense and patchouli, and the single overhead light was fitted with a red bulb. There was music playing, and behind one of the doors, a woman was singing an oriental tune in a high, reedy voice. Brothel or opium den? Francis could almost see Sherlock Holmes in here, losing himself in a golden cloud.

Marni knocked on one of the doors. She didn't wait for an answer, but pushed it open and went in, beckoning Francis to follow her. He didn't know what to expect – a dark and sordid chamber of horrors had sprung up in his mind's eye. But not this. Not a spacious, pale and pristine studio, flooded with natural light. Along the opposite wall, a long row of tall windows looked out over a motley stretch of ill-kept back gardens. In contrast, everything in the studio was sleek and modern – the tattooing chairs and benches were expensive concoctions of steel, leather and wood, while the equipment and light fittings made him think of a luxurious medical facility.

But this wasn't what snared Francis's attention. Something was sitting on one of the plush leather tattooing chairs, staring at him with hostile green eyes. At first glance he thought it was an emaciated and bruised naked baby, a shock that sent a shiver up his spine. But the creature was a cat, completely devoid of hair and thin enough to make every bone visible. Most disturbing of all, as he looked more closely he saw that the bruises were actually tattoos. The creature's back, neck, chest and legs were covered with Japanese pictograms, rendered in dark indigo ink. The cat hissed and showed its teeth to him.

He looked towards Marni for an explanation and then stretched out his hand towards the creature. As he did, it reared up on its haunches and batted at his hand with one paw, scratching the side of his thumb.

'What the—'

The sound of a door opening behind him stopped Francis in mid-flow. He stuck his bleeding thumb in his mouth and turned around to see a willowy Japanese man coming into the studio. He was wearing a dark blue linen kimono. His buzz-cut hair was snow white but his face was unlined, making it difficult to assess his age. He didn't look happy to have visitors.

The man nodded when he recognised Marni, but his scowl deepened as he looked at Francis. He bowed, bending deeply from his waist, and Marni bowed in return, with a flick of her index finger indicating to Francis to do the same.

'Konnichiwa,' the man said. His voice was high-pitched and staccato.

'Konnichiwa, sensei,' Marni replied.

He straightened up from his bow and twisted to face Francis. 'Konnichiwa,' he said, bowing again.

Francis bowed in return, unsure of what to say.

Once they were both upright the man turned straight back to Marni and said something to her in Japanese. To Francis it sounded like he was angry, and whatever he said made Marni frown.

'Yes, I brought a stranger here,' she replied in English. 'Please forgive me, master. We need your help.'

'I don't see you for a year and then you only come when you want something.'

Francis couldn't tell if he was being serious or playful.

'I apologise, Iwao,' Marni said, with another slight bow. 'I'm sorry – I know I should come more often.'

'You should. You're my favourite canvas and you still have

blank skin. You also have a lot still to learn.' Then his face relaxed into a smile. 'How's Thierry?'

Marni smiled in return. 'He's good. Producing some great work at the moment.'

'Tell him to come and see me soon. He's as bad as you are for ignoring his friends. Now, you've brought a visitor. Who is this?'

Chastened, Marni turned to look at Francis. 'Iwao, this is Francis Sullivan.' She switched to Japanese and there was a rapid exchange between the two of them. Eventually they fell silent and Iwao looked at Francis. The cat hissed again, jumped down from the chair and stalked through the room towards the door by which Iwao had entered.

'You are police?' Iwao said.

Francis nodded.

'Get out.'

Marni stepped forward and put a hand on the man's forearm. 'No, please, Iwao. This is important.'

He shook his arm free. 'It's bad luck. Please leave.'

Francis looked at Marni but she seemed to be at a loss, so he turned his gaze to Iwao. 'Mr Ishikawa, we need your expertise in tattoos to help a murder investigation. Let me show you a couple of pictures and then we'll go.'

Iwao screwed up his face. He whispered something to Marni in Japanese. She nodded slowly but her cheeks flamed.

'Give me the pictures,' he said.

Francis opened his document case and pulled out the picture of Evan Armstrong's shoulder.

'We're trying to establish who did this tattoo.'

Iwao took the image from him and went across the room to an immaculately tidy workbench. He held the photo under the glare of a strong desk lamp, then made a soft clicking noise with his mouth as he studied it through a magnifying glass.

Francis looked round at the pictures on the wall. Not

surprisingly, they were all Japanese style and, even with his un-trained eye, he could see that they were something special.

'Are these all by Iwao?' he asked Marni in a low voice.

She nodded. 'He did my back piece,' she said.

'I know who this is by,' said Iwao.

He put the picture down on his bench and pulled an exhibition catalogue out of a nearby bookcase. He flicked through the pages until he found what he was looking for.

Francis found himself holding his breath and glanced at Marni – she was doing the same.

'Yes, here.' Iwao put the brochure down next to the picture and held it open so Francis and Marni could see. 'These two are very similar, certainly by the same hand. See, these triangles here, all distorted slightly in the same direction. The lines have the same weight. The patterns are on a similar scale, same level of intricacy . . .'

Francis looked closer and could see the similarity in the details Iwao mentioned.

'And?' prompted Marni.

'This work is by Jonah Mason. I included him in my exhibition – a great honour for him. But his work is outstanding.'

'I thought it might be one of Jonah's,' said Marni, 'but I wasn't sure. I wanted to see if you felt the same.'

'Is he still working?' said Francis.

Iwao shrugged. 'He's lived in California for the past fifteen years – that's where I met him – but, yes, he's still prolific.'

He closed the catalogue and put it back on the shelf. As he reached up, the sleeve of his kimono slid down to his elbow and Francis caught a glimpse of dark, intricate ink on his forearm.

'You say this tattoo was cut away from the man's body?' said Iwao, turning back to Marni.

'Can you think of any reason why someone might do that?' she said.

Iwao took a deep breath and waited before exhaling. He stroked his chin with slender fingers.

'It's something that happens in Japan,' he said, 'but not like this. People with *irezumi*, usually Yakuza . . .'

'Irezumi?' asked Francis.

'Full body tattoos. Sometimes, when a Yakuza dies, he will have left instructions for his tattoo to be flayed from his body and preserved. There are examples of them displayed in the Bunshin Tattoo Museum in Yokohama. And I know Tokyo University has a collection.'

'But people aren't murdered for their tattoos?'

Iwao shook his head. 'I've never heard of it – in Japan or anywhere else. Now, time for you to go.'

He turned on his heel and left the room without saying goodbye, leaving Francis and Marni to make their way back down the black staircase and out onto the street. When the door had closed behind them, Francis turned to Marni.

'What did he say to you, when I asked him to look at the pictures?'

Marni looked away from him and again her cheeks took on colour.

'It was nothing. He just wanted to remind me of something.'

Francis couldn't begin to wonder what it was and her demeanour didn't encourage him to dig further. They walked on in silence.

Francis's phone vibrated in his pocket. He looked at it and saw a text message from Rory.

Why is Marni Mullins such an expert on prison tatts? She's done time.

vi

I have taken a number of tattoos. I'm turning them into leather –
curing them. They came from different people – dead now, of course
– and they're all at different stages of the tanning process. I've been
curing leather for years. Not human leather, of course – that's a rela-
tively recent thing. But animal skins. And though you might not
believe it, the process is exactly the same. There's nothing different
about human skin and the leather it makes is as soft as any.

For example, the boy's scalp is now bathing in milk of lime to break
down the keratin in the hair and to dissolve the fat. It stinks but it's
an essential part of the process. While that one limes, I'm working
on another. Scudding away hair and rotting flesh from an elegant
sleeve tattoo using a blunted blade. I remember the woman I took it
from. My first victim. I was so nervous but as soon as I started to cut
and peel away her skin, my confidence flooded back. She was a kind
woman – I spoke to her before I killed her – and still graceful when
she realised what was about to happen. Only at the very moment of
death did I see the fear in her eyes and smell her sweat.

I'm at my happiest when working with skins. I learned that fact
when I was working for Ron Dougherty. He recognised my special
talents. He might have been the finest taxidermist in the country
when I apprenticed with him, but he was more than happy to pass
that baton on to me as I honed my skills. But more importantly, we

were a team and he was like a father to me.

He took over my education where my father left off, and was a better father to me in so many ways that I couldn't even begin to list them. When Daddy pushed me out of the nest because I couldn't live up to his expectations, Ron stepped in and picked up the pieces. My pieces. And over the next ten years, he stitched me back together and taught me my craft.

Ron gave me a home and a job, and plenty more. I went to work for him in his studio.

He started me off working on rats and mice. You can buy them alive anywhere – for feeding snakes or lab experimentation – so we had a constant supply. They're cheap so it didn't matter when I made a mistake, though I made precious few. Once I'd learned the basic skills of skinning, curing and stuffing, he let me build my skills on birds and squirrels, on hamsters, and then on kittens. Once I was ready, I was allowed to work on bigger animals. Very few of our clients ever asked where the animals came from. Most of our business came from stuffing people's dead pets, ponies or prize livestock. Sometimes we were asked to make tableaus. People would want a scene from a favourite book or film reinterpreted with dead mice and birds. My favourite was a rat as Don Quixote, riding a hedgehog as he tilted at a windmill. I made it for an old lady from Brixham, who could remember such a piece from her childhood.

Ron died a few years ago. It's a shame he's dead. I kept his skin and tanned it – my first experience with human skin. I always carry a bit of Ron's skin with me now, in my pocket or, more often, pinned inside my clothing, so I can feel it against my own skin. That way we're always together. Never apart.

Ron was the best. That's why he had to go.

Now, according to the Collector, I'm the best.

16

Francis

Francis Sullivan stared at his computer screen with disbelief and swore softly at no one in particular. There was nothing. Not a single mention of a Marni Mullins in the Sussex police database. Perhaps she was in there under another name, her maiden name most likely. But then how the hell had Rory known that she'd been inside? Francis had asked him straight away but he'd just muttered something vague about unsubstantiated rumours. Francis wondered what her crime had been. Shoplifting? Petty drug dealing, like Thierry? He'd had several cautions. Burglary, maybe? Women could be accomplished burglars. He'd have to widen his search to the national database.

He knew he shouldn't, however. He didn't for one minute view Marni as a suspect in the Evan Armstrong murder, and they had no concrete reason to link that murder to the body found under the pier. Sure, both victims had tattoos, but as far as he could make out, so did at least half of the young men who were still alive in the city. And the MOs were completely different. Following up on a prurient interest in Marni Mullins was unprofessional. He could leave that for his unscrupulous number two to do, and he had no doubt Rory would. Francis hardly dared question where he'd got his information about her prison time from.

An email pinged into his inbox and he turned his attention to the cases in hand. It was from Angie Burton and contained the results from an altogether more valid search. He'd asked her to check with SCAS – the Serious Crime Analysis Section – for any violent crimes that involved skin-flaying or tattoo removal. He scanned it quickly for information, taking a sip of coffee as he ran his eyes down the screen.

Nothing stood out as obvious. Victims of all sorts of murders – robberies, pub fights, domestics – were recorded as having had tattoos, but most had been solved and SCAS hadn't flagged any of the tattoos up as having been elemental to the motive. The list of mortal injuries from the database made gruesome reading, but flaying wasn't among them. Most were stabbings or blunt instrument trauma. A woman had had an arm chopped off, another had been pushed under a train, and there were a couple of fatal gunshot wounds. One man had been stabbed in the neck with a tattoo machine, surviving even though the needles had nicked one of his carotid arteries.

Francis skipped down to Angie's analysis of the findings.

. . . no obvious link to Evan Armstrong's death. There might be some sort of connection that would come to light with deeper analysis. However, that would require a substantial commitment of man hours from the team . . .

In other words, Angie didn't want to do it. Francis couldn't blame her – data analysis was becoming a bigger part of the job but it wasn't the reason why most people joined the force. They were interested in hands-on investigating, not sitting behind a desk. But if there was something there, he couldn't afford to miss it on his first case in charge.

He picked up his phone.

'Hollins, in here a moment.'

Two minutes later Hollins appeared in the doorway.

'Can we do it in a sec, boss? It's Angie's birthday and she's about to dole out cake.'

No worries. There's a madman with a flaying knife on the loose but let's all pause the search to eat cake . . .

'Of course.' He got up from his desk and followed Hollins into the incident room. 'Where's the birthday girl?'

Ten minutes later, after he'd joined in with a rousing chorus of 'Happy Birthday' and eaten the thinnest slice of Victoria sponge possible, Angie had intercepted him on his way back to his office and jokingly demanded a birthday kiss. He gave her a peck on the cheek, which was enough to cause his own cheeks to flame. Heading back to his desk, he intercepted Kyle Hollins' attempt at taking a third piece of cake. No wonder there was a slight overhang at the top of his trousers.

'Hollins, my office.'

Rory followed them in, still licking strawberry jam from around his lips. 'Boss? A word?' He spat crumbs as he spoke.

Francis frowned. 'Give me a minute.'

He turned back to Hollins. 'I've sent you a SCAS report based on the markers in the Armstrong murder. I want you to go through it with a fine-tooth comb. Check for anything that could have been missed, especially areas of skin abraded or cut. Cross-reference geography and take a note of any suspects or nominals. Let me know of any linked cases before close of play.'

'But . . .'

'No buts. Just bugger off and do it.'

Hollins reversed out, looking glum.

Rory watched him go with an amused look on his face. 'He was going to tell you that Bradshaw's already got him working on something that needs to be finished on pain of death.'

Francis raised an eyebrow. *The chief was bypassing him and using his staff?*

'It's a tough life. By the way, where is Bradshaw? Seen him today?'

'It's Wednesday. Golf with the Super. Shinning up the greasy pole.'

'Right. What have you got for me?'

Rory planted himself in the empty chair on the other side of Francis's desk.

'Firstly, Tom Fitz from the *Argus* is sitting in reception and says he won't leave until he gets an interview with you.'

Francis sighed. Would the damn man never give up?

'Tell the desk sergeant to throw him out. What else?'

'ID on the headless corpse. I was right – we did have his fingerprints on record.'

'And?'

'He wasn't exactly the gangster I thought.' At least the sergeant could do a nice line in self-deprecation. 'Just one count of joyriding. Thug called Jem Walsh. Local boy, apprentice tattoo artist. Pretty unlikely he was involved in drug wars.'

'Anything to suggest what might have happened?'

Rory paused briefly. 'It turns out he had a tattoo on his head . . .'

Francis's stomach lurched. '. . . And his head was taken.'

'You're thinking what I'm thinking.'

'Maybe – just maybe – they are linked after all.' Their eyes met across the desk. It would need to be thoroughly investigated before they could draw any conclusions, but Francis's heart was pounding. 'Do we know what the tattoo was?'

'A spider in a web that covered his whole skull. And a name, Bel-something. Belial?'

'The Devil. How do we know this?'

'Photos from his parents, guv.'

They both sat still, on either side of the desk. Silence reigned for a long half minute, then both of them spoke at once.

'You go ahead,' said Francis. There was a pulse thudding at the base of his neck and he felt suddenly cold.

'Do you think . . .?' Rory's eyes widened.

A five-second silence. Neither of them wanted to say the words.

Finally, Francis found his nerve.

'One more like this and we'll have a serial killer on our hands.'

17

Rory

They couldn't be certain. They chewed over the known facts for another hour, shooting down their own theories ruthlessly. Despite the public's obsession with them, serial killers were incredibly rare so it wouldn't do to go jumping to conclusions.

'The head might turn up yet,' said Rory. 'It's two murders, different MO, different cause of death, no known link between the victims.'

'To be fair, we haven't looked into that yet. We've only just got Walsh's ID,' said Sullivan. 'And what's the likelihood of two killers working the same patch in the same week?'

'Serial killers start slowly. There's been no time between these two killings.'

'That's true.' Sullivan paused and opened one of his desk drawers. 'Can we see Evan Armstrong's tattoo and Walsh's head as trophies?'

He stared at the notepad on his desk, lost in thought. Rory sat opposite him and pulled a plain black vape out of his pocket. The soft sucking sound his lips made as he inhaled pulled Francis out of his reverie.

'Put that away, Sergeant. You know as well as I do, no vaping.'

Rory scowled as he exhaled but thrust the plastic gadget back into his trouser pocket. God, he hated working for a jobsworth and the new boss was turning out to be just that. There would be no cutting corners with DI Sullivan.

'It's too early to label this yet, or to officially connect the murders.'

The boss going by the rules again. They both knew what the hell it was.

'So we act like it isn't a serial killing and waste valuable time? Ever worked a serial case before, boss?'

'That's hardly the point,' snapped Francis. 'We'll just have to move forward as far as we can, treating them as separate cases until we find something that informs us otherwise.'

'Or until another bloody body turns up,' said Rory.

'Speak to the duty inspectors. Make them aware there's a killer – or even two – at large. We need more uniforms on the street. Both of these happened right in the centre of town . . .'

The conversation was interrupted by the insistent chime of the DI's mobile.

'Bradshaw,' he mouthed to Rory, as he picked up the phone.

'Sir?' Francis nodded a couple of times, his face serious. 'Right away.'

He cut the call and pushed back his chair.

'Come on, we've got to go up and give him a progress report.'

'That won't take long,' said Rory, following him out of the room.

'That's the problem.'

'Are you going to mention our theory?'

'That it's a serial killer? I think not till we've got more to go on. It'll give him a monumental hard-on that I, for one, wouldn't want to deal with.'

The boss certainly had a point.

Detective Chief Inspector Bradshaw's office was on the floor above, though that single floor represented a world of difference. There were no stains on his carpet and he had room for an armchair, a bookshelf and a couple of filing cabinets that together were probably bigger than the boss's shoebox of an office.

Sullivan had knocked and entered without waiting for a reply. Rory followed him in and they both stood waiting in front of Bradshaw's desk as he finished off a phone call. The desk was clear of paperwork but there were several framed photos that featured not a brace of smiling children but the chief on a variety of golf courses. Rory positioned himself slightly behind and to one side of Sullivan – this exchange could get interesting.

'Sit down,' barked Bradshaw. His face was ruddy, possibly windburn from the golf course, more likely from the visit to the bar afterwards. He looked expectantly back and forth from Rory to Sullivan as they took their seats.

'Sir . . .' started Sullivan.

'The Armstrong case. Have you arrested anyone yet?'

'No, sir.'

'Got any names?'

'No, sir.'

'What about Mullins? I thought we had him squarely in the frame.'

'He had an alibi,' said Rory. 'It holds up.'

'Four days on the case and you've made no progress at all. That's about it, isn't it?'

'Not exactly, sir,' said Sullivan.

Bradshaw's face clouded with anger.

'Then, please, fill me in.'

There were rare moments, few and far between, when Rory didn't begrudge Francis Sullivan the DI job. Reporting to Bradshaw was definitely one of them.

'We've managed to identify both the victims, sir.'

'Who was the second? Is there a link that might point to the same killer?'

'We're looking into it.'

Bradshaw sighed. 'But nothing concrete yet?'

'The fingerprint match only came in half an hour ago, sir,' said Rory.

'He's got form, has he? said Bradshaw. I take it you've put a call out to question all known associates?'

'He had a four-year-old charge for joy-riding,' said Sullivan. 'No known associates. No contact with law enforcement since.'

'Jesus Christ, you're treading water. There's a killer, or two killers, out there and you've got nothing.'

'To be fair, sir, DI Sullivan does have a theory,' said Rory.

He noticed a muscle twitch in Sullivan's cheek. He shouldn't have said it.

'Spit it out then, Sullivan.'

'It's nothing, sir. Just speculation. Far too early to make a thing of it.'

Bradshaw glared across the desk. Sullivan's cheeks reddened.

'Simply a discussion we've been having, rather than a working theory.'

Sullivan glanced down into his lap. An avoidance tactic – but he was going to have to spill. When he looked up again, he met the chief's glare. Rory was impressed.

'Evan Armstrong had a tattoo removed from his body. The skin was flayed—' began Sullivan.

'I know all this. Get to the point.'

'The second victim, Jem Walsh had a scalp tattoo that covered most of his cranium. His head has yet to be found. But that makes two missing tattoos, suggesting that our killer, if it is the same person, is taking trophies.'

Bradshaw placed his elbows on the desk and rested the ends of his fingertips against each other. He closed his eyes. He looked to Rory as if he was praying or meditating.

'No.' He hadn't even bothered to open his eyes.

'Sir?' said Sullivan.

Now his eyes sprang open.

'Absolute bollocks, Sullivan. This is not a serial killer taking trophies. I doubt the murders were even committed by the same bloody person. Don't waste your time and my budget on a crackpot theory.' He stood up, glaring. 'Can't you see it? These were two characters on the fringes of crime and I can guarantee that's where you'll find your answers.'

'We're keeping an open mind and exploring every possibility, sir,' said Sullivan.

'And that's your bloody problem. Too much fannying about and not enough focus. Find out who these men associated with and you'll find out why they were killed. After that, it'll be easy.'

'Yes, sir.'

'Don't make me feel obliged to bring in someone more experienced, Sullivan. That would be a failure for both of us. And I, for one, don't do failure.'

'I don't either, sir,' said Sullivan quietly, as he pushed his chair back.

'We'll get your killer for you, sir,' said Rory. 'Whether it's one or two.'

18

Francis

The first thing Francis noticed on letting himself into his sister's flat was a layer of dust on the hall mirror. Guilt washed over him. Robin's flat was usually spotless so this meant only one thing – a relapse, and he hadn't seen her in weeks.

'Is that you, Francis? I'm in the living room.'

Francis went through and his suspicions were confirmed. His older sister was settled in her favourite armchair with a blanket over her knees, but he immediately spotted the crutches leaning against the back of the chair. Five years older than him, academically gifted and, in his eyes, beautiful, Robin was his role model, a woman he looked up to far more than their mother, Lydia. But today his sister looked tired and diminished, her mouth tight.

'Robin, you should have told me, you goose.'

He bent to kiss her cheek and noticed the smell of illness clinging to the clothes that hung loose on her tiny frame.

'Why?' she said. 'Tea and sympathy? Hardly what I want.'

'Speaking of which, I could use some tea.'

He cleared away a meal tray from the coffee table in front of her and tidied the kitchen while the kettle boiled.

'Have you seen Mum?' she said, as soon as he came back into the living room.

He shook his head.

She sighed. 'Come on, Fran. It's okay to ignore me – I've got plenty of friends who care. But Mum? You know you're her only visitor.'

Francis didn't mind getting a hard time from Robin. He deserved it.

'It's work,' he said, pouring tea into two cups.

'Not an excuse,' said his sister.

She stretched forward to take a biscuit from the plate and he noticed her difficulty in picking it up. MS affected her muscles, her co-ordination, her sight and occasionally her speech, when a relapse was bad. He hated what it was doing to her, but he knew better than to comment.

'I know it's not an excuse.'

'And I suppose no social life either?'

Francis shrugged. He always had to endure the gauntlet of Robin prying into his private life.

'You won't find a wife if you don't ask any girls out.'

Why the obsession with marrying him off?

'Work's more important. I'm trying to build a career.'

'So tell me about it.'

This was why he'd finally made the time to come and see her. Robin had always been his sounding board. She could think laterally and make connections that he or the rest of the team wouldn't even stumble across. As they drank their tea, he filled her in on the details of the two murders. By the time he finished he was mournfully resting his head in both hands.

'I'm getting nowhere,' he said, 'and this one's really important.'

'Every murder's important,' said Robin.

'I know. But I've also got a boss who doesn't believe in me and a team who think I'm a yuppy upstart. I've got a lot to prove.'

'As usual. Let me think.'

'Be my guest.'

'It's not, on the face of it, a serial killer,' said Robin slowly, after silently chewing her way through three biscuits.

'Different MOs, timing too close. Sure. Not a serial killer,' said Francis. 'But there's something odd about both of them. No links to crime, no robbery, no sexual motivation.'

'Doesn't mean they're linked.'

'Great. So I've got two killers to catch with the same resources.'

Robin ignored this and pondered over the pictures Francis had brought to show her.

'This,' she said, indicating Evan's flayed shoulder, 'definitely looks like a trophy's been taken.'

'But not Walsh's head? He had a scalp tattoo.'

'I get that. But if the killer just needed a tattoo as a trophy, Walsh had plenty of others to choose from, didn't he? Taking a tattoo off a man's cranium wouldn't be easy.'

'Which is why he needed to take the whole head.'

'Instead of, say, that wolf on his leg?'

Francis was stumped. He went back to the kitchen to fetch the rest of the packet of Hobnobs he'd opened.

'Take a look at this,' he said, holding out a sheaf of papers.

'What is it?' said Robin.

'It's a SCAS interrogation – Serious Crime Analysis Section. Details of other crimes for comparison points.'

'So it would show you anything that might link two crimes together?'

'In theory, yes. But there aren't any other murders with reports of missing tattoos.'

Robin studied the document.

'So in this, your two murders wouldn't be linked, would they? One missing tattoo, one missing head. Any chance of more tea, please, Fran?'

While he filled the kettle and got the tea out, Francis thought about what Robin had said. Evan Armstrong and Jem Walsh's murders wouldn't show up a similar MO but they still had a fact in common.

'Give me the report,' he said, as soon as he'd put the fresh teas down on the coffee table.

Robin handed it to him and he dropped onto the sofa, scanning the information for the umpteenth time.

'What are you looking for?' said Robin.

Francis shook his head. 'I don't know. But there must be something here.'

Something he'd stared straight through five times already. He went back to the top of the report and started reading the crime descriptions again.

Then he spotted it. 'Yes! This!'

'What?' said Robin.

He snatched his phone from his pocket.

'Rory? Rory, open the SCAS report, check out Giselle Connelly – a woman found dead at a golf course. One arm missing, not recovered despite extensive search. Find out if she had a tattoo on the missing arm. Let me know straight away.'

'Francis, you're a genius,' said Robin.

'Not so sure about that. If there's no tattoo, then it means nothing. But if there is, we might have some kind of tattoo-obsessed serial killer on our hands.'

'And all you need to do is work out who it is.'

'Which I do how?'

'By working out why he takes them, of course,' replied his sister.

Of course. It was all that obvious. Wasn't it?

19

Marni

Marni stood outside Tatouage Gris and asked herself what she was doing here. Did she really need Thierry's help in identifying the image of the sleeve tattoo Francis had just given her, or was it simply an excuse to see him? And why was she helping Francis Sullivan anyway? Was she trying to impress him? The answers eluded her, so there was no point hanging around on the pavement.

She pushed open the door and was hardly surprised when a stream of French invective greeted her arrival.

'*Merde!* Can't you leave me alone, *connasse?*'

Even with a scowl on his face, Thierry still managed to look good to her.

'I love you too, T,' she said, ignoring the meaning of his words.

The shop where Thierry worked with Charlie and Noa, plus a rotation of nubile female apprentices, was far bigger than her own and wasn't divided into a front and back section. It would have seemed even larger if not for the fact that the interior was painted entirely black and divided by half-height walls into a series of individual tattooing stations. In one corner stood a partially stripped-down motorbike that Charlie had been working on for as long as anyone could remember.

The place was rarely cleaned and a multitude of familiar smells always hung in the incense-laden air. Curry. Cigarettes. Dope. Disinfectant.

'Marni!' Noa practically sang her name across the studio and then swept her up into a hug. His beard scratched her cheeks as he bent to kiss her but being enveloped in his warm fug felt like coming home. 'It's been too long,' he whispered in her ear. 'When can I steal you away from all this?'

Marni laughed. It had always been their joke, the affair that never materialised.

As Noa went back to the drawing he was working on, Charlie waved at her over the naked torso he was tattooing.

'Charlie,' she said with a nod.

She ignored the apprentice taking an inventory of the ink bottles in Thierry's station. She looked like a punk schoolgirl. It was never worth learning their names. If they were any good they were quickly poached by rival studios who would pay them more, or they simply left over a broken romance with one of the boys. Marni had no time for any of them.

Thierry glared at her but she knew better than to take it seriously. She hung her bag over the back of a stool and wriggled out of her jacket.

'What are you doing here?' said Thierry. 'I don't need to see you every day, do I?'

'The police need our help.'

'Our help?' said Noa.

'Francis sent me a picture of a sleeve tattoo. They're trying to find out who did it. We're the most likely people to know.'

'Francis?' said Thierry. 'The man who arrested me? You're now on first-name terms with him?'

'Whatever.'

Feeling herself start to blush, although she was unsure quite why, Marni delved into her bag and pulled out a rolled-up photocopy. She unfurled it and pressed it out flat on an unused massage bench. It was a typical tattoo-shop shot of a woman's arm with a spectacular biomechanical tattoo.

'Look,' she said. 'This woman was murdered six months ago. Her arm was hacked off.' She pointed to the tattoo in the picture. 'It hasn't been found.'

Noa came over to take a look and even Thierry, despite himself, craned his neck to see the image. He let out a soft whistle. Marni watched him closely, gauging his reaction to the image, but his face told her very little.

'Rad. I knew a guy who had a piece like that, but like the flesh was torn away at the edges,' said Noa.

'That's a sick effect,' said Thierry. 'Wasn't that by Seamus Byrne?'

'Yeah, yeah, it was. He does a lot of stuff like that.'

'But not this one?' said Marni. 'It doesn't quite look like his work to me.'

'Let me take a look.' Intrigued, Charlie had put down his iron and stripped off his gloves to come over. The girl on his bench took the opportunity to stretch out and drink some water.

As Charlie studied the picture, the apprentice stopped what she was doing and slinked up behind Thierry. She snaked her arms around his neck and nuzzled his shoulder. Thierry turned round to kiss her on the mouth. Marni looked away. No one wants to watch their ex playing tonsil hockey. It hurt, but then he always had been an insensitive bastard.

'Hey, guys,' said Noa, reading her discomfort.

Thierry looked round at Marni, then back at the girl.

'Later, babe.'

Marni wondered if he even knew her name.

'How old are you?' she said pointedly.

The girl looked like a deer caught in headlights.

'*Putain*, Marni. Leave her alone.'

Charlie and Noa exchanged looks, and Charlie picked up the image.

'It's good work,' he said. 'Really good.'

'The killer has taste, no?' said Thierry.

Marni forced her attention back to the reason why she was here, and away from thoughts of the last time she'd kissed Thierry. When had that been? A year or two ago, after a drunken night out at one of the conventions?

'That's true. Evan Armstrong's tattoo was by Jonah Mason. He's one of the best at tribal black work.'

'I knew Evan,' said Charlie. 'He was a good guy.'

'Sure,' said Thierry. 'That's why he skipped out without paying.'

'But he was a laugh,' said Noa. 'And you could have got him to pay. You were just too lazy to follow up.'

'I think he probably paid you in dope,' said Marni. 'Plenty did back then.'

Thierry shook his head, but he was laughing.

'You really think the police are onto something? Like there's a killer going around taking people's tattoos? I don't buy it,' said Noa.

'You know you can cure human skin like leather?' said Marni. 'They do it in Japan with Yakuza tattoos.'

'Gross,' said the schoolgirl.

'I'd better get on,' said Charlie, going back to his client. 'But actually, you know who that could be by?'

'Who?'

'There's a guy from Poland. Bartosz somebody. His work is a bit like that.'

Thierry went back to his desk and opened his browser.

'Bartosz? B-A-R-T-O-S-Z?'

'Yeah, that's it,' said Charlie, pulling on a fresh pair of black latex gloves.

'Bartosz Klem,' Thierry confirmed a few seconds later. 'Yeah, this looks pretty similar.'

Marni stood behind his chair and stared at the screen. There was a scrolling column of tattoo images, most of them biomechanical in theme and very similar to the tattoo on the woman's arm.

'It's a pretty safe bet, I'd say,' she murmured.

'So why do the police need to know who did the tattoos?' asked Charlie. 'Do they think the artists had something to do with the murders? Aren't they all by different people?'

'I don't know,' said Marni, with a shrug. 'That doesn't make much sense. I think they're just grasping at straws.'

'But they definitely think it's something to do with the tattoos?' asked Noa.

Marni shrugged again. She rolled up the picture.

'Thanks, guys. I'll let DI Sullivan know. It's up to him whether the information has any bearing on the case.'

'Francis.' Thierry's voice dripped with sarcasm.

'I'm off,' said Marni. She wasn't going to rise to the bait. It would gain her nothing and just give him the satisfaction of knowing he could still press her buttons.

'Come to the pub, *chérie*,' said Noa.

'Not today, darling.'

Marni let the door swing shut behind her. A drink with Charlie and Noa would have been good, but she was damned if she was going to watch Thierry canoodle in a corner with his apprentice. She sometimes wondered if she shouldn't move away to stop the endless pull and push between them, but it always came down to one thing. It wouldn't be fair on Alex. Thierry had already been a part-time father since Alex was six and he was reaching an age now when a father's influence – even one as flaky as Thierry's – was most important.

It wasn't quite dark but there was a sharp edge to the wind now that the sun had dropped away. She hugged her jacket round her shoulders, wondering if there really was someone stalking the town for great tattoos. And that was the thing. They were all good pieces. She knew of the two they'd identified, Jonah Mason and Bartosz Klem. And Francis had shown her another picture, of a spider tattoo on the head of the most recent victim. The lettering was familiar-looking work too.

She passed a tattoo shop she knew on St James's Street and peered in. It was all shut up, no sign of Mandy or Pepe, the tattooists who worked there. There was a scuffed and torn poster stuck to the inside of the window advertising the recent convention. That needs to come down now, she thought to herself as she hurried on towards home.

For the rest of the way, a single thought bugged her.

What joined the dots? Apart from being tattooed, what did these three victims have in common that would make them targets?

But she didn't want to get drawn into things any further, so there was no reason to concern herself with it. Except for the creeping doubt. Could there be more linking her to this case than simply having discovered the body?

20

Rory

'We've made some progress,' said the boss. 'And there's no reason why we can't build on it.'

Seemed like the boss's definition of progress and his own were slightly different.

It was Thursday morning and the whole team were gathered in the incident room for the DI's daily briefing.

He pointed at the incident board.

'We've now got three murders on the board, one of them a cold case from six months ago. Giselle Connelly. The link between all three is tentative but if it holds out – and that's a big "if" – we've probably got a serial killer on our hands.'

There was a palpable frisson of excitement at the words 'serial killer', especially among the younger officers. After all, it was why most of them became detectives. It made Rory remember the first time he'd been involved on a serial killer case. He'd been a plain DC then, but with plenty of cases under his belt, and the DI on the case had been nearing retirement, had seen it all before. But even with a highly experienced team, it had taken months to solve the case. Francis Sullivan might be able to pass exams with his eyes shut, but he wouldn't solve these murders.

The thought depressed him, so he turned his attention back to what Francis was saying.

'We've got to either prove or rule out a link between these three murders. So far, there doesn't seem to be anything to tie the three victims together. Evan Armstrong worked in IT, no criminal record, no known enemies, straight but no steady girlfriend. Giselle Connelly, trainee lawyer, boyfriend out of the country when she was killed, and Jem Walsh, apprentice tattooist. I doubt their paths ever crossed.'

'But even if it's a serial killer,' said Hollins, 'he might be choosing his victims randomly.' He looked pleased with himself at this observation. Rory had noticed before that Hollins was nurturing an ambition to move up the ranks.

'Of course. Most serial killers do. But what I mean is a link between the crimes. Rose Lewis and her team are cross-checking all the forensics. You lot are going to cross-reference every known fact about the victims, how they died, where they died, what they were doing before they were attacked . . . Everything. If we can find any sort of link, it moves us forward. If there are no links, then no serial killer. And if we've got three separate killers, we'll have to work three times as hard.'

In other words, we know nothing.

Rory's phone rang. It was Bradshaw.

'Give me a minute, Sergeant,' he barked and hung up.

Rory's chest felt tight as he climbed the stairs to the top floor. Bloody cigarettes. Bradshaw's door was ajar and he slipped in as the chief finished a phone call.

'Ah, Mackay. I won't take up much of your time.'

'What can I do for you, sir?'

'Just between me and you,' said Bradshaw, in a lowered tone.

Rory closed the office door and Bradshaw nodded at him approvingly.

'I want you to be my eyes and ears in the incident room, Mackay.'

Rory digested what he said. 'How do you mean, sir? We give you daily updates.'

Bradshaw gave him a conspiratorial look. 'What I need is the inside track. You know, how things are going, how Sullivan's getting on. He's relatively inexperienced and could do with a friendly eye on him.'

The chief was asking him to spy on Sullivan.

'Of course, sir. I'll keep you in the know with whatever he's doing.'

Bradshaw nodded sagely, as if they'd made an important joint decision. 'Thank you, Mackay. Now, off you go – I'm sure there's plenty waiting to be done.'

An hour later, Rory and Tony Hitchins were wearing out their shoe leather visiting a list of pubs that Jem Walsh's brother had told them he frequented.

'Yeah, he's a regular,' said the landlord of the Mucky Duck, resting his elbows on the heavy wooden bar. 'Couple of times a week, usually. You after him for something?'

'Unfortunately not,' said Rory.

They showed him the pictures of Evan Armstrong and Giselle Connelly.

The landlord shook his head. 'Can't recall either of them, but we get a lot of tourists and one-off visitors. Don't remember all of the faces that come in here.'

It was the same in all the other pubs they tried. No one that knew Jem Walsh knew either of the other two, and when they went round Evan's local haunts later, the story was the same. Only in one city centre hostelry did a member of the bar staff recognise both Jem and Evan, and he'd never seen them together.

'And Giselle didn't even live in Brighton, did she?' said Hitchins, as they made their way wearily back to the station.

'No. Littlehampton.' Rory scowled. 'Never been in so many pubs without having a drink.'

They met Hollins coming out as they were going in.

'Come across anything useful?' said Rory.

Hollins shook his head. 'Not a bean. No work overlap, no school overlap, no friends overlap, different activities the nights they were attacked. Evan Armstrong was on his way home from a nightclub, Jem Walsh had been hanging out at a friend's house, and Giselle Connelly had been working late. I'm just heading out to talk to the owner of the place where Walsh worked, then I'll visit his old headmaster.'

Rory didn't miss the slightly sneering look on Hitchins' face at Hollins' dedication to the job.

'Looks like no serial killer after all,' said Hitchins, as they climbed the stairs.

'Not necessarily. If he's picking victims at random, there's no reason why they would be linked. Or they could just have a link to the killer but not to each other.'

Hitchins gave him a sceptical look.

'I know,' said Rory. 'This case needs a bloody break. And not in the form of another dead body.'

'There's plenty of speculation going down on Twitter,' said Hitchins. 'Maybe we should take a look through it all.'

'For fuck's sake, Twitter?' said Rory. 'Bloody waste of space designed for conspiracy theorists to sound off on.'

'But what if the killer was on it?'

'Fine. Check it out and see if anyone seems to have inside knowledge that's not public yet. But you can take a bet that if someone does, it'll be an indiscreet PC rather than the killer.'

Rory headed into Sullivan's office to report their complete failure to make any headway.

'Sorry, boss, but there's no link between the victims.'

'Or the crimes, according to Rose,' said Francis. 'She hasn't found a single scrap of matching forensic evidence across any of the cases. Nothing to suggest the same weapons, no DNA or hair or fibres. No fingerprints. Nada.'

'So, no to the serial killer theory?'

'Indeed. I think we're looking at different killers with different motives. This whole business with the tattoos is nothing but a red herring.'

21

Marni

How the hell had that happened? One minute he'd been a baby, now he was sprawled out drunk and snoring across the sofa. Marni fetched a plastic bowl from under the sink and a pint glass of water. Then she shifted Alex's feet to make room to sit down. She tapped on one of his shins through his jeans to wake him up.

'How was the last exam?' she asked, as he started to stir.

'What?' He rubbed his eyes and saw the glass of water.

She waited while he downed it in one.

'The last exam, Alex? Remember, this morning, business studies?'

As he put the glass down, a wide grin lifted the corners of his mouth.

He looked so like Thierry when he smiled it made her heart ache.

'Aced it.'

'Really?' He didn't sound too drunk, she noted thankfully.

'All the right questions came up, everything good.'

'God knows you don't get that from your father or me. Not an A level between us.'

'Dad got his *baccalauréat*, didn't he?'

Thierry was the last thing she wanted to talk about. She'd seen too much of him over the last few days and it was stirring up all the conflicting feelings she'd been trying to leave behind.

'How did it go for Martin and the others?'

'Good too, I think. Liv was moaning a bit, but she always does and then she comes top.'

Liv was Marni's niece, who went to the same school as Alex.

He hiccoughed. 'What time is it? I need to meet them.'

'It's just gone four. But wait, you're not going out again, are you? You're already drunk.'

'Mum!' He screwed up his face. 'I'm not drunk. We had a bottle of champagne to celebrate, instead of lunch. But lots of the others still had an exam this afternoon, so the main party's tonight.'

Marni sighed. Single parenting. She had to be good cop and bad cop rolled into one.

'Well, I'm making you pasta before you go. Come and talk to me in the kitchen.'

The phone rang as she was filling the kettle.

'Marni Mullins?'

'Who's this?'

'My name's Tom Fitz from the *Argus*. I understand you found a body . . .'

Marni hung up. If there was one breed she distrusted even more than the police, it was journalists. *Damn* – how had the man found out that it was her who had discovered the body? And how had he got her number?

By the time the pasta was cooked, the friction between mother and son had evaporated. To be fair, Alex had never been the difficult teenager that some of her friends had to deal with.

'Tell me about your day,' said Alex, once he was ensconced on a stool at the breakfast bar, wolfing down spaghetti. 'Who did you permanently disfigure with your needle?'

Marni laughed. There was no way Alex was going to join the family business. He had nothing but disdain for all things tattoo, which was fine by Marni because she knew it rankled with Thierry.

'Just one poor woman who didn't have the sense to see that getting a tattoo would ruin her life,' she teased.

'Mum, you're the worst. You should have warned her. And now she might fall victim to that tattoo killer. You've just expanded his victim pool.'

'What do you know about that?'

Alex shrugged. 'Everyone at school's talking about it. Each time you tattoo someone, you're giving him fresh prey.'

'I can't see why he'd want to murder someone with one of my tattoos.' *So how and why was he picking his victims?*

'Why not? They're as good as anyone's. If I was going around killing people and collecting tattoos, I'd want one by you.'

'That's sweet of you, but you're warped. Anyway, I don't suppose he cares who they're by.'

'But you said your policeman thought they might be trophies. So it stands to reason you want something decent. Not a piece of shit from a drunk night out in Magaluf.'

Marni cleared his plate into the dishwasher. She knew she shouldn't, that she should make Alex do it. But then it would never get done.

'That's true,' she said. 'He hasn't taken any bad ones yet. They've all been good.'

Alex fell on a bowl of ice cream like he hadn't eaten in a week, his attention lost.

On the kitchen wall behind Alex there was a poster for a tattoo exhibition. It showed a naked woman from behind, her entire back covered by the most spectacular Japanese back piece. It was for a show held the previous year in the Saatchi Gallery, *The Alchemy of Blood and Ink*. She and Alex had gone up to London together to see it. It was of no real interest to him, but he'd taken her for a birthday treat. To one side of the naked woman on the poster ran a list of ten names. These were the ten tattoo artists whose work had been featured in the exhibition.

Rick Glover
Jason Leicester
Ishikawa Iwao
Gigi Leon
Jonah Mason
Polina Jankowski
Vince Priest
Bartosz Klem
Petra Danielli
Brewster Bones

Supposedly the ten best tattoo artists in the world. Subjective nonsense to Marni's mind, but she remembered how put out Thierry had been not to have been included, how he'd raged when he'd seen the poster. She read the list of names again.

'Oh. My. God,' she breathed, and picked up her phone.

22

Francis

What could be so important?

Francis replayed the voicemail in his head as he strode down George Street to reach the corner with St James's Street. Marni Mullins had summoned him without telling him why – but the urgency in her voice had spoken volumes. What did she know? What had she discovered? He was supposed to be going to see Robin this evening, but that would have to wait until next week now. He felt a little guilty that the prospect of a meeting with Marni Mullins appealed significantly more than spending the evening with his sister.

A homeless man reached out for his leg as he passed.

'Spare a copper?'

Francis looked at the man and could see instantly where the money would go. 'I'll buy you some food.' There was a convenience store a couple of doors back.

'Just give me the money.' The man's face was hostile.

Regardless, Francis went into the shop and bought sandwiches, a couple of chocolate bars and a bottle of water. He squatted down to hand them over.

'There's a night shelter at St Peter's church,' he said. 'They'll be able to give you hot food and a bed.'

The man took the sandwiches with mumbled thanks, his dark eyes like hollow shells.

A hundred yards further on, Francis spotted the tapas bar Marni had mentioned in her message, and seconds later he was pulling open the door. It was warm and dim inside. Bare floorboards, exposed brickwork and chunky wooden furniture gave the restaurant a rustic feel. He peered further into the interior and found Marni sitting at a table near the back. There was a bottle of red wine open in front of her, and one of the two glasses on the table was half full.

'Why here?' he said, as he sat down. 'Why didn't you come to the station?'

'I did,' she said. 'They wouldn't tell me where you were.'

This added up – Francis had been up at the morgue, and had only got back to John Street a few minutes before catching Marni's message.

'Who did you speak to? Rory?'

Marni shook her head. 'No. A woman. A prize bitch, actually. Acted like she owned you or something.'

He wondered who it had been. Angie? She could be bit snooty at times, for sure.

'And I needed a drink.'

He looked at her, and she did indeed appear a little shaken by something.

Marni poured wine into the second glass before he had a chance to stop her, but he left it untouched.

Their eyes met. He wanted to hold her gaze but he looked away.

'Tell me what you've got,' he said, feeling flustered.

'This,' she said, touching something on the table that he hadn't noticed when he first sat down.

He picked up a glossy catalogue and held it at an angle so it was illuminated by the candle in the centre of the table. The front cover was a picture of a woman's back, tattooed with a magnificent Chinese dragon, its bright jewel colours standing out from a plain black background. It looked familiar and then he realised it was the same brochure that Iwao had used to show them Jonah Mason's work.

'"The Alchemy of Blood and Ink",' he read out loud. '"Modern masters of an ancient art form."'

Marni nodded, her bright eyes reflecting the candle's flame.

'Why are you showing me this?'

'It was an exhibition, last year, at the Saatchi Gallery. Look inside.'

Perplexed, Francis flicked through the leaflet. Pictures of tattoos in different styles. He found the picture Iwao had shown them.

'Jonah Mason. Evan Armstrong's tattoo artist.'

'That's right.'

'So?'

She took the catalogue from him.

'Look at this.'

She flicked past a couple of pages and then pointed at another picture. It was a biomechanical design, very similar to the one on Giselle Connelly's missing arm.

'Bartosz Klem,' Francis read out loud.

'Yes. One of Thierry's colleagues recognised his style when I showed them the picture. And this.'

She turned to the next page, which displayed a series of highly ornate gothic lettering tattoos.

'These are by Rick Glover, who works round the corner. I'm pretty sure he did that Belial lettering and the spider's web,' she said, then fell into an expectant silence.

Francis took the booklet from her and studied the pictures.

'And?' he said after a couple of minutes.

'Don't you get it?' said Marni impatiently. 'You wanted to find a link between the murders. This is your link. All your victims had tattoos by artists in the Saatchi exhibition. An exhibition of the best tattooists in the world. Someone's collecting.'

'Link or coincidence?'

Marni's eyes widened and she downed the remaining wine in her glass. 'You're not bloody serious?'

'Of course I am – I have to be.' Francis's hand formed a fist on the table. 'Sure, those artists might have done the tattoos on Jem Walsh and the murdered woman, but that's yet to be confirmed. And then so what if they were all in this exhibition? So were . . .' He picked up the leaflet and flicked through the pages. '. . . at least half a dozen other tattoo artists and we don't have bodies to account for those. At this point, you've brought me nothing.'

'And what have you got?'

Playing for time, Francis took a sip of his wine.

'You're drinking.'

'I'm not on duty.'

'But still working.'

A young waiter approached their table warily. Marni reeled off a list of tapas dishes and he went away.

Francis raised his eyebrows. 'We're eating?'

'Helps to keep the body functioning.'

He couldn't help but like her. Nothing if not direct. Perfectly transparent about her likes and dislikes. *What the hell had she been in prison for?* He bit his tongue, on the verge of asking her. He hadn't wanted to press Rory further on the subject in case it betrayed more interest in Marni than he'd like to admit to.

'So your theory is that someone saw the exhibition and is now going around building his own collection? You think we have some sort of *tattoo thief* on our hands?'

'Yes. That's precisely it. A tattoo thief.'

'There's nothing to say there's even a link between these three cases.'

Her eyes widened. 'Can't you see it? *This* is your link between the cases.'

'I doubt it.'

'You can take it or leave it, but you can't deny it's a link. And, I think, it's the only link you've got so far.'

'And so you believe there'll be more victims and that they'll have tattoos by these specific tattoo artists?'

'If my theory's right. And if you don't catch the killer first.'

'How long have you been a tattoo artist?' he said.

The waiter deposited a dish of olives in front of them and Marni popped one into her mouth.

'Nineteen years.' She carried on chewing.

'You must have started very young.'

'I became Thierry's apprentice when I was eighteen. He taught me virtually everything I know.'

'How did you meet him?'

Marni's expression darkened. 'I was working in France, just as a waitress over the summer, to get some sun. I went out a couple of times with his brother, then . . .' Her words trailed off into uncomfortable silence.

Francis didn't want to pry – the scenario seemed pretty clear – so he moved back onto safer ground.

'How many people do you think you've tattooed in those nineteen years?'

She swallowed, eyes closed as she calculated. Then she shrugged.

'Literally thousands.'

Francis tore up a piece of bread, as the waiter rearranged their table to accommodate more tapas.

'Seven more tattooists in the exhibition that your tattoo thief might want a piece of. That means our pool of potential victims is huge?'

'Totally.'

'I'm not sure how much this helps us.'

'Us,' said Marni, a satisfied grin slipping onto her lips as she took another mouthful of wine.

'If it's really even a theory . . .'

'Yes, it's a theory. These are my people under attack, my community. You need to take this seriously.'

'One minute you want nothing to do with it. Now, you're crusading.'

'I don't like seeing people die. People I might know.'

Francis carried on poring over the exhibition brochure. He flicked back to the first page.

'Look,' he said, holding out the introduction for her to see.

'Yes?'

'The curator. It was your friend, Ishikawa Iwao.'

'I know. I went to the opening.'

Francis fell silent. He remembered the tattooed cat snarling at him. If Marni was right about this link, he and his team would certainly have their work cut out for them. But at least they'd have some clear direction to follow.

'Eat,' said Marni. 'And then, Frank, tell me why you became a policeman.'

'Francis,' he said, through gritted teeth.

If you tell me, Marni Mullins, what put you on the wrong side of the law.

vii

One, two, cut a tattoo
Three, four, flay some more
Five, six, my bloody fix
Seven, eight, will not wait

My work demands the keenest blades to enable absolute precision. I only ever sharpen them by hand using ceramic whetstones – never an electric sharpener – and I hum this little ditty to keep my rhythm. I can get a finish like a cut-throat razor, smooth-edged and vicious. I need to keep them keen, just in case I get the chance to use them. You never know when that might present itself, so I work on them regularly, whether I've used them or not. A dull blade will never be your friend.

All my knives are laid out in the right order on one of my work-benches. The short cutting blades and the longer, curved flaying blades. My whetstones are set at just the right angle in a series of clamps on the edge of the bench, so I can quickly move from one to the next. I spend about an hour on each blade, humming my little songs, and I can just lose myself in the repetition.

It's therapeutic.

Just like skin flaying.

It was always my favourite part of the taxidermy process. Removing the skin in one perfect piece. It's a challenge, and success is its own reward. I learned that from Ron. I learned everything about tanning and taxidermy that he could teach me. And some things about life. I soaked it all up like a sponge, till he had nothing left for me.

As well as keeping his skin, I kept his clients. That's how I came to know the Collector. He collects taxidermy, and me and Ron were the best in the business. His requests challenged us to the very limit of our abilities. But I always did my best work for him. Sometimes he watches me work. He's fascinated by the processes involved. He is a very knowledgeable man. Very clever. It's easy to admire a man like that, so it's an honour when he spends time with me, to think that he's interested in the things I show him.

In this way, he's so different to my father and to my brother. They never showed any interest in my work. Everything was about them. What they'd achieved. What they were planning. My ideas and opinions were brushed aside. Ron was better – he was interested in what I did, but that was because he was teaching me. He wanted to see what I had learned. The Collector, though, he admires my work. And I admire him. He has such an eye for beauty and such a great sense for what gives something its artistic merit. It's a bond we share.

I would do anything for the Collector. Anything at all.

He only needs to ask . . .

Ouch! I've cut my finger on the blade. A small globule of blood grows larger, then drips onto the wooden workbench. A stain that will need to be sanded away. Or maybe not.

The smell of my own blood makes me realise how much I need to kill again. It's time.

23

Rory

Eight a.m. in Bradshaw's office. Those had been the boss's instructions, issued by text the previous evening. Rory was here. Bradshaw was here. But the boss was nowhere to be seen.

'So how's he doing?'

Rory's gaze was momentarily fixated on a blob of shaving foam clinging to one of Bradshaw's ear lobes.

'Rory?'

'Sorry, sir. What?'

'Working with Sullivan? You were going to keep me updated.'

'He's very bright, obviously.'

'But?'

'This case, cases . . . It's complicated. We don't know yet whether it's one killer or multiple killers. We don't have a link between them and . . .'

'Go on.'

Rory sighed. 'I'm just not sure that someone with his relative inexperience is really right for this case.'

Bradshaw mulled over his words for a moment. 'Thank you for being so candid with me, Mackay.'

Perfectly done. More fool the kid for being late.

'Of course, that's not to say, sir . . .'

There was a knock and the door to Bradshaw's office opened.

Rory stopped talking and looked round to see Sullivan coming into the room. His suit was as neatly pressed as ever but he was anything but fresh-faced. He stared at Rory with bloodshot eyes that questioned the sudden break in the conversation.

What had he been up to the night before?

'Morning, sir. Sorry I'm late. Morning, Rory.'

Bradshaw grunted his disapproval, checking his watch as the DI sat down.

'Morning, boss,' Rory replied.

'I assume you've made some progress with the case,' said Bradshaw, locking eyes with Francis.

'Has Sergeant Mackay filled you in on where we've got to?'

'No. Rory and I were discussing staffing levels for when Granger goes off on maternity leave.'

The boss clearly didn't believe it.

'We've made some progress, sir,' said Francis. 'I ran a check with SCAS for any possible links to open cases elsewhere, and we've come up with a possible match.'

Bradshaw nodded.

'Last year, a woman's body was found on a golf course with an arm missing. She turned out to be a trainee lawyer from Littlehampton called Giselle Connelly. Twenty-six years old, married . . .'

Bradshaw interrupted. 'What you're telling me is that now instead of two unsolved murders we've got three? Not what I'd call progress. And this one's not even on our patch.'

'The golf course where she was found is. She . . .'

'Exactly. This victim is a woman. The two victims here, who you have so far failed to link in any way, were both men. Serial killers, I would have thought you'd have known, Sullivan, don't switch from killing one sex to the other in the middle of a spree. I've already said, the facts simply don't support a serial killer theory.'

'Sir,' said Francis, in a firmer tone that rather impressed Rory, 'the woman had a sleeve tattoo on the arm that was taken. The missing limb has never been recovered.'

'A tattoo of what?'

'I'm not sure that the subject of the tattoos is relevant, but it was a biomechanical.'

'A bio-what?'

'Biomechanical, sir. It's a tattoo that makes the wearer look like a cyborg, like there's machinery under their skin.'

The boss was starting to sound rather knowledgeable on the subject. Had he been spending more time with Marni Mullins?

'Good God!' Bradshaw rolled his eyes. 'On a trainee solicitor?'

'The point is that all of these victims – Evan Armstrong, Jem Walsh and now Giselle Connelly, who incidentally died several months before our two – all of them had tattoos that were missing when the bodies were found. Although we can't expect to find the skin taken from Evan, whoever took the head and the arm from the other two would still need to dispose of the bones and the skull.'

'I don't buy any of this,' said Bradshaw. 'Your imagination has been working overtime, Sullivan. The tattoo stuff is a coincidence. The woman's murder has nothing to suggest it has anything to do with the two recent killings, and frankly I don't see anything pointing to a link between these two either.' He pushed his chair back from his desk as if to signify the meeting was over. 'You've got three distinct killings that aren't linked and you can't afford to spend any more time trying to put them together. It's lost manpower that should be used considering each case on its own merits.'

'But proving a link would give us the lead we need,' said Sullivan.

'Forget this line of enquiry. Rory, what else could you put the team on?'

Rory cleared his throat and started to speak but the DI cut over the top of him.

'Sir, I think you should see this.' Francis pulled the brochure out of his document case. 'The tattoos that have gone missing were all by artists featured in this exhibition.'

Bradshaw took the leaflet Sullivan held out to him.

What the hell was that? Why hadn't he seen it?

Rory craned his neck to see what Bradshaw was looking at.

'This does give us a possible link between the victims, tenuous as it may be,' continued Francis. 'Certainly, I'm not basing the entire investigation on this premise, but I think we need to bear it in mind. In the meantime, I've got the team investigating and questioning both Evan Armstrong and Jem Walsh's friends and associates. There doesn't seem to be any criminal activity that links the two of them, but just because something doesn't jump out at you immediately doesn't mean it's not there.'

'So you've had no success in finding a connection between the victims,' snorted Bradshaw, tossing the leaflet to one side of his desk, no longer interested. Rory leaned forward to pick it up. It wasn't hard to guess where this had come from – the boss had seen Marni Mullins. He wondered what Thierry Mullins would make of that. The divorced couple still seemed close, as far as he could tell.

'We've interviewed both families about Armstrong and Walsh's friends and habits. Burton and Hollins have been following up with the friends, while Hitchins and I have been round several of the pubs they frequented. Hitchins and Hollins are going to their workplaces today, and Angie's going to look into the Connelly case and check all the victim's social media feeds.'

Bradshaw snorted at the mention of Giselle Connelly. 'And the missing head?'

'Rose hasn't given us anything solid yet, but she's had dog teams all over the beach,' said Rory. 'They picked up Walsh's scent in a parking space on Madeira Drive, less than a hundred yards east of the pier, and followed it down onto the beach. It's obviously strongest around the point where we found the body. It also leads down to the water's edge, which might imply that the head was thrown into the sea. However, there's been no sign of it at low tide and I've sent divers out further, following the undertow patterns, but they've found nothing. If it went into the water, I think there's very little chance of us recovering it.'

'Won't it pitch up at Selsey Bill in a couple of weeks' time?' said Bradshaw.

'Possibly. Possibly not. The coastguard could tell me about the tides, but they didn't have any real expertise on how a detached head would roll along the seabed over time. Not something you can easily run an experiment on.'

'In other words, no fucking progress on any front. What are you doing next? Mackay?'

'Like I said, sir, checking out known associates, workplaces, Giselle Connelly.'

'No identifiable vehicles in the vicinity of either crime?'

'Only partial licence plates. We're working on it.'

Bradshaw frowned. Nothing ever happened fast enough for him. 'Sullivan?'

'I'm going to talk to Ishikawa Iwao again. He curated the exhibition. I want to see what he thinks of the three murders.'

'Nothing better to do with your time? I said to leave that angle alone.'

The boss hadn't got the hang of managing his superior yet – a basic policing skill.

'Sir, this is a credible theory and at this point the only theory. I need to follow it up so I can at the very least either disprove it or see if it has legs.'

'And this Ishikaka character can make a valid contribution?'

'I believe so.'

There was an awkward silence.

'This is the guy who tattoos cats, right?' said Rory, as much to fill the empty space as to make a serious point.

Bradshaw's eyebrows nearly disappeared into his hairline.

'Is that legal?' he said. 'Did you report it to the RSPCA?'

Francis shook his head.

'Sorry,' he said. 'Rory, put one of the Tweedles on it to find out what the situation is with regard to tattooing animals.'

Bradshaw inhaled tightly, his nostrils narrowing. 'You should bring him in for questioning, Sullivan.'

'Over the cat?'

'No, over the bloody murders, you idiot.'

'Cruelty to animals,' said Rory. 'It's where a lot of those fuckers start off.'

'Get him in.'

Bradshaw's tone brooked no argument but that didn't stop Francis.

'We've got absolutely nothing to suggest he's involved. Better I talk to him informally, make an assessment without raising his suspicions.'

He shouldn't have opened his mouth. But it was too late now.

'I said, get him in here.'

'I'll do it, sir, this afternoon,' said Rory.

He didn't miss seeing Francis's hands balling into frustrated fists in his lap.

'Stay out of this, Rory.' He exhaled angrily. 'Sir, we might just have one chance to formally question him. Let's save it for when we have some concrete questions that need answers.'

Francis Sullivan had just said 'no' to a direct order. The results weren't pretty. Bradshaw's brow lowered and his cheeks reddened. He stood up, signalling that the meeting was over. Rory followed his lead with lightning speed.

'You bring him in now. That's an order, Sullivan. You might have made it to DI but don't get too bloody big for your boots.'

Francis said nothing and stormed out of the office. Brave but foolish.

'Don't worry, I'll see to it, sir,' Rory said, closing the door gently as he left.

24

Francis

Ishikawa Iwao bowed to Francis when he came into the interview room. Hugely self-conscious as Rory had followed him in, Francis bowed in return. This time the tattooist wasn't dressed in a kimono but in a pair of unseemingly tight but expensive-looking jeans and a pale blue Oxford shirt that showed off his impressive pecs. It was clear that Ishikawa Iwao looked after himself physically, and Francis had an immediate mental picture of him martial arts training.

Racial profiling. Stop now.

'Thank you for coming in, Mr Iwao,' said Francis. 'This is my colleague, Sergeant Mackay.'

'Don't thank me. I wasn't given any choice in the matter,' said Iwao. He ignored Rory, continuing to scowl at Francis. 'What do you need to talk to me about?'

'Sit down, please,' said Francis.

He and Rory took chairs on their side of the table. Iwao seemed hesitant, but when Francis gave him another nod, he pulled a chair back and sat down. He sat ramrod straight, with his knees together and his feet aligned. He rested his hands on the top of his thighs and looked at the two policemen expectantly.

'I'm going to tape this conversation, if that's okay with you?' said Francis, pressing the record button on the tape recorder.

'Then I will expect a copy of this recording to be lodged with my solicitor's office,' said Iwao. 'I'd also like to know first why you think it's necessary and what my exact status is in this matter. Do you suspect me of having committed a crime?'

'Your solicitor can apply to us for a copy of it,' said Rory, jotting something down in his notebook.

'Your status is that of a witness helping us with our enquiries,' said Francis. 'We'll inform you if we have any reason to change that status.'

Iwao frowned. 'Then there's no reason for you to tape this conversation.'

'Fine,' said Francis. 'If that's the way you want it.'

Iwao seemed to know his rights.

Francis and Rory had discussed a strategy while they waited for Iwao to be brought in. Rather than heading in gently with questions about the tattoo exhibition and the tattooists involved, they would start at the other end – with the murders, and more specifically, his alibis for the time-of-death windows.

'Could you tell me exactly where you were on Sunday twenty-eighth May, between the hours of midnight and six a.m.?'

Iwao looked confused.

'Please repeat the date.'

'Sunday twenty-eighth of May. Last Sunday.'

'Of course,' said Iwao, recovering from his surprise. 'Between the hours of midnight and six? I would have been in bed, I think.'

'You're not sure?'

'In bed or drawing in my studio. I usually retire between midnight and two, and most evenings I spend drawing. I wasn't out last Saturday night, or Sunday morning,' he shrugged. 'I was either in my studio or my bedroom between those hours.'

'Is there anyone who can vouch for this?'

'I live alone.'

Rory and Francis exchanged quick glances. As an alibi, it was non-existent even though it had a ring of truth about it.

'What about last Tuesday night, between midnight and five a.m.?'

'The same.'

'At home, on your own?'

Iwao nodded. 'I was at home, on my own, on Tuesday night.' He held Francis's gaze with steady brown eyes. 'I'm sure you'll be able to check my whereabouts using my mobile if you need to.'

'People don't always take their mobiles with them when they go out,' said Francis, unwavering in his own stare.

'I always do,' said Iwao.

Francis made a mental note to apply for a warrant to investigate Iwao's mobile phone records.

Rory coughed to gain his attention. 'Tell us about that cat of yours. The one with the tattoos. Did you not consider that tattooing an animal would be cruel, and probably against the law?'

'I have two cats like that,' said Iwao, shifting in his chair. 'They were already tattooed when I imported them from Japan.'

'But you think it's acceptable?'

'They came from a rescue shelter. It's not something I would ever do to an animal – it's obvious, animals can't consent. I won't tattoo anyone or anything without consent.'

Francis felt his phone vibrating in his pocket and glanced down at it under the table. A missed call from Marni Mullins. He put it away.

'Can you prove that they were tattooed before you got them?' Rory was like a terrier that had scented a rat.

'Yes, I'm certain there are some pictures in my files that the shelter sent me before I offered to take them.'

'We're still going to have to report your cats to the RSPCA,' said Rory.

Iwao stared at him blankly.

Francis was beginning to sense the entire interview was a wild goose chase. He pushed Marni's exhibition catalogue across the table for Iwao to see.

The tattooist looked down at it, recognised it but didn't bother to pick it up.

'You think all this has something to do with my exhibition?' he said.

The phone vibrated in Francis's pocket. It was Marni Mullins again. She would have to wait.

'Why didn't you mention it when I visited you with Ms Mullins?' said Francis.

Iwao's eyebrows shot up. 'Why should I have done? You asked me about one tattoo. The exhibition didn't seem particularly relevant at the time.'

'We think there might be a link.'

'Between the exhibition and what exactly?'

'A number of murders.'

Francis could almost see a succession of thoughts pass across Iwao's face. The questions about his whereabouts, the questions about his cats, a potential link between the victims. His features twisted with disbelief.

'You think *I* could be involved?'

'You were the one that told me about how Yakuza tattoos are removed from the body after death for preservation.'

Iwao pushed his chair further back and crossed his arms and his legs. A classic defensive posture. 'I want my lawyer. I'll say nothing more until he arrives.'

Francis's phone vibrated insistently.

He went out into the corridor and dialled Marni's number.

'You fucking bastard,' she hissed as soon as they were connected. 'I take you into my confidence, introduce you to my friend and you arrest him?'

'Marni ...'

'First Thierry, now Iwao? What the hell is wrong with you? Can't you find any suspects of your own?'

'It wasn't my idea to question him.'

'Like I give a shit. I've called Iwao's lawyer and he should be with you any minute. That man wouldn't harm a fly – he's a practising Buddhist. Can I suggest you let him go and focus your attention on finding the real killer? And you should be warning people with tattoos by those artists that there's a murderer on the loose instead of pulling innocent men in for questioning.'

She hung up on him. He'd blown his one contact in the tattooing community. And he was beginning to feel now that these killings might somehow be connected to the victims' tattoos.

Rory appeared in front of him.

'Iwao's lawyer is in reception,' he said. 'God knows how he got here so quickly.'

'The tattooing grapevine. Aka Marni Mullins.'

An hour later they were back in Bradshaw's office, having just escorted Iwao and his lawyer off the premises.

Bradshaw was all bluster. 'We had one suspect and you let him go.'

'We had no grounds to hold him,' said Francis.

'He had alibis?'

'No. But . . .'

'So he's still in the frame?'

'Technically, yes. But I don't believe he did it.'

Bradshaw rolled his eyes. 'Lord save us from cops who follow their hunches.'

'We've come across nothing connecting him to either one of our murders, or the earlier one that might be linked.'

The guy was weird but did that make him a killer?

'That's true, sir,' said Rory. 'And he had a slick lawyer. Not worth tangling with that one.'

'What now?' said Bradshaw. 'We're back at square one, aren't we?'

'Sir, I want to propose a press conference,' said Francis. 'We need to warn people that there's a killer on the loose, and that he's targeting people with tattoos by certain tattoo artists.'

'Absolutely not.'

'Sir?'

'You want to let the killer know that we're on his trail for the sake of an unproven theory? Even if there's something in it, a press conference will push him straight into hiding and we'll lose any initiative we've got.'

What initiative would that be?

'He's killed two people in the space of a week.'

'He could be planning his next killing already,' added Rory. 'I think the DI is right about putting out a warning.'

'And I didn't ask for your fucking opinion, Mackay. This whole serial killer theory is very sketchy. I'm not convinced.'

'It seems just as likely as three separate murderers, sir.'

'Well, forget the bloody theories and get out there looking for evidence. You need to find something before there's another murder.'

'Jesus,' said Rory under his breath as they left Bradshaw's office. 'You know who he'll blame if someone else dies?'

The twitch in Francis's jawline said it all.

25

Marni

'You're sitting like a champ!'

Marni's favourite lie tripped off her tongue as Steve tried not to squirm under the points of the needles. She realised she was being a little aggressive and took a deep breath to calm herself down. It was just that she was so angry about what had happened. But that wasn't Steve's fault. It was their third session and she was working on a cluster of chrysanthemums that formed the background to the full sleeve tattoo of a Japanese-style tiger. There would be at least one more session before she finished.

'Right, we'll call it a day. I've finished this patch and you can come back in a week or two for the final push.'

Steve sat up on the massage bench and swung his legs round to the side, rotating both shoulders to get his circulation going.

'Thanks, darling,' he said, looking at the new work with a delighted smile.

Marni dismantled her tattoo iron, putting the used needles in her sharps bin and peeling off the disposable plastic covering that kept it clean from blood spatters. As she wrapped Steve's arm in cling film, she wondered how old her client was – he was practically bald but his facial features still appeared youthful and his eyes were bright behind the thick lenses of his glasses. He seemed quite old for a first tattoo, but then people were getting them done at all ages these days.

'Cash?' he said.

'Please,' said Marni. 'That was three hours, pretty much to the minute.'

While Steve counted out the notes, Marni stripped off her latex gloves and washed her hands. It had been a long day and her fury at Iwao being taken into custody had made her tense. What the hell was Francis Sullivan playing at? He couldn't seriously think that Iwao had any involvement in the murders, could he? Iwao murdering anybody was even less likely than Thierry having played a part. A lot less likely, to be honest. She worried about Thierry . . .

The bell rang at the front of the shop, announcing a new arrival. Her stomach lurched. Damn, she thought she'd locked the door when she started tattooing Steve. She peered through from the studio and saw Francis Sullivan coming towards the counter. The sight of him did nothing to improve her mood. Was he going to arrest her next?

'What do you want?' she said, without preamble.

Behind her, Steve was gingerly feeding his freshly tattooed arm into the sleeve of his jacket. Francis stopped in the connecting doorway, taking in the scene.

'I can wait till you've finished,' he said.

'Steve, this is Detective Inspector Frank Sullivan. Frank, this is Steve, one of my very favourite clients.' She would do everything she could to wind him up and she noticed with satisfaction how he grimaced at being called Frank.

'Hi, Frank,' said Steve, sticking out a hand.

Francis Sullivan took hold of it as if it were something the cat had dragged in.

'You're that policeman, aren't you? The one investigating the tattoo murder.'

Francis gave the most imperceptible of nods.

'I can't believe Marni found the body,' continued Steve. 'Got anyone for it yet?'

'Only the wrong people,' snapped Marni, continuing to tidy up. *When the hell were they going to find the right one?*

'The paper said it was something to do with tattoos. Is that it? Is that right?'

Francis looked pained by Steve's babbling and gave Marni a meaningful stare.

She ignored him.

'If you don't mind,' said Francis to Steve, 'I need to talk to Ms Mullins.'

'Got it. I'm sorry.'

'Aftercare, Steve. Remember.'

As the main door slammed behind him, Marni stopped what she was doing and faced Francis.

'I have nothing to say to you, Frank. What you did was outrageous.'

'I want to talk to you about something else.'

'Why would I talk to you?' She turned her back to him and started screwing the caps back onto the plastic ink bottles.

'Marni, two people were murdered in Brighton in the last week. There's reason to suspect that the killings are somehow linked to the tattoos they had. You know that.'

'So you believe my theory now?' said Marni, glaring over her shoulder at him. 'But does that give you the right to ride rough-shod over the community here? You're arresting people for no reason at all.'

Francis sighed. 'I haven't arrested anyone yet. But we need information, so I have to question people who I think might be able to help me. That includes you.'

'You want help, from me, from us, and this is the way you go about it? You're simply alienating people. You can't seriously think for a moment that me, or Thierry, or Iwao were involved in the murders?'

'I've got to explore every possibility.'

Marni slammed a bottle of disinfectant down on her workbench. Was she angry at him or at her own suspicions? Or perhaps it was fear that was making her react in this way.

'What you should be doing is warning people. If there's a killer on the loose who's targeting people with tattoos, they should at least know about it. I haven't seen anything in the papers or on the TV telling people to cover up and be careful. Why not?'

'My boss . . .'

'Your boss? I thought you were the one in charge of the case.'

He winced. 'I don't work in a vacuum. There are certain expectations to be fulfilled in the pursuit of a case like this.'

'Policing by numbers. I get it. I've seen it before.' *It had happened in France. It was happening here too. Taking the path of least resistance.*

She finally stopped what she was doing and turned to face him.

He looked furious. 'You don't get it. You know absolutely nothing about the pressure I'm under to produce fast results. And I've got the press snapping at my tail, too.'

'It's part of your job description, being able to handle pressure. Yeah, produce some results and save another damn person from being murdered. For a start, you could put out a warning that this is happening.'

'I can't do that. It could start a panic.'

'If you don't, I'll talk to Tom Fitz. He'll write another story to warn people. All he's had so far are the basic details of the bodies found. He's looking for something more meaty to give to his readers.'

Francis sighed. 'Stay away from him, Marni, please. Let the

police decide what information goes out when. The rumour mill's already in overdrive.'

'Then do something soon.'

She'd made her point but he didn't answer her. Instead, he sat down on a spindly wooden chair in the corner of the room. He rubbed his eyes with both hands, the fatigue and stress showing. But Marni's sympathy fell short. She *had* seen what could happen when the police went for quick and easy results. She had experienced perhaps not a miscarriage of justice, but certainly a level of justice that was misaligned with the facts.

'How about a coffee?' he said.

In a small coffee bar, two doors down from the studio, they found a corner table and ordered – a black Americano for him, and a triple macchiato for her.

'So what do you want to ask me?' Marni let her hostility show in her voice.

'Tell me how you know Iwao didn't do it.'

Marni shook her head. 'No way, Frank. You have to prove who did do it. It's not up to me to prove who didn't do it. There's nothing I can say to convince you – I just know Iwao. He's simply not capable of behaviour like that.'

'But Thierry is, isn't he?'

'Fuck you.'

She stood up.

'Marni!' The rip of anger in his voice made her tentatively sit down again. 'I'm not saying I think he did it. But I need to know more about him. According to our records, he's been convicted of drug dealing and of GBH. Tell me about those.'

'The drug dealing is self-explanatory. It was never big time, just a bit on the side, out of the studio. Money was tight when Alex was born. I couldn't work for several months.'

Frank nodded his understanding.

'He got caught a couple of times. End of.'

She wasn't going to tell him that the dealing had been one of the reasons she'd divorced Thierry. One of many. Like the other women. And the drunken outbursts that reminded her a little too often of Paul. That part of her life was none of Francis Sullivan's business.

'And the other?'

'He beat a guy up in the Heart and Hand. It was a long time ago.'

'Why?'

Marni bought time by taking a mouthful of cold coffee. 'There'd been some stuff in the papers and this guy, we didn't really know him, took a pop at us over it.'

'Stuff about his dealing convictions?'

'No. Stuff about me. The guy came up and made a few out-of-order comments so Thierry decked him.'

'And that was all?'

'That was all.' Marni wanted to change the subject. Desperately. The last thing she wanted was Frank Sullivan nosing around in her past. Or Thierry's.

Francis finished the last mouthful of his own coffee and stayed silent for a few minutes.

'Marni, can I ask you something?'

'Sure.' *No.*

'It's not about Thierry.'

'Go ahead.' *Please stop.*

'You were in prison once, weren't you?'

The one thing Marni had wanted to avoid talking about. 'Yes.'

'But I can't find any record of it in the police database.'

She visibly bristled. 'It was when I lived in France.'

'That explains it. What did you do?'

'Does it matter?'

'No, but . . .'

'I stabbed a man.'

Her bravado crumpled as the memory flared up in front of her eyes. The dull sheen of the blade. The blood, and then so much more blood. Sirens wailing in the small hours. Policemen speaking French too quickly for her to understand. She fought for air and then found her voice again.

'Did you hear what I said? I stabbed a man.'

The colour had drained from Francis's face. He looked like a man who wished he could take the question back.

viii

Do you ever actually wonder what it's like to flay the living skin off a human body? I don't suppose you do. I think about it often. When I'm doing other things. When I lie in bed at night. In quiet moments like this one. I'm waiting in my car for the next one on my list to finish work. I'm collecting his habits so I can read his character and formulate a plan. He's tall and goes to the gym a lot. Every day, in fact. I'm looking forward to taking the skin from his body, to peeling his tattoo away. Like peeling an apple.

In fact, it's not quite like peeling an apple. Live human skin is more flexible and elastic than apple peel. And the technique is completely different. The hardest part is getting started once I've made the outline cut around the area I want to flay. I tease the edge of the skin up with the point of my blade, moving it from side to side to create a small pocket between the raised skin and the tough white muscle sheath beneath. Or, in the case of some people, the layer of subcutaneous fat. Then, when I can get a grip on the loosened flap of skin, I can start to peel it back, gently teasing with my blade to separate it from the flesh.

Depending upon where it is on the body, there may be a little blood or it might be awash with it. I do nothing to staunch the bleeding. What's the point? My victims always die in the end and the most important thing is to release the tattoo without damaging it. Nothing beats the satisfaction of making the final cut with the knife that frees the piece of skin I'm working on. Then I can hold it in my hand, still warm and wet, steaming even if we're out of doors on a cold night, and I can see how it will look when the skin has been cured and tanned.

Not everybody is lucky enough to love their work the way I do. I suppose one might call this my dream job. The pay's good, but in all honesty, I would do it for free. I would do almost anything the Collector asked me to, but luckily he recognises where my special skills lie and this work satisfies both our needs. He loves the pieces I've given him so far – we're building a very special collection together.

The man I'm watching emerges from his office building and starts walking towards his parked car. His tattoo isn't on show – he wears a cheap black suit to work. I doubt whether the people in his office even know he has a tattoo. He sells insurance over the telephone and then compensates for his stultifying days by engaging in unwise activities by night. I've watched him in the clubs, where he shows off his tattoo and his moves. I've seen him buying drugs in the public toilets and disappearing down dark alleys with other men searching for oblivion. Or cheap kicks.

He'll be an easy enough target when the time comes. A ripe fruit, ready to be split and peeled. Then I'll strip it away from him, inch by inch, an entire body suit in two huge pieces. God, he'll bleed. I can almost taste it in the air.

It needs to be soon.

26

Francis

Francis knew he ought to be praying, but his head was still spinning. *Marni Mullins stabbed a man.* She'd said little more about it and what she had said didn't make sense. He'd assumed it had been in self-defence, but she was quite clear that wasn't the case – and she had, after all, gone to prison for it. He desperately wanted to know more but information was proving elusive. *Who? Why? Under what circumstances?* He tried again to turn his mind to prayer but could only concentrate for a moment.

He gave up and pushed back from a kneeling position to sit next to Rory on the hard wooden bench. They were in the back row of pews in St Peter's. Although it was not his own church, Francis knew it well and had been to services here before. Rory squirmed uncomfortably beside him. Clearly he wasn't a churchgoer. However, funerals and memorial services were part of the job. The murder team needed to show their respect to the victim's family – and take the opportunity to assess who else was present at the funeral.

St Peter's was a huge neo-gothic concoction designed by Charles Barry, with soaring columns and a stunning stained glass window at the top end of the nave. Francis loved it and if he hadn't felt compelled to stay at St Catherine's out of loyalty to Father William, he might well have swapped allegiance. As it was a memorial service, there was no coffin – but a large blow-up photograph of Evan Armstrong stood on an easel on the altar steps, with extravagant floral displays on either side. People shuffled past in silence, and despite the sunshine pouring in through the windows, the atmosphere was sombre.

'What percentage of murderers do you think go to their victims' funerals?' whispered Rory from behind his hand.

Given that most killers were intimately acquainted with their victims, the percentage was probably high. Francis pressed a finger to his lips and concentrated on studying Evan Armstrong's family and friends. Dave and Sharon Armstrong were in the front row, with a young woman who Francis guessed was Evan's sister. None of them were dressed in black. Dave was in a navy suit, which was at least sombre enough for the occasion, but Sharon wore a bright magenta coat. Her face, in contrast, looked wan and pinched, the lines scored deeper than Francis remembered from when he'd first met her just a week ago. She'd leaned heavily on Dave's arm as they'd walked up the short aisle, and he'd lowered her gently to a sitting position as if her legs were about to give under her. The daughter, weeping soundlessly into a ball of tissues, was in a melange of brown and green layering, with muddy brown boots peeping out from under a rust-coloured ankle-length skirt. She looked as if she'd been interrupted doing the gardening. Francis held firmly to the opinion that one should wear black to a funeral – after all, black clothes were hardly a stretch for anybody's wardrobe these days – but he got the feeling that the Armstrongs weren't a religious family anyway.

There was an obvious gulf between Evan's wider family and his friends. The former were cut from the same mould as Sharon and Dave, everyday people whose lives had been cruelly disrupted by the loss of one of their own. A lot of them went up to the front to embrace Sharon and shake Dave's hand, then found a place to sit down in respectful silence.

Evan's friends, on the other hand, formed a gathering just beyond the doors of the church, as if unwilling to go in and confront the death of someone they knew. A lot of them, Francis noted, as he stared round to assess them, could have been from the crowds he saw at the tattoo convention – black clothes, shaven heads or brightly dyed hair, excessive piercings and, despite the solemnity of the occasion, tattoos on display. They were more vocal, too, with the girls crying loudly – possibly a little competitively, Francis thought – and the men talking urgently in low undertones.

Gradually, once the organ started playing, they made their way into the church and sat down. Francis noticed Marni and Thierry Mullins arriving together, with two heavily tattooed men who were speaking in French with Thierry. Rory jabbed him in the ribs with an elbow, signifying that he'd seen them too. Once they were seated, Marni turned to glare at Francis. He gave her the smallest of nods, but she'd already turned her back on him. Iwao came into the church in a discreet black suit and joined the end of Marni's bench. *Had he known Evan?* The tattooist looked at Francis with vitriol and then whispered something to Marni.

The stragglers filled up the final pews at the back, and Francis and Rory were obliged to slide along their bench to accommodate a well-built woman dressed in head-to-toe black, including gloves and a small hat with a black net veil. Even sitting down, she was nearly a head taller than Francis. He pegged her as a maiden aunt who'd lost her way or hadn't been able to work out where to park. She mouthed her thanks to them just as the vicar stepped forward and started talking. A few more latecomers tiptoed in, standing at the back as the short service got underway.

Francis listened to the vicar dispensing words of comfort to the bereaved and wondered how soon he would be at another memorial or funeral. It would be different, though, when it was for his mother – she had already planned the service with him, several years ago, and it would take place in the tiny country church where she'd worshipped every Sunday of her married life, and where Francis had discovered his own faith as a child. Did that mean it would be any easier for him and his sister to say their farewells? It was where his parents had got married, but he doubted his father would even bother to show up. Distracted by these thoughts, Evan's service was over before Francis realised it, and he was woken from his reverie by the procession of the vicar down the aisle.

Outside afterwards, the two tribes kept their distance from each other, although there was some overlap as a few of Evan's friends went to have words with the family. Francis and Rory stood to one side, watching quietly. Francis had Hollins parked just across the road from the church, filming the proceedings on a zoom lens. Rory's point about the likelihood of the killer attending the service was something Francis took seriously, and he would have the resulting film analysed until he knew who every single person was and their relationship with Evan Armstrong. Tom Fitz presumably shared this ambition, as he wandered among the mourners taking picture after picture.

'Still searching for your killer?' Ishikawa Iwao materialised at Francis's side. 'How will you know him when you see him?'

He melted away before Francis could answer.

Francis found his eyes drawn back time and again to Marni Mullins. She was talking to a short man with a bright, fresh tiger tattoo on his right arm, the man he'd met in her studio the previous evening. But all he could think about were the words echoing through his head. *Did you hear what I said? I stabbed a man.* As if she could hear what Francis was thinking, she paused in her conversation and looked him straight in the eye. The look she gave him wasn't a friendly one. He turned away and walked across the road to have a word with Hollins, who was filming, not particularly surreptitiously, through the driver's open window.

'Make sure you get everybody on camera, Kyle.'

'Boss.' He didn't look up from the viewfinder.

'Especially the tattooing fraternity.'

'The focus of my attention.'

Francis felt a tap on his shoulder and spun round.

Marni Mullins wore her fury like a weapon.

'You're filming us? You shouldn't even be here. You never even met Evan Armstrong when he was alive.'

'Did you?'

She looked taken aback and her mouth worked for a moment before she found her answer.

'He was one of Thierry's clients and friends with Charlie and Noa for a while. We have a right to be here. You don't.'

'I was under the impression Thierry wasn't that keen on him, over the unpaid bill,' said Francis. 'In any case, we do have a right to be here. We're trying to track down his killer.'

'Here, at a memorial service? Have some respect.'

'These are the people Evan knew.'

'Apart from you and your men,' she snorted.

'I thought we were on the same side, Marni.'

'What side are you on, Francis?'

'Justice. The right side.'

The words seemed to imply something he hadn't meant them to. Marni narrowed her eyes momentarily, then turned on her heel and stomped back to where Thierry stood talking to Evan Armstrong's sister.

Francis watched her go, wishing he hadn't come over to the car and drawn attention to their presence. He still felt stung by her anger and shocked by her aggression. But as she spoke urgently to Thierry, he could see a certain vulnerability to her that he hadn't appreciated up to now. There was darkness in her past, he knew that for certain. But what of the present? Did she hold the key to the case?

ix

I'm at the funeral. Everyone who knew poor Evan Armstrong is here. And, looking around, it appears quite a number who didn't. The police are here in number. After all, who else wears AirWear-soled shoes with a suit? They're looking for me, obviously, but they don't really know what — or who — to look for. I feel a little sorry for them.

But while they're not watching me, I get to watch them. There seems to be an interesting dynamic at play here. The older one that I assumed was in charge isn't. He's clearly taking direction from the much younger one. Oh yes, the redhead might look fresh out of school, but he's got smart dripping off him like sweat off a pig. Not to be underestimated.

Still, he's whistling in the wind when it comes to finding out whodunit.

The family look devastated and I feel proud that it's all my doing. This whole gathering is a result of my work. I'm the cause of all the tears streaming down that poor woman's face, the tremor in her husband's hand as he reaches out to support her. My sharp blade has scarred their hearts as thoroughly as it carved Evan's flesh. This pain is their appreciation of my work. I wish Ron was here to see what I've done, what I'm doing. And in a strange way, I wish my father was here too. Certainly, he'd be shocked, but it would make him realise that I do have some talent after all. The thought of him leaves a bitter *taste in my mouth, so instead I turn my attention to the people that are here.*

The great and the good of the skin community, all in one place at one time. Pretending to forget about their petty jealousies and back-stabbings. Pretending to be sad because someone most of them hardly knew has died. And all the little groupies, sobbing into their black hankies as if they mean it. When in fact it's just an excuse for a piss-up at the pub afterwards.

Not Marni Mullins though. There are no tears on her cheeks as she sweeps past me to leave the chapel. She's beautiful but her body vibrates with suppressed anger. I wonder who she's angry with, and why. I'll see.

There's a lot you can find out by lurking at a funeral. Some people are genuinely raw, emotionally flayed. Others are performing, fulfilling what's expected of them. Interactions are intensified and, with the addition of alcohol at the wake . . .

I watch and I learn.

Marni Mullins is talking to the young policeman. He's blushing. It's hardly a friendly exchange. She's still angry when she walks away, but he just looks regretful. What does he have to regret when it comes to Marni Mullins? His eyes follow her around like a puppy dog.

Be still my beating heart. The Collector is here.

27

Marni

The wake was held at the Heart and Hand as, apparently, it had been Evan's favourite watering hole. It was hardly big enough to accommodate the number of people that came from the service, and drinkers quickly spilled out onto the street corner. The irony of the pub being the setting for Thierry's alibi for Evan's murder didn't escape Marni. Francis had told her about the girl with the mermaid tattoo and she had no doubt that the bitch would be here today. She sucked in a breath and bit on her lower lip. That wasn't really fair. She and Thierry had been apart for years, so why should it matter to her who he slept around with? The problem was, it did seem to matter.

Freed from the solemnity of the church, the wake took on more of a party atmosphere. With drinks in their hands, Evan's friends from the tattooing community were catching up and exchanging gossip. New tattoos were shown off and either complimented or mocked, and stories swapped from recent conventions. The girls who had been so conspicuously crying were now laughing just as loudly, and Marni felt a little sorry for Evan's family who sat huddled in a corner.

She looked around the crowded bar, frowning as she wondered whether Thierry would be with the mermaid girl or the studio's new apprentice. She didn't have to wait long – she spotted him huddled in the corner whispering in his junior's ear. She turned away, bile rising.

'She is over eighteen,' said a voice in her ear. 'Just.'

Noa materialised at her side and tilted his hand up and down to ask her if she wanted another drink.

Why the hell not. She hadn't come by car and she wasn't tattooing this afternoon, so she might as well have another. She wasn't sure she could face an hour or two here without having the sharp edges softened slightly.

'Sure. Thanks.'

As she waited for Noa to return, Iwao came up to her.

'Did you know him?' she asked.

'Evan? No. But I spoke to Jonah Mason about what had happened and he asked me to represent him here.'

'He's in California?'

'Yes. I've passed on his condolences to Evan's parents. Jonah feels terrible that his tattoo could be the cause of Evan's death. He's thinking of putting up a reward for information that leads to the killer.'

'Seriously? But it's not his fault that some psycho decided to hack that tattoo off Evan's body. The guy could have taken any one of his other tattoos.'

Iwao pursed his lips. 'Not if your theory about the exhibition is right, Marni. It would suggest that this killer is being very specific over which tattoos he takes. And from that we can assume he's being specific in his choice of victims, too.'

Over Iwao's shoulder, she could see Francis Sullivan approaching them.

'Damn! I can't believe the police are still here. It's so disrespectful.'

Iwao glanced back and grimaced.

'He's just doing his job, Marni. But you'll forgive me if I don't hang around.'

He ducked away swiftly and, at the same time, Noa arrived with her glass of wine. He took the empty from her and put it on the bar.

'There, my darling. Now tell me how you've been.'

She kissed him on the cheek.

'Give me a minute, Noa. I just want to send this bloody policeman packing.'

Francis Sullivan was hovering in her peripheral vision and it was irritating the hell out of her. In his drab suit, he looked completely out of place among the tattooing fraternity. He could have taken off his jacket and tie. *What a stiff.*

'You've got a nerve,' she said, turning to him.

'We all want this killer caught, don't we, Marni?' he said.

He wasn't even holding a drink or trying to blend in.

'Some things are sacred.'

Francis looked around the crowded bar, at the people tucking into sausage rolls and downing pints, but made no comment.

Marni took a large mouthful of wine. She was starting to regret the help she'd given him so far. He seemed far too willing to just pin the crime on anyone with a tattoo, rather than turning up any real evidence. That was what the police were supposed to do, wasn't it? Dig up the evidence that would lead them to the killer. Not pick the killer and then start looking for the evidence.

'How many of the tattooists from Iwao's exhibition are here?'

Marni swallowed her wine.

'Iwao's here,' she said. 'He's representing Jonah Mason, who's in California. Rick Glover's here, but none of the others, I don't think.'

'He did Jem Walsh's spider tattoo, right?'

'That's right.'

'Can you introduce me to him?'

Marni felt anger flushing her cheeks.

'So you can arrest him tomorrow? That seems to be how this works.'

Francis sighed. 'Marni, we look at everyone who might be linked to the case and then we try to eliminate them from the enquiry.'

'In other words, you want me to introduce you, so you can check out his alibi for the night Jem died. No fucking way, Frank.'

'Listen, love, you need to get down off your high horse for more than five minutes at a time. There's a killer out there, targeting your community.'

'You're right,' she said quietly. 'I don't want anyone else to die. But by not sharing the information you have, you're putting us all at risk. Please, at least put out an official warning.'

'It could have an impact on the killer's behaviour.'

'It could save lives.'

Talking to him was like talking to a brick wall.

'Excuse me,' she said. 'I have other people to speak to.'

But as Marni made her way across the bar, blood roared in her ears and her heart rate soared. This wasn't right and she wasn't going to stand by idly and wait for the next person to die.

'Noa, grab me that chair, would you?' She pointed at the chair currently occupied by Thierry's apprentice.

'Sure thing. Excuse me,' said Noa, gripping the back of the chair and unceremoniously tilting the girl into Thierry's lap. Her skirt was so short Marni could practically see her knickers. The girl scowled, but Thierry laughed and snaked an arm around her waist. Seeing that fuelled Marni's anger to further heights.

'Where do you want it?' asked Noa.

'Right here by the bar, that's fine.'

Marni climbed up onto the chair and looked around the noisy pub. Looking for something to grab people's attention, she picked up a fork and banged it on the side of her glass.

'Quiet for a moment, quiet,' shouted Noa in his rumbling bass tones. 'Marni's got something to say.'

Heads turned towards her, and Marni noticed Sharon and Dave Armstrong giving her puzzled looks.

'Hi, hello,' said Marni, as the general hubbub in the bar settled down. 'I think most of you know me, but for those who don't, my name's Marni Mullins, of Celestial Tattoo. I have to admit that I didn't really know Evan, but I'm here today because I know a lot of people who did. And I've got something really important to say to you all – and I want you to spread this around to all your friends who aren't here today.'

She reached down to the bar behind to put down the wine glass and the fork. A sea of faces looked up at her expectantly. At the back, Francis Sullivan's face showed intense disappointment. His sergeant was standing next to him, looking outraged.

'Marni, please don't do this,' said Francis. He continued to speak but his words were drowned out by a flurry of excited murmurs.

'Listen up,' said Marni. 'The police believe that the man who killed Evan might also have been responsible for two more murders. Tattoos were missing from those bodies, and the tattoos that have been taken have one thing in common. They were done by tattoo artists who featured in the recent *Alchemy of Blood and Ink* exhibition.' Marni spotted Rick Glover looking shocked at the back of the room. 'There's a very good chance that a serial killer might be targeting people with works by the tattoo artists involved, namely Ishikawa Iwao, Jonah Mason, Bartosz Klem, Brewster Bones, Polina Jankowski, Rick Glover, Gigi Leon, Jason Leicester, Vince Priest and Petra Danielli. I want to warn you because the police won't. If you have a tattoo by any of these artists, take extra care when you're out at night. Don't go out on your own. I'm scared and you should be, too.'

She took a sip of wine and caught her breath as people took in the list of names. Most people were shaking their heads, but one or two talked in hushed, urgent tones, indicating a tattoo here and there by someone on the list. She saw one of her clients, Dan Carter, downing a near-full pint of beer with fear flashing in his eyes. Frank Sullivan and Rory Mackay, however, were nowhere to be seen. No doubt they'd scurried back to the nick to work out what to do now their closely guarded secret was out.

'Evan Armstrong and Jem Walsh were both killed here in Brighton within the last couple of weeks,' she continued.

'Jem Walsh?' said a girl standing near Marni's chair. 'Jem's *dead*?'

'No way,' said someone else, as a flurry of gasps spread through the crowd – obviously, despite the coverage in the local press, quite a few of the mourners hadn't heard about it. The door slammed as someone rushed outside.

'I'm so sorry,' said Marni.

The girl slumped against the man next to her, who just managed to prevent her slipping to the floor.

'What's going on? What are the police doing about it?' someone called from the back.

People started firing questions at Marni and pandemonium broke out. Thierry helped her down from the chair. Her job was done.

'Why the hell did you do that?' he said. 'You'll have Sullivan on your case now.'

'It's his own bloody fault. Hopefully, I've saved someone's life. And if Frank doesn't like it, he knows what he can do with it.'

'You shouldn't have done that. He'll just take it out on the rest of us, poking his nose in where he's not wanted.' He hadn't let go of her hand from when he helped her off the chair. 'I wish you'd never got involved with this, Marni. It worries me.'

She pulled away from him and he frowned.

What was Thierry's problem with the investigation – and with her? So many mixed messages. His temper flared whenever the subject was raised, but other times he seemed more concerned for her. What was going on?

Did she really want to know?

28

Rory

Rory wouldn't have believed it possible for the boss to come into work looking any worse than he had the previous morning. However, he was wrong. Francis was in early but his suit was rumpled and his hair unwashed. When Rory arrived, the boss was already at his desk with a super-sized black coffee, poring over pages of notes in front of him.

'You okay?' said Rory, trying to edge close enough to see what he was working on.

Francis looked up, noticing him for the first time. 'Do we know where Bradshaw is today?'

'Not around. He's got a high-level strategy meeting with a couple of DSs.'

'Do you know where?'

'Hollingbury Park.'

His golf course of choice.

'Good.' He went back to studying his notes.

Rory waited for further explanation but the boss ignored him. Fine. He had plenty of his own work to be getting on with. But five minutes later, before he'd even properly started on anything, the boss called him back into his office.

'Rory, I've been up most of the night, wrestling with my

conscience. I want to do right by my job, but that's not the only consideration.'

Rory squirmed in the chair. *Where was this going?*

'People are panicking and rumours are flying round after Marni's little announcement. If the killer strikes again and we've done nothing, we'll have blood on our hands. We need to take control and calm things down.'

'What are you going to do?'

'I'm calling a press conference.'

'But the chief explicitly forbade it. You go against his word and he'll string you up for it.'

Francis shrugged. 'I realise that – but I won't let another person die just because I was too weak to speak out. Our theory's been leaked anyway. Marni saw to that. But we need to make it official – she's right, people need to know and protect themselves.'

Jesus. This was going to cause an earthquake.

'I'll understand if you want to step back from this, Rory. You've got a family, so you can't risk your job.'

'But you'll be risking yours.'

'That can't be helped.'

Of course, Sullivan was right. They had a duty to act if they could potentially save someone's life. But what Francis was proposing to do went against a direct order from a superior. That could get him not only kicked off the case, but out of the force if Bradshaw went to town on it. Down in the stairwell, out of sight and earshot of the incident room, Rory pulled his mobile out of his pocket.

He dialled Bradshaw's number.

Press conferences were always held in the largest ground floor room at the John Street police station, but even that wasn't big enough to accommodate the unprecedented number of journalists that had crowded in, clutching a variety of tech devices and stubby pencils to record the official version of events. Two murders in the space of a week was big news – it effectively doubled the number of killings in the city for the year so far. As the grim details had started to leak out, which they always did, the local journos had been joined by a number of hacks from the nationals.

Rory scanned the room from the door at the back and then retreated into the corridor to try his phone again. The chief hadn't answered his message, and there was no one else in the station with the authority to shut this down. He went back into the room.

Francis had made some attempt to look less creased. He'd taken his suit jacket off and rolled up his shirtsleeves – not that his shirt looked much better – and he'd slicked his hair back with water. He tapped the microphone on the table in front of him to check whether it was switched on. An expectant hush fell among the excited journalists.

'Good morning,' said Francis, to test the microphone level.

There were a few muttered replies.

'My name is DI Francis Sullivan of the Major Incident Team, and my unit has been tasked with investigating the two murders that have taken place here. Evan Armstrong, a thirty-three-year old-man from Hove, was found dead in the Pavilion Gardens on Sunday, twenty-eighth May. Jem Walsh was discovered underneath the Palace Pier two days later. He had been decapitated.'

'Are you working on a link between the murders?' said a young woman in the front row.

'I'll take questions at the end of my statement,' said Francis.

'I've heard he's taking tattoos from the bodies.' It was Tom Fitz. If he hadn't actually heard Marni's speech at the wake, he certainly would have picked up the gist of it later. News like that would have become the main talking point across the city's bars and pubs.

'I realise that a number of rumours have been circulating since Evan's funeral yesterday,' continued Francis, 'which is why I called you all in.'

The door at the back of the room opened and Francis paused. Bradshaw stepped into the room, shut the door and came to stand next to Rory. He was wearing a pale yellow sweater and blue chinos, and he still had his golf shoes on his feet. His expression was furious but he didn't speak.

His appearance made Francis momentarily lose his stride. A whisper of impatience rolled through his audience as he paused to pick up the thread.

'We have reason to believe that the individual responsible for the killings is indeed removing tattooed parts of his victims' bodies and taking them away. As yet, we have no understanding for the motive behind this but we're looking closely at who he's chosen as victims and which tattoos he's taken.'

'Marni Mullins said something about the recent *Blood and Ink* exhibition,' said Tom Fitz. 'Is there a link between this and the killings?'

'That is just speculation, and implying otherwise would be irresponsible. We have nothing concrete to suggest this is the case. However, it is one of the reasons for talking to you. We need to put out a warning to anyone with a tattoo, regardless of the artist who executed it, that they need to be careful. Avoid walking through the city alone after dark, keep your tattoos covered in public, watch out for each other.'

As he stopped speaking, pandemonium broke out in the room. Everyone seemed to have a question at once, hands went up in the air, and towards the back, people were standing up and pushing forwards. Bradshaw started to make his way up the side of the room towards the podium.

'I'll take a handful of question,' said Francis.

'Do you have any suspects yet?' said an out-of-towner.

'Can I have your name and who you work for?'

'Simon Epson, *Telegraph*.'

Francis could see the slant that his article would take.

'Do you have any suspects, Officer?' repeated the journalist.

'I'm sorry – I can't discuss the operational aspects of the case with you at this time,' said Francis.

'In other words, you have no idea who this tattoo thief is?'

'No comment.'

'Lizzie Appleton, *Mirror*. Apparently, you arrested the exhibition's organiser, Ishikawa Iwao. Why was that?'

'No one has been arrested in this case, Ms Appleton. Ishikawa Iwao is among a number of individuals who have been helping us with our enquiries.'

As far as Rory was concerned, Ishikawa Iwao was most definitely still a person of interest.

'Like Marni Mullins?' said Appleton.

'As I said, we've received help from several individuals but I can't go into specific details with you.'

'I think it's time we wrapped this up, ladies and gentlemen.' Bradshaw practically pushed Francis sideways and took over the mic. 'Thank you for coming. Please report responsibly and don't start a panic across the city. We want people to take sensible precautions, not live in fear.'

There was a stampede for the door as the reporters realised they weren't going to get any further titbits for their columns. Rory watched Francis, now white as a sheet, trying to make a swift exit before Bradshaw could collar him. At the door, the boss turned momentarily and glared at him, eyes like daggers. Rory waited a second, then made his own escape. The boss clearly knew it was him who had called Bradshaw.

Climbing the stairs, Rory felt bad about what he'd done. Calling the press conference had been the right course of action, morally speaking. Quite possibly, Francis had saved someone's life. And it had taken guts to go against a direct order. Rory sighed. He wouldn't go so far as to say alerting Bradshaw had been the wrong thing to do. But it had left a bad taste in his mouth.

Then he heard footsteps behind him, coming up fast. He knew it was Sullivan.

'You bastard!'

29

Francis

The fact that Rory had so evidently run straight to Bradshaw made Francis's blood boil. The chief would have found out about the press conference, no matter what – but that didn't mean the little shit had to spill the beans before the damn thing had even kicked off. It wasn't surprising the case was getting nowhere fast – how was he supposed to work without the support of his team? The buzz in the incident room fell silent as he walked in, all eyes fixed upon him. Rory followed him in, with Bradshaw hot on his heels.

'My office. Now. Both of you.' Bradshaw's voice was far louder than it needed to be and he didn't wait for an answer.

Francis looked at Rory, who shrugged.

'If I'd kept quiet, I would have been in for a bollocking too.'

It didn't come close to an apology. And the fact was, Rory hadn't done any harm to his career by making the call to Bradshaw.

'So it would have been okay with you to let potential victims wander around unaware of what was happening?' Francis said. 'Makes me wonder how you sleep at night.'

They followed Bradshaw up the stairs at a safe distance, Francis's heart pounding in his chest as he took the steps two at a time. Whatever was coming his way, he probably deserved it.

But at least he could look himself in the eye with the knowledge that he'd done the right thing.

Walking into the chief's office, there was a palpable chill in the air. Bradshaw had dropped into the chair behind his desk with a heavy sigh. Neither Francis nor Rory dared sit as they waited for the tirade that was coming. Bradshaw looked from one to the other, but it was on Francis that his eyes finally settled.

'What in God's name were you thinking?'

Francis steeled himself. 'I was thinking that we might save someone's life. Sir.'

'We discussed it. I forbade it.'

It wasn't a question, so Francis said nothing.

Bradshaw turned his attention to Rory. 'You did the right thing, calling me.'

'I thought you needed to know what was happening,' Rory replied, but his eyes were downcast.

'Informing the public wasn't your decision to take,' said Bradshaw, redirecting his attention to Francis. 'It's probably caused widespread panic.'

'Marni Mullins warned them at the wake,' said Francis. 'Rumours have been flying and people were already panicking.'

Rory rolled his eyes. It made Francis bristle with anger.

'I stand by what I did,' he continued. 'Hopefully it's saved a life.'

Bradshaw was clearly unimpressed. 'It didn't cross your mind that the rumours alone would be enough to stop people from taking unnecessary risks?'

'With all due respect, sir, I felt that we should be in control of the flow of information.'

Bradshaw snorted. 'All you've done is alert the killer – if it is indeed a single killer – to the fact that we've worked out what he's doing. He'll just go to ground and we'll have less chance of catching him than before.'

'I don't agree, sir.'

'Your wealth of experience tells you otherwise?'

'My training tells me that serial killers are attention seekers. If – underlined heavily – these killings are linked in the way that we think they might be, the publicity will play right up to the Tattoo Thief's ego. Rather than go to ground, it could draw him out. My plan is to flood the city centre with plain clothes and monitor the CCTV live. Hopefully we can catch him before he kills again.'

'You mean, catch him in the act?' Bradshaw shook his head. 'That's a high-risk strategy.'

'Not in the act,' said Francis. 'Now everyone's been warned, he won't have the opportunity. People are alert and on the lookout. He'll get desperate, he'll take more risks and give himself away.'

'I bloody hope so. You need to think of the crime stats. I'm under pressure from above to bring all crimes, especially violent crimes, down.'

'Which we'll do by flushing out the killer and arresting him.'

Bradshaw clasped the bridge of his nose between finger and thumb and pursed his lips. 'I don't see that working,' he continued. 'Put out someone to act as bait and you might have a chance, but just taking away his opportunity to kill won't help you catch him. I can't do anything, Sullivan, other than take you off the case. Mackay, you're acting officer in charge until I can get a new DI transferred.'

'But, sir, the DI called the press conference with the best intentions.'

It was way too little, too late, and Rory obviously knew it.

'I don't give a monkey's brass balls – you're in charge now and you'll take instructions from me. Get that Japanese tattooist back in custody and get some forensic evidence that'll hold up in court.'

'There's no reason to think it's him.'

'Shut up, Sullivan. Get out, both of you.'

'You can't do this, sir.' Speaking through gritted teeth, Francis could hardly form the words.

'I can do what I bloody well please, Sullivan. Mackay's in charge.'

The interview was over.

Outside in the corridor, Francis gave full vent to his anger. 'Damn, damn, damn!'

He was off the case. Bradshaw and Mackay were barking up the wrong tree, which meant the killer would have the freedom to carry on unhindered. He punched the wall with a balled fist. An explosion of pain shot up his arm.

'Damn it!'

x

I knew that once the project got going, I'd need to move fast. The Collector has given me a list of tattoos to gather in, and I need to harvest them all before the police get too clever. Once I have them, I can make a safe retreat – they'll never know where to look for me. It's the harvesting of the tattoos from the bodies that's the most risky part of the operation.

The Collector and his list. He has such an eye for beauty on the human body and he's creating a private collection the likes of which will never have been seen. The taxidermy and the tattoos are just the start – I know he has other ideas. Last time we spoke, he was wondering if it was possible to take a person's face. I said I thought it was entirely possible. If I complete this task, perhaps he'll have more for me to do. I will have gained his trust. He needs to realise that I could be his right hand, that he can rely on me. He must know by now of my devotion to his cause. But the more successful I am, the more he'll notice me. I need to snag his attention. And the way to achieve that is to do his bidding to the very best of my considerable ability. It's time he showed some appreciation for what I've done so far, I think.

I'm making good progress and tonight should net me another one, if my target behaves in character. I've watched him over the last few weeks, drinking in the Victory Inn on the corner of Duke Street and Middle Street. He stays in there with a group of friends till it closes, then they all go their separate ways. I've followed him three times. He takes the same route home, cutting through the Lanes to get to Old Steine and across to Kemptown. Only tonight, I'm not following him. I'm lying in wait for him.

The Lanes suit my purposes admirably. The smaller ones are steeped in darkness and virtually deserted at this time. Dan Carter obviously feels that it's safe enough to cut through them – you can still hear rowdy drunks laughing and catcalling on North Street. But that doesn't mean they'll hear you. Especially when a hand goes over your mouth from behind and smothers your face with an ether-soaked rag.

I chose this spot with care. The alleyway is narrow, but just to the left of the doorway where I'm standing, there's an iron gate which leads to an isolated yard. I've already dealt with the lock on the gate, so I can just pull Carter through it. The yard will give me somewhere to work, undisturbed, for several hours. All the equipment I need is already stashed there in a bag. Carter's tattoo is large and even if I work fast, it's still going to take a considerable time. But it will be beautiful when it's done, probably the most beautiful one on the list, maybe apart from . . .

I hear footsteps approaching. His. I've learned the cadence of his walk while I've been watching him. Everyone has a unique foot-fall, their own rhythm of putting one foot in front of the other. I shake ether onto the cloth in my left hand and brace myself against the doorframe behind me. The footsteps get louder, closer, and as they are virtually level with my hiding place, I step out into his path, jostling him hard with my shoulder against his torso. As he turns to remonstrate, I clamp the cloth over his nose and mouth from behind. He struggles but it only takes a few seconds after he's inhaled to feel his body slump against mine. I drag him through the gate into my secret courtyard.

Now he's unconscious, the real work can begin. Time to come out and play, my beloved blades.

'The vorpal blade went snicker-snack.'

I love that poem. Sometimes it seems as if Lewis Carroll wrote it just for me. It so suits the work I do. My vorpal blade . . .

What the hell? I can hear voices, close by. A couple, whispering sweet nothings to each other. And if I can hear their sweet nothings that means they're too close. And they're blocking my escape route.

Damn it.

Damn it. Damn it. Damn it.

30

Francis

Francis loved St Catherine's at night. He had a key to the church and in the small, silent hours when he couldn't sleep, he would sometimes let himself in to spend an hour or two in quiet contemplation and prayer. Mindful of the church's electricity bill, the small reading lights in the choir stalls were enough to cast a soft glow through the chancel, and Francis found the crowding shadows to be a comfort where others might not.

But tonight, comfort was in short supply. Perhaps his prayers for success in his new job had been too self-centred and the altruism with which he'd thought he'd acted nothing more than a cover. Was the uncomfortable reality that he craved success and recognition for its own sake? His prayers had gone unanswered, because it was clear he was making a total screw-up of his first case. Being removed from command this early wasn't something his career could easily survive. At best he'd be sidelined, or worse still there would be a drip feed of pressure for him to apply to another force or even find another career. What did a failed policeman do with his life? There weren't many options after such a short-lived tenure.

Rubbing his bruised fist, Francis gazed up at the crucifix to find Jesus looking sad and regretful.

Fair enough. He'd been in thrall to his vanity, squandering his time on self-aggrandisement, looking for justice for the dead while ignoring the living who needed him more. He'd missed his last two visits to his mother and there couldn't be much time left. He'd ignored a couple of calls from his sister and, while she might not admit that she needed him, he knew his presence in her life was one of her mainstays of support. These women were alive and they needed him. They didn't ask for much, just that he be there, and these past two weeks he hadn't been.

He would visit his mother and phone his sister tomorrow. He dropped to his knees on the altar step and bowed his head in prayer. The smell of incense from an earlier service drifted through the chancel and he heard a door softly closing. He gave the slightest of nods when Father William joined him at the rail, then carried on praying. He took the priest's arrival as a sign that God hadn't abandoned him but had instead sent counsel – and he gave thanks.

'I saw the light and I knew it was you,' said Father William, when Francis returned to sit in the choir stalls.

'God told you?'

Father William laughed. 'No. It's only you and the verger who have keys, besides myself. And he wouldn't miss a wink of sleep to give comfort to a dying nun.'

Francis smiled. He knew the verger, a charming man who never let piety get in the way of afternoon tea with the parishioners.

Father William put both his hands over the hand Francis was resting on the rail.

'So tell me what brings you into the house of God at two in the morning?' he said. 'Maybe I can offer some more practical answers than him upstairs.' He raised his eyes momentarily to the crucifix above them.

Father William was a man of great wisdom and years of experience when it came to the workings of the human heart. If Francis's own father had abandoned him, it could only have been to make way for Father William's appearance in his life.

Finally allowed to unburden, Francis spoke for nearly an hour in the half-darkness of the empty church. Father William listened and nodded as he outlined his failings, first in the case and then with regards to his mother and his sister.

'I want to catch this killer more than I've wanted anything in my life, Father. Is that so wrong? But there are no leads and I'm off the case with even less chance of catching him now.'

'It's not wrong to want to succeed at what you do,' said the priest. 'And in succeeding here, you'll surely be saving further lives. The motives that rule our hearts are never singular. Most altruism is tied up with images of self-worth and we've all felt pride, which is a sin, for doing something good and righteous.'

'I understand,' said Francis. 'And I believe that if I can succeed at my job, I'll be making our community a safer place. But right now, I can't even do that. We're at a dead end and the killer's sure to strike again.'

'Never give up, my boy. If you know in your heart that what you're doing is right, then just do it and don't hold back because of what the world might think of you. God is the only one whose opinion matters.'

'You mean carry on regardless?'

'That's exactly what I mean.' There was determination in Father William's voice and Francis took strength from it. 'Now, give my love to your sister, and I'll tell your mother you're on your way when I see her tomorrow.'

The priest dropped to his knees in the choir stall, his hands still resting on Francis's.

'Domine Iesu, dimitte nobis debita nostra, salva nos ab igne inferiori . . .'

Save us from the fires of hell.

He wouldn't give up now.

31

Rory

He was in charge. Sullivan was off the case. And there'd been another attack.

This time, however, they'd cut a break. The victim was still alive – just – and Rory was waiting outside his hospital room for the chance of an interview. The doctors were insisting that the man would be in no fit state to talk, but Rory had heard that before. He decided to wait, but now, pacing the dimly lit corridor, he was feeling a little unsure of himself.

This was the lead they'd been waiting for. An attack survivor, a fresh crime scene as the killer had been disturbed in his work, and a drunk couple in an interview room at John Street, who hopefully weren't too far gone to remember what they'd stumbled into. He'd called all the team from their beds to capitalise on this stroke of luck. And much as he hated to admit it to himself, the boss's take on things wouldn't go amiss, either.

But one thing was certain. It blew the Iwao theory out of the water. He'd had two PCs sitting outside his house all night and they'd reported that he hadn't left the premises.

He texted Francis and caught him coming out of church. *Did he bloody live there?*

Fifteen minutes later, Francis joined him in a side room at the County Hospital. Rory fed some coins into a drinks machine and handed his former boss a cardboard cup of coffee.

'I shouldn't be here, Rory. If Bradshaw finds out . . .' Francis's tone was grim, with a clear implication.

'He won't. But two heads are better than one.'

Rory's actions had got Francis thrown off the case. It made him wonder how helpful he'd be if their roles were reversed. He'd half expected the boss to tell him where to go when he got back in touch. Instead, Francis dropped wearily onto an uncomfortable-looking chair upholstered in red plastic and listened as Rory filled him in.

'I can give you opinions, that's all. You'll have to make all the decisions. What did the doctor tell you?'

'It's serious,' said Rory. 'The man – his name's Dan Carter, apparently – has a severe concussion and the bastard had made a series of deep cuts, resulting in substantial blood loss. Apparently, Carter's got a full body suit tattoo, so if our drunk lovers hadn't arrived when they did, it could have been really nasty.'

'Is any of the tattoo missing?'

'The doctor said the cuts were all around the edge . . .'

'Just like we saw around Armstrong's tattoo site.'

'. . . and the killer had started peeling away the skin from the top of the shoulder. The doc said they had to cut away part of the tattoo and replace it with a skin graft from Carter's thigh.'

Francis winced in exactly the same way as Rory had when the surgeon explained the grisly details to him.

'When will we be able to talk to him?'

'The doctors would rather we didn't.'

There were footsteps in the corridor outside, and a nurse pushed open the door.

'They're in here,' she said.

'Thank you,' said a woman's voice.

Marni Mullins walked into the room, hair tousled, with her dark eye makeup conspicuously smudged.

'What's she doing here?' said Francis.

'Charming,' said Marni. 'Do you think I wanted to be dragged out of my bed at four in the morning to help you? Hospitals are not exactly my favourite places.'

She looked rattled.

'I called her,' said Rory. 'I want Marni to look at the victim's tattoo. The killer seems to be speeding up and we need to work out who his next victims might be.'

'Well, then thank you for coming,' said Francis, making Rory acutely aware of his own lack of manners.

The DI had stood up when Marni came into the room, and now he stepped forwards and placed a hand briefly on her upper arm. There was a slight change in the atmosphere that got Rory wondering. Quickly he brought Marni up to speed on what had happened.

'How many tattooists were featured in the exhibition?' said Francis, sitting down again.

Marni thought for a couple of seconds. 'Ten.'

Rory pulled a notebook out of his pocket.

'Give me their names,' he said.

Marni counted them off on her fingers. 'Iwao, Bartosz Klem, Rick Glover, Gigi Leon, Brewster Bones, Jason Leicester, Polina Jankowski, Jonah Mason, Vince Priest and . . .' She struggled to remember the last one and rubbed her forehead. 'I've got the catalogue at home . . . Wait, it was another girl.' She sat down opposite Francis. 'Got it. Petra Danielli. Italian, working out of Milan.'

'And whose work has the killer taken so far?'

'Evan Armstrong was tattooed by Jonah Mason,' said Francis. 'And Bartosz Klem did Giselle Connelly's arm.'

'Jem Walsh's tattoo was by Rick Glover,' added Marni.

'Which basically means, if our theory holds true, Dan Carter's tattoo must have been by one of these others,' said Rory, tapping his pencil on the list he'd just written.

'And if it's not by any of them?' said Marni.

Rory shrugged. 'Your theory crumbles.'

'We've now got two witnesses and a survivor,' said Francis. 'They'll have information, and with any luck it'll help us find the bastard.'

The door opened and a tall man in shirtsleeves, with a stethoscope round his neck, came in. As he glanced between the three of them, he looked almost as tired as Rory felt.

'Who's in charge here?' he asked.

Francis nodded his head in Rory's direction.

'Right, Mr Carter is awake, if not entirely lucid. I can give you five minutes with him but then he has to rest.'

'Will he be okay?' said Marni.

'A brain scan later will answer that question – he appears to have sustained a slight head injury, probably from falling,' said the surgeon. 'However, the cuts were only flesh wounds. They'll heal, but the skin graft will leave scars.'

'Mentally as well as physically,' muttered Rory.

'Well, that's not my department,' said the surgeon. 'Follow me.'

Dan Carter was in a private room a little way down the corridor where they'd been waiting. Everything in the room looked dull grey in the scant light of dawn, even the white sheets and bandages in which the latest victim was swaddled. Of his tattoo, there was no sign whatsoever – the only flesh on show belonged to his face, neck and hands. One arm was strapped in a sling across his chest. His face was grey, gleaming with an unnatural sheen of sweat.

As the surgeon left them alone with him, Marni stepped forward.

'Hi, Dan.'

'Hi, Marni,' the man said. He spoke slowly, still drugged. 'What are you doing here?'

'Helping these guys,' she said with a nod over her shoulder at Rory and Francis.

She knew him? How incestuous was the tattooing community?

'Police?' said Dan.

Marni nodded. 'Can you show me part of your tattoo, Dan?'

'Sure,' he said, nodding down at the arm that wasn't in the sling.

Marni gently pushed up his hospital gown to reveal a brightly coloured Japanese sleeve tattoo. She studied it for a while.

'That's gorgeous. Petra Danielli?'

'Yes. One hundred and seventy hours with her. But now . . .' He broke off his speech with a grimace.

Francis stepped forward at the other side of the bed. 'Dan, can you tell us exactly what happened?'

Dan Carter frowned as he let the sleeve of the hospital gown drop back down to his wrist.

'I'll try. I was in the Victory with a couple of mates.'

'Their names?' said Rory.

'Pete. Pete was there, I think. No, no, not Pete . . .' His eyelids drooped heavily.

'No worries,' said Francis. 'Can you remember what time you left?'

'Can't remember leaving. We were all outside . . . The bar had closed. I remember smoking a cigarette.'

'Were you walking with anybody else?'

'No, I don't think so.'

'Did you see any other people out on the streets?'

Dan shrugged helplessly.

'What happened?' prompted Francis again.

He shook his head. 'I'm sorry. It's a total blank. There's nothing after standing outside the Victory.'

'The doctor said he thought you'd been knocked out, probably with ether, and then hit your head on the ground. What do you remember from when you came round?' said Rory, at the end of the bed.

'There was a woman screaming and a man bent over me, looking at me. He asked if I was okay. My shirt was gone and I was in pain. It was freezing cold and I was bleeding. I could feel the warm blood running down my arm.'

'You don't remember anything of your attacker?'

'He was gone. The man told the woman to shut up a few times. They called an ambulance and I passed out again.'

'And that's all you remember?'

Dan Carter closed his eyes. The door opened and a nurse came into the room.

'That's enough now, folks. Mr Carter needs his rest.'

'Thank you, Dan,' said Rory. 'We'll come and talk to you again tomorrow. You might have remembered more by then.'

Dan opened his eyes. 'There was just one thing. I don't know if I'm remembering this or imagining it.'

'Tell us,' said Francis. Rory heard the tension in his voice.

'It's just this image . . . A pair of hands in white latex gloves, moving in front of my face. I could see something through the gloves, like tattoos on the back of his hands. Dark red, large tattoos. Kind of like roses . . .' He shrugged, forgetting his shoulder wound, then winced in pain.

'Out,' said the nurse. 'Come back tomorrow.'

32

Marni

Roses. One of the most common subjects to be tattooed on any part of the body. Marni had long ago lost count of how many she'd done herself and, unless an artist specialised in tribal or black work, every tattooist would have done their share. But tattoos on the backs of hands were probably a little less common. She didn't know anyone personally with roses like that and she breathed a sigh of relief.

So, was there any chance of her finding a man with roses tattooed on the backs of his hands by searching the internet? She had to give it a shot. Dan Carter had been lucky but the next person the killer targeted probably wouldn't get such a break. If the killer had failed to acquire Dan's Petra Danielli tattoo, would he target another one of her designs or move on to the next artist he had yet to harvest tattoos by? She shivered and goose bumps broke out on her arms.

After being called out to the County Hospital at four in the morning, Marni had lain awake until gone seven, fighting off the growing dread that usually stalked her in the small hours. Institutions always unnerved her, and as she dozed off she'd imagined herself back in the darkness of a prison cell, walls closing in, ceiling like a weight suspended above her. She sat up with a jolt. She closed her eyes again, but the same thing happened.

When she finally slept, it had been deep without being restful and she woke at midday feeling jittery and tired. Thankfully it was Sunday, so she wasn't working. But the images in her mind of rose-tattooed hands wielding a knife propelled her to her studio anyway. This man was hurting people she knew. Something had to be done to stop him.

Sullivan and Mackay seemed to be getting nowhere. There was scant forensic evidence and they had no one in their sights. But this new information could make all the difference. She couldn't recall anyone locally with roses on their hands, so perhaps the killer came into town from somewhere else. He'd killed Evan Armstrong during the convention, and Jem Walsh a couple of days later. She settled Pepper under her desk with a dog biscuit and flipped open her laptop. Once it had booted up, she typed 'Brighton Tattoo Convention 2017' into Google Images. Might the killer have attended? It seemed plausible. And if he had, the chances of him having been photographed were reasonably good – there were literally thousands of images online and if someone, her, took the time to trawl through them, just maybe they could track the bastard down.

She quickly sent an email to Thierry, Charlie and Noa, asking them to do the same, but it was Sunday lunchtime. They'd either be in bed, nursing hangovers, or in the pub creating them. No matter. She started scrolling down the screen, scanning each image for hands and for roses. All the tattooists were wearing black latex gloves while they worked, but their customers' hands were often on view, and when the artists weren't working, the gloves were off. She wondered if the killer was actually a tattoo artist, or just a collector.

'Jesus, Pepper, look who I've found here!'

The dog grunted on hearing his name. Marni was momentarily distracted by an image of a tattooist she'd been on a couple of dates with the previous year. It had come to nothing, but he'd been a nice guy and she still counted him as a friend.

'And here I am, working on Steve.'

Pepper wasn't interested but Marni dwelled on the picture for a minute. There was a row of punters at the front of the stand, watching as she layered colour along the tiger's back. Could one of them be the man she was looking for? Had the killer stopped in front of her booth and watched her at work? A chill ran up her spine. She checked the hands visible in the image and found no roses. Even so, she felt unsettled. She kicked off a shoe and rested her foot on Pepper's shoulder for comfort.

The afternoon wore on and her eyes grew tired from staring at the screen. She stopped a couple of times to make coffee, and had a ten-minute break to take Pepper out and smoke a cigarette. She'd seen plenty of tattooed hands, but no roses yet. Possibly this was just a wild goose chase. Perhaps the Tattoo Thief hadn't even come to the convention. And if he had, she'd be sifting through a crowd of more than seven thousand attendees on the off chance that he'd been photographed, or more specifically that his hands had been caught on camera.

She'd never seen so many tattooed hands. But most of them were continuations of sleeve tattoos that stretched up the whole arm, or calligraphy flowing across knuckles – LOVE, HATE or GOOD, EVIL; LONE WOLF or WHAT IF, IF ONLY.

It had been cloudy all day and dusk drew in early. Marni flicked on the Anglepoise lamp on her desk, still intent on scouring every single picture taken at the convention. Pepper sighed in his sleep, a sound sweet and reassuring to Marni's ears. She was working more slowly now as fatigue set in, sometimes having to check the same image twice as her concentration lapsed. Perhaps just another hour and then she would resume her search in the morning . . .

Pepper bolted out from under the desk, a low growl rumbling in his chest. He ran to the front of the shop, barking, and by the time Marni caught him up by the door, he was trembling all over. Panic washed through her, shortening her breath.

'Hey, Pepper, what is it? Did you hear something?'

Through the window, the street outside looked deserted. It was raining now and water flecked the glass, forming rivulets that raced each other down the pane. She peered around, looking for an explanation for the dog's behaviour. There! A movement in a doorway, three buildings along on the opposite side. A dark figure sinking back into the shadows. She stared at the place until black spots swam in front of her eyes, but she saw nothing else. It was a shop door and the shop was shut. There was no light on in the building, no movement in the doorway.

Had she really seen something or had she imagined it? She was so jittery these days – the whole business had put her on edge.

'It's nothing, babe,' she said, turning her attention back to Pepper. 'Probably just a seagull diving for rubbish.'

Marni turned and went back to her desk, but Pepper stayed where he was, trembling as he guarded the entrance to the shop. She could still hear him muttering and growling as she sat down. Pepper wasn't the brightest spark and she should take no notice of his stupid imaginings, but she was unsettled now and her hands were shaky on the keyboard. Since finding the body, she'd become drawn deeper and deeper into the case. How clever was that? Her watch read close to half past seven. She'd give it another half hour and then go home.

It was when her thirty minutes were virtually up that she saw it. A forearm in the process of being tattooed. The artist's hand was in the way so she couldn't make out what he was working on. But that didn't matter, it wasn't what caught her attention. She stopped scrolling down the page for one reason only. The back of the sitter's hand was heavily tattooed in dark red. Marni squinted at the image, trying to see whether it was a rose. She clicked the cursor to enlarge the image.

The tattoo might match what Dan Carter had described. But as she stared at it to make out what it was, she realised it wasn't a rose after all.

It was anything but a rose.

33

Francis

It was more than a little unusual for Bradshaw to put in an appearance at the station on a Sunday evening. In fact, it was practically testament to how worried he was about solving the case. He was looking for the reflected glory of a timely arrest and no doubt well aware that if the case went cold, it was the chief's career which would suffer most. Rory had reluctantly confided in Francis that he was being constantly harassed to bring people in and find the evidence against them.

'Rather than find the evidence, draw conclusions and then make the arrests,' said Francis. 'Has he forgotten everything he learned in training?'

'Trouble is, the evidence we've got so far tells us nothing,' said Rory with a sigh. 'A bit of information on the types of blades and no leads.'

They were sharing an uneasy truce in the incident room, drinking tea and mulling over the events of the past twenty-four hours, when Bradshaw swept in. He looked surprised to see his new OIC fraternising with the one he'd just pulled off the case.

'What are you doing here, Sullivan? You're not on this case.'

Rory stood up so he could meet the Chief's glare, eye to eye.

'I called him in. He's not currently assigned to anything and I felt I could use his existing knowledge to analyse what happened last night. No point leaving an officer idle who might be able to contribute.'

Thankfully this appeared to remind Bradshaw what he was doing in the station on a Sunday evening. 'I want a progress update on all of that, Mackay. Come to my office in five minutes.'

After he was gone, Rory sat down again and drained his cup of tea.

'I want you back on the case, Sullivan.'

Francis shrugged. 'You'll have to convince Bradshaw of that.'

Rory narrowed his eyes. 'No. *We'll* have to convince him.'

Francis knocked on the door of Bradshaw's office and went in. His heart was pounding and adrenalin jangled his nerves. Rory followed him in.

Bradshaw was reading a report and didn't look up.

'Sit down, Rory,' he said.

Francis coughed. It was enough to make Bradshaw realise that Rory hadn't come on his own.

'What are you doing here – I asked Rory for a case update. I didn't include you, did I?'

'You need to put me back in charge.'

Rory's head whipped round in anger. 'What the fuck . . .? That's not what I meant.'

'I'm the ranking officer in the department. I should be running the case.' Francis turned and looked at Rory. 'You want me back on the case? Then you'll be working for me. Got that?'

Bradshaw tried to interject but Francis gave no ground and continued.

'Last night we got lucky, very lucky indeed. A couple coming home after pub closing time disturbed the Tattoo Thief at work. He got away, of course. But he left us with a survivor and two witnesses. Don't let their testimony go to waste.'

'Rory can manage that information without your help.'

'The victim of the attack was a man called Dan Carter. He has a full body suit by a tattooist based in Italy called Petra Danielli. She was one of the tattooists in the Saatchi Gallery exhibition. It pretty much proves the theory that the killer's collecting tattoos by an exclusive group of artists. The theory that neither you nor Rory put much faith in. It's time to admit that I was right.'

Bradshaw narrowed his eyes, looking from one to the other of them. 'All right, what else have you got, Sullivan?'

'The attacker had outlined the tattoo with cuts, using, we believe, a short-bladed knife. He then changed knives and started to flay Carter's shoulder. The blades used are certainly similar in style to those that were used on Evan Armstrong, though there's no way of knowing if they were in fact the same ones. The pattern of the cuts suggests that he was intending to remove the entire body suit in two pieces – the front and the back – if he hadn't been interrupted.'

'Body suit?'

'A Japanese-style tattoo that extends over the entire torso, arms and legs.'

'Jesus.'

'Mr Carter couldn't tell us much as he was attacked from behind and rendered unconscious. But he does remember one thing from a moment of lucidity. The killer was wearing white latex gloves and Carter could see through them – the man has tattoos on the backs of both hands, dark red, most probably roses.'

'So you have a possible identifier for him.'

'On my advice, Mackay has put Hollins and Hitchins on an image search to find people with similar tattoos. Tomorrow, they'll visit all the local tattoo shops and ask if anyone remembers doing tattoos that could match Carter's description. I feel confident, sir, that we'll be able to pick up some leads.'

'That Rory will be able to pick up some leads, Sullivan. What about the couple, what did they have to say?'

'They ducked into an alleyway in the Lanes to find some privacy. They weren't really looking further down the alley but the killer, presumably perceiving them as a threat, rushed past them to get away. At the same time, they heard a moan in the distance and the man went to investigate. They basically saved Carter's life.'

'What about the attacker? What did they see?'

'Not much. He was carrying a hefty bag – nearly knocked the girl over with it – and he had a baseball cap pulled on low to shield his face. He was taller than the man, probably at least six foot. They didn't hear his voice and it was too dark to catch his hair or eye colour.' Francis shrugged. 'It's the information from Carter that should really enable us to move forward.'

Bradshaw steepled his hands on the desk. 'So you think I should reinstate you? Rory's been doing a decent job without you, and nothing you've just said changes that.

'Rory, are you ready to step down?' said Bradshaw, not bothering with niceties.

'No, sir,' said Rory. 'I'm the more experienced officer, after all.'

'Tough decision,' said Bradshaw.

Clearly it was tough working out which course of action would be better for his career, rather than most likely to solve the murders. Francis despised him.

Bradshaw went over to the window and looked out, his back to the two officers.

'Rory's in charge. You take the rest of the week off, Sullivan. I'll reassign you on Monday.' He couldn't even look them in the eye.

'Thank you, sir,' said Rory. 'You've made the right choice.'

Smarmy little git.

There was nothing for Francis to say.

'Now we know whose work the killer is targeting, we should be able to tempt him into the open,' said Rory.

'What you're implying is entrapment,' said Francis, 'using a potential victim as bait.'

'Shut up, Sullivan.'

'But it's a totally unethical way to proceed.'

Bradshaw glared at him. Francis wondered if he'd gone too far. At this rate he'd never get back on the case.

'So you think we should rely solely on a hunch based on Carter's blurred memory of an obscured hand?' sneered Bradshaw.

'It's ridiculous,' said Rory.

In his pocket, Francis felt the familiar vibration of a missed call.

'It's our best lead to date,' he said.

'Mackay, you do what you think is right, and report back to me.'

'Yes, sir.'

The phone vibrated in Francis's pocket again.

'And I'm sure there will be plenty of forensic evidence once Rose has finished with the attack site. Focus on that.'

'Yes, sir,' said Rory.

'Right, Mackay, you and your team have got precisely twenty-four hours to bring me something concrete. Don't fuck it up, Sergeant. I don't give second chances.'

'I won't, sir.'

'Sullivan, I don't want to see your face in here again until I've assigned you to another case.'

As soon as they were out of the room, Rory headed for the stairs at speed without saying a word. Too angry too talk to him, Francis hung back and pulled his phone from his pocket. It vibrated again in his hand – someone was desperate to talk to him.

There were text messages. All of them were from Marni

Mullins. He opened the most recent and an image filled his screen. It was a hand. A tattooed hand.

The tattoo wasn't a rose.

Deep red, harsh black outlines, black contouring.

It took Francis a couple of seconds to process the image, and then he saw it. It was a human heart, anatomically accurate and practically still pulsating. Dripping with dark rivulets of blood.

Was this the hand of the killer?

34

Marni

When Marni arrived at the station, she was escorted to the incident room by Angie Burton. The policewoman hardly spoke to her on the way up the stairs, giving Marni the distinct feeling she was looking down her nose from a great height. No matter. She was used to it – a certain section of the population had no time for people with tattoos.

Rory Mackay escorted her to an empty desk, where she got out her laptop.

'Francis said you'd found some images that might be the attacker's hands,' he said.

Marni looked round. 'Isn't he here?'

'He didn't tell you?'

'What?'

'He threw a press conference against the chief's orders, so now he's off the case.'

'I saw it. It was just what was needed. He shouldn't have been taken off the case for that.'

'Yes, but the press has gone to town. These are now "the Tattoo Thief" killings, apparently. Top brass are furious.' He changed the subject abruptly. 'Show me the pictures.'

Marni scrolled through her files and opened her picture gallery.

Rory stared at the enlarged image of the human heart tattoo on the screen. Marni watched him. She'd spent the last hour gazing at the picture – she didn't need to look at it again.

'Ever seen anything like it before?' said Rory, shifting his weight from one foot to the other.

'Sure. Human hearts are common, most often on chests. But I've seen them in all the usual places for a tattoo. Can't remember seeing them like this, on the back of someone's hand, though.'

'Do you think this is what Dan Carter could have seen through the attacker's glove?'

Marni shrugged. 'Maybe. But that doesn't mean there aren't a hundred other people with roses or hearts or something else tattooed on the back of their hands.'

'Does the work look familiar to you?'

'Not at all, but I've emailed the image to Thierry, Charlie and Noa to see if they have any thoughts on it. Really, we've got more chance of getting a lead from the guy who's tattooing him. This picture was taken at the convention – that immediately cuts it down to the tattooists who were there.'

'How many's that?'

'About three hundred and fifty.'

'Great.'

'But nearly half of them were women.'

Rory glanced back at the picture. She was right – the hands of the tattooist were big and brawny, with heavy forearms stretching from his black gloves. The picture didn't extend far enough to include his face, but they could see the T-shirt he was wearing – an Iron Maiden tour T-shirt, its black background faded to dark grey with age.

'Angie, Tony, come and look at this.'

The two detectives came across to where Marni was sitting and peered at the screen over her shoulder. Hitchins let out a long, low whistle.

'Nasty,' he said.

'Angie, get a memory stick, would you? Then try and find a match to the guy tattooing with artists that were at the convention.'

'Sure, boss,' said Angie, turning to go back to her own desk. She came back a moment later and, without checking whether it was okay with Marni, stuck a memory stick into the side of her laptop.

'Download them, please,' she said.

Marni wasn't thrilled by her tone.

'This'll be like looking for a needle in a haystack,' said Hitchins.

'Then get to it.' Rory turned to face Marni. 'Thank you for bringing these in, Ms Mullins. We'll be in touch if we need anything else.'

Angie pulled the loaded memory stick from the laptop and Marni realised she'd been dismissed. Fine. They didn't need Francis any more and they didn't need her. It seemed more than a little unfair that he was off the case for just warning people of the danger, but wasn't this what she'd come to expect from the police? Now, if they didn't need any more of her help, she wouldn't offer it. But they'd better catch this damn lunatic before he struck again.

Alex was watching football when she got home. It was past eleven o'clock but she could see from the way he was dressed – black bondage trousers and a ripped Bob Marley T-shirt – that he was planning to go out.

'Where are you off to?' she said, dropping onto the sofa next to him with a glass of wine and a bag of crisps.

'Liv's boyfriend's having a party before he goes off travelling.'

'Sounds good.'

'Can I take beer?'

'Do we have any?'

Alex shrugged but wasn't interested enough to stop watching the match to find out.

Marni sipped her wine, ignoring the football. She'd spent enough time in front of a screen today. Once Alex had gone, she could indulge herself with a long, hot soak in the bath. She leaned back against the cushions and closed her eyes.

'Mum!'

She sat up with a jerk, splashing wine on her lap and the adjacent cushion.

'Doorbell!'

'Well, get it then.'

Alex frowned at her but hauled himself off the sofa. Marni dabbed at the spilled wine with her sleeve, hoping it wasn't Thierry at the door.

'It's for you – that cop,' shouted Alex from the hall. 'I'm off now. See you tomorrow.'

'You staying over?'

'Probably.' Alex stuck his head back through the door. 'And even if I come home, you'll be asleep.'

She got up and managed to kiss him on the cheek as he turned to go. Francis Sullivan was standing in the hall – and for some reason the unexpected sight of him made her momentarily flustered. As the door banged shut behind Alex, she beckoned him into the living room.

'Hi,' she said. 'Come through.'

Pepper gave an excited bark when Francis came into the room, and heaved himself up from the hearth to sniff a trouser leg. Francis ignored him.

'Sorry to come round so late, but Rory just sent these over to me and I thought you'd want to see them.'

So at least one of the team appreciated her efforts. Then she remembered he wasn't even on the investigation any more.

'Rory told me you're off the case.'

Francis put his laptop down on the coffee table.

'Officially, yes. But in my mind, it's still my case.'

'Wine?'

He hesitated for a moment before answering. 'I'd better not,' he said finally.

She ignored his answer and got a glass for him. Then she topped up her own, and sat down next to him on the sofa.

'Look at these,' he said. 'This is the tattooist that was working on the man we think could be a suspect.'

Marni studied the pictures he brought up on the screen. There were several shots of a muscular tattoo artist working on a number of different clients. Some showed him in the faded T-shirt and he had the same brawny forearms with tribal tattoos on them.

'Oh yes,' said Marni. 'The T-shirt's the same as in the picture I found. It didn't take long for you guys to find him.'

'Rory put the whole team on it. The advantage of having man-power. He's called James Diamond. Heard of him?'

Marni shook her head. She didn't recognise the name or the man in the picture. 'So what happens next?'

'We get in touch with this guy and find out who he tattooed at the convention. And that should give us our killer.'

'Maybe. If the heart tattoo is what Dan saw through the glove.'

'Of course. And if it wasn't, we're back to square one.'

'Where does he work?' said Marni.

'Out of a studio in Guildford. Fancy a trip there tomorrow morning?'

'I thought you were off the case?'

'It's not a line of enquiry Bradshaw approves of. Rory will concentrate on the direction Bradshaw wants to take. He won't get round to it for a day or two.'

'Seriously?'

'We can steal a march on him. I'm still determined to solve

this case and this could be an important lead.'

Francis Sullivan had something to prove.

'Sure, I'll come with you. It's in my interests to get this killer under lock and key, given I'm likely to know half his victims.' She sipped her wine and thought for a moment. 'It makes the hours spent looking through those photos worthwhile.'

'It's the basis of good police work. Leave no stone unturned. Check the details endlessly.'

'Boring.'

'But worth it when you pinpoint the one tiny detail that makes the case fall into place. It might be finding a single hair that matches the killer or the victim, it could be discovering a single CCTV frame that shows up someone's alibi to be a lie – whatever it is, it gives you a rush.'

'I get it. Like when I do a highly detailed tattoo. Hundreds of chrysanthemum petals, virtually all the same. But when the tattoo's finished, it's great to watch your client seeing it in the mirror for the first time.'

'Assuming they like the results,' he said with a half-smile.

His flash of humour took her by surprise. She hadn't known him very long but this was the first time she'd seen him come anywhere close to making a joke at her expense.

'Why are you always so serious?' she said, thinking aloud.

'What?' He looked genuinely surprised.

'You are. That was the first funny thing I've heard you say. And it wasn't that funny.'

'Right.' But it was accompanied by a proper smile this time, a smile that Marni unexpectedly hoped to see again.

Whoa! That's not somewhere you want to be going.

Marni stretched and looked at her watch. It was beyond midnight and she needed a cigarette. Because of Alex, she didn't smoke in the house.

'Just going outside for a fag. Want to stretch your legs?'

'Sure.'

Out in the garden, she lit up and inhaled deeply, aware of Francis watching her.

'Want one?' She offered him the packet, then nearly dropped it in surprise when he reached out a hand towards it.

'Haven't had a fag since I was at school,' he said, extracting one slowly.

'You mean you've actually had one?'

'Just the one,' he said, grinning ruefully.

'So you don't really want one now.'

'Something came over your face when you took that drag,' he said. 'Contentment. Relief. Pleasure. I want to see what it was. Call it research.'

Contentment and pleasure were clearly not what Francis Sullivan experienced when he inhaled on his second ever cigarette. During the inevitable coughing fit, he dropped the cigarette on the ground and had to bend double. For a moment Marni, as incapacitated with laughter as he was with coughing, thought he was going to be sick. Pepper, who'd joined them for the break, started barking and running round the small garden as if he'd seen a cat.

'That good, was it?' said Marni, finishing her own cigarette and stubbing it out in a small pot of sand by the edge of the patio.

Francis made a hacking noise as he tried to clear the smoke from his lungs.

'Don't let me have another one. Ever.' His voice was rough and hoarse.

'I won't. It was a waste of a perfectly good cigarette.'

She was standing in front of him and, without thinking, she brushed his hair back from his forehead. Their eyes met as she let her hand linger at his temple.

What are you doing?

He seemed to lean towards her and Marni felt arousal spreading through her like wildfire. She wanted to kiss him. He looked as if he wanted to kiss her, as if he was about to kiss her. But a sudden sharp growl from Pepper brought them both back down to earth with a bump.

'What is it, boy?' said Marni.

'Your dog's jealous?'

Marni shook her head. At least Francis was acknowledging what had just almost happened.

'Not usually. I don't think it's that. I think something spooked him. He was acting strangely earlier this evening.'

Francis looked around the small back garden.

'What's beyond the fence?'

'There's a small service alley for access from the road.'

'I can't see anything. Maybe he saw a fox or a cat.'

The spell broken, they went back into the house. Marni offered Francis coffee but he declined.

'I'd better be going. I'll pick you up first thing and we'll track down James Diamond.'

Seeing him out of the front door, Marni was once again overcome by an urge to kiss him but held herself back.

What the hell was going on?

It took her longer than usual to fall asleep once he'd left. Not because of her usual rotation of night terrors, but because she couldn't stop imagining what it would be like to kiss Frank Sullivan and where it might lead. She told herself it meant nothing. But she couldn't get one image out of her mind. His unruly hair falling across his forehead and how completely natural it had felt to brush it aside.

xi

I can't breathe.

I hear my father's voice in my head, telling me I've made a mess of things. Over and over. I always make a mess of things. I always get things wrong. The Collector's saying the same thing now, in my father's voice. This can't have happened. It can't be happening.

I'm fighting for a single breath.

The process. I have to keep my mind on the process. To stop myself from going mad. I'll keep it there until I'm ready to think about things. And about what I need to do next.

The process.

But everything is ruined. Everything is FUCKED UP.

I take a clean knife and make a swift cut to my forearm. Blood erupts over the spider's web of scars. This is the only way I can calm myself. The pain soothes me and my anger slips away.

I bandage myself up, then I'm ready to get on with my work.

The skin in my hands is the scalp with the spider's web tattoo. It's slippery at this stage, a little rubbery, and my fingers glide across the surface as I move it around the board to inspect it, inch by inch. I love the feel of it under my fingertips, soft and pliant, wet. I should be wearing gloves – it's just come out of a vat of sharpening agents. The hair and fat that cling to it are partially dissolved and its own stink is masked by the strong smells of the sodium sulphide and sodium hydroxide. Later, I'll pay the price for not wearing gloves. My hands will be red and sore, the skin will be dry and cracked. But I deserve the pain.

My task for tonight is to clean the skin, to clear away any hair that's left and remove any grease so it's ready for tanning. A lot of the hair is already gone but there is always a slight fuzz clinging to the surface at the end of the liming process. I remove it by 'scudding' – scraping it with a blunted knife. It's a delicate operation. There's a huge risk of grazing or nicking the skin, which could ruin the whole piece. Concentration is everything. I can't let it wander for a moment, which is why I find the process so therapeutic. No other thoughts intrude, so it will give me time to calm down.

I try to lose myself in the process but my mind won't settle.

I can hear that woman screaming, over and over. 'He's dead,' she kept shouting. 'He's dead.' He wasn't dead then, not by a long shot, and I watched from a doorway a little way up the street as the police and ambulance arrived. I saw them carry him out with an oxygen mask over his face and blood on their scrubs. He's not dead and that might be good for me, or it might be bad.

Damn! Damn! Damn!

That should never have happened. I despise that couple. Prepared to fuck in the streets like animals, so overcome with lust and alcohol. They stank of it.

No! Is that a small graze on the skin? I need to focus my mind on what I'm doing or I'll ruin the job.

I can't tell the Collector what happened. Not yet. I know I must. I know it will be in the newspapers that a fresh attack by the Tattoo Thief has been foiled. That's what they've started to call me in the press. The Tattoo Thief. The whole city is living in fear of my knife. But I'm nearly done. Just a few more names on my list and then I'll sink away into obscurity again, having made my mark and provided the Collector with his heart's desire.

It's a good thing Dan Carter is still alive, on balance. I think it's safe to assume that he didn't have any useful information to give to the police. And once he's out of hospital, I can take a second shot at him.

His name is still on my list.

35

Marni

It didn't take long to realise that the reason Francis Sullivan had invited her along on the trip to Guildford was for her car. He arrived at her house on foot the next morning and explained that his car belonged to the force and that he'd be breaking rules if he used it for such an irregular outing.

'Just as well I haven't lent mine to Alex then, isn't it?' she said, grabbing her keys off the kitchen counter.

Francis didn't seem to appreciate her left-hand-drive Citroën Deux Chevaux or her scrappy driving style. Either way, he was a bad passenger. They'd hardly pulled out of Great College Street when Marni noticed his white-knuckled grip on the edge of his seat. The engine was noisy and the suspension close to non-existent, but Marni had brought the car back from France with her when she and Thierry had moved to England. The memories of driving it down tree-lined country roads, with Thierry singing along to the radio and a picnic on the back seat, were the only happy memories of France she had, and she was determined to drive it for as long as she could.

'This car is on its last legs,' said Francis. 'Are you sure it's safe?'

'Perfectly,' said Marni. She changed the subject with a grin. 'Last night was good, wasn't it?'

Francis's head whipped round to look at her.

'Finding the tattoo artist, remember?' *Did he think she was referring to the almost-kiss?*

Francis stared out of the window, but she could see his cheeks were burning.

It was raining heavily in Guildford when they arrived, and when they located the tattoo studio ten minutes later, Marni was less than thrilled to see a double yellow line outside it.

'We'll find a car park,' said Francis, as she was about to park illegally.

'You're police. Surely you can sanction parking on a double yellow for the sake of a murder investigation.'

Francis swiped a glance across at her. 'No. Being in the police doesn't mean you get to break the law at will.'

'Parking on a yellow line?'

'I might get away with it in an emergency. But this isn't an emergency, Marni.'

'I think it is. There's a killer on the loose.'

Francis ignored her, pointing to the entrance of a high-rise car park. Marni grumpily pulled into a space. A ten-minute walk through the rain, which could have been avoided if he hadn't been such a stiff. Most of the policemen she'd ever come across wouldn't have thought twice about parking on a double yellow.

She was even more annoyed when they discovered the tattoo parlour wasn't open yet. They stood glumly in the rain, peering in through the windows. It was a nice-looking place, with all the tattooing gear neatly lined up in ordered rows. Marni never trusted an untidy studio. An untidy tattooist might be sloppy about hygiene, too.

Francis banged on the glass door and then rang a bell next to it several times.

'Try phoning,' said Marni. There was a phone number stencilled on the door glass.

As he dialled, a door opened on the left-hand side of the shopfront and a man's head appeared in the gap. He'd obviously just woken up. The hand that held the door open was tattooed with Polynesian banding.

'Man, we're shut. Come back in the afternoon.' He had an Australian accent.

'Are you James Diamond?' said Marni.

'Sure am.'

'I'm Marni Mullins.' She stepped towards him.

He opened the door wider to reveal that he was just wearing a T-shirt and boxer shorts. His arms and legs were covered with black ink.

'I know your work – great stuff. Hi.'

'And this is DI Francis Sullivan.'

Francis stepped forward.

'I'm investigating the recent murders in Brighton,' he said.

Diamond's eyes widened. 'The Tattoo Thief?'

'Yes. Can we come in and talk to you for a minute?'

'Listen, mate, I've got nothing to do with any of that.'

'You're not a suspect,' said Marni quickly. 'We just want to ask you about a picture from the convention. We're trying to identify someone.'

Diamond breathed an audible sigh of relief. 'Sure. Let me get dressed and we can talk in the studio.'

He reappeared at the shop door two minutes later in jeans and a fresh T-shirt. They followed him inside and Marni looked round. It was easy to guess Diamond's speciality – it was like stepping into a 1950s tiki lounge, with rattan furniture and Pacific Island decor on the walls. Polynesian masks stared down at them, and there was a flash gallery of tribal designs along one end of the shop.

They showed him the picture and he stared thoughtfully at it for a couple of minutes.

Marni watched Francis, who was looking round the studio

with more interest than she would have credited him for. She wondered if he was starting to get it. Maybe, with a little bit more time, she could persuade him to get a tattoo himself. She wondered what he would choose if he ever did.

'Yeah, I remember this one. A bit weird actually.'

'How so?' said Francis.

'Twitchy, not at all talkative while I was tattooing.'

'What did you tattoo?' said Marni.

'It was a symbol I'd never seen before. Brought it in, hand-drawn on a scrap of paper. I don't know what its significance was.'

'Do you keep records?'

James shook his head. 'Not for walk-ups at a convention. You just do the tattoo and take the cash.'

'So no name?' said Francis.

Diamond thought for a minute. 'Sam. Sam Kirby or Corby, I think. Mentioned living out of town on Ditchling Road, on a farm . . .' He tailed off with a shrug.

Francis was almost bursting with excitement as they walked back to the car park.

'Finally. Finally, we've got ourselves a decent lead.'

'You really think this could be our man?'

'God knows.' He glanced upwards apologetically. 'It's probably not his real name, if he was planning to do a runner from the start. And Ditchling Road goes for miles. He might have moved. It might not even be the guy we're looking for – so if we do find him, he could have rock solid alibis. But at least the case is moving and we've got something to do.'

He pulled his mobile out of his pocket.

'Angie, can you check a name for me against addresses in Ditchling Road . . .'

A shiver ran up Marni's spine. The game was afoot and she'd be damned if they'd let this killer strike against her community again.

36

Marni

Ditchling Road originated in the city centre and ran north for eight miles to the village of Ditchling. Beyond the city's edge, it climbed steeply into the rolling countryside of the South Downs, where Victorian villas were replaced with fields and farmhouses.

As they drove back from Guildford, Angie Burton called Francis back.

'No, don't mention it to Rory. This is strictly off the books.'

Marni strained to hear what Angie was saying on the other end of the line, but she couldn't make it out.

'But you got something? Good. Right. Thanks, Angie, I'll owe you a favour . . . All right, a drink then.'

'Got an address?' said Marni.

'Yes. You'd better take me back to the station. I can't turn up looking for a suspect with a civilian in tow.'

'But we can go straight down Ditchling Road on the way back to Brighton.'

'Marni, it wouldn't be professional. If you were on the scene it could jeopardise the case. And if we ran into the killer . . . No way. It's not an option. I'm not putting you in danger.'

'I'll stay in the car. But you can't waste time. What if Diamond actually does know Sam Kirby or Corby and phones him a warning? He could get away.'

'Kirby,' said Francis. 'Angie found an address for a Sam Kirby.'

He went quiet for a moment, then he twisted in his seat to face her. She gave him a sideways glance.

'All right, we'll give the property a drive by, check out the lie of the land. If it looks like there might be someone at the address, I'll call Rory to bring backup so we can make an arrest. But whatever happens, you'll stay in the car.'

'I'll stay in the car.'

For sure. She would definitely stay in the car.

They drove back from Guildford choosing a different route that brought them to the village of Ditchling. The road that lay between them was Ditchling Road, winding across the farmlands and heathlands of the South Downs.

'What's the house number?' said Marni, as they left Ditchling village behind them.

Francis laughed. 'They don't have house numbers out here. It's a farm. Stone Acre Farm we're looking for.'

The houses became sparser as they climbed toward the Ditchling Beacon, the third highest point on the Downs. The road wound its way up the wooded slope until they came out at the peak. The long descent into Brighton lay ahead of them, and Marni could see a number of farmhouses set back from the road on either side.

They passed a couple of houses that didn't seem to have names, but certainly didn't look as if they qualified as farms. The next was an obvious farmyard and had a sign – High Croft Farm.

'Pull in here,' said Francis. 'I'm going to ask where Stone Acre Farm is.'

An old man crossing the farmyard with his dog stopped to see what they wanted.

'You're looking for Stone Acre? It's the next farm down. That's Tom Abbot's old place.'

'Do you know Sam Kirby?' said Francis.

'No, never heard of the bloke. But Tom's kids have been renting the place out since Tom died. I took the fields off 'em but they've had several different tenants in the farmhouse these past few years. Go on two hundred yards, take the track off to the right, then follow it for a quarter or so of a mile. Can't miss it.'

They followed his directions and at the head of the track was a wooden sign that read Stone Acre Farm. The paint was split and peeling, and the signpost stuck out of the verge at an angle. It was evident, as they drew into the yard of Stone Acre Farm, that the place was no longer operational. The slumping gate was propped open and weeds had invaded cracks in the concrete surface of the yard. The farmhouse garden was overgrown and the scattering of outbuildings all looked in need of repair. There was no car on the hard standing next to the house, no open windows and, frankly, no sign that anyone lived there at all.

As Francis got out of the car, Marni stayed seated. She wound down her window. The farmyard was silent – the noise of traffic on Ditchling Road was muffled by a dense copse, and in the lee of the hill, the wind hardly made a sound. Her skin crawled. Something seemed off. It was a feeling she knew well enough not to ignore, so she felt happy to be confined to the Deux Chevaux. A single raindrop hit the windscreen and then the heavens opened.

Between the creaky sweep of the windscreen wipers, she watched Francis stride across the concrete yard to the covered porch of the farmhouse. He pulled on a wrought iron bell pull and Marni heard a distant clang. The whole place reminded her of Cold Comfort Farm.

There was no one at the house, or at least no one answered his ring. Ignoring the rain, Francis came back to the car and stood by Marni's open window. He pulled out his phone.

'Rory? I'm at Stone Acre Farm, a mile on the Brighton side of the Beacon.' He listened for a moment. 'No, nothing to speak of. But I think you should get the team up here. I'll call you when I've got more.'

He strode off across the yard in the direction of three near-derelict outbuildings. Marni watched him with slow dread seeping through her capillaries.

He disappeared into the first of the structures, a corrugated iron lean-to on the side of the far larger barn. As he disappeared from her view, Marni felt increasingly nervous. She looked around the car for something she could use as a weapon, should the need arise. There was nothing on the back seat, but she remembered there was a wrench in the boot.

As she got out of the car to fetch it, Francis reappeared and gave her a questioning look.

'This place is creepy,' she said, opening the boot.

'Stay in the car,' he said. 'There's nothing here. I'll be done in a moment.'

Marni grabbed the wrench and climbed back into the driver's seat. She felt reassured with the heavy metal balanced across her lap.

Francis circumnavigated the main barn looking for an entrance, sniffing the air.

'Something, somewhere round here, really stinks,' he called out to her.

Marni stuck her head out of the window and inhaled. The rain must have dampened down the farmyard smells, but there was still a tang in the air that caught at the back of her throat.

'We're on a farm,' she said.

He came a few steps towards the car. 'With no animals.'

'A dead animal?'

'Maybe. But something else. Chemicals of some kind.'

234

He disappeared round the side of the barn but reappeared almost immediately.

'The barn door's locked. Shiny new padlock.'

'You'll need a warrant, won't you?' said Marni.

The tone of his voice had suggested he'd rather not wait. However, the law-abiding side of him won over and he spent ten minutes on the phone to Bradshaw explaining what he was doing there and convincing him to apply for a warrant.

Rory arrived with a couple of PCs, whom he instructed to make a safe perimeter around the area. Francis got out of the car to talk to him. Marni listened through the open window.

'What the fuck is she doing here?' Rory said, on seeing her, sitting behind the wheel of the Deux Chevaux.

'She was with me when I found Kirby's name and address,' said Francis. 'I wasn't going to waste time taking her back to Brighton first. She'll stay in the car.'

'Jesus wept,' said Rory. 'First rule of policing – no civilians on crime scenes. If you allow her to contaminate the scene, we could lose the case.'

Francis wasn't interested. 'She's an expert witness now. And, like I said, she'll stay in the car.'

Expert witness? Bugger that!

Not for the first time, Marni regretted the moment she'd laid eyes on Evan Armstrong's body, not to mention her subsequent call to the police.

It took a further hour for Hitchins to deliver the warrant. Tension ran high between the two policemen, and Rory sat on the cramped back seat of the Deux Chevaux, poisoning the air with resentment at being forced to smoke his e-cig outside in the rain.

Hitchins had been instructed to bring bolt cutters. Francis and Rory took them and all three disappeared around the barn, leaving Marni once again alone in the car. Only this time, she'd had enough. She opened the driver's door, willing the hinges not to squeak, and, still clutching the wrench, scurried to the corner of the barn and looked round it. As she watched, Rory made short work of the padlock and the door swung open with a low hiss. Francis led the way inside, followed by the other two.

Forgetting her curfew, Marni hurried after them. As she caught up, she heard Rory's gasp of shock, and when Francis reappeared in the doorway, she could read fear in his eyes.

'Go back to the car, Marni,' he said on seeing her. There was a tremor in his voice.

As she continued towards him, Rory appeared at his side. He understood Marni's intent and stepped forward with his arms outstretched.

'This is a crime scene,' he said, blocking her path.

She needed to see what they had found. She tried to look beyond him, through the doorway, but she was overwhelmed by a wall of putrid air.

It was the smell of death.

The smell of death, and of something far worse.

37

Francis

Never had Francis been so relieved to step away from a crime scene. The overpowering stench as they opened the door had told him enough – and he pulled Rory back straight away. Three minutes later, appropriately kitted out in white suits, overshoes and masks, they were as ready as they could be.

Francis took an experimental breath as they reached the open door. He'd pasted the inside of his mask with Vapo-Rub. The fumes were stinging his eyes and each breath he took in carried the sharp cut of menthol. Having done the same, Rory was coughing and there were tears running down his cheeks, saturating the top edge of his mask.

'Right, let's do it,' said Francis.

He faltered on the threshold, feeling both dread and compulsion over what they were about to find. Rory crowded behind him, forcing him to take the plunge.

There was a switch just to the right of the door and he flicked it with a gloved hand. Strip lights, suspended from a joisted ceiling, flooded the space with a harsh white glare. It was instantly apparent that the inside of the building had been renovated, even if the outside hadn't.

Francis glanced around the cavernous space. The first thing that snagged his attention was a row of white plastic fifty-litre barrels that lined the left-hand wall of the barn. Then he noticed that the walls were covered in blown-up images of tattoos. *What the hell had been going on in here?* He hardly dared walk across the smooth concrete floor towards the barrels. As he came closer he could see that each was full to the brim with liquid. Here was the source of the putrid smells. He could barely breathe and he knew without looking what they would contain.

'Jesus,' said Rory, following him in. 'I know what this is. Took Liz and the kids to Marrakesh last year and got taken round the tanneries. Stank just like this.'

'Someone's curing leather?' said Francis.

He fought against the impulse to head straight for the door and drive away from the hellish place as fast as he could.

Instead, he edged forward and forced himself to look inside the first bin. Below the surface of the dark liquid, he could see pale shapes drifting, like dying fish in polluted water. One of them slowly twisted to reveal the dark outlines of a tattoo on its other side. Bile rose in his throat and he had to look away.

'He's curing human skin,' he said, as everything fell into place – why the killer was taking tattoos, what he was doing with them afterwards.

Rory stood next to him. 'Oh, fuck.'

With gritted teeth, Francis looked along the remaining barrels. There were different liquids in them but not all of them contained tracts of skin. It was hard to tell which of the barrels was the culprit for the smell, or if it was a combination of the fumes. The SOCOs would send all of them for chemical analysis, but the precise nature of the chemicals hardly mattered. The crime was obvious.

Francis turned away, sickened. There was a workbench along the opposite wall, cluttered with bottles and vials of unnamed chemicals, wooden boards with dark stains, a knife block and a container of assorted surgical instruments. A cardboard box of latex gloves. A row of books on taxidermy, and there was also a stuffed squirrel at one end of the bench. At the other end of the bench was a large stone sink. Francis hated to think what had been sluiced down that drain.

'Boss?'

'Yes?'

Rory was at the far end of the workbench.

'You need to see this.'

He was pointing at a shallow dish. Francis went over.

There are things a policeman sees that can never be unseen and Francis had come across his fair share of them. But nothing like this. Crumpled in the glass dish, protected from drying out with a layer of cling film, was an orb of skin that looked like a deflated balloon. The web tattoo on it was unmistakeable, even though the skin appeared white and bloated. Rory pushed the dish with the end of his pen and the tattoo quivered like a jelly.

'We've got him, haven't we, boss?'

Francis shook his head. 'He's not here.'

Rory pulled out his phone. 'Hitchins, when SOCO arrive I want that farmhouse to be taken apart and stripped right back to its bones. I want every inch of this property to be taken to pieces. We need to have the drains inspected. Look for slurry pits, look for signs of digging or burials, and find out who the hell this person is . . .' He'd had to lower his mask to talk on the phone, so he covered his mouth with his hand to take a breath. 'Yes, overtime is authorised. Get every man that John Street can spare up here, now.'

Rory had warmed to his task as the man in charge.

After he hung up, they both gazed at the wall of tattoo images. There were pictures of the tattoos that had been taken from Evan Armstrong, Giselle Connelly and Jem Walsh. There were pictures of Dan Carter's body suit. There was a large poster from the Saatchi Gallery exhibition. And among them, there were pictures of other tattoos that Francis didn't recognise.

'Future victims or bodies we haven't discovered yet?' said Rory. 'We need Marni in here.'

'No way. Her presence will contaminate the crime scene.'

'Not if she's in here in her capacity as an expert witness.'

'No.'

'Come on, Rory. She was right about the connection between the victims and she could give us vital information on these tattoos that could well end up saving a life. I'm going to fetch her.'

Rory scowled but did nothing to stop him.

Five minutes later, Marni was standing next to him, studying the images tacked to the wall. Her face above the mask had gone pale but she'd stayed calm even when she'd realised they were in the killer's workshop. Rory had gone outside to make a call, and Francis could only guess who he was speaking to.

'These all look like tattoos by the artists from the exhibition,' she said. 'We were right with our theory.'

'Your theory,' said Francis.

Marni shrugged.

'What about these ones we've not seen before?' he continued. 'They must be his future targets. If we can identify them, we can protect them.'

Marni walked along the row of images.

'Recognise any of them?' he asked.

'I can hazard a guess at the artists – after all, we know who they are from the exhibition. But the people in these pictures . . .' She shrugged helplessly.

Rory came back in and joined them.

'Well? What can you tell us?' His tone verged on aggressive.

Marni ignored him and continued looking at the images.

'There are more tattoos here than there are artists,' said Francis. 'He seems to be giving himself choices.'

'I expect some of them are easier to track down than others,' said Marni. She was looking at a full leg sleeve, the woman's image cropped to show no more of her body. 'This one's definitely by Iwao. It's the Japanese mythology he specialises in.'

'And this one?' said Francis, pointing to a man's back. The tattoo was black and grey, showing the fall of Lucifer.

Marni looked at it and looked away.

'Sorry,' she said. 'I can't breathe through this mask.'

She looked shaky on her feet.

'This is a beauty,' said Rory, on his return.

Marni and Francis turned in his direction. He was pointing at a picture of a woman's back piece, Japanese in style, featuring a pair of fiery orange koi carp in a pool and the figure of a kneeling geisha with tears falling from her face into the water. The branch of a maple tree arced across the top left corner, shedding its distinctive leaves across the scene.

'Iwao again?' hazarded Francis.

'Frank, I think I'm going to faint.'

He only just caught her.

xii

I have a sense of foreboding. It nags at me all the way up Ditchling Road. I trust these intuitions – I'm very attuned to disturbances in my equilibrium. Recent events have taken a toll on my psyche. I have to recognise that. What happened in East Street knocked me off balance. I need time alone with my skins to ground myself.

I can't shake off the feeling that something's wrong.

Because something is wrong. A car pulls out from my lane and I'm immediately suspicious. A silver Mitsubishi. The only vehicle, other than my own, that ever comes down the track is the post van. I slow down as it passes me in the opposite direction.

I know the driver. It's one of the plods who was at Evan Armstrong's funeral. And I know the passenger. It's Marni Mullins. What the hell were they doing on my property?

I drive straight past the farm and on towards the Beacon. My hands are shaking. I need one of my pills, so I pull into the Beacon's parking area.

Switch off the engine.

Breathe.

Lean forward and rest my head on the horn to cover the howl of rage I can no longer contain.

When I feel better, I take my binoculars from the glove compartment and a knife from my pack. A fifteen-minute walk through the *fields brings me to the boundary of the farm. From the top field, I can see down into the yard. There are more cars, some of them police cars, some unmarked. A van. And people, swarming over my property. Coming in and out of the house. Emerging from the barn.*

I feel like something inside me has been ripped away. And I can't even begin to think of how I can tell the Collector.

And there's the man who's done this to me. The red-haired policeman, standing in the middle of it all, giving out directions and feeding on the information. Like a spider in the centre of his web. I know him. I know what he wants. But he isn't going to have it. I won't be caught so easily. My work is too important to allow a little man like that to interrupt it.

My blood sings for vengeance.

38

Rory

How dare he? Sullivan was acting as if he was in charge again. He should have kicked him off the site as soon as backup had arrived. Him *and* Marni Mullins. Instead, he'd allowed Mullins into the crime scene, and she'd passed out. After which he'd lost Hollins for a couple of hours as someone had had to drive her home. What a screw-up. And letting Sullivan and Mullins have the information that had led them to Diamond and Stone Acre Farm had been another screw-up. There was no doubt in Rory's mind now that Sam Kirby was the man they were looking for and they'd broken the case. They had enough evidence in that barn to put him away for life. Somehow, he'd have to make sure he took the credit for the discovery, along with Bradshaw.

Rose Lewis arrived and parked her van at the entrance of the yard, and Francis and Rory went out to meet her. The yard itself was now counted as part of the crime scene and the SOCO boys and girls would be all over it in a minute. They led Rose into the barn, waiting in silence for a few minutes as she took in the enormity of the find. One of her SOCOs slowly circumnavigated the barn, taking multiple photos of the vats and the workbench.

'He's processing leather here, right?' said Francis, when Rose finally signalled she was ready to talk.

'There are more steps to the process than people would imagine,' Rose said. 'Most of them involve soaking the skin in a variety of chemicals – to remove the fat and hair, to neutralise the pH, to cleanse it of previous chemicals, to stabilise the proteins in the skin . . .'

'How long do all of them take?' said Francis.

'It depends on the chemicals and the quality of the skin being tanned. Anything from a few hours to several days.'

'And the process is the same for human skin as it is for leather?'

Rory grimaced. The whole subject matter was making him feel sick.

'Of course. There's no difference between human skin and animal skin as far as processing is concerned. I expect you'd need to treat it in a similar way to pigskin.'

'How many of the tattoos do we have here?' asked Rory. Anything to change the subject.

'Definitely Jem Walsh's scalp but no sign of Giselle's arm or Evan's tattoo,' said Francis. 'However, the search is by no means over.'

A SOCO came over and beckoned Rose.

'Excuse me,' she said and ducked away with him.

'What's your next move?' said Francis to Rory.

'We've got to locate Kirby and get him into custody. We've got plenty of evidence for an arrest warrant and I've already been onto the station to put out an APW for him. Angie Burton's trying to find a picture of him to circulate.'

Now Sullivan would learn how an experienced cop handled things.

'Do you think he'll attempt another kill?' said Rose, coming back to them.

Francis looked across at the wall of images. 'He definitely seems to be targeting work by the Saatchi artists. However, once he realises we're here, he'll more than likely go to ground. In the meantime, you'll need to identify every individual in these pictures and offer them protection.' He was looking at Rory. 'Maybe get Hollins to make contact with each of the tattoo artists in question and see if they can tell us who the pictures are of.'

Trying to take over again.

'Already spoke to Hitchins about that.' Rory made a mental note to do it ASAP. 'Have you been inside the house yet?' he added.

Francis shook his head. 'Not yet.'

The inside of the farmhouse was crawling with SOCOs taking pictures and dusting for fingerprints. A white-suited sergeant came over to Francis and Rory as they stepped into the hall.

'Nothing in here so far that obviously connects with the crimes,' he said. 'But there's very definitely someone currently living here. Remains of breakfast in the kitchen which could only be this morning's. Paperwork we've found so far all relates to one Sam Kirby. Seems he pays the bills, has his bank statements sent here.'

'Thank you, Officer. Found a diary or a calendar yet?'

The SOCO shook his head and went back to his duties.

'I wonder where he is,' said Francis. 'Looks like we were unlucky to have missed him.'

'I think you mean lucky,' said Rory. 'Remember, you and Marni arrived on your own with no backup. Incredibly irresponsible. He could have answered the door with a knife in his hand.'

'Well, he's not going to come home now, with all this going on.'

'Sir, sir!' A uniformed policeman burst through the front door.

'What?' said Rory.

'A man's been spotted up at the far end of one of the fields. Looks as if he's watching the property.'

'Come on,' said Francis, heading straight for the door. 'It could be him.'

'Unlikely,' said Rory. But he wasn't going to miss the chase.

The PC led them out of the house and diagonally across the yard. He pointed over the fields that sloped upwards in the direction of the Beacon and immediately a tall man in dark clothing broke cover and started running awkwardly up the hill, away from them.

'Idiot,' muttered Francis. 'Now he knows we saw him.'

He set off at a run up the side of a ploughed field in the direction of the man. Rory followed but he had a decade-and-a-half, plus forty pounds, on Francis, so there was no hope of keeping up. And he detested running up hills. He could feel his chest tightening after the first fifteen metres.

Francis was widening the gap between them, but not making any ground on their quarry. He reached the top corner of the field and Rory saw him looking about for a way over the hedgerow. There was no gate or stile – that was at the opposite corner – and as Francis made a couple of abortive attempts to clamber over the barrier, the man who'd been watching them disappeared over the brow of the hill.

'Damn it!' Francis pulled out his phone. 'No fucking signal up here,' he stormed, as Rory finally reached him.

Rory bent double with his hands on his knees, panting loudly.

'Looks like you need a fitness assessment,' said Francis shortly, heading off back down the hill.

Rory remained where he was for a moment, swearing silently as he waited for his breath to return. There was something glinting at the bottom of the hedgerow.

'Wait.'

Francis turned back. Rory traversed the shallow ditch at the bottom of the hedge and reached his hand through. His fingers grasped on cold metal, something sharp.

'Ow!'

He pulled his hand back and looked at what he held. It was

a knife, the blade so sharp it had cut his index finger across the middle joint on contact. Blood was dripping down onto the handle.

'Nice work,' said Francis.

'Thanks,' said Rory.

Francis pulled an evidence bag from the pocket of his SOCO suit and held it out. Rory deposited the knife gently inside the bag.

'That wasn't a fucking compliment. You've just contaminated what might be the most important piece of evidence we have.'

39

Francis

Petrol station flowers wouldn't be the thing, but Francis didn't want to arrive empty-handed. He'd taken Marni into a distressing crime scene and now he was going to disrupt her evening by asking her to look at pictures of it. He settled on vodka. She'd mentioned a favourite brand once and he'd be able to pick it up at the Asda superstore on his way back into the city from Ditchling.

The SOCOs had just about wrapped up for the day, though they'd be back in the morning. He'd arranged an overnight watch on the property in case Sam Kirby decided to return and spoke to Rose from the car. She was now back in the cool, calm ice palace of the morgue, examining Jem Walsh's part-cured tattoo and a number of other pieces of tattooed skin they'd retrieved from the various barrels of chemicals. She'd already sent tissue samples off for DNA analysis, but there was no doubt in either of their minds that what they had found was Jem Welsh's scalp. They'd also discovered what was presumably his flayed head – red and raw with open, staring eyes – in the freezer.

'Keep me posted with whatever you find,' he said to Rose and hung up, pulling into an empty space a few metres down the road from Marni's house.

Rory had been on and off the phone to Bradshaw for most of the afternoon and, from what Francis could gather, the chief had actually sounded pleased with the case's progress.

'He thinks it's a shame you didn't wait for the bastard to get home before you went in,' Rory reported, with a wry grin.

'There was no way for us to know when we approached the house whether he was in or not,' Francis had replied.

Typical bloody Bradshaw.

There was no answer when he tried Marni's door, even though he could see lights on upstairs. He dialled her number.

'Hello?'

'I'm at your door.'

'I've got the house to myself and I'm in the bath, Inspector. Go away.'

'Marni, I wouldn't be here if it wasn't important. I'll wait.'

Ten minutes later she opened the door and ushered him inside. She was bundled in a thick tapestry robe and her hair was gathered up in a damp ponytail. She smelled of sweet-scented bath oil.

'I'm sorry,' he said, as he followed her through to the kitchen. 'I shouldn't have taken you inside that barn today.'

She shook her head vehemently. 'It's fine. It was more the mask over my face that was the problem than what you were showing me. I get claustrophobic and I couldn't breathe.'

'I brought you this.' He held out his peace offering and her eyes lit up.

'Now you're absolutely forgiven. I was going to offer you wine, but after today's experience maybe a couple of shots would be in order.'

Francis generally tried to avoid spirits but it had been a long day – and humouring Marni was certainly in order, seeing as he was about to ask for her help again.

'Sure, why not?'

Marni cocked an eyebrow and took two shot glasses out of a cupboard. 'Come on.'

They went through to the sitting room and Francis looked around. It was even more of a magpie's lair than her studio – a snug hippy parlour that appeared to have been imported piece by piece from Rajasthan, Kathmandu and the Inca trail. He sank into a pile of kilim cushions on the deep sofa.

Marni lit an incense stick, then filled the two shot glasses to the brim. Francis noticed a slight tremor as she poured. Maybe the scene at the farm had had more of an effect on her than she was prepared to admit. She handed him one.

'Neat?' said Francis, with a barely suppressed shudder.

'Yes, neat. But you don't have to down it in one.'

He had no intention of doing so. He took a tentative sip, expecting a harsh burn at the back of his throat, but the sensation was surprisingly smooth. Marni sipped hers, looking relieved as the alcohol hit the spot.

'I'll corrupt you yet, Frank Sullivan.'

'I think it'll take more than a vodka shot to do that.'

She became suddenly serious.

'Tell me what you discovered at Stone Acre Farm,' she said.

He filled her in on what they'd found in the barn and the evidence that was emerging from the farmhouse. She'd grown pale as he described the various vats and their grisly contents. He noticed her hand shaking as she poured herself another drink.

'It seems that Sam Kirby was watching us work. One of the PCs spotted a man in a field above the farm.'

'Couldn't have been a farmer, by any chance?'

'Peering over the hedge with binoculars?'

'Okay, not a farmer.'

'We went after him but he got away. He did drop a knife, though.'

'Do you think you'll be able to link it to the murders?'

Francis shook his head. 'It's not likely to be admissible as evidence, because that idiot sergeant picked it up, cut himself on it and bled all over it.'

'Rory? Is he okay?'

'Put it this way, the cut is nothing compared to his embarrassment.'

Francis finished his shot in a large gulp. This time he did feel the burn, but he rather enjoyed it.

'I need your help again.'

Marni refilled his glass. 'I know,' she said. 'The pictures – the tattoos that he hasn't taken yet.'

Francis pulled his laptop out of his document case and opened it on the coffee table in front of them. He'd photographed each of the images pinned to the wall in the Tattoo Thief's barn, and now he wanted Marni to tell him which ones she recognised.

'It's a long shot,' she said. 'Even the artists who did them might not have kept records of their clients' contact details.'

'Fair enough,' said Francis. 'But we've got to find out any way we can, so we can offer these people protection. Until we've got Sam Kirby in custody, we have to assume they're in danger.'

'What are you doing to catch him?'

'Rory's just rolled out a massive manhunt. He's heading up a task force and seeing if his vehicle can be traced. It's hard to know where he'd hide, so it's just as important to find these potential victims. Unfortunately, one of them might lead us right to him.'

Marni spent the next hour poring over the pictures but she didn't know who any of them were. 'Email them to me and I'll share them round,' she said. 'Someone will know who they are.'

Francis shut his laptop and finished his shot.

'I'd best be going.'

'Have you eaten since we had breakfast?'

'No.' He hadn't really noticed it up until now but at the thought of food his stomach cramped with hunger.

'Pasta?'

Apparently pasta couldn't be consumed without red wine in the Mullins household and, though Francis did his best to decline, Marni would hear none of it.

'Where's your son?' asked Francis, sucking spaghetti through pursed lips.

'Staying at a friend's.'

'So he's not going to follow the family trade?'

'He won't even have a tattoo,' said Marni, laughing.

'No doubt he'll see sense when he's older,' said Francis wryly. 'Tell me about your family.'

Where to begin?

'I've a mother, and a sister.'

'Do they live in Brighton?'

'They both have multiple sclerosis. My mother's in a care home in Saltdean, and my sister lives in a sheltered housing scheme in Hove. It means she can keep her independence but know there's help around if necessary.'

Marni nodded. 'At least they're close enough for you to see them.'

'I don't go as often as I should.'

'And your father?'

'He's long gone.'

'I'm sorry,' said Marni, pouring him some more wine.

Francis shook his head ruefully. 'He's not dead. He left us after my sister got her diagnosis, when we were both still teenagers. Seemed like he couldn't cope with having two invalids to care for.' Despite all the years that had passed, it was a struggle for Francis to keep the bitterness out of his voice.

'Leaving you with a heavy burden?'

'They're not a burden,' Francis snapped. 'I'll always be there for them, and they're the reason why I take my job so seriously.

I want to make sure they get the very best care that's available, and that costs money.'

'I'm sorry. I didn't mean to hit a nerve. And you've been successful so far, haven't you? You're young for a DI.'

It was a hard question to answer.

'Well, a lot of people at John Street thought I was promoted above my ability. Now I've been taken off my first case, so that could be it as far as my career goes. Successful isn't quite the word I'd use.'

'But today you made a big break. Surely Bradshaw will see that.'

'Knowing who the killer is and having him in custody are two different things. He's on the run – he might simply vanish. Or he might kill himself. We need to get him into a courtroom. Anything less than that's a cock-up. And Bradshaw and Rory will be doing all they can to take the credit if it's a success.'

He didn't talk to people about his family or his job, ever. So why was he doing it now, with Marni Mullins? Exhaustion washed over him.

'Sorry to bore you with all that.'

'Other people's lives are never boring,' said Marni. 'I couldn't be a tattoo artist if I thought that.'

'People tell you things while you tattoo them?'

'Always. It's almost a form of therapy for some people.'

'Did you tattoo people in prison?'

She looked shocked by the question.

'Sorry. I shouldn't pry.'

'No, it's fine,' she said. Then she shook her head. 'No, I didn't tattoo anyone in prison. I was in no fit state. I couldn't cope and the other women in there treated me like a pariah. I was the English bitch who'd stabbed a Frenchman – no one ever bothered to ask why, or what had happened. They made their own minds up.'

'How long you were there for?'

'It wasn't long – just a few weeks. I was in the late stages of pregnancy with twins.'

Francis was appalled. 'They sent you to prison when you were about to have twins?'

'The judge wasn't a particularly sympathetic man.'

'You knew you were having a multiple birth?' She'd mentioned the fact that she'd lost a child, but Francis was shocked to learn that it had been one of twins.

She nodded. 'I was attacked in the shower block, and I miscarried one of the babies. They moved me to a hospital to monitor the remainder of my pregnancy. By the time Alex was born, I'd served most of my sentence and a judge released me.' She fell silent for a moment. 'It was a bad time.'

'I'm sorry,' said Francis again.

The conversation lapsed. Francis tried to think of a way of changing the subject without it seeming contrived. Marni fidgeted with a paper napkin.

'Have you . . .?'

'Did you know . . .?'

They both started talking at once, then stopped again.

'You go,' said Francis.

Marni shook her head. 'No, you.'

But Francis had forgotten what he was about to say.

'Look, I'd better be going. Thank you for the food and the wine.'

He stood up and made a move to pick up the empty supper plates. His leg caught on the corner of the coffee table and he staggered slightly.

'Whoa!' Marni steadied him with an arm and they stood facing each other.

Francis grinned. 'I think I'm a little bit drunk.'

'I think you're a lot drunk, Frank.'

'Don't call me Frank.' He studied the face in front of him, realising for the first time how much he liked it. 'I'm sorry. I don't usually drink, so I haven't a head for it.'

'That's fine,' she said. 'But you can't drive. I think you'd better stay here.'

It seemed like a good idea to Francis. Such a good idea that he thought he'd better kiss her.

So he did. She kissed him back. To Francis, it seemed like the start of something.

Something good.

xiii

When my father used to get angry with me, I hated him for it. When I was young, it was my school work. As I got older, it was the decisions I made. When I started working for him at the family firm, I couldn't do anything right. 'You sent out the wrong order.' 'You used the wrong leather.' 'That colour you chose for that bag is disgusting.' The more often it happened, the more my feelings of love turned into something else, hard-edged and bitter, until that was all that was left.

Now the Collector's angry with me. I had to tell him what happened and, over the phone, I could hear first the disappointment in his voice and then something with a harder edge. I could picture his frown, his sneer, and I wanted to disappear or turn back the clock. Of course, with the Collector, it's different. He has a right to be angry with me. I've made mistakes that are unforgivable and now Jem Walsh died for nothing. His precious scalp is simply a piece of evidence with a number, instead of a beautiful work of art.

Francis Sullivan is the name of the policeman who's to blame. I watched his press conference on the television. I watched him trespassing on my property, contaminating the only place where I feel safe, and then running up the hill behind me. He's ruining everything I've worked for.

He'll regret it, I'll make certain of that.

Seeing his car outside Marni Mullins' house feeds my anger. What was she doing at Stone Acre with the police? Why's he with her now?

I'll sit and wait until he leaves.

But the lights have gone off downstairs and he still hasn't left.

I can hear laughter through an open window. Her laughter.

I can wait.

The lights have gone off upstairs.

I have to wait. I have no choice. But my anger burns bright and soon I will have to act.

40

Francis

Francis pulled the duvet cover over his face. Why did his bed smell different, perfumed? Still under the protection of the covers, he opened his eyes. He was in his boxer shorts. This wasn't his bed. He didn't recognise the sheets.

Something thudded onto the end of the bed and scrabbled across the duvet. Francis sat up in a hurry and found himself face-to-face with Pepper. The dog barked excitedly and started to lick his cheek.

It all flooded back. The vodka shots, the pasta, the red wine. Kissing Marni.

Why had he thought drinking vodka was a good idea?

He pushed Pepper away and checked his watch. Damn. He should be in the office by now and he would need to go home first for a change of clothes. Pepper renewed his attack and the pains in his head migrated to the back of his skull.

He lay back down with a groan. Wine and vodka? It wasn't like he'd never had a hangover before. Of course he had. But today wasn't the day for one. It wasn't even the week for one.

'You awake, Frank?'

He opened his eyes to see Marni drifting into the bedroom from the en suite. She was naked, coming towards the bed as if she had every intention of climbing back into it. There were parts of last night that seemed a blank, but surely if anything else had happened between them, he'd remember it? All he could think of was that long, lingering kiss. Nothing else.

Marni sat down at the end of the bed, facing him, and he tried to look anywhere but at her breasts. He failed miserably. They were beautiful and they were causing significant stirrings under the duvet. He opened his mouth to speak, but before he could think of anything to say, the doorbell rang.

'At this hour?' said Marni. She stood up and headed for the bedroom door where a couple of robes hung on a hook.

Frank couldn't take his eyes off her. Not because she was stark naked, though that was obviously reason enough. Not because he wanted to see where she was going. That was clear enough too. But because, when she turned her back to him, he saw her back piece for the first time. Of course, he knew she had a back piece by Iwao, but he'd never thought to ask to see it. Her tattoos were none of his business.

Only this one was.

He recognised it in an instant and his heart stood still.

He'd seen it before. In the killer's barn.

Marni Mullins was a target.

Marni Mullins was on the killer's list.

The tattoo on Marni's back was in one of the images the Tattoo Thief had pinned up on the wall – the orange and gold koi carp twisting in the swirling blue and green waters of the pond, and the crying geisha in her scarlet kimono and black obi. Only in life, moving sinuously as Marni walked across the room, it was much more spectacular than the flat image he had seen.

The killer was still at large and he wanted to take the tattoo off Marni's back.

'Marni …'

'Just let me deal with whoever's at the door. Then I'll get us some coffee.'

Francis fought to stay calm.

She pulled on the tapestry robe she'd been wearing the evening before and he heard the stairs creaking as she went down.

Recovering himself, he looked around the bedroom and saw his clothes in a crumpled heap near the window. Ignoring the pounding in his skull, he swung his legs from the bed to the floor and gingerly stood up. The room spun and then stabilised as he steadied himself with deep breathing. When he was able to, he went over to the pile of clothes and dug his mobile phone out of his trouser pocket.

It took him three attempts to get his passcode right but then he was in. He pulled up the images he'd taken the day before at Stone Acre. Yes, he was right. The living tattoo he'd just seen on Marni's back was on the killer's list. No wonder she'd fainted when she'd seen the picture on the Tattoo Thief's wall. How could he have been such an idiot not to realise? And why the hell hadn't she told him? At the thought of Marni in danger, a wave of anxiety washed through him.

He dialled Rory. She needed round-the-clock protection, from now on until they had the killer in custody. There was no answer.

His brain was working in slow motion today. He bolted from the room, trying to remember frantically where the staircase was. Pepper started to bark and charged after him, weaving between his legs to make every step hazardous.

'Marni! Marni, wait! Don't answer the door.'

He took the stairs two at a time, Pepper tumbling down under his feet.

'It could be the killer . . .'

But he was too late. Her hand was on the latch and she pulled open the door before the word 'killer' had left his lips.

Thierry Mullins, clutching a bag of croissants and two take-away coffees, was standing on the step. He looked them both up

263

and down, registering the fact that Francis was only in his shorts. Then he looked Marni squarely in the eye.

'*Qu'est-ce qu'il fait ici, lui?*'

Pepper positioned himself in front of Francis, a low growl rumbling through his chest.

41

Marni

Marni looked from one man to the other. Francis looked as if he'd seen a ghost. He was out of breath and staggered against the hall wall. What the hell was wrong with him? Thierry wore an expression of murderous intent, but Francis wasn't afraid of him surely. Before anyone could speak, Alex pushed past his father into the hallway. Pepper rushed up to him, tail wagging and panting.

'Hey, Mum,' he said, planting a kiss on her cheek.

God, this wasn't embarrassing at all, to have your teenage son marching through a stand-off between your ex-husband and the man who'd just spent the night in your bed. She wanted to say 'No, I didn't sleep with him', but that would hardly be appropriate.

'Hi, darling,' she said, hugging him. 'How was your stay?'

What else could she say?

Alex stepped back and looked at her incredulously. Then he looked from Thierry to Francis and back to Marni.

'Mum?' In a single word, he asked every question she didn't want to answer.

No one spoke. It was awkward. Beyond awkward.

Alex's expression flitted between angry and confused. 'Come on, Pepper. Let's get the hell out of Dodge.'

He dropped a bulging backpack onto the hall floor and took the coffee and the croissants from his father's hands. A slavering Pepper followed him in the direction of the kitchen.

Thierry was scowling at Francis with a look Marni knew all too well, his brows lowered, and he was biting his lip against the release of a string of French invective. Francis inched backwards into the darker recess of the hall, but she could see his cheeks were flaming.

Thierry raised himself up to his full height so he could look down on Francis.

'This is how you protect my wife from the Tattoo Thief? In her bed? Is that what you call close protection?'

Finally he was getting a taste of his own medicine.

'Ex-wife,' said Marni. 'Which means who I sleep with is none of your goddamn business.'

But she regretted the words the moment they were out of her mouth. She knew Thierry's temper. He'd always been a jealous man, and even though they were divorced, he clung to the contention that, as a Catholic, he would forever be her husband. When it suited him. She could literally hear him grinding his teeth.

'You have a son to think of, too.'

When he pushed past her into the hall, however, it was a step too far.

'Thierry!'

He was squaring up in front of Francis, his fists already clenched. Francis, in just his shorts, was at a distinct psychological disadvantage, let alone the physical disadvantage in terms of height and weight.

'I suggest you leave my house now, or I'll kick you out,' said Thierry.

'It's not your house,' said Marni, furious.

She tugged on Thierry's shoulder but he shook her off as if she were a minor irritation.

Francis had raised his arms into a defensive position. He looked like a poster boy for the Queensberry Rules and Marni could see that it was never going to be an even fight. Thierry had always played dirty and he hated the police almost as much as she did.

'Stop this now,' she roared.

'You're not an occupant of the house and, as a police officer, I'm asking you to leave,' said Francis, his tone sharp.

Oh God, that was never going to work.

Francis's head snapped against the living room doorframe as Thierry's fist glanced off the side of his nose and across his cheekbone. He slid to a sitting position, clutching his nose with both hands and gasping for breath. Marni watched in horror as blood trickled out from between his fingers.

'Fantastic, Thierry. You've just assaulted a police officer. You'll end up back in the nick.'

Thierry was nursing his knuckles with his other hand and deigned to reply only with his infamous grunt. It was all too typical and reminded her why things could never work between them.

'Alex,' called Marni. 'Can you bring some kitchen roll?'

She knelt down beside Francis and gently pulled his hands away from his nose. It was bleeding copiously and a swelling had already started bulging out on one side of it.

'I don't think it's broken,' she said, taking a handful of tissues from Alex, who slunk out of the hall again as fast as he could. She gave them to Francis to staunch the flow. 'You're not going to arrest him, are you?'

'Not if he gets out now,' said Francis, his voice thick with blood and mucus.

'Enjoy your breakfast,' said Thierry, turning to leave.

'Wait. There's something I need to tell you.'

Thierry ignored her and headed for the door.

'Thierry, you're on the killer's list!'

There was an edge of hysteria to her voice that made Thierry stop in his tracks.

'What the hell are you talking about?'

Francis stared at her, wide-eyed with shock.

'The Tattoo Thief, Thierry. You're one of his targets.'

They sat side by side on the sofa. Francis still mopping blood from his nose, Thierry too stunned to speak until he'd downed the shot of whisky Marni placed in front of him.

Alex came in silently with a tray of coffees. He conspicuously handed the cups to his parents and then just dumped Francis's on the table with a clatter. The air was frigid.

Marni shredded a couple of tissues nervously, waiting for the two men to gather their thoughts.

Francis recovered first.

'So let me get this straight. You saw a picture of your own tattoo and a picture of Thierry's tattoo on the killer's wall?'

Marni nodded, biting her lip.

'Which one is Thierry's?'

'The fall of Lucifer tattoo.'

'So you're both targets. That's why you fainted, isn't it?'

'Yes.'

'But you didn't think to mention this fact to me? Even when I showed you the photos later in the evening?' His words were clipped but there was no missing the underlying fury. 'I can't believe you kept it to yourself. There's a very real, very skilled killer out there – and he's coming after you.'

Marni's stomach clenched painfully. *Why hadn't she told him? Because she didn't want to admit the truth to herself? Because she thought she could keep herself safe?*

Thierry groaned loudly. His hands were shaking.

'Marni, why didn't you tell me as soon as you knew? Why didn't you tell me?'

'I . . .' Marni didn't know what to say.

'Either one of us could have been killed in our beds.'

She'd really fucked up.

'Damn it, Marni, you were here on your own last night before I arrived,' Francis continued. 'What if it had been the killer at the door, rather than me?'

'I wouldn't have opened it. I knew it was you, because you phoned.'

'I can't handle this,' said Thierry, heading off towards the kitchen.

'Stay here,' snapped Francis. 'I need to talk to both of you. On a professional level. You need protection. Marni, make some more coffee while I get dressed.'

Damn men. They all thought they could take over. This was her house and he had no right to issue orders. She needed a nicotine hit, so she lit a cigarette and went and stood outside the back door.

'Tell me, what's going on with him?' said Thierry, following her out and leaning on the door jamb.

'None of your business,' she said, exhaling a cloud of smoke. 'All you need to know is that you're on the killer's hit list, so please be careful.'

'So sweet of you to care.' He had recovered from the shock. Now he was just angry with her.

'You're Alex's dad. I wouldn't want to see him getting hurt if anything happened to you.'

Thierry had left by the time Francis came back downstairs and it was hard to tell if he was relieved or annoyed. Marni poured them both fresh coffee.

'Give me his home address and where he works – I'll make sure there's someone keeping an eye on him until this is over.'

'Thank you,' said Marni. Then she cocked her head. 'Same

treatment for me? A policeman shadowing me?'

'Absolutely.'

She frowned. 'I have Pepper. I don't need a bodyguard.'

'You don't get a choice.'

'Will it be you?'

'No, it won't. I need to run the case, not trail around after witnesses.'

'No personal protection then?'

He was so easy to tease. His face went scarlet.

'Look, what exactly happened last night?'

'Oh, Frank, don't you remember?'

'I remember kissing you.' He looked like he'd sucked on a lemon.

Really? It was that bad?

'There's no need for you to worry. Nothing else happened. You passed out after that and, believe it or not, I'm not in the habit of having sex with unconscious policemen. Or any policemen, come to that.'

Frank stared at his feet, his cheeks blazing afresh. 'I'm sorry.'

'Don't be. I'm sure it's a relief to you. I could see how much you were panicking when Thierry thought we'd slept together.' She finished her coffee in one gulp, determined to play it cool given his obvious regret about the whole thing. 'Now, I know you've got a lot to do, so why don't you run along and sort me out a big, strong bodyguard?'

It was a shame they wouldn't be repeating the exercise, because with Frank Sullivan's soft drunken snoring in her ear, Marni had enjoyed her best night's sleep in months.

He gathered up his belongings and left without saying another word.

As soon as the door shut behind him, Marni hammered a fist against the wall.

'Damn you, Francis Sullivan!'

42

Rory

Rory had spent most of the night at a police roadblock on
Ditchling Road, stopping cars not so much in the hope of apprehending the killer, but to find out if anyone had seen anything
unusual and to warn the local community to be on their guard.
As the traffic died off in the small hours, he'd come back to the
station to review CCTV findings and to draft a statement for
Bradshaw to release to the press. It was hard work. Press releases
were more Sullivan's forte than his, but he hadn't heard from him
since before midnight. Finally, he'd managed to slope off home
for a quick shower and a short kip but now he was back – and
more determined than ever to track Sam Kirby down.

He checked his phone for the umpteenth time and found that
he'd missed a call from Francis on the drive in. No message. No
text. He called back, but the door of the incident room swung
open before there was an answer.

'Hang up, Rory. I'm here.'

It was Francis Sullivan, but not as he'd ever seen him before.
His hair was tousled, his suit looked slept in and his nose was
swollen and skewed off centre. As he came across the room,
Rory could see the faint shadows of two black eyes starting to
blossom.

'Jesus, what happened to you? Don't tell me you found him?'

Francis dropped into a chair.

'Could we have some coffee?' His voice sounded a little slurred.

'You're hungover.'

Francis slumped forward, his head in his hands.

'And you've been in a fight.'

The DI groaned and Rory failed to suppress a snort of laughter.

'How does the other guy look? And who was it?'

'Thierry Mullins.'

There was only one reason Rory could think of for Thierry Mullins to have punched Francis on the nose. He would never have had Sullivan pegged as a ladies' man.

'I'll get coffee.'

By the time he got back from the canteen, it was clear Francis had taken control of himself. His suit jacket was hanging on the back of the chair, the front of his shirt was spattered with water and his hair was wet. Hollins had arrived in the meantime and was sitting at his desk staring at Francis.

Rory put down the two coffees he was carrying and extracted a comb from his jacket pocket. He handed it to Francis.

'Thanks.'

'Hollins, stop gaping and get to work.'

'Yes, Sergeant.'

Rory briefed Francis on the night's activities.

'Right, first priority is close protection on Marni Mullins. She's on the Tattoo Thief's hit list.' Francis pointed to the pictures of the relevant tattoos pinned up on the incident board. 'Oh, and if you can spare anyone, Thierry Mullins is also on the list.'

'I'll get that sorted,' said Rory. 'Um . . . Do you want Mullins to be charged with a Section 89?'

Of course, he was fishing to find out what had gone down between them.

'No.'

Rory raised his eyebrows.

272

'I'm not discussing it.'

As Sullivan turned his attention to a file, the door to the incident room opened again. This time Bradshaw was standing on the threshold.

'Please tell me you at least know where Kirby is.' He looked Francis up and down with disdain. 'And what the hell are you doing here?'

Rory stepped forward. 'I'm using him on the case,' he said. 'We need all the manpower we can get for this one.'

Bradshaw bristled.

'In fact, sir, it was Sullivan who discovered Kirby's identity and that he lives on Stone Acre Farm. I need him back on the case.'

Even though he didn't care for Sullivan personally, Rory was beginning to recognise that the boss was damn intelligent and knew what he was doing. And a bad feeling was niggling at him over the way he'd shopped Francis for holding the press conference.

'So what are you saying now? That Sullivan's doing your job better than you can do it?'

'Not exactly,' said Rory, looking as if he'd surprised himself, 'but he does have something to offer.'

Sullivan's mouth fell open, then closed abruptly.

Hollins, who was listening surreptitiously from his desk, knocked over a cup of coffee. Bradshaw was momentarily distracted but then turned back to Rory.

'Not what I expected of you, Mackay,' said the chief. He looked at Francis. 'Right. This goes totally against my better judgement, but you're back on the case.'

'In what capacity?' said Francis.

'You're the senior ranking office in this team, so obviously you'll be in charge. Do I have to spell everything out?'

'No, sir. Thank you, sir.'

'Don't thank me till you've solved the case. How are you going to proceed?'

'We're continuing to question drivers on Ditchling Road and the team is reviewing all CCTV city-wide around the clock. We've already put out footage from the night Evan Armstrong was killed, of a hooded individual we're pretty certain is the killer. We've also identified a couple of the target pictures we recovered from Kirby's barn – Thierry and Marni Mullins – and we're putting them under close protection. Burton's doing what she can to identify the subjects in the other images.'

'What about vehicles registered to him?'

'Nothing in his name,' said Rory. 'He obviously does have a vehicle – but it's not registered with the DVLA, and we've got no insurance information coming up. We're checking tyre tracks picked up at Stone Acre, but they won't provide much information to narrow the search down.'

'Damn it! He could be miles away by now.'

Francis didn't say anything.

'Right, Sullivan, you might be back in charge, but from now on, you run everything by me. You need some experience at the helm.'

'Very well, sir,' said Francis. His voice was frosty. 'Do you have anything in mind?'

'We need to be proactive – we should be drawing the killer out.'

Straight away Rory could see where this was going.

'How do you suggest we do that, sir?' said Francis.

'It's obvious, isn't it? We know the identity of some of the people he wants to kill next. We could dangle Marni Mullins under his nose as bait.'

Francis's eyes widened. 'I don't think we should do that, sir.'

'You don't?' Bradshaw's voice was heavy with sarcasm.

'No, sir. That would be putting civilian lives in danger, Marni's life in danger. That's not why I became a police officer.'

'Don't be ridiculous, Sullivan. We'll have her covered. She won't be in any danger at all.'

'Sorry, sir. As far as I'm concerned, it's not an option.'

Bradshaw's face darkened. 'I'm not giving you any choice in this. It's my final decision.'

'Then you'll have to take me off the case again, sir. I won't deliberately put Marni Mullins in the path of a serial killer.'

Rory was about to add that the same went for Thierry, but he was interrupted by his phone. It was Hitchins.

'We've had a response to this morning's TV witness appeal . . .'

'Wait. I'm putting you on speaker.'

'A man's called in. He saw a person who he thinks could be Sam Kirby – apparently looked similar to the CCTV images we put out.'

'Where?' snapped Francis.

'At the marina.'

'We're on our way.'

xiv

My knife. My knife! The vorpal blade.

I know where I dropped it but I can't go back for it. I can never go back to Stone Acre. They'll be watching for me. And even if I could go back, I won't find it. They'll have it by now. The SOCOs are like ants, crawling over every inch of my world, dismantling, judging my work. Judging me.

They'll be impressed. Damn them all.

I have other knives. Of course I do. But that one was special, my favourite blade. The Collector brought it back for me from a trip to Japan. It'll take a couple of months to sort out a replacement. First, however, I need a place to stay. The Collector has a small boat at the marina, just one tiny cabin, a sleeping bag. It gives me breathing space, a few days. As long as he doesn't find out I'm using it. I don't think he would be pleased, even though it's so I can carry on with his assignment. He's still very keen that I finish this part of his collection. He's hinted that he wants to move forward with his next plan. He's such an ambitious man – it's one of the things I admire about him most. He told me something once, a story from his childhood. When he was at school, he collected Top Trumps cards. He had the best collection, of course, but he was missing one rare card that carried a particularly high points score. When his best friend got hold of it, he was furious. On the way home from school later that week, he hung his friend over the balustrade of a bridge, thirty or forty feet above a wide river, holding onto him by just one ankle until he promised to give up the card. The Collector always gets what he wants. I fear him and worship him in equal measure. I'll just have to be very careful when I speak to him not to let slip exactly where I'm staying. And I must, above all, complete my task for him.

I'll come and go in the shadows. And I'll kill again, very soon. My fingers are itching for it.

43

Francis

It was beginning to get dark as Francis and Rory pulled up outside the marina's security office. A uniformed guard was standing in the doorway and he stepped up to introduce himself as they got out of the car.

'Police?' he said.

Francis nodded.

'I'm Alan Chapman. I made the call.'

Francis came round the car to the pavement side. 'Tell us where you saw him and what made you think it was the Tattoo Thief.'

'I'll show you,' said Alan.

As they walked along the promenade past rows and rows of jetties, he told them the details.

'I saw your witness appeal on the TV and the CCTV footage with it. I always take notice of things like that because we have so many people coming and going at the marina. Not that I particularly thought your man would be here.'

He took a left turn off the promenade and led them along a wide jetty that had two levels. There were narrow wooden walkways branching off the main structure on either side, all crammed with boats of varying sizes. Down the centre of the top level there were a number of two-storey buildings made from corrugated iron, painted white and yellow.

'What are these?' asked Rory.

'Showers, toilets, launderette,' Chapman answered.

'What did you see and where?' said Francis.

'It was down here,' he said, pointing along one of the narrower gangways. 'Pretty sure it was this one, because I recall the big boat at the end. It's moored there permanently. I was here, looking back towards shore, and I saw a figure, dark clothes, a hoody with the hood up. Just walking fast down the jetty.'

'But what made you suspicious of him?'

'It was something about the way he was moving. He had a slightly rolling gait that reminded me of the CCTV stuff on the news. And his clothes were similar to the description you put out. He looked around a few times as if he was worried that someone was following him, or he didn't want to be seen.'

'Did he get onto one of the boats?' said Francis.

Chapman shrugged. 'I looked away. There was a boat coming into its berth on the other side and they were making rather a meal of it. When I looked back this way, the man had disappeared. He could have gone onto one of the boats or he might have made his way back to land.'

Rory rubbed his chin. 'I'm still not sure why you think it could be our killer. Hoodies are not uncommon.'

'I've been in security for a lot of years. You get a sense for when someone's uncomfortable with what they're doing. When I got back to the office, I looked at your CCTV footage, at the shadowy figure you pointed out in New Road. Like I said, the man's gait was similar, his clothes were similar, and he had that vibe. Look, I could be totally wrong, but it has to be worth checking.'

They walked down the narrow jetty to the end and back, but all the boats were quiet, with no sign of any of the owners on board.

'Thank you for reporting it,' said Francis. He turned to Rory.

'Call the team down here – let's have them check all the boats along this jetty and the adjacent two. See if there's anyone that matches the description.'

They made their way back to the security office.

'Could you furnish us with the names and addresses of all the boat owners that are currently moored here?' Francis said to Chapman.

'Certainly.'

'And do you have CCTV on all the jetties?'

'No, not covering every single one. We've got one at the entrance of the marina, a couple along the promenade, and a number covering the car parks.'

'Can we take a look at them?'

A couple of hours examining CCTV footage and the combined efforts of Hollins and Hitchins talking to boat owners and checking boats yielded precisely nothing.

It wasn't that Francis doubted Chapman's word. In fact, he felt sure Chapman had seen what he claimed to have seen. But there was no sign now of a shady figure in a hoody and no conclusion to be drawn from the sighting. Francis dropped Rory back at John Street and then looped back the way he came. He wanted to check there was a protection detail parked outside Marni's house.

When he got there, he was happy to see there was a car on duty. He had a quick word with the two PCs, who had nothing untoward to report. As he was going back to his own car, Marni's front door opened.

'Frank?'

He walked over to her.

'I saw you talking to them,' said Marni, without preamble, as he stood on the bottom of the three steps that led up to her door. 'Please call them off. Everywhere I go, they're shadowing me. It's not good for my mental health.'

'Seriously? They're there to save your life. I thought they'd give you some reassurance.' He toyed with one foot on the second step, wondering if she'd invite him in.

'I can look after myself.'

'I bet Evan Armstrong thought that too. He was well over six foot.'

Marni sighed. 'I've asked them to leave me alone and they won't.'

'They told me, but they follow my orders, not yours.'

'And I get no say?'

'No.' He stepped backwards onto the pavement.

Marni scowled.

'You might thank me, when they intercept a killer who's intent on taking that beautiful tattoo off your back. At the moment, we have no idea where he is. We've been chasing up sightings all over Brighton and along the south coast. One guy thought he saw him down at the marina, another called an hour later to say he was in Shoreham. And until I have him in a cell, you're going to have protection.'

'I have a dog and I've taken self-defence classes.'

'Pepper will hardly be very effective against a man with a knife. And a couple of self-defence classes probably won't help either.'

Marni stared at him, lips pursed. She made a move to shut the door, but then thought better of it. 'The reason I took self-defence classes was because I was in danger. It wasn't some stupid fitness fad. I took classes from an ex-Israeli army guy. *Krav maga* is their self-defence system.'

'I'm impressed.'

'I had no choice. There was a man who posed a very real threat to me.'

'The one you were charged with stabbing?'

She nodded, her face pale and tense.

'What happened?' he asked gently.

She shook her head. 'Not much. Just a man who developed an obsession with me.'

'Where is he now?'

'He's in prison for something totally unrelated.'

'Who was he?'

'Thierry's twin brother. He raped me. I stabbed him.' Her gaze was unflinching and unforgiving. 'Now please call off your dogs.'

44

Marni

A faceless man carried Luke – the baby she'd lost – in the crook of his arm. In his other hand, he held a long curved blade that glinted with a blinding light. They were running. Sometimes Marni was pursuing them, at other times they were coming after her. Alex beckoned her from the distance but no matter how hard she ran, he never seemed any closer.

She woke up drenched with sweat and went across the room to open the window. Below her, on the street, the squad car sat and she could see the driver inside, sipping coffee out of a cardboard cup.

Coffee would fix things. She checked the time on the radio alarm on her bedside table. She was due at the studio in half an hour. She had a full day of appointments ahead and she needed to make some money. Coffee and a shower.

Forty minutes later, she tapped on the window of the police car.

'You might as well drive me to work,' she said, when the disgruntled officer lowered his window. 'You'll be going there anyway and I'm running late.'

'Hop in then,' he said, without cracking a smile.

She could hardly blame him. What sort of an existence was it, sitting in a small car for eight hours at a stretch, watching someone else live their life?

Her first appointment was waiting for her at the door and it was non-stop for the rest of the day, despite a no-show. It felt good to be working again. The past couple of weeks had seemed disjointed and she'd had to rearrange a number of her regular clients because of her dealings with the police. Hopefully they'd catch the bastard soon and life could return to normal. Steady, quiet and uneventful. Just the way she liked it.

Her afternoon appointment was with Steve to finish off the tiger tattoo she'd been working on at the convention. It would be a glorious piece when it was done – the orange tiger standing out from the flurry of deep magenta chrysanthemums, blood dripping from its teeth and claws.

Steve was early and had already been waiting twenty minutes by the time she'd cleaned away and taken payment from her previous client. He climbed up onto the massage bench impatiently.

'Do you think you'll be able to finish it today?' he asked.

'Possibly,' said Marni, with a shrug. She studied the work so far. 'Still needs four or five hours, so it depends if you're up for it.'

For the first hour of tattooing Marni simply switched off. Steve was explaining to her what his company did, some cutting-edge programming technology that Marni had little chance of understanding and absolutely zero interest in. He droned on, hardly pausing for breath, and it seemed to be mostly about how much better his company was than the competition. She immersed herself into her art, and the stresses of the previous days began to diminish as her mind cleared.

'What's happening in your world, Marni? How's Alex?' said Steve, invading her thoughts. She hoped he couldn't tell she hadn't been listening all this time.

'He's good. Just finished his A levels, so life's one long party.'

'Good times. Remember them well. What's he going to do next?'

'Uni hopefully – geography.'

'Geography? Not a lot of careers in that. You should send him to have a chat with me about working in programming.'

'Sure,' said Marni, trying to concentrate on her work.

'What about you? What's the latest on that tattoo thief killer?'

Her hand jerked slightly and he winced. At the same moment, she heard the flap of the letter box and Pepper rushed through to the front of the shop barking.

'Give me a minute, Steve. If I don't rescue the post, Pepper will eat it.'

'No worries.'

She didn't really care about the post but it was the perfect excuse not to discuss the murder with him.

There was only one letter and Pepper was shunting it across the floor in an effort to gain purchase on it.

'Give up, Pepper. It's not for you,' she said, stooping to pick it up.

The French postmark had her clutching at the shop counter for support. Fear prickled across her scalp and tightened her chest as she recognised the handwriting of the address.

It was another letter from Paul.

She couldn't read it. She could hardly bear to touch the envelope. But she looked at the postmark. The letter had been posted in Marseilles. She knew that was where Paul was in prison. She wondered how he'd smuggled it out and who had posted it for him. A bent guard, probably. She felt short of breath, but forced herself to count slowly to settle the rhythm. She put the letter face down on the counter and closed her eyes.

What did he want? Why couldn't he leave her alone?

She felt dizzy and opened her eyes again, fixing her gaze on a black mark on the floor.

'Everything okay out there?'

Damn! She'd forgotten about Steve.

'I'm fine. With you in a sec.'

She went through to the studio and shoved the letter into her bag. A long cold drink of water helped, as did an assessment of her work so far.

'Listen, Steve, I don't think we can finish today. I'm sorry, but I'm exhausted, so I'm not really up for a long session. I'll book you in for a spot in a couple of weeks, yeah?'

Steve grimaced. 'Seriously, Marni?' He looked down at his arm. 'There's hardly any more to do. Please can we get it done today? I'll pay you extra.'

'It's not about money. It's just that if I keep working when I'm tired, you won't be getting my best work.' Tired *and* stressed. And she needed food – her blood sugar was dipping.

'Take a break then. Have a coffee, and then we'll have a final push. I'd really like to have it finished.'

'Why?'

'There's someone I want to show it to.'

This Marni could understand. Everyone getting a tattoo always wanted it finished as quickly as possible. She was feeling drained, but she hated to send a client away disappointed.

'Okay. You want a coffee too?'

It was the last thing she wanted to do but coffee would make it more bearable.

'Sure. Thanks, Marni. You're tattooing like a champ.'

XV

She has a police guard, sitting in a car outside her studio. It makes it easier for me to tell where she is. They were outside her house last night, having followed her home at walking speed from drinks with friends. They discreetly tailed her earlier when she picked up her son from the school sports ground. But, frankly, life would be easier without their constant presence.

I've just had the go-ahead from the Collector. He called to say he wants to push on with the harvesting. He's trying to sort out a new place for me to set up the curing operation as quickly as he can. He was much calmer than last time I spoke to him – all business, no more recriminations. We have more tattoos to take now, replacements for the skins the police have got hold of, so I have a new list. Marni Mullins is at the top of it – the Collector had told me to wait before cutting her, but now he's set it as a matter of priority. And it has to be said, her tattoo is a beauty if the pictures of it are anything to go by.

Giving her bodyguards must have seemed like a necessary precaution once they found her picture at Stone Acre. But the policemen are outside the studio and she's inside. They're about ten metres from the shopfront, watching a locked door. I'm watching them while I decide what to do about them. Circumvent them or kill them first?

It's all about weighing up the risks in light of the reward. The Collector has set a high price for Marni Mullins' back piece. But *it's not about the money. I let him down. The police are on my trail and our completion date needs to be set back. It's imperative that I prove to him that I'm still up to the task, that I'm still worthy of the commission.*

It's late for Mullins to still be working in her studio. I can watch her if I go into the alley at the back of the row of shops. She's drawing, designing new tattoos to offer to her clients. All alone at the back, while her minders sit drinking coffee and smoking cigarettes out at the front.

They won't have a clue when it happens. In another couple of hours, they'll be bored and dozy. If the girl works much longer, tonight could be the night.

I wonder how much she'll struggle. I wonder how much she'll bleed.

45

Marni

Finishing off Steve's tattoo had made it a long day and all Marni really wanted to do was head for home and a hot bath. But she knew she'd have trouble getting off to sleep. Her thoughts were unsettled and there was a gnawing anxiety in her stomach that wouldn't let go. Instead, after dropping back to the house for a quick supper with Alex, she went back to her studio to work on some drawings. It was the only way to find the peace of mind she so needed. Besides, it was time to bring things to a head.

For an hour, she tried to concentrate on the drawing in front of her, rather than on the darkness creeping into the corners of her studio. She sat alone, in a small pool of light, with her back to the window. She was wearing a halter neck top which showed off the upper portion of her tattoo – anyone who walked down the alley at the back would be able to see it. This was on purpose, even though the evening had turned the air a little cooler.

Frank Sullivan was in no position to tell her what she could and couldn't do. But she felt compelled to do what she could to draw the killer out. She'd been a victim far too many times in the past – the unopened letters from Paul in her dressing table told her that. Now she was going to take control. She wasn't going to let Paul scare her and she wasn't going to let the Tattoo Thief scare her. Let the bastard come for her. She'd meet him head on.

But what if it was someone she knew? Something tugged at one corner of her mind and as much as she needed to find out the identity of the Tattoo Thief, she was also terrified of what that knowledge would bring.

The drawing. She was letting her mind wander and she needed to focus. A new client had asked her to design a Japanese-style sleeve featuring her mother's favourite flowers and, as always with commissioned work, it was important to interpret the client's wishes rather than freestyle with her own ideas. She drew an explosion of overblown peonies, and in her mind's eye, she could see deep pinks and magentas, set off by a scattering of emerald green leaves at the edges. She added a cluster of butterflies around the top and tucked in a small frog looking out from under the petals at the bottom. When she looked up at the clock an hour had passed.

But her thoughts turned back to the case, and then to the letters that had come from France, and her pencil faltered. She felt vulnerable.

She put the peonies to one side and started on a fresh sheet of paper. If she was going to find it hard to concentrate, she should at least give her pencil hand free rein. She started with a series of sweeping curves across the page, then squinted at them through half closed eyes to see what they suggested.

The sweep of a blade through tattooed skin. A tide of crimson in its wake.

She opened her eyes fully and looked away from the page.

Pepper snorted under her desk, so she bent down to scratch his ears. Nothing was going to happen. There was no one out there in the darkness, staring in.

She rotated the piece of paper on her desk and saw the form of a rolling Hokusai-style wave. She picked up her pencil again and started to draw with more purpose, and this time she was able to quell the anxiety churning inside her. Time passed and the pile of drawings at the side of her desk grew. She took Pepper outside with her when she needed a cigarette, then, after giving herself an insulin jab and with a fresh cup of coffee beside her, returned to the flower design she'd abandoned earlier. It was close to one a.m. and Pepper was grumbling to get home, but now she had hit her stride.

A loud crack from the direction of the back door unleashed a powerful surge of adrenalin. Her stomach contracted and hair rose along the back of her neck.

'Hello?' she called, pushing her chair back and rising cautiously.

Pepper growled and scurried out from his shelter. They both stood staring as the back door of the studio burst open and a black-clad figure flew towards them. Marni saw a flash of silver approaching. Every part of her body constricted and tightened. She couldn't breathe and she couldn't think. Everything went into slow motion.

The knife was in the attacker's right hand. His left hand was clutching a balled-up cloth. His face was obscured by a balaclava. Without thinking, Marni moved her feet into a defensive stance. *Short, simple, repetitive blows.* The mantra ran through her head as she raised her arms to ward off the man.

Pepper made first contact. He leapt up in defence of his mistress, barking harshly until his mouth landed up against the man's leg. Marni took advantage of the man's shock to try and kick his other leg out from under him, but she wasn't quite close enough to get the drive she needed. The man brought his knife down fast, cutting into Pepper's back, right between his shoulder blades. The dog let go of the leg with a howl of pain, turning his head away as the man drew the knife out. This gave the cut a wider arc and blood gushed out onto the white fur of Pepper's back. He fell to the floor with a thud, moaning as the air was knocked from his lungs.

'Damn you!' shrieked Marni.

The man lunged at her with his knife and she felt it scrape across her arm. She turned to avoid it and took a step back, trawling her memories for the self-defence techniques she'd learned.

She knew what to do now. Hard, sharp slaps against the man's knife arm made him lose focus for a moment. Another kick. But the man stepped back fast and stretched out the arm holding the cloth. He dropped his knife and spun sideways, giving him the reach to pull Marni into a neck lock. She saw the cloth moving in towards her face. Even bunched up it would cover her mouth and nose. She struggled against his arm but he was stronger than her and taller than her by almost a foot.

Where in God's name were those bloody police protection boys when you needed them?

The tang of petroleum caught in her nostrils. The material pressed against her face and Marni knew that if she breathed in, it would be her last conscious breath. She could hold her breath for maybe a minute and a half, less though if she was struggling. She relaxed her body, pressing her weight against the man, pushing slightly. The man was forced to take a couple of small steps back. Marni sensed where his feet were in relation to her own and then stamped down hard on the bridge of his right foot.

He yelped and in that split second, Marni was able to pull his arm away from around her neck. She turned to face him and they grappled. Marni could still smell the ether residue on her face and it fuelled her anger. She wasn't going to let this happen. She jacked a knee sharply into his groin but he didn't loosen the grip he had on her upper arms.

Pepper grunted and tried to move, making Marni glance in his direction. Around the dog was a slick of blood, black in the half light, spreading across the floor. Taking advantage of her distraction, the man kicked against her legs so she collapsed to the floor in a heap. A second later he was on top of her, straddling her, the hand with the ether-soaked cloth bearing down.

'Why?' she gasped, struggling under his weight. 'Why are you taking them?'

Even though the man's face was covered by a balaclava, he still bowed his head and turned his face away from Marni, as if to hide his features.

'You sick bastard!' Anger powered her to fight back. She struggled desperately underneath him, lashing her head from side to side to avoid the ether. She wasn't going to let it happen to her. She wasn't going to die here. She wasn't going to die now.

But the man was in control. He punched her hard in the side of the head and the room spun. She gasped as through clouded vision she saw the hand holding the cloth descending on her.

'NO . . . NO . . .'

She shrieked as loud as she could, letting the words become a scream.

Her mind scrambled for a way out, but her arms were immobilised under his body. She could kick with her legs but they couldn't bend back far enough to be able to hit him. She writhed underneath him but it was useless.

The balaclava had two eyeholes and a slit at the mouth. The man was grinning, peering down at her as he bent closer. He was taking pleasure in her fear – she could see it in his eyes as well as his smile. She'd seen this look before on cruel, weak faces.

She wasn't going to let this be the last thing she saw.

She took a deep breath that filled out her chest and clamped her mouth shut as the cloth reached her face. Then, summoning every last reserve of strength in her body, she thrust her head forward and up. Her forehead smashed against his nose. There was a crunch and his head snapped back. The impact hurt like hell, but a high, sharp scream of pain told her it hurt him more.

The cloth fell away from her face as he put both hands to his nose. She could breathe again. She felt the weight of his body shift and used his distraction to pull her arms free from under him. She rolled to one side, unbalancing him enough to be able to push him off.

Despite the overwhelming impulse to clamber to her feet and run away, she knew this was the last thing she should do. He would take her down in a matter of seconds. Instead, she scrambled on top of him and grabbed at his arms, effectively pinning him down.

They were both panting heavily and Marni realised that when he regained his breath, he'd make a more concerted effort to escape. She needed to put him out of commission quickly. She grabbed a handful of the balaclava at the back of his head and slammed his face down into the floor. His cries were muffled by the floorboards. She did it again and then three more times for good measure.

But she didn't care. She was in survival mode and his pain meant nothing.

His struggling slowed down but didn't stop entirely. Marni glanced around, desperately trying to work out what to do next. Something glinted under her desk. It was his knife. She slowed her breathing to calm down her heart rate, wondering if she could reach it while still maintaining enough pressure to hold the man in place.

And then what? Stab him?

There was a noise at the front of the shop and the two police minders crashed through the front door. They quickly took hold of the man and helped Marni off him. As one of them cuffed him, Marni lunged across to where Pepper was lying motionless in the pool of his own blood.

'No, no, please . . . come on, Pepper, please be alive.'

She gently pulled him towards her and cradled his head. His chest moved with irregular shallow breaths.

'Call a vet, please, please!' she cried out to one of the policemen.

'In a moment, love.'

With her assailant rendered harmless, the constables called for backup.

Marni closed her eyes. She couldn't bear to lose Pepper. She cradled him in shaking arms, her heart pounding, panting hard as her body was still flooded with adrenalin. Within minutes the shop was overrun with police.

'Marni?' It was Frank's voice. 'What the hell happened? Your arm's bleeding.'

'I'm all right,' she said shakily, without bothering to look at the wound. 'Is it him? Have you got the Tattoo Thief?'

One of the uniforms pulled the attacker to his feet. Francis stood facing him. The man was far taller and bulkier than Francis – well over six feet.

'Sam Kirby?'

The man said nothing. Francis stretched up and grasped the top of his balaclava. He pulled it off and gasped.

They all gasped.

The Tattoo Thief was a woman.

46

Francis

Sam Kirby. *Samantha*. The Tattoo Thief. SHE. Francis couldn't get his head around it. In all this time, since Marni had first found Evan Armstrong's body, it hadn't crossed his mind for a second that the killer wasn't a man. Why hadn't it? That was easy enough to answer – these killings had been physically demanding. Dead bodies are dead weight and the killer had overpowered the victims, chopped off limbs, flayed skin and then dumped them. If anyone had suggested the murders had been committed by a woman, they would have been laughed out of the department.

Of course, now he could see it, given the size of Sam Kirby. Tall, broad, muscular. Certainly she probably had the strength for the task – but for a woman to have the necessary aggression? Female serial killers were comparatively rare, and most of those documented used poison or were killing infants or the elderly. He couldn't remember coming across a female killer who attacked and murdered men in the way Sam Kirby had.

Furthermore, Marni Mullins had deliberately done what he asked her not to do, and for that alone Francis was furious. How could she have put herself in harm's way without telling him? How could she have thought of doing it at all? It was irresponsible beyond belief and Francis had had to suppress the urge to take her by the shoulders and shake her.

'What if she'd succeeded?' he'd shouted at her in the confused minutes after the unmasking. 'This might have been a murder scene and I might have been looking down at your bloody, skinned back.'

Later, Francis had felt scared by his own reaction to what had happened, by how deep his feelings had become. He couldn't bear the thought of Marni being the Tattoo Thief's next victim. Thank God the protection detail had heard her screams. Marni might have been in control by the time they arrived, but the fight could so easily have gone the other way.

Francis was still feeling shaky as he made his way up to Bradshaw's office. That the woman they'd arrested the previous evening was the Tattoo Thief, he had no doubt. She'd broken into Marni's studio with a knife, and just outside the back door they'd discovered a kit bag with a set of knives, plastic sheeting and ziplock bags. In one of the side pockets was a packet of pills with a prescription sticker on it – beta-blockers prescribed for Sam Kirby. And as they removed the latex gloves she was wearing, the two bleeding heart tattoos on the backs of her hands were revealed. This gave them their link to the attack on Dan Carter and Rose Lewis was already having a field day linking the forensic evidence from the bag, the farm and the earlier crime scenes.

Francis knocked on Bradshaw's door and went in.

'Where's Mackay?' said Bradshaw, before he was even through the door.

'Coming up behind me. He just wanted to make sure all the custody paperwork was in order.'

Bradshaw nodded approvingly.

'Good work, Sullivan. I had no doubt you'd catch the killer in the end. See, I was right about using one of the targets as bait. It drew the killer out. Well done.'

'Thank you, sir.' Francis gritted his teeth to answer civilly, sitting down on one of the chairs opposite Bradshaw's desk. 'But in fact, the credit should go to Marni Mullins. We just arrived in time to pick up the pieces. And it's not a ploy I would ever have sanctioned if she'd discussed it with me first.'

Bradshaw raised his eyebrows at this, but Francis wasn't going to tell him how infuriated he was with Marni.

'However, are you sure this woman is really the killer? It seems doubtful to me. And if you think she is, don't you think she might have had an accomplice?'

'At this point, the evidence suggests very strongly that she's the person we've been looking for,' said Francis. 'Forensics will confirm either way later today.'

'And an accomplice? Anyone in the frame for that?'

'We haven't come across anything yet that would suggest there was an accomplice involved.'

'But a woman acting alone? These were very physical murders.'

'Sir, she's a powerful woman. Tall, strong, heavily muscled. I would guess she does a lot of weight training.'

'Mmmm . . .' Bradshaw didn't seem convinced. 'None of the footage from the night Evan died or the witness statements from the aborted attack suggested it was a woman.'

'Like I said, she's got a masculine build. The CCTV images are grainy, and as to the witness statements – they were expecting it to be a man and the brain just fills in the gaps.' Francis shrugged. 'I'm entirely sure it's her, sir.'

Rory came in while he was speaking and, with a nod to both of them, sat down on the remaining vacant chair.

'Everything in order?' said Bradshaw.

'I's dotted and T's crossed,' said Rory. 'They're putting her in an interview room as soon as they've cleaned up her face.'

'Does she need medical attention?'

'The duty doctor's seen her. Broken nose, but apparently an icepack is all they'll do now. They'll assess the damage more thoroughly in a few days when the swelling's gone down. She's had some painkillers.'

'Right, we'd better get down there. Sullivan, you take the lead. Rory, sit in. I'll be watching so just make sure you don't fuck this up. We need a solid conviction on this and if you do anything to jeopardise it . . .' He trailed off. They knew what he'd do and it didn't need spelling out.

Francis stood up and Rory followed him out.

'The chief thinks she might have an accomplice,' said Francis, as they took the stairs, two at a time.

'Don't see it myself,' said Rory.

'Me neither. She looks tough. I think she could have man-handled those bodies on her own.'

Sam Kirby was already in the interview room by the time they arrived, her hands cuffed together as she held an icepack up against her nose. Her cropped grey hair was an unruly mess and her blood-spattered clothes had been replaced by a shapeless grey tracksuit. She sat like a man, legs wide apart, and she was breathing noisily through her mouth.

'Can we take the cuffs off?' said Francis to the duty sergeant at the door.

The sergeant came in and unlocked the handcuffs. Francis noticed that Kirby didn't particularly co-operate with him, even though it was for her own comfort. She rubbed her wrists and glared at Francis and Rory from red, watery eyes, purple bruises already spreading underneath them.

Rory switched on the tape recorder and recited the time, date and names of those present in the room. He read Kirby her rights. Kirby watched him, unmoved.

'Can you please confirm your identity as Sam or Samantha Kirby?' said Francis.

When addressed, Kirby switched to staring at a corner of the ceiling beyond them. Francis repeated the question, though he guessed he wouldn't get an answer.

'Miss Kirby,' he said. Her face took on a sneer. 'We're investigating your attack on Marni Mullins in the small hours of this morning. We're also investigating a number of murders and an attempted murder that have taken place in Brighton over the past few weeks. You would honestly be helping yourself if you co-operated with this interview.'

Her fake smile looked more like a grimace on her bruised mouth, but it was her first acknowledgement of their presence in the room.

'Could you account for your whereabouts at the following dates and times? Sunday the twenty-eighth of May, between twelve a.m. and five a.m.? Tuesday—'

'It isn't over until it's over.' Her voice grated, loud and harsh as she cut across him.

Francis looked at her fingers and saw dark nicotine stains. 'Can you explain what you mean by that statement?'

She didn't answer, but followed his gaze down to her hands. She rubbed her wrists again – they were thick and the cuffs must have been a tight fit – and then resumed looking at the ceiling.

'Do you mean the killings aren't over?' said Francis. 'We know you had other targets from the pictures we found in the barn. But you won't be able to kill them now, will you?'

'It isn't over until it's over. It isn't over until it's over.'

Francis rubbed his eyes with his thumb and index finger.

Rory opened a folder that was on the table in front of them. He showed her a photo of Evan Armstrong, the one his parents had given them of him showing off his new tattoo.

'Do you recognise this man?' he asked.

Kirby didn't even look at the picture. 'It isn't over till it's over.'

Rory glanced at Francis.

There was a knock at the door and the duty sergeant came in.

'Can I have a word?'

Outside in the corridor, the sergeant introduced Francis to a slickly dressed man with an expensive briefcase. He was balding and his dark beady eyes were quickly assessing Francis and his surroundings.

'This is Mr Elphick,' said the sergeant.

Francis raised his brows. 'Yes?'

'I'll be acting as Miss Kirby's counsel,' said the man. 'I'd like to see my client, check that she's not been mistreated in any way. I understand that she was injured during the arrest process.'

Francis gave him a disdainful look. 'Not during the arrest process. Your client, if she instructs you, was injured in the course of attacking Ms Mullins, who thankfully was able to defend herself and apprehend Miss Kirby.'

'That's your interpretation of events. I'm sure my client will have a different story to tell.' He swept past Francis into the interview room.

If she bothered to share it with us.

Rory flicked the tape recorder back on.

'Resuming interview at three fifty a.m. Now joined by . . .'

'George Elphick, lawyer for the accused,' said the lawyer. He knew the drill.

Kirby, Francis noticed, was now looking as smug as anyone with a split lip and broken nose possibly could.

'I'll continue my questioning,' said Francis. 'Miss Kirby, do you know or have you ever met Jem Walsh?'

'It's not over.'

Elphick leant across to his client and whispered something in her ear. She shrugged and he nodded his head vigorously.

'No comment,' she said.

And that was it. *It's not over* was swapped for *no comment.* Francis knew better than to continue trying. With the lawyer in place, they wouldn't be getting anything useful out of Sam Kirby.

Not that it mattered. There was plenty of forensic evidence and now they knew what to look for – an exceptionally tall woman – he felt sure they'd be able to pick her out on more of the CCTV footage of the nights and locations in question.

'Interview suspended,' he said and Rory flicked off the recorder.

Rory stood up, staring down at Kirby, who was focusing on her own hands.

'I know where I've seen you before,' he said. 'You were at Evan Armstrong's funeral, weren't you?'

Of course. Something had been niggling at the back of Francis's mind and it was just this. He'd seen her before, and Rory was right – it was at Evan Armstrong's funeral. She was the giant woman who'd sat next to them at the back of the church.

George Elphick stood up. 'I want to request a full psychiatric evaluation of my client before you ask her any more questions,' he said. 'There's a very good chance that she's not fit to stand trial.'

It was hardly a shock tactic but the door burst open and Bradshaw blustered into the room. 'Mr Elphick, if I think for one minute you're obstructing my officers in the commission of their duty, I'll have you charged for it, mark my words.'

'I don't think that will be necessary,' said Elphick. 'Any judge will see that evaluation is in my client's best interests. Goodnight.'

He left without a word to his client and she didn't seem to care if he stayed or went. But as the sergeant handcuffed her to take her back to the cells, she started to laugh. And as she did, she finally made eye contact with Francis.

'I've changed my mind.'

'About what?'

'Do you want to know who I am?'

xvi

This is the man who's brought me down and now, as I stare him in the face, I feel compelled to make a connection with him. I will kill him, at some point in the future. But first I need him to understand who I am. Too many people have misunderstood me and underestimated me in the past. This time, this one won't. I'll make myself known, like I should have done when I had my father's attention, or even back in the days when I had his love.

The policeman looks shocked at my sudden change of heart. But of course, there's no way he can understand it.

We sit down in the interview room again, just him and me.

'So go ahead,' he says. 'Tell me who you are.'

I tell him my story. I gauge his reactions to things I say and those responses show me who he is. Know your enemies, Ron always said.

'You want to know what made me who I am today?'

He nods. I can see the triumph in his eyes. He thinks he's getting a confession. But I don't think this will be admissible in court – Mr Elphick will see to that.

'My family has always worked with skin. Kirby Leathers. Set up by my great-great-grandfather a hundred years ago. The company should have come to me, but it went to my brother, Marshall. Daddy's favourite. Do you have a sibling, Detective Sullivan?'

He gives an imperceptible nod. He knows better than to get drawn in, but he wants to keep the information flowing. This is the game we'll play.

'Tell me about him,' I say.

'Her. I have a sister.'

'Do you love her, Detective?'

Revulsion sweeps his features at the way I say it.

'Tell me about your brother,' he says, and I can't resist.

'Marshall stole my birthright. He should never have been born. He ousted me from the family business and then he ruined it. He mechanised every step of the production process. He bought cheap skins and made bad leather, creaming off the profit until the business had to be sold for a pittance.'

'What did you do?'

'I was pushed from the nest.'

Just saying it drags me down.

'Was your father your role model?' I ask.

A fleeting look of pain sweeps his features. All the answer I need.

'And when you left home?' he says.

'I became an apprentice to Ron Dougherty. He had the taxidermy shop out in Preston, right by the park. Did you know it?'

'I remember it.' The answer is tight and contained.

'I worked there for years as Ron's assistant. He was a father to me in so many ways. He gave me a home and a job, and plenty more.'

'You became a taxidermist?'

'He taught me all I needed to know. It's fair to say that we were the best in the business.' I'm bored now. 'Tell me, why do you hate your father?'

'I don't.'

He's lying. I laugh.

'You know this thing's not over.'

47

Marni

'Marni?' Thierry pronounced her name in a way that no one else ever had. Hearing his voice puzzled and reassured her. She opened her eyes.

She was lying in bed in a hospital room. The only other bed, directly opposite her, was empty. Sunlight streamed in through the pale, ill-fitting curtains and she blinked as she focused. There were people sitting on either side of the bed. Thierry and Alex on one side, Francis on the other. At which point she became aware of an atmosphere in the room that you could cut with a knife.

It all flooded back. The Tattoo Thief bursting into the studio. The struggle. The unmasking of a furious woman with bloody heart tattoos on the backs of her hands. Marni gasped.

'I can never forgive you for putting yourself in such danger,' said Thierry.

She ignored this. He was being overdramatic.

'Where's Pepper?'

Thierry shuffled his chair forward and took one of her hands. 'He's fine. But you acted recklessly.' He stroked the back of her hand with his thumb, such a familiar gesture.

'Where is he?'

'*Merde*. The dog's not important. You could have died. I was so scared, *chérie*.'

307

'Leave me alone, Thierry. I'm perfectly alive as you can see.'

Marni glared at him and pulled her hand away from his. Thierry looked bereft and tried to take it again, but she slipped it out of reach under the sheet.

Alex stared at her with wide, anxious eyes. 'How could you have done that, Mum? You should have told us.'

'You would have stopped me.'

'Bloody right, we would,' he said.

'I don't need a ticking-off from you, thank you,' she said testily. 'I'm the parent, remember.' But his concern brought a warm glow inside her, and more than a twinge of guilt.

Francis coughed. 'I'll need to take a statement from you at some point, Marni. When you're up to it.'

'No! You got her into this mess, now leave her alone. She needs to rest. I don't know what you're even doing here.' Thierry stood up and there was something threatening in his posture.

Francis frowned at him across the bed. 'She's an important witness in a multiple murder case.'

'This is your fault. You put her in danger.'

'He didn't,' said Marni. 'He had no idea what I was doing.'

Thierry snorted derisively. He sank back to his chair and tried again to take her hand.

'When can I go home?' she asked.

'That's up to the doctors,' said Francis. 'You may have had a slight concussion.'

Marni looked down at her left arm. It was swathed in bandages. 'And this?'

'Nine stitches. Your sleeve will have a scar on it,' said Thierry.

'Damn!' She turned to Francis. 'When do you want to do the statement?'

'Whenever you feel up to it.'

'I'm good. If I can get some coffee, we could do it now.'

'*Non*. You need to rest. This is ridiculous,' said Thierry.

'Thierry, I can decide whether I'm up to it or not. You need to back off.'

Thierry stood up abruptly. 'Okay. So I know where I'm not wanted. Come on, Alex.'

'Will you be back later?'

Thierry glared at her, but he nodded. 'Let me know when he's gone.'

When he reached the door, he turned back to the room. 'Inspector, can I have a word with you?'

Francis stood up and followed them out.

Marni's head was throbbing. The last thing she needed was two men fighting over her, especially as she wasn't particularly interested in either of them. *Was she?* Suddenly she felt exhausted. She closed her eyes and consciously relaxed the tension in her jaw. She was safe now. The killer was in custody and there was nothing here for her to be afraid of.

The door opened and closed.

'Marni?' It was a woman's voice.

She opened her eyes to see Angie Burton holding out a cup to her. 'Francis told me you wanted some coffee.'

She pushed herself up the pillows. 'Thanks. Where is he?'

'I'm sure he'll be in to see you when he's ready,' she said. The apparently friendly smile didn't quite reach her eyes.

The door opened again and Francis came back in.

'Thanks, Angie,' he said.

'No problem. Let me know if there's anything else you need.' Now she was positively simpering and Marni knew the score. Well, Angie was welcome to him.

'You all right, Marni? Do you need painkillers?'

'I'm fine. What did Thierry want?'

'Just to threaten me with grievous bodily harm if I put you in danger again.'

Marni snorted. 'Ignore him. He's all mouth.'

'He was worried about you. Rightly so. What you did was idiotic.'

Marni pushed herself up against the pillows. 'It got the Tattoo Thief arrested, didn't it?'

'And it almost got you killed.'

'You know what, instead of being angry with me, you might just bloody thank me for doing your job.'

Francis bristled but didn't say anything. He looked like someone had rammed a poker up his arse.

'Fuck you,' she said. 'I'm tired and I think it's time you left. And don't bother coming back again.'

xvii

They've taken me away from Brighton. Squashed like a sardine in a crappy police van. Handcuffed all the way. That shit lawyer should have stopped it. A stinking prison in the middle of nowhere. Fucking get me out. The Collector has to get me out. My chest feels tight. I can't breathe.

I'll hurt anyone that lays a finger on me. Guard or prisoner.

This needs to end. GET ME OUT OF HERE.

Where is he? He said that he would protect me. His lawyer told me they would get things sorted, get me out. I can't stay here, I won't survive.

The Collector won't let me down. He won't.

This is Marni Mullins' fault. My fingers itch for a knife. I want to slash her beautiful tattoo. Rip her back to pieces. Shred her skin with a blunt blade. Make her feel it. Hear her screaming as her warm blood runs all over my hands.

I'll have my time with her. I'll carve her into pieces. And that red-haired policeman. I'll have them both.

It's not over till it's over.

Where's the Collector? Where is he? Why doesn't he come?

48

Marni

The doctor was young and good-looking, making Marni wonder if she'd reached that age where all public sector employees would start to look younger than her. But when he shone a small, bright light into her eyes and declared that he wanted her to stay under observation until the next morning, she didn't warm to him at all.

'Seriously?' she said. 'I feel fine.'

'Headache?'

'Apart from that.'

He peeled the bandage back slowly from her arm and Marni winced as she saw a long, raw cut in the flesh, puckered at regular intervals by tight black stitches. It cut right across the lower portion of her sleeve tattoo, slicing through the wing of the vengeful angel wrapped around her arm. It was Thierry's work, the first of several he'd done for her – and looking at it brought back memories of falling in love. She wondered if she'd ever feel anything with the same intensity again. But with those memories came the memories of Paul that couldn't be disentangled – the dark third side of the triangle – and the lengthening shadows of all that had followed.

The doctor sucked in his breath. 'It's a little red for my liking.' He felt the skin on either side of the cut. 'It's hot. I think there's an infection – but we've given you antibiotics, so it should calm down over the next twenty-four hours. I'll send a nurse in with a clean dressing, and I'll come back and see you in the morning.'

'You can't be persuaded to change your mind?'

'It's for your own good, Ms Mullins. You've had a shock so we want to monitor your blood sugar levels for a while, too. Please bear with us.'

When he'd gone, Marni looked at the cut. She flexed her wrist, feeling pain shooting up her arm. The cut looked deep in places. Thank God it had been on her left arm, rather than her right.

A nurse came in and bandaged it. Marni was patient until she left. It was time to put her plan into operation.

She got gingerly to her feet and the room swam, as the jack-hammer in her head responded to every move. Through an open door, she could see a bathroom. She took tentative steps towards it, clasping the doorframe gratefully when she reached it. She propped herself up at the basin for a few minutes before splashing her face with cold water. In the mirror, she looked pale and tired, and maybe a decade older. Her hair was a mess and the previous day's eye makeup was smudged on her cheeks.

She wasn't going to stay here. The killer was in custody and she needed to get home, have a bath and then sleep in her own bed. That was the only way she was going to start feeling better.

She went back into the bedroom and looked around for her clothes. They lay crumpled on a chair by the window. There were splashes of blood on her top and on her jeans but she didn't care. They felt better than the short hospital gown, with its open back. Her bag was in the small cupboard by her bed, and a tub of painkillers stood on the nightstand. They were prescribed to her, so she dropped them into her bag and zipped it shut.

No one challenged her as she left the hospital, though every moment she expected someone to shout her name. The police protection had been called off now the Tattoo Thief was in custody, and no one had any reason to keep tabs on her. Down in the main lobby, she thought about calling Thierry to come and fetch her, but he would probably try and persuade her to stay here for another night. There was a taxi stand outside the front entrance. She checked that her purse still had money in it before joining the queue. She'd be home in minutes and, with the front door shut and locked behind her, the rest of the world could go to hell.

However, once she was sitting in the taxi, a shiver ran through her. She realised she didn't want to go back to an empty house. Alex was at Thierry's and Pepper was still at the vet's.

'Can you take me to Gardner Street instead, please?'

'Sure,' said the driver.

She would go to the studio and do some drawing. Drawing was the only way she'd be able to make sense of the emotional turmoil she was experiencing – the attack, what she'd seen at Stone Acre Farm, Pepper, Frank Sullivan, Thierry, the ever-present spectre of Paul . . . None of this was tied to her past but there was a lingering anxiety that always brought those events to the surface when she felt threatened.

The driver dropped her off outside the studio and she knew, the moment she opened the door, that it had been a mistake to come here. She had to peel crime scene tape away from the door – she wasn't even sure she was supposed to be in here. The events of the previous evening flooded back and she was confronted with all the evidence of what had happened – Pepper's blood, the massage bench lying on its side. Her desk was a chaotic mess and there were dark smudges of fingerprint powder on every surface.

But this was her space, and she wasn't going to let what happened leave her cowering in a corner.

Wearily, she started cleaning up, sponging Pepper's blood

from the floor, doing her best not to breathe in the stink of it. She tugged the massage bench up to standing with her one good arm and wiped away the black fingerprint powder coating wherever she saw it. She couldn't help but cry. Pepper's bravery was touching, and she felt proud of herself, too. She'd been attacked before, but this time she didn't fold and crumple. She'd used the skills she'd made herself learn and she'd managed to save her own life. Maybe a few others, too, now that the Tattoo Thief was behind bars. While the police were trying to pin the blame on the wrong man, she'd done what had been needed to safeguard her community.

Clearing up took her a couple of hours and by the time she finished her head was throbbing again and there was no way that she'd be able to focus on drawing. Empty house or not, she was ready to go home and crawl into bed.

With fortuitous timing, her mobile chimed.

'Yes?'

'Marni, where the hell are you?' It was Thierry.

'At the studio.'

'I'm at the hospital. They told me you checked yourself out.'

'I did. I couldn't stay there a minute longer.'

Thierry grunted. 'Idiot.'

'Did you call me just to insult me?'

'I'm coming to get you. I'll take you home.'

'Thank you.'

He wasn't always so bad.

She picked up her bag and some drawing supplies to take with her and checked that the back door was locked. Someone, at Francis's behest she imagined, had sorted out a temporary padlock to make good the damage that had been done when Sam Kirby had kicked the door in. A more permanent fix could wait till later in the week.

She went out by the front and stood on the pavement to wait

for Thierry. It was getting dark and the shops and cafés nearby were mostly closed. Halfway down Gardner Street, a pair of giant legs in red and white striped stockings stuck out above the street from the fascia of a comedy club – they always brought a smile to her face. She'd snapped up the tattoo studio here when she and Thierry had first broken up and she had to leave Tatouage Gris. Now she couldn't imagine ever wanting to work anywhere else.

She watched for Thierry's ancient Jag. At least it would be a comfortable ride home.

Headlights came up the road towards her but passed by. It wasn't the Jag, just a white tradesman's van, and so she carried on watching. Her headache had receded slightly out in the fresh air and she thought longingly about a warm bubble bath. She smiled. She felt proud of herself, good about the future. She'd proved something to herself and she would never forget it again. She wasn't a victim.

I'm nobody's victim any more.

Pain exploded in the back of her head and she staggered forward. An arm caught her. Something pressed against her mouth and, as she gasped for air, the world turned black.

49

Francis

The service wasn't acting as a balm to Francis in the way he'd hoped it would. This was the first time he'd encountered a person so thoroughly evil up close. Of course, apprehending killers was the focus of his job, and had been since he'd first become a detective constable. But this time was different, a more personal adversary because he'd been in charge of the case, and on a scale of depravity he had never seen before. The revulsion he felt for all he'd seen at Stone Acre Farm and for the smile Sam Kirby flashed at him when he finished questioning her had left him feeling dirty.

He felt calmer for being inside St Catherine's, as he always did, but none of the prayers or readings that evening spoke to him. They did nothing to quench the pain and even Father William's sonorous voice offered no comfort. His question was always the same. How could such evil exist? A question humanity had asked throughout the ages, but one that God never chose to answer.

His thoughts drifted to his sister, then to his mother. His mother never held it against him when his work prevented him from visiting, but his sister had made her feelings quite clear. Of course, he felt guilty – he didn't do half enough for either of them. He'd taken Robin to visit their mother just before coming to the service and it hadn't gone well. His mother, almost completely blind and confined to a wheelchair, had cried for most of the time they spent with her. She wanted to know if they'd heard from their father, which of course they hadn't. It had been years since he left, but he was still the focus of their mother's thoughts in a way that was painful to witness.

Robin had reproached him for not visiting frequently enough, but each time he left his mother, alone in her own world, confined to her lonely room, he felt terrible. This afternoon had been no exception. His mother's interest in the world beyond four walls had diminished, and Robin covered her own fear of this future with brusque irritation. His mother's cheek, when he kissed her goodbye, was wet with tears. The future held nothing for her.

He let his eyes drop and bowed his head. Father William was reciting the final prayer, 2 Corinthians 13. Francis shifted his weight on his knees, sorry that the service was over so quickly.

As the small body of worshippers filed out, he sat back on his chair, contemplating the painted angels behind the crucifix. The church was silent apart from the noise of shuffling feet as the organist didn't play at evensong. He bent forward to rest his head in his hands, praying for Robin and his mother, and for the strength he needed to do his job well, asking for forgiveness for the times he'd fallen prey to distractions and disillusionment. Father William gave his shoulder a quick squeeze as he walked back up the aisle towards the altar.

It was not the time for his phone to ring, so of course it did. Father William's head whipped round, a look of silent reprimand plastered across his face. Francis switched it off immediately, but not before glancing at the number. Thierry Mullins. Ringing him to issue another threat? He put the phone back in his pocket and bent his head in silent prayer again.

Half an hour later, when he emerged from the church, it was overcast outside and much cooler than it had been earlier. St

Catherine's stood on the brow of the hill with its churchyard sloping down towards Dyke Road and, beyond it, North Street. Feeling less anxious, Francis strolled down the worn brickwork path, then ducked through the stone archway at the bottom that led onto Wykeham Terrace. He walked up the path to the front door of his father's imposing Victorian gothic house. He'd always loved this house, though he'd spent scant time here as a child. The grey and white paintwork and crenellated eaves had made it virtually a castle in his youthful eyes. His father had left it empty more than a decade before, so moving into it when he wanted a place of his own had made sense – as a temporary measure. That had been three years ago and he hadn't even started looking for an alternative.

He pulled his phone out of his pocket and switched it back on. He was thinking about what he had in the fridge for supper when a text message bounced in.

Marni missing – call me.

It was from Thierry, and had been sent two minutes after his phone had rung in the church. Another one followed.

Call me. This is serious.

Then another two, similarly worded.

Francis hit the button for Thierry's number.

'Thank God,' said Thierry as they were connected. 'She checked herself out of the hospital and went to the studio. I was going to pick her up but she's not here.'

'So maybe she got tired of waiting for you and set off on foot,' said Francis. He tried to keep the anxious edge out of his voice.

It's not over . . .

'She's not answering her phone. And she wasn't waiting long – it only took me ten minutes to get here. I've been up and down the street. There's no sign of her. She hasn't had time to get home and, anyway, why leave when you've got a lift coming?'

'What do you think has happened?'

'How would I know?' snapped Thierry. 'Please, get a missing person's report out on her.'

'You're not telling me everything, are you?' There was something in Thierry's voice that suggested he knew more than he was letting on.

'I don't think this has anything to do with it, but you should know, my twin brother is due to be released from prison round about this time. There's bad blood between them.'

'Your brother was the man she stabbed, right?'

'She told you what happened?'

'Only some. Are you suggesting that your brother might come here? To do what?'

'No . . . I don't know. I just need to know she's safe.'

'I'll meet you at the studio.'

Ten minutes later, Francis drew up outside Marni's studio on Gardner Street, not caring that he was parking on a yellow line. Thierry was waiting for him inside the front of the shop.

'Was the door left open?' said Francis, as he hurried in.

Thierry shook his head. 'I've got a key. I used to work here with her sometimes.'

'Any sign of where she might have gone?'

'Nothing.'

Francis went through to the back. 'She must have spent some time here – she's cleared up all the mess from yesterday.'

'Apparently, she left the hospital at about five o'clock.'

Francis checked his watch. It was nearly half past seven.

'When did you last speak to her?'

'At about seven. I was at the hospital and she was here. But she was gone by the time I got here.'

It didn't make sense. The Tattoo Thief was behind bars. Marni shouldn't have been in any danger. Francis wanted to believe that she'd just decided not to wait for Thierry. But then why wasn't she answering her phone?

'Your brother Paul is still in prison in France?'

'Yes, as far as I know.'

'But you're not sure?'

'My mother would know if he's out.'

Thierry quickly dialled a number and then spoke rapidly in French. When he hung up, his face was relieved.

'Paul's still in prison. He's due for parole but that hasn't happened yet. That's all my mother could tell me.'

So it wasn't Paul. But that in itself hardly helped – Marni was still missing. Francis was scared. There were multiple possibilities. He got out his phone again.

'Rory, put out an ATL on Marni Mullins. Missing from her studio on Gardner Street since around seven.' He listened for a moment, frowning. 'Yes, I do think she might be in danger. Now just do it.'

It's not over . . .

50

Marni

Did she dare open her eyes? Was she back in the hospital? She was on a cold, hard surface. She was lying on the floor, on her side, and a moment's impulse from her brain to her limbs told her she couldn't move. Panic, and a rush of adrenalin. She tried to bring her right hand to her face but she couldn't. It was secured to her other hand at the wrist, behind her back. She was tied up and a moment's experimentation revealed that her ankles were also bound together.

She screamed for help. Nothing emerged from her throat but a dry rasp.

She opened her eyes. It made no difference – her world was black. She must be blindfolded. She rubbed the side of her face against the top of one arm and felt a strip of fabric bound round her head, but she couldn't shift it enough to see underneath. No chink of light slipped beneath the blindfold. She opened her eyes against the fabric but there was nothing.

The night terrors times a thousand.

She shut her eyes more tightly. She thought she heard a baby crying – Luke. Alex appeared in the distance. He was running away from her, taking Luke, and she was powerless to follow them. She bit her cheek and the pain made her snap out of it.

She listened. The silence became its own sound, hissing in the dark and ringing in her ears, a persistent earworm that pulsed with the rhythm of her blood in her veins. The only way to banish it was to concentrate on the sound of her own breathing. She needed to move. She rolled from her side onto her back, crushing her arms, then onto her other side. The floor was cold. The hip and shoulder on which she'd been lying ached.

Marni bent her legs up towards her body and shifted her weight, struggling into a sitting position. Now she could lean forwards and rest her head on her knees. She took a few deep breaths and felt better. She could think more clearly. Maybe if she shuffled around on her haunches, she would be able to work out where the door was.

This thought shocked her – how quickly had she normalised the situation she was in? Where the hell was she? Who had done this to her? Fear was like a cold shower of needles piercing her skin. Her enemy wasn't the darkness or the silence. It was the person who'd put her here.

That could be only one person. Paul.

No. That couldn't be.

She started to scream for help again and this time her voice rang out loud and clear. She yelled for a minute, then stopped, listening, hoping she would hear someone coming. But what if it was Paul? She regretted making a noise.

If it wasn't him, who the hell else would do this to her. Why?

It was cold. It was dark. She desperately needed water. She was alone. Before very long she'd need insulin and food, in the right order. And she was scared. She knew only too well what he was capable of.

For the next hour, she shuffled round and mapped out the confines of her captivity. It was a large room, and she bumped into various items of furniture, one or two of which were chairs, but there were also other pieces she couldn't identify. On one wall, she felt a doorframe and a door. With this discovery, she pushed herself up onto her knees and, by pressing one shoulder against the door handle, was able to manoeuvre herself up to standing. She turned around and felt for the handle with her hands. She pushed it down and tried pulling, then pushing the door. It didn't move. It was locked.

Disappointment flooded through her. Her bladder released. Hot urine rushed down her legs and soaked into her jeans, the stink of it assaulting her nostrils.

She sank back down to the floor and started to cry.

51

Rory

The boss flew into the incident room, his usual pallor exaggerated, his breath rasping from running up the stairs.

'Nothing?' he said to Rory.

Rory shook his head. 'The ATL's only been out a short while.'

'CCTV?'

'Just getting to it.'

'Come on, Rory. You know as well as I do, if we don't find her soon our chances of finding her diminish fast.'

Rory knew that and more. Like the fact that the more time that passed, the more likely it was she'd show up dead. That even if they found something on the CCTV, it would only tell them where she was then – not where she was now. Things the boss didn't need to hear, given the state he was in already.

'Angie,' said Francis, 'I got this list of numbers from Thierry Mullins – friends, family, people she might have called. Run through it and see if any of them have any idea of her whereabouts.'

Angie took the list back to her desk and started to work the phone.

'What about the kid?' said Rory. 'He might know something.'

'Thierry's gone back to his flat to ask him. He'll let us know.'

'Her sister doesn't know anything,' said Burton, starting to dial the next number on her list.

Rory got the CCTV feed for Gardner Street up on his screen. Francis studied the footage over his shoulder. Unfortunately, the camera angle meant that the entrance to Celestial Tattoo was just out of shot.

'Goddamn it – this won't show us anything.'

'Let's take a look,' said Rory, staying calm. 'If she left on foot, we'll see her coming down the road this way or, if she went the other way, she'll show up on one of the other cameras when she turns the corner into North Road.'

Rory set the footage in motion. He started it at seven, exactly the time when Thierry had called Marni from the hospital. There were a few people walking up and down the road, but most of the shops and pavement cafés were closed by then. Vehicles came down the road intermittently – it was a narrow, one-way street, too narrow for parking, which at least gave them a clear view of the pavements and doorways.

Francis fidgeted behind him.

They watched it several times, scanning the pedestrians for Marni, but there was no sign of her walking. As Rory had expected, the footage yielded nothing useful.

'What about North Road? Can you load the film that covers its junction with Gardner Street?' asked the boss.

They ran through the new footage for another half hour, desperately trying to see her.

'It's like she's vanished into thin air,' said Francis.

'Could she have left by the back door?'

'No, it was padlocked from the inside. She came out at the front. Start all over again, Rory, and take down all the vehicle licence plates.'

A couple of hours passed, though it felt far longer.

Francis paced the incident room, barking questions at the

team and talking to Thierry on the phone. Alex knew nothing, nor did anyone else Thierry had called.

'Talk to me, Rory.'

'Nothing yet, boss. The first three cars – I've checked them on the database. They're all local, no obvious connection.'

The golden hour had passed long ago and if Marni had been abducted, her chances of survival were growing slimmer with every passing minute.

'Boss?'

'What is it?'

'This one,' Rory said, pointing at a small white van. 'It's coming up as registered to a hire company.'

'Let's go.'

As Francis led the way out, he almost ran straight into a uniformed officer coming in.

'Inspector Sullivan?'

'Yes?'

'This has just been handed in at the desk.' He held up a large red shoulder bag. 'A man found it after pub closing in an alleyway off Gardner Street. It appears to belong to the missing woman, Marni Mullins.'

Francis didn't need the information – he recognised the bag immediately.

As the officer handed it over to him, the sound of a mobile phone ringing came from inside. Francis dropped it onto the nearest desk and rummaged through it for the phone. Thierry's name showed on the screen, and Francis pressed answer.

'Marni? No, who's this?' came his panicked voice, struck with a moment of hope.

'Francis. Her bag's just been handed in. Found in Gardner Street.'

'*Merde, merde!*'

'We've got a lead. A hired van drove up the road at around

about the time she went missing. The car hire office is in Cannon Place. It opens at six a.m. – meet us there.'

He was about to hang up when Thierry said, 'Wait.'

'What is it?'

'Is her medication in the bag?'

'Medication?' Francis pulled the two sides of the bag wide open so he could see inside.

'She's diabetic. She needs insulin shots.'

'I had no idea she was diabetic.'

'You don't really know her very well at all, do you?'

At the bottom of the bag, Francis could see a small clear pouch containing medical paraphernalia. He pulled it out. 'What happens if she misses it?'

'If she doesn't control her blood sugar levels, for even a few hours, she'll fall into a coma.'

52

Francis

Rory worked the phone as Francis drove. 'No answer, boss. They're not open yet.'

'Keep trying.'

It was no distance and the streets were empty. Francis hit the accelerator and flipped his blue lights.

'I need details on who rented the following van from you ...' Rory had finally got an answer and reeled off the registration number. 'Police. We suspect it might have been used in a crime.' He was silent and then hung up the call with a string of expletives. 'Fucking data protection. Need a warrant. The guy's obviously been watching too many crime dramas.'

'He's bloody right, of course,' said Francis. 'Hopefully seeing a warrant card will be enough to convince him.'

He was driving too fast down Old Steine and then failed to give way as he should have at the roundabout. Marni's bag, with her medication inside, slid from one side of the back seat to the other. An angry Vauxhall driver sounded his horn as Francis sped away up Kings Road and along the front.

'Anything from Hollins yet?' Francis had called him out to question the owners of the other vehicles they'd seen on the CCTV, though he doubted it would yield anything of use.

'No, boss. He only left home ten minutes ago and he's got further to go than us.'

'Shit! I can't help wondering . . .'

'What?'

'All that *it's not over* stuff.'

'But Kirby's locked up. We've found nothing to suggest an accomplice. I don't see how it can be connected.'

Francis shook his head. 'I've got a bad feeling, Rory.'

The white regency splendour of the Grand Hotel passed in a blur, and the brakes shrieked as Francis made the sharp right into Cannon Place. The car hire office was located at the top end of the road. Francis screeched to a halt, half blocking the entrance to the small yard in which the hire cars were parked. They jumped out of the car and ran to the office door, becoming aware of the sounds of an altercation inside.

'*Putain!* Tell me now who's got a white van out on hire from you,' came Thierry's unmistakeable tone from inside.

'I can't.' The second voice sounded strangled.

As Francis and Rory entered the office, they could see why. Thierry had hold of a young man by the two sides of his shirt collar and was practically dragging him across the chest-height counter.

Rory heaved him off and strong-armed him back against the opposite wall. The young man rested against the counter on his side, panting. His name badge announced him as Amit.

Francis got out his warrant card and held it out for the young man to read.

'Jesus, that was fast. I only just called you,' Amit gasped.

Francis exchanged a glance with Rory. 'We called *you*.'

'I just dialled nine nine nine for help: this guy came in and started threatening me.'

'Just get the damn information,' shouted Thierry.

'I can't just give out information to you, sir,' said Amit, less afraid now he realised he had the backup of two police officers.

'Shut it,' said Rory to Thierry. 'Leave it to us.'

Francis turned back to Amit. 'I need to know who hired this van.' He passed across a slip of paper with the registration details written on it. 'We have reason to believe it may have been used in an abduction yesterday evening.'

Amit stared at the paper, looking unsure as to what he was supposed to do.

Francis flashed his warrant card again. 'This is an emergency. A woman's life might be in danger.'

There was a brief scuffle and Thierry broke away from Rory. He came and stood by the counter next to Francis. 'My *wife's* life might be in danger.'

'Of course. I'm sorry,' said Amit. 'I was following the company rules.'

Francis gave Thierry a warning look. 'That's okay. Now, please, give us the information.'

Amit turned to his computer and typed in the details. 'Got it. It's hired out to an IT company called Algorithmics. They've had it for a couple of weeks.'

'Got an address?' said Rory.

Outside the office, a police siren sounded loudly and seconds later two uniformed PCs rushed in.

'Right, what's going on? Are you the one that called in?' The older of the pair addressed Amit, while glaring at Francis, Thierry and Rory.

Francis pulled out his warrant card for the third time. 'DI Sullivan.'

'Sorry, sir,' said the cop. 'We got a call to come out here. Threatening behaviour.'

'We've got it covered. Thanks for turning out but it's sorted.'

'Right, guv.'

The two uniforms backed out.

Amit handed a printout to Francis. 'That's the address for the company.'

Francis read it out loud. 'Gorse Avenue, East Preston. Where the hell is that?'

'East Preston? Out Littlehampton way,' said Rory.

'Let's go,' grunted Thierry.

'Thank you, Amit,' said Francis, as they headed for the door.

'I hope you save the lady,' Amit called after them.

As Francis got back into the driving seat, he heard the passenger door opening behind him. He looked round to see Thierry climbing into the back seat. 'What the hell are you doing?'

'I'm coming too.'

'No. No way. This is a police matter.'

'I'm not getting out. Now drive.'

'Three's better than two,' said Rory. 'Who knows what we'll find there?'

'That's exactly what worries me,' said Francis, gunning the car into gear.

'Along the front, then the A259,' said Rory. 'Blue light?'

'Blue light,' said Francis. 'And seat belts.'

He put his foot down on the accelerator and offered up a silent prayer. A plea. He would bargain anything to see Marni safe.

53

Marni

Had she slept or had she just been drifting in some sort of fugue state? It was hard to say and it didn't matter. Marni was awake now, the hard floor digging into her, a heavy blanket of cold air making it difficult to move. She stank and her jeans were tight and clammy and damp. She felt sick, but hungry at the same time, though fear killed her appetite the moment she became aware of it.

She struggled to sit up and was immediately dizzy, yellow spots floating in front of her bound eyes. Her sense of time and place had lost their anchors and she had no way of working out how long she'd been here. She didn't even know if it was day or night, but she needed food and water and, even more urgently, insulin.

She took a deep breath and shouted for help at the top of her lungs, making it last for as long as she could. Breathe and repeat. Breathe and repeat – until she felt light-headed again and had to lie down.

Her mind started to slip away and her thoughts spun out of control. *Should she start gnawing at her own arm, like a rat in a trap? Could she eat her hair, bite into her cheek?* The danger of slipping into a coma was seductive and she fought against it. But then she couldn't remember what the danger was, why she was fighting. *Surely it would be easier to slip away?*

A sudden noise, as sharp as the crack of gunfire after all the hours of silence, dragged her back to consciousness. It was a door opening. A light went on and at the bottom of her blindfold she could make out a thin, pale line.

'Help me,' she croaked.

Footsteps came towards her.

'Help me. I need water. I need food.'

She struggled to sit up. A hand on her shoulder made her start. It pushed her back down to the floor.

'Shhhhhhhhh.'

She tried to push back against it, but she didn't have the strength.

An arm cradled her head. Then the rim of a plastic bottle was pressed to her lips. She drank gratefully. Cold, cold water. It was painful to swallow but so welcome she almost sobbed with gratitude. She drank her fill but still the bottle was pressed against her lips, so she drank more.

But why didn't the person untie her or undo her blindfold?

She turned her head away from the water and heard the bottle being placed on the floor.

'I'm diabetic. I need food. I need insulin.'

The supporting arm lowered her back to the floor and footsteps receded.

Whose arm? Whose footsteps? It felt strange to be attended to by someone so completely anonymous, with intentions unknown. *Could it have been Paul?*

'Why don't you untie me? Why don't you help me?'

The door closed and the footsteps were muffled, on the other side of it. Panic rose in her gullet. She was afraid she would vomit up the water she'd just drunk. Whoever that person was, they were her captor, not her rescuer. Her head spun, her world spun. The floor tilted underneath her and she started to hyperventilate.

The door opened again and the footsteps came back towards her. The man – something about the footfall made her think it was a man – heaved her up into a sitting position. Something soft and sugary was pressed against her lips. She took a small bite. A doughnut? It was stale but she attacked it ravenously, not caring as jam ran down her chin. It would take ten or fifteen minutes for the glucose to hit her bloodstream, but relief flooded through her.

When the doughnut was finished, the man left her slumped against the wall. She could hear him moving around the room, though she couldn't work out what he was doing. What would happen next? What were her chances of escaping from him? Should she try and form a connection with him, and beg him to release her?

'Thank you for that,' she said, still licking the sugar from around her lips.

He didn't reply.

'Who are you? What do you want from me?'

Still no answer.

'Please just let me go. I haven't seen your face. I don't know who you are. Please don't do something you might regret.' She hated the fear that crept into her voice as she spoke.

The silence was broken by a sound she recognised. The clatter of a blade against a whetstone, rhythmic and steady. Fear clutched at her, tightening her throat, grinding her insides as sharply as the stone ground the metal.

'Please . . .'

'Marni, I have no intention of regretting a single thing I'm going to do to you.'

A slow, lazy drawl. Familiar. Male. She'd heard this voice before, but where? It wasn't Paul. The accent wasn't French.

'Please, you can untie me. You've had your fun, but now I think you'd better let me go.'

The sound of the knife on the stone didn't miss a beat.

'What do you want with me?'

The sharpening stopped. Marni held her breath.

'What do I want with you? I would have thought that was obvious.'

That voice.

The footsteps came towards her.

'As you won't be leaving here alive, there's actually no need for this.' He yanked the blindfold from her face. Marni gasped as a few hairs were pulled away along with it.

After hours in the dark, she was blinded. She closed her eyes tightly and waited for the white flashes to clear, then opened them slowly, head down, looking at the floor. Polished cement glinted up at her as she focused her blurred vision on her own feet and lower legs. She felt suddenly conscious of her damp and stinking jeans.

Glancing to one side, she saw another pair of feet. New trainers, hardly worn, with chinos, too long, rippling at the ankles. Slowly, she let her eyes travel up the man's body – he was a little knock-kneed and his trousers were too tight at the waist, pushed down at the front where his belly spilled over the top. He was wearing a black polo shirt with a company logo she'd never seen before. He had a tattoo on his arm. A tattoo that she'd finished only a couple of days ago. Steve smiled down at her as their eyes met and she felt chilled to the bone.

Oh my God!

'St-Steve?'

Steve? The computer geek with the tiger tattoo?

Her blood sugar spiked with a rush of adrenalin.

'Beautiful Marni. All mine.'

He turned away from her abruptly and went back to a table where she could see a knife and a whetstone lying.

Fear made her mouth dry. Words weren't forming in her mind.

She instinctively struggled against her bindings, then stopped. All thought of escape left her as she started to look around the room and take in her surroundings. Rational thought of any kind was no longer an option. Fear had taken the driving seat.

The room was a large rectangle, larger than she'd imagined from her limited shuffling around when she was blindfolded. There were no windows – were they underground? The black walls were lined in some sort of high-tech rubberised cladding. She'd seen it before in recording studios. Soundproofing. Ice crept through her veins. The ceiling was an industrialist nightmare of aluminium pipes and grids. Along one of the short ends of the rectangle, there was a white screen and in front of it a couple of slumping sofas upholstered in deep red velvet. A private cinema.

But that wasn't all. Behind the sofas, taking up the central portion of the room, stood a row of seven highly polished concrete plinths, each one about four feet high. Marni blinked and refocused, tearing her eyes from one to another. Bile rose in her gullet, burning her throat. On each plinth stood a framework of thick silver mesh, polished and gleaming in the sharp light. The frames were formed in the shape of human body parts – an arm, a leg, a torso, a head. One, standing taller than the rest, was shaped like an entire body. Four of the frames were just that, nothing else. But the other three appeared to be draped with pieces of soft, buttery leather. Tattooed leather.

Marni fought the urge to vomit as she realised exactly what she was looking at.

The 'leather' was human skin. Giselle Connelly's arm with its detailed biomechanical tattoo. Evan Armstrong's shoulder with its Polynesian design, and a leg she didn't recognise with an elegant watercolour of a peacock. Human skin turned to leather, preserved and put out on display.

The room spun and she slumped onto her side.

'Ah, I can see you're appreciating my collection. Amazing, aren't they?'

'You . . .? But these are Sam Kirby's pieces.'

'Of course. But I commissioned them. She was working for me.'

It didn't make sense. She didn't understand.

'And, you, Marni Mullins, you will be the most beautiful of them all.'

He walked towards her and she shoved herself back against the wall. When he reached her, he bent down, pushing his face towards hers. As she cowered and whimpered in front of him, he kissed her gently on the lips. Then he softly pressed a folded cloth over her mouth and nose. The tang of ether hit the back of her throat. Her world returned to black.

54

Rory

Rory had been on enough emergency runs through Brighton not to be a nervous passenger. But that was before he went on a blue light run with Francis Sullivan at the wheel. They'd hardly pulled out of Cannon Place when he swerved precariously to avoid a delivery driver who stepped out from behind the open doors of his van.

Thierry hurriedly did up his seat belt in the back.

'Jesus, boss, you have passed your advanced driving, haven't you?'

Francis frowned and squinted at the road ahead. Almost immediately they came up behind a minibus. Francis sounded the siren.

'Come on,' said Thierry. 'Pass him!'

Francis gave another blast of the siren and finally the minibus driver slowed down and pulled across onto the pavement.

'Now go!' urged Thierry.

Francis put his foot down and they sped through Hove, blue light flashing, with the sea on their left and the just-stirring town to their right.

'Rory, try Hollins.'

Rory called and listened to his phone for a few moments. Hollins had seen the owner of the first car that had shown up on the CCTV footage.

'Just a school-run dad,' he reported as he hung up, 'picking up his daughters from swimming training. Says the swimming instructor will vouch for him collecting the girls. It's not likely to be him, in Hollins' view.'

'What about the second one?'

'Hollins is en route there.'

Francis slammed on the brakes as a BMW pulled out in front of them. Rory's phone flew into the footwell and Thierry swore softly in French. The siren went on again and then they were past it.

'You're sure we are going to the right place?' said Thierry.

'No,' said Francis. 'Not at all. But it's the best lead we've got.'

'Stands to reason,' said Rory. 'If you're going to abduct someone, a van's better than a car. And the timing seemed right.'

'*Merde!*'

Rory couldn't tell if this was a comment on the boss's driving or on the fact that they were acting on a hunch. But it didn't matter. All that mattered was getting to the address and finding Marni.

They crossed the bridge over the River Adur, after which the road widened and ran dead straight. It was empty of traffic. Blue light still flashing, Francis let rip.

'How much further?' he asked Rory.

Rory checked the map on his phone. 'Four or five miles, but we've got to go right through the middle of Worthing.'

The small coastal town was starting to come to life for the day and the road suddenly hit junction after junction. The tension in the car rose still higher as Francis skilfully wove the vehicle through a series of obstacles.

'*Putain!*' Thierry's swearing became louder. 'Where did you learn to drive?'

The blue light in the front of the windscreen carried on flashing and Francis hit the siren intermittently to let the other road users know they were coming. Finally, they seemed to be through the worst of it, past Worthing and Goring, and the road joined a stretch of dual carriageway.

'Left at the third roundabout.'

The turn took them south, back in the direction of the sea. As Francis sped up again, Rory saw red lights flashing ahead. A bell started ringing.

'Level crossing, boss.'

'I know. I see it.'

'It's closing.'

'I know.'

'We won't make it.'

Francis didn't reply but continued accelerating.

Up ahead, the barriers were already starting to come down.

'Frank! Stop now!' The panic sounded in Rory's voice and he gripped the dashboard with white knuckles, pushing himself back in his seat.

'No, no way,' said Thierry, sounding just as terrified.

'We're not going to fucking make it!'

The barriers were down and it seemed as if Francis was just going to smash through them.

Acting on instinct with no thought of the consequences, Rory grabbed for the wheel and tugged it sharply towards him. With his other hand, he grappled for the handbrake. Francis tried to fight against him but was taken by surprise. With an ear-splitting screech, the car spun out of control, barrelling sideways into the low wall of the adjoining station car park. The train rushed by with its horn blaring. Rory let go of the wheel and slumped back in his seat, suddenly aware that the airbag in front of him had deployed.

He looked at Francis, who was scrabbling to get his own airbag out of the way. When he couldn't wrench it off the steering wheel, he attempted to start the stalled engine. It bit first time and Francis threw the car into reverse. The blue light was still flashing in the car, and the crossing's red lights were still flashing beyond. The bell sounded louder than ever.

Rory turned in his seat.

'Are you okay?' he said to Thierry.

Thierry came out with a rush of expletives that meant nothing to Rory. But at least he was alive and conscious. There was blood gushing from where he'd bitten through his lip on one side of his mouth.

Francis manoeuvred the car through a three-point turn so they were facing the right way again. The bell stopped ringing. The red lights stopped flashing. The barriers came up and Francis hit the gas.

'Don't you ever call me Frank again.'

55

Marni

Marni felt two sensations – pain and cold. Sharp pains spasmed through her wrists and shoulders – they seemed to be bearing all her weight. Tight strictures were cutting into the flesh of her wrists. Her arms were high above her head, twisted unnaturally. Her hands were blocks of ice, almost numb, while the long cut in her left forearm burned. A cord of pain throbbed in the crease of her neck where her head had been lolling back unsupported. She was standing up, tied to something. And she was freezing. She could feel cold air on her skin. All of her skin. Realising she was naked, she snapped her eyes open, fear quickly dwarfing the other sensations and galvanising her to lash out against her bindings.

She was still in Steve's basement cinema, tied to a St Andrew's cross, facing one of the walls. All she could see was the rubber soundproofing material, a few inches in front of her face. While she was unconscious, Steve had removed her clothes and tied her up to this contraption. She could smell an unfamiliar floral scent. It was rising off her skin and she realised she was feeling the cold so acutely because she was damp. God forbid, he'd washed her down. The stink of urine was gone but she retched at the thought of his hands on her body.

She felt dizzy. The doughnut had prevented her from sinking

into a coma, but without a shot of insulin, she wasn't going to benefit from much of the energy it should have given her. She knew it wouldn't be long before the black spots would rain down behind her eyelids and she'd lose consciousness again.

Maybe that would be better.

The room was silent. Fear made her feel faint but pain kept her mind sharp. She raised herself onto her tiptoes to take the pressure off her arms, reassured by the burning pain as some blood managed to get through. She thought about what she knew of Steve, if that was even his real name. She'd spent more than twenty hours tattooing his arm and she tried to remember what they'd talked about. He'd certainly been very interested in tattoos and the process of tattooing, but there was nothing unusual in that with people who sat for her. He hadn't been great with pain, though by no means the worst. He'd talked a fair bit about himself, though when she thought back on it, she couldn't remember much in the way of concrete facts. He worked in computers – boring – and the rest had all been opinions – what he thought of this, what he thought of that, why his opinion was necessarily more valid than others'. She remembered with a shudder how he'd asked her about Evan Armstrong's body, knowing all along exactly what had happened to him.

There had been no empathy for anyone else in any of the conversations she'd had with him. Not that she'd particularly noticed it then. It was only now, thinking back, that she realised how self-centred he'd sounded. At the time, she'd only given half an ear, at best, to what he was saying, concentrating most of her attention on what she was doing.

But how could she turn this knowledge to her advantage? How could she use it to prompt him to let her go?

She heard the door opening and her stomach lurched. Footsteps came towards her and then he appeared in her peripheral vision. He was smiling, but it wasn't a smile. It was a leer.

'You're so beautiful, Marni, it's almost a shame to desecrate that perfect body. But your tattoo will be the jewel of my collection.'

Marni's blood ran cold and she involuntarily thrashed against her restraints.

He stepped towards her and ran a hand down her spine.

'Shhhhhh.' His voice was so close to her ear that she shuddered.

'Please, Steve . . .'

'Please what?'

'Please let me go. I can carry on tattooing you. I could give you an amazing back piece. You don't need to do this.'

'Ah, but I do. I need to complete my collection because that idiotic woman fucked up.'

There was a sudden flash of anger in his tone that made Marni even more scared.

'S-Sam Kirby?' She needed to keep the tremor out of her voice.

'She was supposed to collect all the tattoos, then disappear. I paid her well enough.'

'She's been arrested.'

'I know. I'm paying for her lawyer.'

Marni had to keep him talking. He would find it harder to kill her if he related to her at a human level. But she couldn't expect empathy with the position she was in. It would have to be about him. She wondered, for the briefest second, if anyone was coming for her. Thierry was expecting to pick her up – surely he would have told the police.

She pushed those thoughts out of her head. She had to act for herself. Time was running out, her blood sugar was plummeting again.

'And now I have to finish the job without her.'

'You don't have to. The pieces you have are enough.'

'It's not the entire collection. The police have some of them, taken from Stone Acre Farm, and besides, I particularly want *your* tattoo. And also Thierry's.'

Marni's blood ran cold. If she didn't get out of this, if she couldn't put an end to this here and now, this madman would go after Thierry. She thought about Alex and her heart broke.

'Do you know how to do it? How to cut the skin from my body, how to cure it? Don't you need the Tattoo Thief to do it for you?'

She guessed this would make him bristle and she was right.

'Of course I can do it myself. I've watched her flaying skin. I've watched her tanning it. It's hardly rocket science.'

'Only, if you're going to take my tattoo, I don't want you to ruin it.'

He took a step closer to her and she shivered. Fear had made her forget the pain of being suspended by her wrists, but each time that fear was ratcheted up, her mental agony became greater. He ran both his hands slowly over her back. She pressed herself against the wooden cross, but there was nothing she could do to escape his touch.

'Marni, perhaps I should explain. The human body is a work of art in itself. Yours especially. But when a tattoo is added, it takes it to another level. Living works of art, warm to the touch. No other art form is as dynamic as a tattoo.'

'But you kill them. Surely that goes against what you've just said.'

'When people die, their tattoos die with them. They rot like any other piece of flesh. By doing this, I'm saving great works of art. It's what they do in Japan, with the Yakuza tattoos. The preserved skin thus becomes superior to the living skin.'

'Only you're killing people to do it. In Japan, they wait for them to die naturally.'

'Art is more important than people. I've known that since I was a child. The human body is nature's ultimate work of art, and when we adorn it with our own works, its beauty is magnified. Art must endure through time in a way that people never can.

347

And art is pure and true, while people lie, brag and fornicate. I'm keeping what's important, discarding what doesn't matter. I'm creating the ultimate art collection. Surely you understand that, Marni? You're a great artist yourself.'

Pretentious crap, she wanted to shout, but she knew she had to humour him.

'And if you kill me, no one else will benefit from my art.'

'Another advantage of your death. My tattoo will become a more rare and precious object.'

'You're wrong, Steve. And what you're doing is wrong.'

She felt the force of his blow before she saw it coming. He smashed a bunched fist into the side of her head. Stars exploded in front of her eyes.

Steve walked away from her. Blood roared in her ears. She couldn't hear what he was doing. Time was running out. Deep breaths. Slowly, not quickly. Don't hyperventilate. Pain radiated out in waves from where his fist had hit her. She bit down hard on her lip to counter it, tasting blood in her mouth.

This couldn't be the end. She had so much more living to do. She wasn't going to let this bastard have his way. Somehow, she'd get out of this. Somehow.

'I'm sorry if I hurt you, Marni.' He was coming back to her. 'This will soothe you.'

He pressed something soft against the side of her face, a cool caress.

'Wh-what is that?'

'This?' He smoothed it against her cheek. 'This is Evan's tattoo, Evan's skin.'

Marni recoiled. It felt like the softest chamois leather.

'Sam did a good job with this one. She was so talented and now it's all going to waste.'

Marni felt physically sick. Her mouth flooded with saliva. As she breathed in, she caught the scent of the human leather,

348

strong and piggy. She retched and acid vomit burned the back of her throat. She gritted her teeth and pressed her lips together tightly, determined to remain calm.

'Your skin will be even softer when I've finished preserving it,' he said. 'So soft, so beautiful.'

His other hand was on her back again and she could feel his fingers tracing the shapes in her tattoo.

'Oh Marni, it's hard for me to decide if I want you or if I want your tattoo more. You're special to me, and you're a creator of art. My other victims carried art on their bodies but nothing in their minds. However, you, you're the embodiment of art itself. A creator and a living work of great beauty. But if I let you live, you'll betray me. So much as I want you – and I do want you very much – it's only the artwork on your body that I can trust.' He grabbed a handful of her hair and yanked her head back so that he could look her straight in the eyes. 'That means, my darling, you're going to have to die.'

56

Francis

Despite a major dent along the passenger side of the car, Francis barely moderated his speed as they cut a swathe through the narrow, sharp-cornered lanes of the village of East Preston. In the back, Thierry nursed his lip in silence, while Rory studied the map on his mobile to work out the quickest route to Gorse Avenue.

'Left onto Vicarage Lane.' The tyres screeched as Francis took the corner too fast. 'Right onto Fairlands ... left at Sea Road ...'

A couple of young mothers chatting on the pavement with their pushchairs were left open-mouthed as the car sped through, blue light still flashing, and on Sea Road Francis had to slam the brakes on to narrowly avoid hitting a cat.

'Jesus,' muttered Thierry.

Finally, they came to Gorse Avenue.

'Kill the light,' said Rory. 'Slow down.'

Lined on either side by large houses, Gorse Avenue went nowhere. It was a wealthy cul-de-sac of extensions, conservatories, tennis courts and outdoor pools. The houses on the south side of the road fronted onto the beach and it was easy to picture the gin-and-Jags lifestyle of the local residents.

'I thought we were looking for a business address,' said Francis.

Rory shrugged. 'Probably some entrepreneur who runs his company from home.'

After the intensity of the drive across from Brighton, their slow, silent progress through privilege felt surreal. They didn't meet another car and there were no pedestrians along the side of the road, or people in their gardens.

'That's it,' said Rory, 'on the right.'

He pointed to a sprawling contemporary structure that looked completely out of keeping with the Edwardian villas and art deco lodges they'd been driving past. Clad in corrugated steel, with sharp angles and curving buttresses, the building seemed to have no windows at all – at least not on the road side. Francis pulled the car up on the verge in front of the house next door. He didn't want to lose the element of surprise by turning into the drive.

'How are we going to handle it, boss?'

Francis sighed and rubbed his face with his hands.

'Depends if anyone's home. We don't have a warrant, so we need to play it by the book. Thierry, you wait here.'

'I'll be damned if I do. I'm coming with you.'

'No. This is police business.'

'Marni's my wife. And she needs insulin.'

'Ex-wife.' What was it with these two? It wasn't the first time that Francis wondered why they'd divorced.

Francis got out of the car. Rory and Thierry did the same. Thierry had the little pouch containing Marni's insulin-injecting kit in one hand.

'All right. No fireworks, no histrionics.' Francis was looking at Thierry when he said this. 'Look for the van, then follow my lead.'

They walked along the road – there was no pavement, just neatly mowed grass verges – and into the driveway. A pale blue Aston Martin was parked conspicuously in front of the house.

'He does alright for himself, then,' murmured Rory.

There was no sign of the van, but there was a garage off to one side. Its door was closed. Francis pointed towards it and they changed direction.

Rory tried the main garage door. 'Locked.'

Francis skirted round the side. A footpath led to a side door, the top half of which was glass. He peered into the garage. Beyond a stripped-down Harley, he could see a small white van. It looked the same as the one on the CCTV footage, but seeing it from the side meant he couldn't make out the plates to confirm it.

Rory came behind him. 'That's definitely it. Must be.'

'Right, time to question Mr . . . what's the owner's name?' said Francis.

'Harrington. Steven Harrington,' said Rory. He was tapping into his mobile. 'Comes up on Google as the owner of Algorithmics, the company that hired the white van.'

They walked in silence back around the house, towards the front door. A small silver name plaque stated 'Algorithmics'. Underneath it there was an intercom button. Francis pressed it.

'We're sorry. There is no one working here today.' The voice was female, robotic. 'Please call the telephone number below to talk to someone.'

Francis glanced down. There was a number embossed in the metal fascia of the intercom.

'Shall I call it?' said Rory.

'No. Wait here, in case someone comes. I'll have a quick recce. And call for some backup, fast.'

Francis set off around the house again, Thierry following silently at his shoulder. As they progressed down the side of the building, the garden came into view – an unadorned lawn leading down to the sandy beach some fifteen metres away. There was an empty concrete terrace at ground level that didn't look like it was ever used – there was no furniture on it. However, there was a larger terrace at first-floor level, though this only boasted a solitary chair facing out to sea. The back of the house, in contrast to the front, was all glass and no metal. It put Francis in mind of a vast aquarium. Goldfish-bowl living taken to the extreme but, of course, there was no one around here to see in through the vast windows. He wondered if it was a private beach or whether members of the public could settle with their picnics and spend an hour or two watching how the rich passed their Sunday afternoons.

He looked through the windows. The ground floor was given over entirely to a single open-plan office. There were banks of computer screens arranged in semicircles across a line of desks but only one, high-tech, ergonomic office chair. Did only one person work for Algorithmics, generating the cash income for such a lavish lifestyle?

'Thierry, try all the doors on ground level. If you find one open, come and get me. Don't go in.'

Francis started to climb the steel staircase which gave access to the first-floor balcony. Each footfall made a soft clang on the metal, so he moved slowly to minimise it, not wanting to give his presence away in case there was someone in the house. The one chair on the balcony was perfect for sunrises or sunsets, no doubt. But it was the view inside the house that took Francis's breath away.

He put his hands up to the glass window to cut out the glare of the early-morning sun and stared in breathlessly. He wouldn't even know how to describe it. An art installation? A tableau? There were stuffed animals. Rank upon rank of them. Not in glass cases like the ones he'd seen at the Natural History Museum as a child, but out in the open. A battle had been staged, animal against animal, fighting with scaled-down human weapons, wearing miniature human clothing. The Roundheads versus the Cavaliers. Dogs against cats. A rabbit taking on a

353

mongoose. Foxes fighting snakes. Big cats wrestling. Animals were wounded, skewered, decapitated. Tooth and claw ran red with blood. Animal body parts were strewn across the carnage.

It was both extraordinary and twisted, and indicated strongly that a very warped mind had created such a scene. Francis's heart pounded and he tasted fear. Not for himself. But cold terror at the thought that Marni might be somewhere here, at the mercy of whatever creature had created this for his entertainment.

'*Putain!*' Thierry gasped as he came up beside Francis.

Francis put a finger to his lips, then tried the handle of the glass door that led onto the balcony. It opened and, without a moment's thought, he stepped inside. Thierry followed.

The room had a fusty smell, like old fur coats, and dust motes drifted across the floor. But he had a sense, a strong sense, that they weren't alone in the house. There was a faint smell of coffee, and somewhere, an open window was causing a draught. Without bending down, Francis used each foot to lever off the opposite shoe. They passed through the room and came to a landing with a staircase in either direction.

'You go upstairs, I'll go down,' he whispered to Thierry. 'Shout if you need help.'

Thierry nodded. 'We've got to find her. She needs insulin, desperately by now.'

He cautiously set off to check the next floor.

In his stockinged feet, Francis made no sound as he moved down the stairs. And for the first time in his career as a police officer, he wished he had a gun.

57

Marni

Marni took a deep breath.

'There is a way of having both, Steve,' she said. She made her voice a little breathy. She wanted to throw up. She couldn't believe what she was contemplating but her survival instinct was stronger than any revulsion she felt.

'What do you mean?' His eyes narrowed.

'Like you said, my tattoo's a living work of art. Keep me alive and you can see it every day. You can touch it and it'll be warm. You can watch it move when I move. Imagine having a living exhibit in your gallery.'

Steve didn't say anything. He was obviously considering the possibility and his breathing got faster. He caressed her back again, this time letting one of his hands stray round to the side of her naked breast.

Marni bit down hard on her lip to stop herself from retching.

'I could keep you down here in a cage. My own little zoo exhibit. I like the idea.'

'Yes,' said Marni, that single word a struggle to spit out.

'I could make love to you every day.'

Daily rape. Was it really a better option than death?

'It's a very clever idea, my dear. We could try it for a few days, couldn't we, to see how it would work.'

He sighed, pressing himself up against her back. Marni felt one of his hands exploring between her legs, and she jolted, smashing her hip against the wood of the cross. Steve withdrew his hand and slapped her hard on one buttock.

'It would never work,' he said, his voice hissing, 'because you wouldn't be a willing participant. I would have to watch you like a hawk. You would be always looking for your chance to get away. Hardly the pretty picture you just tried to paint.'

'But if you let me live, I would owe you so much . . .'

'A pity fuck? Don't take me for a fool, Marni.'

He stepped back from her and walked away.

'And it would deprive me of using this on your downy skin.'

She heard him picking up something and coming back. She didn't need to see it to know what it was, but he was going to show her.

The silver blade glinted and flashed as he twisted it in the light, holding it up just inches from her face. The cutting edge curved back from the hilt and was engraved with complex watermark patterns. Marni had never seen a knife like it before.

'Sam taught me all about knives – about the best blades for cutting and the best blades for flaying. They're two quite different processes, you know, and require different tools. I'll tell you about how I'm going to do it.'

Marni shut her eyes tight, wishing she could do the same with her ears.

'First I'll make a perimeter cut around the expanse of skin I want to take. So in your case, right around the edge of your gorgeous back piece. I'll just use a short, straight blade for that. Then I'll swap and use this one.' He thrust it under her nose.

Keep him talking.

'But do you know the full curing process?' Marni's flesh crawled. It was an impossible conversation, even though it might

356

somehow save her life. 'Tell me about Sam and what you learned from her.'

'Sam is a gifted taxidermist. I've been buying pieces from her for years – I collect stuffed animals.'

Marni thought of the old taxidermy shop near Preston Park. She used to go and stare in its window sometimes, before it closed down.

'But she wanted to expand her range of skills, and we soon discovered we had a shared interest in skin. She showed me how she cured animal skins and we started to talk about whether you could cure human skin. Idle chatter at first, but gradually I began to understand it was something she would be willing to do. When I put it to her that I wanted to collect some tattoos, she was more than willing.'

Marni's tongue stuck to the roof of her mouth. She couldn't say a word.

'Sadly, now she's been arrested, I'll have to finish the job myself.' He teased the tip of the blade against the wood of the cross. It left a small white scratch in the varnish. 'Once I've flayed the tattoo from your back, I'll soak it in saline solution and then the succession of chemicals that will break down the proteins in your skin and flush out the grease.'

A wave of nausea left Marni reeling. She was lightheaded and her blood sugar was now dangerously low. If she passed out, there was a very real chance that she'd never come round again.

Steve was droning on but she couldn't concentrate on what he was saying. '. . . changes the pH . . . a blunt tool for scraping hair . . . made Sam teach me just in case . . .' Darkness cloaked her vision but she was determined not to succumb. She bit her cheek and gasped with the pain.

'But the most important thing she taught me was how to sharpen a knife properly. It's critical to use the sharpest blade. This one is like a diamond.'

He took hold of one of her cold, limp hands and held it steady against the wood of the cross. Before she realised what was happening, he'd made a slash across her palm with the knife, the blade long gone before she felt the sting.

'See?' he said. 'Sharper than a scalpel. More precise.'

Marni sobbed. She couldn't help herself. Hot blood ran down her arm.

Steve watched it entranced. Then he stepped forward, pushed his tongue out beyond his bottom lip and licked the blood away.

'Oh Marni,' he said. His voice was thick with arousal. 'I think it's time for my fun to begin.'

58

Francis

The house was unnaturally still and silent. Rory was waiting at the front for backup and Thierry was somewhere on the upper floors. Francis felt as if he was entirely alone, with only the faint hum of the air conditioning to accompany his silent progress. He went down a flight of stairs to investigate the office level, heart pounding.

Most of the monitors were off, but there was one left on, softly glowing, showing CCTV feeds from the outside of the house. He could see Rory on the front drive, speaking into his mobile. At the far end of the office area, there were several doors. Two of them were locked, but one was fractionally ajar, so he pressed his ear to the space and listened. As he did, a woman's sharp scream rent the air from beyond the doorway.

Marni!

He couldn't be sure it was her, but whoever it was needed help. He pushed the door open to find himself at the top of another flight of stairs. He could hear the woman moaning and then. above it, the sound of a man's voice, though he couldn't decipher the words. He paused. He needed a plan, but without any idea of what lay below, that was difficult. Looking down the stairs, he could see another half-open door at the bottom. That at least would afford him some cover, and he might be able to see what was going on before making himself known.

Don't waste time. Go!

He skittered down the stairs as fast as he could, praying he wouldn't give himself away. The creak of a step could be catastrophic and not necessarily for himself. The thought of Marni at the mercies of the madman responsible for the bloody tableaux above made his heart pound and strengthened his resolve. He'd never been in a situation like this before. The arrests he'd experienced had usually been carefully planned and involved full backup. God, he hoped that was what Rory had been doing on his mobile.

He offered a silent benediction as he stood poised by the second door, crossed himself, then slipped into the room.

All of it hit him at once – Marni on the cross, her back a bright red sheen, the cured tattoos on their wire frames, a man standing with his back to him, wielding a curved knife that dripped with blood.

'Stop! Police!'

The man turned and looked Francis up and down.

Never had Francis felt more naked for want of a weapon. If only Thierry and Rory were with him. It had been a mistake to split up.

'Frank, is that you?' It was the voice of desperation, hoarse and cracked.

'Yes, Marni.'

'Oh sweet,' said the man. 'You know each other already. Well, Frank, I'm Steve. Remember? We met at Marni's studio.'

He lunged forward, the bloody blade in front of him. Francis had expected an attack like this and side-stepped to put one of the concrete plinths between them. Steve snarled and changed his course to catch Francis on the other side of the plinth. Francis charged with his shoulder low, barrelling into the stone column and sending it over. It glanced into Steve's hip, but he was already moving away from it, so it fell harmlessly onto the concrete floor with a crack. The silver frame and its precious cargo bounced across the floor and hit the opposite wall.

Marni was straining her neck to see what was happening.

'Help me,' she screamed.

In a split-second decision, Francis ran to help Marni, rather than turning to confront Steve. He grabbed a second knife from a low table and quickly slashed through the cable attaching one ankle to the cross before Steve got too close. At least now he was armed. He straightened up and held the knife out in front of him, knees bent in a defensive stance.

With a roar of anger, Steve launched himself again, coming at Francis almost sideways, leading with his left shoulder, while following through with the knife in his right hand. Francis stepped forward diagonally, ducking low to plunge at Steve's centre of gravity. They clashed and sprawled together on the floor. Steve's blade clattered from his hand but he was lashing out with his feet, landing heavy kicks in Francis's stomach, aiming for his groin to incapacitate him. Francis swung his knife hand in a sweeping curve and ripped into Steve's trouser leg, dragging the knife down as he pushed it in deep to achieve maximum damage. Steve gasped and shuffled backwards, moving out of reach. Francis had to pull the knife out of his calf or risk losing it.

They were both panting heavily. Steve grabbed for his own blade and staggered to his feet. With wild eyes and flared nostrils, he bore down on his opponent, who was still lying winded on the floor.

Gathering all his reserves, Francis rolled onto his front and pushed himself up to his hands and knees. Steve lunged at his back and Francis felt the scraping of the knife through his jacket. He twisted suddenly and sprang to his feet, facing Steve, who looked at him in dull confusion. Francis had a split second of grace before the next onslaught and he stepped forward, meaning that Steve wouldn't have the space to stab him in the chest. It did, however, also mean that he'd be able to reach round to stab him in the back. Then he remembered the knife in his own hand.

Use it. Use the damn thing.

He wasn't quick enough. Steve anticipated his action and brought one of his forearms down hard on the front of Francis's shoulder. Francis's blade clattered to the floor as he heard his collar bone snap. His right arm was now a dead weight and pain screamed from his shoulder down to his wrist. Steve grinned excitedly and followed up his advantage. He shoved Francis back against an empty concrete plinth and then pressed the blade of his knife to the base of the policeman's throat.

'Any last words?'

Nothing was further from Francis's mind than making a speech. He lunged forward and raised a knee to Steve's groin. It wasn't the hardest or most accurate of actions but it got the blade away from his throat. Steve yelped and staggered backwards, putting space between him and Francis as he tried to regroup. He looked down and slapped a hand over his blood-soaked chinos, pressing the earlier knife wound to staunch the bleeding. His face was grey and he glared at Francis with angry red-rimmed eyes.

Francis picked up his knife clumsily with his left hand. He struggled to cut Marni's other foot free. Then, with equal difficulty, he sliced through the ropes securing her wrists. Thank God the knife was as sharp as it was. Gasping, she dropped to the floor in a heap, barely conscious.

'Don't touch her,' shrieked Steve. 'She's mine.'

Francis looked round frantically. Neither of them would be safe until he'd shut Steve down. He switched the knife to his useless right hand, and pulled his mobile out of his pocket. He hit Rory's speed dial, not taking his eyes off the other man. Engaged.

Damn!

He was taller than Steve, by a good three or four inches. That would mean he had a longer reach. Not that it would be worth much, now he was reduced to using his left hand. Furthermore, Steve was heavier than him, all brawn, and had a lower centre of gravity. How could he play for time until Thierry arrived? Surely he must have come back down by now.

'Thierry?' he yelled.

Steve was on his feet again, moving in a slow curve across the room, coming closer and closer.

If Francis went to him, it would leave Marni vulnerable. But if he stayed by Marni until Steve got to him, it put her within reach too. He inched forwards. Could he draw Steve away from Marni or would she be his prime target?

She hadn't moved since she'd dropped to the floor a minute ago. He couldn't hear her breathing and he couldn't risk turning round to see if her chest was rising and falling. The long cuts running down each side and across the top of her back were still bleeding – he could see blood spreading on the floor out of the corner of his eye. She urgently needed a medic.

Only too late did he realise what Steve was up to. By calling for Thierry, Francis had given the game away that he wasn't there alone. It had been a major error. Steve wasn't making a run for it – he was ensuring that help couldn't arrive. He slammed the door shut, turned the key in the lock, then shoved the key into his pocket.

'Your arrival changes everything,' said Steve. He stood with his back against the door, still breathing heavily. The leg that Francis had cut wasn't bearing any of his weight and his trainer was soaked with blood. 'Marni was going to be the only one who'd end up dead in here. But now you've got to die too.'

Francis considered his options in less than a second.

Get him away from the door. Get him down. Get the key. How much chance did he have of doing that?

'Come on then, you bastard!' It was a risky strategy that might see him dead. He had to hope that blood loss would dull Steve's reaction times.

But he was wrong.

Steve came at him like a fury, blade flashing in the light. Francis stepped away, putting the first of the plinths between them. Steve feinted in one direction, Francis moved in the other. They circled the concrete stand until Francis lunged forward and gave it a hearty shove. It crashed to the floor, missing Steve's good leg by a hair's breadth.

'Cheap shot,' hissed Steve, retreating behind one of the sofas.

Francis ran forward, planted one foot on the back of the sofa and launched himself through the air. He didn't have a plan – but if he didn't act, he and Marni would both be dead.

Their bodies collided and crashed to the floor. Francis struggled to overpower Steve but as they rolled across the concrete, Steve hooked Francis's right arm and yanked it back. A shooting pain ripped through Francis's shoulder. His head spun and he slashed at Steve's arm with his knife. Steve let go and used his superior weight to flip Francis onto his back. He straddled him, pinning him to the floor by placing his knees on Francis's shoulders, further crushing the already broken collar bone.

Francis writhed underneath him, trying to find a way out. His left hand flailed, failing to make contact with his opponent.

There was a loud banging at the door and the sound of voices.

Steve pushed down more heavily on Francis's chest. He held his curved blade against Francis's throat.

'You only have yourself to blame,' said Steve. 'You broke the cardinal rule, coming here without backup.'

The door handle rattled.

'Boss, are you in there?'

Francis tried to answer but Steve instantly replaced the blade with a forearm across his windpipe, crushing down. A strangled grunt was the best Francis could do.

There was a heavy thud against the other side of the door.

Steve fumbled with his knife, dropping it momentarily on Francis's chest. At the same time, Francis felt his own knife being taken from his hand. He glanced up and saw Marni crouching behind Steve's left shoulder, an index finger against her lips warning him to keep quiet. She was bone white, her face made pearly by a sheen of sweat, and her whole body was shaking, but the determination in her eyes gave Francis a moment's hope.

She held the knife up and steadied her position. At the same moment, sensing a change in the man underneath him, Steve twisted round to follow his gaze.

'I never thought I'd have to do this again in my lifetime,' said Marni.

She didn't hesitate. The blade ripped into Steve's pectoral muscle, slicing down across his breast. He dived off Francis onto the floor to get away and Marni fell on his back, stabbing at him again. Steve turned to wrestle with her as Francis rolled into both their bodies. His intention was to push Marni off Steve before Steve could apply his blade to her. The three of them tangled on the blood-slick floor. Francis felt pain. Marni screamed. There was the sickening noise of a knife scraping bone.

The door burst open and Rory and Thierry rushed across to them, pulling them apart, skidding in the blood as they did so. Thierry pulled Marni into his arms as Rory slammed Steve's arm on the floor until he released his grip on his knife.

His chest burning for breath, Francis looked down to see that the front of his white shirt was drenched in blood. He slumped back against the side of one of the sofas. Marni was motionless in Thierry's arms, her eyes open, eyeballs rolled back. Steve clutched at his neck, blood spurting from between his fingers.

'Boss?' said Rory.

'I'm alive,' he gasped.

59

Marni

Waking up in hospital was turning into a nasty habit. Marni blinked and looked around. She was in the same room as last time, except the view from the window was different. Thierry was holding her hand and he smiled gently as he realised she was awake.

'Take me home?' she said. It came out as a croak. Her throat felt as if she'd swallowed a pack of razor blades. Unwrapped.

'Not a chance, babe. And no checking yourself out, either.'

He held a plastic beaker to her lips. The water was tepid and stale but it tasted perfect. She took several greedy sips before he took it away.

'Easy,' he said.

'How long have I been here?'

'Two days. You were in a coma when they brought you in and you'd been stabbed. The tip of the knife caught your spleen and tore it.'

His words made Marni aware that the whole of her torso felt tender. She gingerly lifted the sheet that was covering her, but she was in a hospital gown, so she couldn't see the injury. Her back felt lacerated and her left arm was throbbing painfully.

'They operated on you,' said Thierry. 'I think it was touch and go, thought they wouldn't admit it to me.'

Marni didn't want to believe it, but his face was so serious. He looked scared. She closed her eyes.

'Mum, how do you feel now?'

She hadn't noticed Alex sitting beyond him in the shadows.

'Alex, come here.'

He came forward to the bed and gave her the gentlest of hugs. She winced.

'I feel like I need to sleep for a thousand years.'

'So you won't run away this time?' said Thierry.

She opened her eyes and shook her head. She smiled at them – seeing them together was a comforting presence, and feeling Alex's hand warm on top of hers was the best thing in the world.

'Mum, we were worried about you. No more of this part-time policing, right?'

'I promise.'

'I'm hungry,' said Alex. 'But I want the full story from you when I get back.'

'Of course,' said Thierry. 'Now you know your mum's okay, you can get back to what's important.' He fished change out of his pocket. 'I think there's a vending machine by the lifts.'

Marni watched Alex leave the room and then spoke.

'There's no way Alex can hear the full story.'

Thierry nodded. 'What do you remember?'

'Being tied up. Steve and Frank fighting. There was so much blood.' Her breath caught in her throat. 'Is . . .?'

'Francis is fine. Steve, not so much, but still alive. What is it with you and knives?'

He was smiling at her the way he used to, before their marriage had blown up into a storm of angst and recriminations.

Her eyelids were heavy and her whole body seemed to be

one giant ache. She felt safe enough to let herself slip back into sleep's warm embrace with a sigh.

It was night outside when she woke up again. The room was in semi-darkness, with just a small pool of light at her side coming from the Anglepoise light on the nightstand. She felt cool. The sheet had been kicked down to the end of the bed and the hospital gown barely covered her. As she pulled herself up into a sitting position to straighten things out, a sharp, stabbing pain in her side made her gasp.

At the same moment she became aware of a dark figure slumped in an armchair in the corner of the room – her cry had roused whoever it was from sleep.

A moment's panic swept through her.

It couldn't be . . .

'Thierry?'

The figure stood up and loomed at the end of her bed.

'It's me, Francis.'

Relief washed through her. 'Frank.'

He came and sat in the chair that Thierry had left at the bedside.

'Thierry said you'd woken up, but you were asleep again when I got here. I didn't want to disturb you.'

'How long have you been here?'

'Since seven-ish.' He looked down at his watch. 'It's just gone ten.'

He took both of her hands in his.

'You saved my life, Marni. If you hadn't taken the knife from me and used it, Steven Harrington would have killed me.'

Flashes of memory came back to Marni. 'But you saved my life, too. He was about to cut the tattoo off my back when you arrived.'

'We only just made it in time.'

'Thank you.'

'Don't thank me. I let you down. I should have realised you were still in danger.'

'But how could you have known? Sam Kirby was in custody.'

'And she basically told me the whole thing wasn't over.'

Marni shrugged. It hurt like hell.

'Am I going to be charged?' she said. She didn't really want to know the answer.

Francis frowned. 'With what?'

'I stabbed Steve, didn't I? What if he dies?'

'Jesus, Marni, that was self-defence. Of course you're not going to be charged. You'll have to be a witness at his trial, but that's all.'

'He'll go to trial?'

'I spoke to his doctor before coming here. They're confident he'll recover so, yes, he's going to trial. He'll be charged with murder by Sam Kirby's side – even if he didn't kill the victims himself, he commissioned the crimes, which makes him every bit as guilty in the eyes of the law. They'll both go away for a very long time.'

'You solved the case.'

'Of course. What would you expect?'

They both laughed and then, quite unexpectedly, Francis raised one of her hands to his lips and kissed it. The laughter died in Marni's throat, replaced by something more overpowering. Their eyes met.

Francis said, 'You know, there's an old proverb, that if you save someone's life, they belong to you. I don't know where the proverb's from . . .'

'So, in this theory, we belong to each other?'

He smiled at her. 'Might be the case.'

'Really?' Marni said, pursing her lips. 'You belong to me?'

'And you to me.'

'That's nice.' She leant back on the pillows and closed her eyes.

'What are you thinking, Marni Mullins?'

'I'm thinking about which part of your body I'm going to tattoo first.'

Francis's mouth fell open. 'No, no, that's not how it works.'

'It is.'

'Not.'

'You're mine. I get to tattoo you. I get to choose what.'

'No.'

Marni dipped the needles into the black ink. She was going to enjoy this very much. He wasn't, but then that was the price you paid for a tattoo.

'Ready, Frank?'

'As I'll ever be.'

She tattooed the first black line on the pale skin of his back and laughed.

'Ouch.'

'How does it feel to be tattooed?'

'You can stop now. I didn't realise it would hurt this much.'

She carried on tattooing.

'Don't worry. You're sitting like a champ.'

Acknowledgements

I owe many people large debts of gratitude for their support and help over the course of bringing *The Tattoo Thief* into existence, but two people stand out for their unswerving belief in the potential of a three-minute pitch to become something more, and for the unstinting support they gave me through the writing process. My wonderful agent Jenny Brown, of Jenny Brown Associates, through her involvement with Bloody Scotland, gave me the chance to pitch my idea in the first place and offered me representation on the promise of what was to come – you have my eternal gratitude. The other person is my amazing editor Sam Eades, of Trapeze – she was present at the initial pitch and shepherded me through the creative process with patience and insight, drawing the best from me and then demanding more – thank you – you've made me a better writer by setting such a high bar.

I also owe a great deal to the Bloody Scotland International Crime Writing Festival – the value of being able to pitch, as an unknown and unproven writer, in front of a panel of publishers and agents cannot be underestimated. I'm not exaggerating when I say that those three minutes pitching my idea on the stage at Bloody Scotland changed my life.

Thanks and admiration to my stalwart copy editor Sophie

Wilson, who never once complained at having to change thousands of em dashes into en dashes and double quotation marks into single quotation marks – rest assured, that won't be necessary in the next manuscript. She also helped me to avoid multiple disasters by spotting plot holes and correcting my most heinous errors. And gratitude to my accidental and enigmatic proof reader Mac, who picked up all the errors I certainly would have missed.

Thanks are due to numerous other folks. In particular, I want to thank my very gifted tattoo artist, Matt Gordon, who not only tattooed the brilliant octopus on my arm but also, over 25 hours of tattooing, imparted a huge amount of information on the art and the people who pursue it. Thank you also to Woody of the Brighton Tattoo Convention, not only for helping me with my research and checking the manuscript for authenticity, but also for never complaining that I have hijacked his convention for the purposes of fiction. Jess Stocker of Chapter XIII in Brighton gave me insight into what it's like for women working in a male-dominated industry and how women tattoo artists are becoming more of a force.

I'm extremely grateful to Superintendent (Retired) David Hammond of Staffordshire Police for ensuring no major errors in my police procedure and also to Doctor Jo Harris of Imperial College School of Medicine for similarly advising me on medical matters.

Thanks are due to Marion Urch of Adventures in Fiction, who imparted a great deal of writing wisdom to me over the course of her mentorship and made me the writer I am today.

Finally, many fellow writers, friends and family members have earned my gratitude. They have acted as sounding boards, readers, cheerleaders and purveyors of the necessary quantities of gin that fuelled this endeavour. In particular, I'm grateful to my wonderful friend Madeleine Mitchell for many hours of discussion of plot, writing technique and much else, and to Crystal Hill Nanavati for reading and endless encouragement. Also to the members of my book group for making me read things I didn't want to and for their massive enthusiasm for *The Tattoo Thief* – thank you, Diana Barham, Amanda Hyde, Jo Harris and Sue Cunningham. Thank you to Carol Ridler for providing me with my hermit's cottage where I was able to hide myself away and write uninterrupted over the long cold winter – and thank you for providing gin and encouragement while I did this. I must also thank Caroline Wilkinson and Niamh Paris for their friendship and support throughout the process. And last but not least, a million thanks to Mark, Rupert and Tim for their enduring support and the belief that one day I would make it.

If you should have been mentioned here and I've missed you – you still have my gratitude and I'll buy you a large drink when you point it out to me!

Reading Group Guide

1. What is the effect of hearing the story from the voice of the killer in those short chapters? How did it make you feel?

2. Marni is a complex character, damaged by her past. Is she a hero or a villain? Do you like her?

3. Brighton feels like an extra character in the novel. Discuss how the seaside setting is used in the story.

4. How does the author ratchet up the tension throughout the novel? Were there particular moments when you were on edge?

5. Discuss the relationship between Marni and DI Francis Sullivan, and how it changes over the course of the story.

6. Did you suspect who the murderer was? What hints did the author make?

7. Discuss the role of tattoos in the story. What did you learn?

8. Share your favourite films/TV programmes/books about detective duos.